Km/mu
KENGLSS
060104

Dickens the Journalist

Other titles by this author:

DICKENS' JOURNALISM, VOLUME 4: The Uncommercial Traveller and Other Papers, 1859–70 (edited by Michael Slater and John Drew)

Dickens the Journalist

John M. L. Drew
Lecturer in English Literature
University of Buckingham

macmillan

First published 2003 by
PALGRAVE MACMILLAN
Houndmills, Basingstoke, Hampshire RG21 6XS and
175 Fifth Avenue, New York, N. Y. 10010
Companies and representatives throughout the world

PALGRAVE MACMILLAN is the global academic imprint of the Palgrave
Macmillan division of St. Martin's Press, LLC and of Palgrave Macmillan Ltd.
Macmillan® is a registered trademark in the United States, United Kingdom
and other countries. Palgrave is a registered trademark in the European
Union and other countries.

ISBN 0–333–98773–X hardback

This book is printed on paper suitable for recycling and made from fully
managed and sustained forest sources.

A catalogue record for this book is available from the British Library.

Library of Congress Cataloging-in-Publication Data

Drew, John M. L., 1966–
    Dickens the journalist / John M. L. Drew.
        p. cm.
    Includes bibliographical references (p.) and index.
    ISBN 0–333–98773–X
        1. Dickens, Charles, 1812–1870–Prose. 2. Dickens, Charles,
1812–1870–Knowledge–Journalism. 3. Journalism–Great
Britain–History–19th century. I. Title.

PR4592.P7D74 2003
828'.808–dc21

                                                            2003046920

10   9   8   7   6   5   4   3
12   11   10   09   08   07   06   05   04

Printed and bound in Great Britain by
Antony Rowe Ltd, Chippenham and Eastbourne

For Philip, Lindsay, and Coro,
with love

Contents

Acknowledgements

The British Academy provided funding for my initial research into Dickens's later journalism from 1992–94. I am no less grateful to my grandmother, the late Ruby F. Gathercole, for what John Dickens would have called, ahem, pecuniary assistance, during those years. And for excellent advice and friendly hospitality at the same time, I owe much to Andrew Sanders and the late, much missed, Edwina Porter.

I acknowledge the importance to this study of the 'Dent Uniform Edition' of Dickens's journalism in my introduction, but this is the place to thank Michael Slater for the invitation to work on the final volume, and for the tremendous amount I feel I have learnt from his scholarly acumen, enthusiasm, knowledge of Victorian journalism, and of Dickens in particular. It may not show much in the book, but the encouragement and advice is much appreciated. Likewise, I'm very grateful to the anonymous Palgrave reader for the project, whose comments and suggestions have been invaluable throughout the drafting process.

Cathy Waters and Leon Litvack have been most kind in sharing with me their forthcoming work on aspects of Dickens's journals and journalism. I'm also grateful to David Paroissien, editor of *Dickens Quarterly*, for permission to reproduce part of my essay 'Voyages Extraordinaires: Dickens' "Traveling Essays" and *The Uncommercial Traveller*' which appeared in Volume 13 of the journal (1996).

It is a pleasure to thank my supportive colleagues Stefan Hawlin and Kate Mattacks, who have been unfailingly helpful and interested in the project. I must also record my very great debt to colleagues in the University of Buckingham Library, particularly Jackie Harris, for handling and arranging loans, tracking down obscure material, and generally lightening the load: thank you all.

My final acknowledgement has been anticipated by the Dedication: the book would not have been produced without inspiration from all three, to whom none of the blame attaching to its defects, however, can possibly be referred. My interest in Dickens's journalism began in 1984 when I proofread my father Philip Drew's landmark article on *The Uncommercial Traveller* (*Essays and Studies*, 1985), which rightly claimed it as a neglected work. It is nice to feel, a few years later, that this may no longer be the case.

Introduction

This is a book about Dickens's journalism and the journalistic career which produced it. The trajectory it traces differs significantly, in its dynamics and uncertainties, from the familiar contours of the career of Dickens the novelist. However, the aim of the study is not to offer partial thoughts on Dickensian biography, nor a critical reading of the relationship of the journalism to the novels, but to survey the texts which compose the 'canon' of Dickens's journalism themselves, and the contexts of their production, as a three-dimensional field of its own. I think this is worth doing because, notwithstanding the wealth of important twentieth-century studies illuminating myriad aspects of the writer's life and craft, a book of this kind has never been published before.[1]

The omission seems remarkable, but is connected to the likewise remarkable fact that no dedicated edition of Dickens's journalism existed until the 1990s. David Pascoe's one-volume anthology for Penguin Classics (1997) and, in particular, the *Dent Uniform Edition of Dickens' Journalism* (4 volumes, 1994–2000), a project masterminded by Michael Slater, have, for the first time, put the majority of Dickens's journalistic output into the public domain in a scholarly and annotated format. Before this, readers could only turn to skimpily-edited reprints of collections republished by Dickens during his own lifetime (*Sketches by Boz*, *Reprinted Pieces* and *The Uncommercial Traveller*) or attempt to track down the increasingly rare collections called *Miscellaneous Papers* or *Collected Papers*, gathered by B. W. Matz in 1908 and Arthur Waugh *et al.* in 1937. For most of the last century, as Slater observes, 'the great mass of all this vintage Dickens writing has remained largely unobtainable outside libraries.'[2] In its timing and conception, the present study is thus predicated upon the Dent edition, and indebted to its achievements.

This is not to say, however, that research has never taken Dickens's journalism into account. Much has been written on the subject, but relative to the letterpress inspired by Dickens's novels and short fiction, it is not well known, and it is very widely scattered. It takes the form of

1

unpublished doctoral research,[3] scholarly articles (often forensic rather than critical in approach) printed in different journals or collections and over a long period, insightful comments in monographs with other priorities, and two books about a small part only of the canon (the papers collected and repackaged as *Sketches by Boz*).[4] If the present study successfully documents, assimilates and draws conclusions from this disparate material in the interests of an overall critical and historical profile of Dickens the journalist, it will have achieved a major part of its purpose.

In the process it has been necessary to confront, and sometimes to ignore, some of the theoretical implications of attempting to define and critique a journalistic canon. Difficulties of definition may have been circumvented in practical terms by the establishment of a *Uniform Edition*, with its 'Complete listing of Dickens's known journalism, December 1833–August 1869,'[5] but even this may be subject to debate. It is by no means certain, for one thing, that all Dickens's anonymously-published journalism has been identified, so the careful detective work carried out by B. W. Matz, W. J. Carlton, Philip Collins, Alec Brice, K. J. Fielding, Patrick McCarthy, and others, still needs continuing. Furthermore, it may be argued that Dickens's editorial addresses, poetic squibs, letters to the newspapers on public issues, travel writing published in volume as well as in periodical form (*Pictures from Italy, American Notes for General Circulation*), should also be brought under consideration, as being essentially journalistic in intention and execution. More significantly still, are 'journalism,' 'journalistic' and 'journalese' not terms that can, and have, been applied to many passages in Dickens's novels and tales – pointing towards the conclusion that with Dickens in particular the frontier between journalism and forms of writing usually defined in generic terms (fiction, poetry, novel, short story, etc.) is a virtually impossible one to police? For almost everything that Dickens published, by virtue of appearing in newspapers, magazines, or 'numbers' could be technically classified as journalism.

It has, of course, long been a topic of debate whether the writings of an individual 'in the public journals' (*OED*), or journalism is general, can be said to constitute a distinct genre, or whether journalism is simply a form of printing and distribution which can transmit texts conforming to any of the established 'literary' kinds. This fuzzy interface worried both F. R. Leavis, whose doctoral thesis scrutinized 'The Relationship of Journalism to Literature' (1924), and, in its application to Dickens's fiction, G. K. Chesterton, who articulated the problem in characteristically pithy manner:

> Dickens's work is not to be reckoned in novels at all. Dickens's work is to be reckoned always by characters, sometimes by groups, oftener by episodes, but never by novels ...[6]

More recently, commentators have looked to the insights of post-structuralist theory, with its emphasis on the printed text as a 'methodological field' where formerly self-contained disciplines meet and merge, to rethink the relations between the nineteenth-century periodical press, 'Literature,' and the impression of popular culture they help constitute. The conclusions reached recognise provisionally how material conditions of press production interact with generic patterns of narrative in a way which allows, for the purposes of this study, the canon of Dickens's journalism to be construed as a hybrid 'publishing genre.'[7]

Given this canonical instability and generic permeability, the present study needs to take a wide view of the field of Dickens's journalism and thus includes some discussion of his travel books, public letters and topical poetry published in newspapers, as well as of the structural and stylistic debt that the opening numbers and conduct of the serial 'novels' owe to Dickens's parallel work in newspapers and magazines. While it draws a general distinction between journalism and imaginative literature, and focuses on the former as a conspicuous area of neglect, it by no means seeks to reinforce the qualitative assumptions underlying traditional distinctions between the two, in which the former is disadvantaged. Indeed it will argue for recalibration of our scales of literary value as they apply to Dickens, in line not only with the exceptional press response to the material contained in the Dent edition (discussed in the final chapter), but also with current attempts to deconstruct the binary divide between these ideologically burdened concepts.[8] Recognition of journalism's crucial role in the constitution of the equally contested concept of modernity is an important step in this underlying argument.

Although the abstraction for study of a famous individual's contributions and relations to the periodical press clearly militates against the drawing of universal conclusions, – this is one disadvantage of the selective tradition – where a writer is, like Dickens, equally celebrated for representing as for transcending the dynamics of his age, the results may bear a broader application.[9] Furthermore, the continued attempt to isolate and reinsert Dickens's journalism into the fabric of the periodical press and its sense of its own development, is one, I hope, which shows (something postmodern criticism is perhaps reluctant to concede) that Victorian commentators were as acutely self-conscious of their own modernity as we are, and sought to articulate it as cleverly and as frequently, using the terminology and conceptual frameworks at their disposal, and where those failed, inventing new ones. That Dickens the journalist played a part in this process is, I contend, undeniable. Readers will need to judge critically whether they believe it was also a conspicuous one. This study certainly makes it seems so.

As an illustration of this last claim, it is worth revisiting a well-known paragraph of the critic Walter Bagehot, which comes from the middle of his lengthy review of Chapman and Hall's 'Cheap Edition' of Dickens's fictional works up to 1858, and which treats them from the outset as the creation of a man 'whose genius is essentially irregular and unsymmetrical.'[10] Bagehot's interdisciplinarity is exemplary, as he describes (but denigrates) the operation of Dicken's literary genius as one which borrows structures from another discursive field, the grubby world of newspapers, and then links both to the perception that, through the latter's graphological correspondence with the layout of the city, Dickens is uniquely placed as a mediator of modernity:

> Mr Dickens's genius is especially suited to the delineation of city life. London is like a newspaper, Everything is there, and everything is disconnected. There is every kind of person in some houses; but there is no more connection between the houses than between the neighbours in the lists of 'births, marriages, and deaths.' As we change from the broad leader to the squalid police-report, we pass a corner and we are in a changed world. This is advantageous to Mr Dicken's genius. His memory is full of instances of old buildings and curious people, and he does not care to piece them together. On the contrary, each scene, to his mind, is a separate alertness of observation that is observable in those who live by it. He describes London like a special correspondent for Posterity.

The assertion that, Dickens 'does not care to piece … together' any connections between characters and buildings in the city is one which can quickly be overturned, if applied to carefully-plotted novels like *Bleak House* or *Little Dorrit*. It is one which Dickens himself powerfully rebuts in 'Curious Misprint in the *Edinburgh Review*.'[11] But if, along with the rest of the paragraph, applied to Dickens's journalism, it has particular resonance. The question of whether it is part of the journalist's job to piece together, and interpret, the interaction of individuals and the contemporary scene, or simply to record it, is one which Dickens engages with repeatedly as shorthand-writer, reporter, leader-writer and editor.

1
Copying and Reporting Life (1830–1833)

London, 1830. In the topographical watercolours of George 'Sidney' Shepherd and George Scharf, the city is depicted not as a placid, neoclassical panorama – a civilization resting on its laurels – but as a place of accelerating change and incongruous juxtapositions. It looks like a spectacularly unregulated building site, what Dickens was later to call in an article about the engineering works at Euston, 'an unsettled neighbourhood.' It was unsettled physically and also politically, with the death of George IV in June, a General Election in July, newspaper reports in August of the Paris revolution, the reassembly of Parliament in October, and, in November, after 47 years out of office, the return of a Whig-led government, bringing representatives of radical new partnerships between the middle and working classes into untried alliance with the party aristocracy. Planned legislation, much of it imbued with Benthamite social philosophy acting through the newly-appointed Commissions, included reform of Parliamentary representation, a complete overhaul of town corporations, 'improvements' to the Poor Law, and, in return for the support of the hundred Irish MPs under the fiery leadership of Daniel O'Connell, its corollary at every turn was the condition of Ireland and the Irish. By 1832, armed rebellion, revolutionary uprisings in major cities, were not just a 'spectre' imaged by later historians, but a real and present danger. Not only was the reform programme furiously debated, but the precise manner in which the contests were recorded and mediated to the country was the subject of intense, and, in stylistic terms, subtle scrutiny.

With so much attention focused on Westminster, the early 1830s saw the shifting back from Edinburgh to London of publishing initiatives, an intensification in the production of political prints, and 'a watershed in the history of British journalism' as the unstamped press battled for the abolition of the fourpenny newspaper stamp.[1] This was the heyday of parliamentary reporting, when the press itself vied with government in information transfer, when Lord Chancellor Lyndhurst pronounced Barnes of *The Times* to be 'the most powerful man in the country.'[2] Parliament was sitting for longer than ever before: twice as many days annually and nearly three times as many hours as it had in the mid 'twenties.[3] At a time when most of the young men destined to shape public opinion in the mid-Victorian period were studying classical literature and law, the eighteen-year old Dickens was already at work, and fully programmed into the information transfer, but as yet a mere cog in the wheel of the mighty engine of the press.[4]

He began as a copyist, but family connections secured him a place as one of a small number of parliamentary reporters – a demanding if unofficial profession which created in the reporter 'a sort of universality of talent,' in default of the university education that birth and the family misfortunes denied him.[5] He found himself (as David Copperfield would later complain) wallowing in words, his own thoughts and opinions wholly swallowed up by the *Mirror of Parliament*, the *True Sun* and, initially, the *Morning* and *Evening Chronicle*.[6] But as he emerges from the obscurity of London's millions as an individual, as he travels from anonymity towards becoming a recognized 'author,' as his words distinguish themselves from the millions of other words that were spoken, written or printed in this period, one begins to identify a gymnastic voice: adept at assimilating all the different languages and forms – the different discourses – that were available for reporting this social and political flux, and developing a new metalanguage to comment archly upon it.

I

Dickens's journalistic career had in fact begun several years before, some-time after March 1825 and before October 1826, on a London morning paper called *The British Press*. Samuel Carter Hall, the self-styled 'father' of the English newspaper press, and a reporter on the paper, recalled how '[n]ow and then there came to the office a smart, intelligent, active lad, who brought what was then called ... "penny-a-line stuff;" that is to say, notices of accidents, fires, police reports, such as escaped the more regular reporters, for which a penny a printed line was paid.'[7] This was the young Charles Dickens, aged thirteen or fourteen, newly entered as a pupil at Wellington House Academy in Mornington Place and released from the shameful drudgery of Warren's blacking factory. None of the penny-a-line items in the paper can be attributed to Dickens with any surety, but the following notices illustrate the kind of report which may have come from his pen:

> Mr Hayes, of Trentham Farm, near Bushy, was found drowned in the Regent's Canal on Saturday, near the Beames-lock. He left home for London on Wednesday, and was not heard of after. There were no marks of violence upon the body, and there was 3l. in the pockets of the deceased. An inquest will sit upon the body this day.

ALARMING FIRE – About one o'clock yesterday morning, a fire was discovered in the extensive warehouses of Mr. Curling, fellmonger, of Dockhead, which soon attained such an ascendancy, as to throw the whole of the surrounding neighbourhood into the utmost dismay ... but by the great exertions of the firemen, who worked their respective engines with uncommon effect, the flames were in a short time altogether subdued.

Yesterday, a gentleman of the name of Gilham, resident near Brentwood, was thrown from his horse and killed on the spot, not far from his residence. We are sorry to hear he has left a widow and a very numerous family.

On Wednesday last, another very large pike was caught, by a party from Aylesbury, at the Weston reservoir, near Wendover. The fish weighed nearly twenty-seven pounds, and measured three feet nine inches and three quarters in length. Thirty-eight persons partook of it.[8]

The choice of the *British Press* was an obvious one. It had become a ministerial paper earlier in the decade,[9] and John Dickens had found employment there soon after his pensioned retirement from the Navy Pay Office, and he held positions on the journal's 'parliamentary corps,' and, for a period of two months before the paper's collapse on 1 November 1826, in the unlikely guise of its 'City Correspondent.' A series of a dozen articles critically exposing the St. Patrick's Assurance Company, Dublin, for 'doing business greatly beyond its capital,' and extolling the virtues of Lloyd's of London as underwriters of marine insurance, can be identified as his work.[10] While Carter Hall recalled John Dickens, with Pecksniffian periphrasis, as 'a gentleman of no great intellectual capacity,' Dickens himself told a friend in 1827 that his father was 'a first-rate shorthand writer on Gurney's system, and a capital reporter.'[11] John Dickens's metamorphosis from clerk to reporter was at least as remarkable in fact as his son's accomplishment of that same feat on leaving his junior posts in the offices of the solicitors Ellis & Blackmore and Charles Molloy sometime in 1829. There were two key elements in this Daedalian transformation of father and son. One was knowledge of the magical art of 'Gurney's system' of shorthand, which they both studied;[12] the other was an enterprising and successful journalist who had become a relative through marriage, John Henry Barrow.

II

Although the Gurney system – as well as its name, 'Brachygraphy' – was superseded during the nineteenth century first by Taylor's stenography and then by Pitman shorthand, for well over a hundred years it was the most prestigious and popular system used in Britain and the colonies. It was 'the means of doing the greater part of the official reporting for parliament and the government, most of the evidence in the blue-books having been taken down by the Gurneys and their staff.'[13] Thomas Gurney's adaptation of an even older shorthand technique had gained him, in 1737, the post of shorthand writer at the Old Bailey; in 1750 he published the first of many editions of *Brachygraphy* ('or Swift Writing Made Easy to the Meanest Capacity'), and his son Joseph was responsible for the revised 9th edition of 1778, which remained unaltered through successive reprints issued by the family. The edition used by Dickens was probably the 15th edition, published in January 1825, which reprinted a fulsome dedication to George III, along with a series of four extravagant neo-classical Odes to the Author of the work:

> In less enlighten'd ages hadst thou liv'd,
> GURNEY, thine art had witchcraft been believ'd;
> With doubtful fear they'd view'd the strange design,
> And thought enchantment dwelt in every line.
> ... Thus GURNEY'S art contracts the mighty plan,
> And sinks th'immense of science to a span.[14]

Dickens later looked back nostalgically on this period of his life in various partially-autobiographical passages of *David Copperfield*. Although the Romantic orientation of the künstlerroman meant that much factual, if not emotional detail, was suppressed, Dickens nevertheless coloured David's description of learning the Gurney system with similar images of the occult:

> I bought an approved scheme of the noble art and mystery of stenography (which cost me ten and sixpence); and plunged into a sea of perplexity that brought me, in a few weeks, to the confines of distraction. The changes that were rung upon *dots*, which in such a position meant such a thing, and in such another position something else, entirely different; the wonderful vagaries that were played by *circles*; the unaccountable consequences that resulted from marks like *flies' legs*; the tremendous effects of a *curve* in the wrong place; not only troubled my waking hours, but reappeared before me in my sleep. When I had ... mastered the alphabet, which was an Egyptian Temple in itself, there then appeared a procession of new horrors, called *arbitrary characters*; the most despotic characters ever known; who insisted, for example, that a thing like the beginning of a cobweb, meant expectation, and that a pen and ink sky-rocket stood for disadvantageous.[15]

Despite being dressed up in its later stages as an opium-eater's nightmare worthy of De Quincey, David's account accurately states the basic components of the system Dickens studied. In the Gurney alphabet, '[t]he only distinct marks, which can be made use of are a *point*, a *circle*, a *straight line*, and a *curve*. These may be varied by position.' Once these have been learned from the first and second pages of the four-page table, the '*Arbitrary Characters*, on the remainder of the second and third pages, should be got in memory.' There, indeed, a sign like a sky-rocket on page 3 represents 'advantage' or 'advance' arbitrarily, while the complex sign for 'expectation' – or 'xp*ctsn*' as it is abbreviated – features in the final paragraph of one of the sample texts included for practice purposes.[16]

III

The man who claimed to have taught Dickens shorthand was John Henry Barrow, a younger brother of John Dickens's great friend Thomas Culliford Barrow, whose sister he married in 1809. Barrow was a Gray's Inn lawyer, called to the bar in 1828, but like many of his peers he earned his bread as a journalist rather than practising, and developed a specialist knowledge of eastern affairs. By 1819 he was a Doctors' Commons reporter engaged on *The Times*, and in March 1820 may have helped John Dickens to secure publication there of his first-hand account of a terrible fire at Chatham.[17] Later that year Barrow reported the sensational trial for adultery of George IV's official wife, Caroline, as it 'dragged its foul length along week after week [and] swallowed up every other topic from June to November.'[18] The *Times* reports were avidly read, and Barrow attracted favourable notice from those politicians who championed the Queen's cause, such as Charles Tennyson.[19] By 1822, he was also contributing articles to the *British Press* on Indian affairs, and again may have used his influence to recommend John Dickens as a contributor in 1825. His good offices also included, he later told John Payne Collier, teaching his 'extremely clever' nephew 'Gurney's shorthand, which he wrote well.'[20] Barrow has thus been hailed as Dickens's 'literary mentor,' but while it is doubtful that Dickens learnt much about writing fiction from the example of *Emir Malek, Prince of the Assassins* (1827), his uncle's only and unsuccessful novel, it is clear that for the next few years, as Barrow's career reached its peak, he generously acted the part of master-craftsman during his nephew's informal apprenticeship in parliamentary reporting.

Crucial to this was Barrows's establishment in January 1828 of an ambitious new weekly publication dedicated to printing verbatim reports of the speeches (where possible, corrected by the speakers themselves) given in both Houses of Parliament. Invoking what is now called the 'reflective model' of conceiving the relationship between politics and the periodical press, he named it *The Mirror of Parliament*.[21] Although the publication remained studiously apolitical and pledged to 'the principle of absolute and uncompromising impartiality,' it was nevertheless a risky as well as toilsome undertaking. The Commons' standing order of 1738 which declared it a breach of Parliamentary privilege for anyone to print 'any Account of the Debates, or other Proceedings of this House,' and the various orders prohibiting the entry of strangers into the Galleries, were still technically in force, and hence until as late as 1875 reporters were liable to exclusion by the Speaker if a single MP drew attention to their presence.[22] To avoid such inconveniences, and because of the sheer expense of supporting a permanent roster of shorthand-writers, the well-known monthly compilation of unofficial *Parliamentary Debates* published by T. C. Hansard and son were produced by a group of out-of-house 'collators,' working mainly from different newspaper reports and sometimes from corrected proofs and notes supplied by MPs. Barrow's project, by contrast, necessitated a dedicated team of employees in the galleries – 'sixteen or seventeen picked reporters' who 'worked in guinea turns of three-quarters of an hour each' – as well as those who, like John Dickens, were employed in liaison with members to verify draft reports of important speeches. During the twenty or so weeks a year when Parliament sat in the early 1830s, the *Mirror*'s reporters could earn as much as fifteen guineas a week.[23]

In the winter of 1829–30, however, when Dickens left his solicitor's clerkship to set up as a freelance short-hand writer, his brachygraphy was not sufficiently reliable for him to enter the Gallery straight away. Parliamentary reporting not only required complete mastery of note-taking at speed, but a similarly rapid ability at writing out accurately from one's own notes for the compositors. Dickens was not yet proficient in this aspect of the craft: a common problem recorded by trainee stenographers, paralleled by the young Joseph Crowe's recollection that he 'made fair progress in writing, though but slow progress in reading my own hieroglyphics.'[24] In the interim, shorthand practice was needed where the pressure was less intense and the consequences of inaccuracy less damaging. This Dickens found, for a period of between eighteen and twenty-four months, working in a variety of ecclesiastical and Admiralty courts sitting in the College of Advocates and Doctors of Law, in Great Knightrider Street, near St Paul's churchyard. The college was better known to Londoners as Doctors' Commons.[25]

IV

The question 'what is Doctors' Commons?' was one which Dickens later answered in a variety of ways in journalistic satires of its antiquated proceedings, the first of which, 'Doctors' Commons,' was published in *The Morning Chronicle* on 11 October 1836. Thereafter, it recurs – like the mentions of Warren's Blacking manufactory and other London places of particular personal resonance – like a signature, in *Pickwick Papers*, in *Master*

Humphrey's Clock, and as the setting for David Copperfield's courting of Dora, during his employment there as an apprentice proctor articled to Mr Spenlow.[26] In the novel, it is man-of-the-world Steerforth who first opens the innocent David's eyes to the existence of the College, summing up its business as 'always a very pleasant profitable little affair of private theatricals, presented to an uncommonly select audience.' This cynical perspective is one which David comes to adopt, and reflects less the viewpoint of a proctor than that of the kind of detached observer which Dickens himself became, as a freelance short-hand writer employed by the proctors to make notes of cases on their clients' behalf. The parallel between the courts and private theatricals also has its own, biographical, logic. 'It wasn't a very good living,' he later told Forster, '(though not a very bad one), and was wearily uncertain; which made me think of the Theatre in quite a business-like way': practising 'four, five, six hours a day' and going to 'some theatre every night, with a very few exceptions.' Other free hours were spent in the Library Reading Room of the British Museum, for which Dickens acquired a reader's pass on the day of his eighteenth birthday, at once settling down 'to the acquirement of such general literature as I could pick up.'[27]

In order to be close to his new daily forum of business, from November 1830 or before, Dickens shared an office with, and carried out work for, a proctor called Charles Fenton, at 5 Bell Yard, Doctors' Commons, commuting from temporary lodgings in the Adelphi.[28] From 1831 until 1844, the name 'C. Dickins' was registered, along with the above address, under the heading 'Shorthand Writers' in the annual *Law List*.[29] The cases on which he reported were heard before the High Court of Admiralty, the Court of Arches, the Consistory Court of the Bishop of London, the Delegates Court, the Prerogative Court, and the Court of Faculties, such reports being in demand not only for administrative purposes but for summaries in the daily press. One biographer also records that Dickens carried out freelance work in Chancery at this time, noting that 'his first employment as a reporter was in the Lord Chancellor's Court taking notes of the cases, and here Mr. Blackmore, the solicitor, says he occasionally saw him after he left his service.' Dickens later recalled that some of the speeches made by Lord Lyndhurst during his first term as Lord Chancellor were 'models of grace and dignity.'[30]

Transcripts made by Dickens of sentences delivered in a Doctors' Commons case survive. On 18 November 1830, Dr Stephen Lushington gave judgements in two separate cases brought in by Fenton and 'promoted' by one Jarman, churchwarden of St Bartholemew the Great's, against two ratepayers, Bagster and Wise, whom Jarman accused, under the Statute 5 and 6 Edward VI, c.4, of 'quarrelling, chiding and brawling by words in the Vestry-room' of the church, over the levying of a disputed Poor Law rate. Dickens took the sentences down in shorthand, afterwards writing them out in full and binding them in two parchment booklets, which he signed and dated.[31] The case is quintessential Dickens material, and it is not surprising to find it transmogrified into the Arches Court Case of 'Bumple against Sludberry' in Dickens's later sketch for the *Morning Chronicle*.[32] The differences between the report and the sketch are slight; in both, the reader detects a structural irony in the clash of registers, as lively common oaths are rephrased in periphrastic legal language. Dickens is also believed to have reported at least one sensational murder trial at the Old Bailey in his Doctors' Commons days, and a detailed description of the demeanour of the prisoners as they were called to hear sentence pronounced 'bears evidence' of Dickens's hand. The familiarity with proceedings later shown in 'Boz's' sketch of 'The Old Bailey' for the *Morning Chronicle* in October 1834, certainly suggests that it was more than 'curiosity' which 'has occasionally led us into both Courts at the Old Bailey.'[33]

V

Within months of recording the parochial and essentially trivial arguments of Jarman, Bagster and Wise, Dickens found himself in the galleries of the old Houses of Parliament in St Stephen's Chapel, which had accommodated the Commons since the Reformation, and in Westminster Hall, where the Lords had been in residence since 1800. There he would begin recording arguments on topics of utmost national concern and gravity, and hear the leading British and Irish politicians in action. Sir George Hayter spent several years perfecting a grand historical canvas of the 'House of Commons, 1833,' with portraits of Aberdeen, Edward Stanley, Gladstone, Earl Grey, Lyndhurst, and dozens of other dignitaries. Although an older reporter noted the nineteen-year-old's 'exceedingly reserved' manners, from the first, the new scene does not seem to have struck Dickens as particularly venerable.[34]

For one thing, the Chapel was manifestly inadequate for its adapted purpose, as the same colleague recalled:

It was dark, gloomy, and badly ventilated, and so small that not more than four hundred out of the six hundred and fifty-eight members could be accommodated in it with any measure of comfort. When an important debate occurred, but especially when that debate was preceded by a call of the House, the members were really to be pitied; they were literally crammed together, and the heat of the house rendered it in some degree a second edition of the Black Hole of Calcutta. On either side there was a gallery, every corner of which was occupied by legislators; and many, not being able to get even standing room, were obliged to lounge in the refreshment apartments adjoining St Stephen's, until the division, – when they rushed to the voting room in as much haste as if the place they had quitted had been on fire.[35]

In October 1834, there was in fact a fire, which substantially destroyed both chambers.[36] As the new Parliament buildings were not finally completed until 1860, for the remainder of his stint in the galleries Dickens enjoyed the same kind of makeshift and temporary lodging at work, as he did at home.

'There never *was* such a reporter!' exclaimed Thomas Beard, the first friend Dickens made amongst his new colleagues. Anecdotes abound of his 'great splash' in the small pool of Gallery reporters.[37] Almost as important as this first, confidence-boosting success was the impact made on him by the rhetoric of prominent politicians such as Henry Brougham, Daniel O'Connell, Earl Grey, and Edward Stanley. 'Brougham in his prime,' for example, Dickens later told a friend,

> was by far the greatest speaker he had ever heard. Nobody rivalled him in sarcasm, in invective, in spirit-stirring eloquence. He was the man, too, he said, who of all others seemed, when he was speaking, to see the longest way before him.

His emphatic but periphrastic delivery ('not the shadow of a shade of a doubt,') and his placing 'parenthesis within parenthesis,' were features Dickens recalled and often imitated, though not, apparently, connecting his far-sightedness with the evils of telescopic philanthropy.[38] The story is also told that Dickens was so moved while reporting O'Connell's account of the outrages committed on the Irish peasantry that he 'put down his pencil ... and declared he could not take notes of the speech, so moved was he by its pathos.' O'Connell's 'fine brogue, which he cultivated,' his passion and melodrama, won Dickens's approval on a speaking campaign in the early months of 1836,

> and though he repeated [his speech] ... upon the wrongs of Ireland ... many, many times during the three months when I followed him about the country, I never heard him give it twice the same, nor ever without being himself deeply moved.[39]

By contrast, the elderly Whig Prime Minister's style of oratory, 'his fishy coldness, his uncongenial ... politeness, and his insufferable though most gentlemanly artificiality' angered him by its coolness; '[t]he shape of his head (I see it now) was misery to me and weighed down my youth.'[40] Another Whig, soon to cross the house to the Tory benches, was the Secretary of State for Ireland, Edward Stanley, whose six-hour speech during the first reading of the Suppression of Disturbances Bill in February

1833, was so imperfectly reported in the Commons that he later summoned Dickens to take it down in full. Nearly twenty years later, as Prime Minister and the 14th Earl of Derby, his orotund style was one Dickens recalled well enough to mock in the speech of 'our honorable friend ... the member for Verbosity.'[41]

The first major airing of the Bill for the Reform of Parliament, introduced in the House of Commons by Lord John Russell, took place between 1 and 9 March 1831. On the seventh, Dickens wrote to a friend apologizing for breaking an engagement, with the excuse that 'I was so exceedingly tired from my week's exertions that I slept on the Sofa the whole day.' In spite therefore of Forster's assertion that Dickens's 'first parliamentary service was given to *The True Sun*' (a paper which did not commence publication until 5 March 1832) it seems clear that by early 1831, Dickens was working late turns in the galleries for Barrow's *Mirror of Parliament*, in tandem with freelance work at Doctors' Commons and other courts of law. On different occasions, Dickens himself recorded that he had made his 'debut in the Gallery (at about 18, I suppose), engaged on a Voluminous publication ... called *The Mirror of Parliament*,' or, while still 'a boy, not yet eighteen.'[42] James Grant recalls that prior to *The True Sun*, 'Mr Dickens had been previously engaged while in his nineteenth year, as a reporter for ... *The Mirror of Parliament*, in which capacity he occupied the very highest rank among the eighty or ninety reporters for the press in Parliament.'

Another contemporary notes that in addition to reporting for Barrow's *Mirror* 'throughout the great Reform debates of 1832,' Dickens also

> ... acted as a sort of sub-editor of the work. It was a great object to get it before the public in advance of its rival, and by means of the good system the new hand established it was usually done.
>
> The connection thus established made him well known at many editorial rooms, and soon procured him an engagement as a reporter upon *The True Sun*, a London evening paper then lately established.[43]

By December 1832, Dickens had sufficient authority on the *Mirror's* staff to write to one job hunter promising him work 'when the session commences; and as soon as our arrangements ... are completed.' A year later, he described himself to a friend as 'busily engaged' for over a week amongst 'masses of papers, plans and prospectusses' assisting his uncle at his house in Norwood.[44] The *Mirror of Parliament* had now established a reputation amongst MPs in both houses as 'a work containing the most faithful and accurate account of the proceedings of Parliament'[45] and Barrow's next project – with which Dickens seems to have been involved – was to secure some kind of official recognition for its services. A petition to this end was presented to the House on 12 May 1834 but rejected by the Speaker; a motion presented on 22 May commanded some support in debate, but was finally defeated by eighteen votes. The failure was due in part to fierce rivalry from *Hansard*, but also perhaps to a trend against verbatim reporting of debates (as opposed to précis, selection and even the parliamentary sketch) setting in at this time.[46] More certainly, it marked a downturn in Barrow's career, and after a break in publication in 1839, *The Mirror of Parliament* eventually folded in 1841. Barrow estimated that he had lost £5000[47] – a small fortune – on the venture.

VI

Whilst much evidence indicates that Dickens's experience on the *Mirror of Parliament* helped secure him a simultaneous appointment to the reporting staff of the *True Sun* from 5 March 1832, the scope of his work for this paper remains uncertain, and no contributions have previously been identified. Given that this stamped, sevenpenny evening paper, 'overflowing with talent,' was shortly to become 'unequivocally the most radical London evening paper,'[48] and (unlike the *Mirror*) gave its parliamentary reporting a strong political bias, Dickens's relations with it are worth investigating. Charles Kent (a journalist friend of later years who was not yet ten in 1832) has claimed that Dickens's 'labours upon the *True Sun* were at the most but slight and perfunctory. He occupied a position on its reporting staff ... in effect of a supernumerary, who is liable to be called upon in the event of an emergency.' Yet early biographies suggest that Dickens did make an impression on the paper: that he was 'soon found to be one of the most ready, rapid and reliable of its reporters,' and that

> with the managers, he soon became noted for the succinctness of his reports, and the judicious, though somewhat ruthless, style with which he cut down unnecessary verbiage, displaying the substance to the best advantage, and exemplifying the well-known maxim ... that "speeches cannot be made long enough for the speakers, *nor short enough for the readers*"[49]

John Forster, who was the *True Sun's* dramatic critic from the summer of 1832 and 'regularly acting' as one of the editors by 1833,[50] confirms that Dickens held a position of some influence. When 'a general strike of the reporters' threatened the paper, 'on the staircase of the magnificent mansion we were lodged in' Forster not only saw Dickens for the first time, but learned that the employee known familiarly as 'young Dickens' 'had been spokesperson for the recalcitrant reporters, and conducted their case triumphantly.'[51] The incident is not dated, but may have been in late July 1832, when Dickens punned to Henry Kolle that the 'Sun is so obscured that I intend living under the planet no longer than Saturday Week next.'[52]

As there are no later references to the paper in Dickens's correspondence, it may be that his connection with the paper lasted no longer than the end of the Parliamentary session on 16 August. Yet even these few months of contact would have constituted a political baptism of fire for a young parliamentary reporter, with the final passage of the Reform Bill through the Commons and Lords in March, the 'Days of May' crisis (Earl Grey's resignation, Wellington's recall, the mobilization of the Political Unions and preparations for armed rebellion, and Grey's eventual reinstatement), followed by the implementation of the Act in England, Scotland (July) and Ireland (August).[53] Throughout, the paper kept up, in its detailed reports, editorials, and letters to the editor, a self-conscious display of its own policies and reporting practice, boasting its successes, and bemoaning its financial instability in a covert appeal for funds.

The paper's first proprietor was Patrick Grant, whose unsuccessful legal struggle with Murdo Young for ownership of the *Sun* (a Tory daily which had gone over to the Whigs when they took office in 1830) gave birth to the new paper, but dogged its fortunes. In addition to fitting up the paper's offices on the Strand 'in a style of splendour which little accorded with the ultra Democratic principles which the paper advocated,'[54] Grant hired extravagantly, employing in addition to Forster the staunch Whig Laman Blanchard as Literary Editor, William Carpenter the prolific radical pamphleteer as sub-editor, and, from 1834, Leigh Hunt as reviews editor. Douglas Jerrold and William Maginn were among the paper's early and more boisterous contributors.[55] The *True Sun* sold itself partly on the speed with which its very full reports of the readings of the Reform Bill were expressed to the provinces,[56] but side-by-side in its columns, ran anti-Tory satirical sketches and poetic squibs about politics and reporting. One of these, from the hand of a 'rhyming reporter,' shows the confidence with which the Gallery was able to cry *tu quoque* when accusations of reporting bias and spin were made by politicians:

> His brethren and himself have been accused
> Of being prejudiced, corrupt and partial;
> Of giving speeches, that had much amused,
> A serious tone; and rendering others martial,
> That were intended to be very tame;
> Of putting in unauthorized "Hear, Hears!"
> And filling lines with "Opposition cheers";
> ... Of twisting facts, in short, the way we please.
> By which it would appear that all M.P.'s
> ... Are virtuous, gifted, lofty, libelled martyrs
> To that most horrid clique – the base Reporters.
> *We* are that luckless, libelled race, alas!
> *We* are that sorrowing, short-hand writing class![57]

The authorship of this piece is unknown, but there is compelling evidence to attribute to Dickens some other comic verses published in the *True Sun* – not, indeed, forming part of its news coverage, but featuring prominently amongst its front-page advertisements, and constituting Dickens's first known publication in any genre.

The evidence rests with the *Morning Chronicle* reporter John Payne Collier, whose *Old Man's Diary*, published in 1872 (the same year as the first volume of Forster's *Life*), is not without its confusions over dates, but contains circumstantial information concerning Dickens's early career which there seems little reason to doubt. As a Shakespearean scholar, he was exposed as a forger in the early 1860s, but it is difficult to see how he might have forged the following coincidence, concerning Dickens's authorship of a poem advertising, of all things, Warren's boot blacking:

> July 24 [1833]. ... I asked Barrow where his nephew had been educated, but he could not exactly tell me. ... I inquired his nephew's qualifications, and the reply was that he was extremely clever, and that he (Barrow) had taught him Gurney's short-hand, which he wrote well, as had been proved on the *True Sun*, a newspaper which, strange to say, I had seldom seen....
>
> I asked how ... he had been employed before he had connected himself with the *True Sun?* The answer was rather ambiguous: the uncle only knew that his father's family distresses had driven Charles Dickens to exert himself in any way that would earn a living: that at one time he had assisted Warren, the blacking-man, in the conduct of his extensive business, and among other things, had written puff-verses for him. In this way, as well as in others, he had shown his ability; and Barrow jocosely referred me to the rhymes (possibly his) which accompanied the wood-cut advertisements of Warren's blacking, containing the figure of a dove ... looking at a polished boot, and mistaking the reflection of itself for the real appearance of its mate....[58]

Collier then quotes a four-line stanza, commenting that he 'thought the lines very laughable and clever for the purpose ... [t]he bold transition, or apostrophe, from the dove to the blacking is sublime, and, if not Pindaric, at least Peter-pindaric,' and the good impression they made led to a request to meet the young parodist, as the following chapter explains. Researchers have since uncovered various details illuminating elements of Collier's anecdote,[59] but never the rest of the poem from which he quotes. Forster himself recorded that, in 'after-talk' concerning the 'autobiographical fragment' incorporated in the *Life*, Dickens had explained how 'the poets in the house's regular employ he remembered, too, and made his first study of one of them for [Mr Slum] the poet of Mrs Jarley's wax-work.'[60] Apart from Collier's report of Barrow's claim and sample lines, however, there has been nothing to suggest that Dickens himself was one of their number – until the recent discovery of a series of ten puff verses published in *The True Sun* at roughly weekly intervals, during the first three months of its publication and during Dickens's brief employment on its staff. Like the hand-bills advertising Jarley's, several of them are 'couched in the form of parodies on popular melodies,' including the first, 'The Turtle Dove,' set to the 'Air – Jessy of Dumblain.'[61] More significantly, it also contains, as its final verse, the lines which Barrow, *pace* Collier, attributed to Dickens:

> As lonely I sat on a calm summer's morning,
> To breathe the soft incense that flow'd on the wind;
> I mus'd on my boots in their bright beauty dawning,
> By Warren's Jet Blacking – the pride of mankind.
> ...
> On a maple-tree near sat a turtle bewailing,
> With sorrowful cooings, the loss of her love;
> Each note that she utter'd seem'd sadness exhaling,
> And plaintively echo'd around the still grove.
>
> When lo! in my boots the lone mourner perceived
> Her form, and suppos'd that her lover was there;
> Even I, that the vision was real, half believed –
> The Blacking reflected her image so clear.
> ...
> How wild were her cries, when the fairy illusion
> She found but a cheating and transient shade;
> Like Hope's airy dreams but a faded delusion,
> That shone in the bloom Warren's Blacking displayed.
>
> I pity'd the dove, for my bosom was tender –
> I pity'd the strain that she gave to the wind;
> But I ne'er shall forget the superlative splendour
> Of Warren's Jet Blacking – the pride of mankind.[62]

The product message apart, in conception and manner 'The Turtle Dove' exactly parallels Dickens's known, non-professional, 'literary' output at this period – 'The Bill of Fare,' written for the Beadnell's dinner-party in Autumn 1831, parodying Goldsmith's 'Retaliation;' the eight-verse parody of Southey's 'Devil's Walk' written in Maria's album in November 1831; the doggerel poems and songs to be sung to Irish melodies which make up the surviving scraps of *O'Thello*, Dickens's Shakespearean burletta written in 1833.[63] Three of his later poetical squibs on political topics, published in *The Examiner* and *Daily News* (to be discussed in due course), likewise take the form of new lyrics for old songs, and one – 'Subjects for Painters (after Peter Pindar)' – is as openly Peter-pindaric as Collier could have wished.[64]

Back in 1823, the so-called 'Blacking Laureate' Alexander Kemp had been paid 'Two shillings and Sixpence each!' by Robert Warren for the 'above two hundred' puff verses he wrote for the business.[65] Writing of the 'very expensive' work of Mr Slum in the 27th chapter of *The Old Curiosity Shop* in August 1840, Dickens would award him only three-and-sixpence per poem. In 1835 he mentions, in a slum sketch of 'Seven Dials,' a shabby-genteel man leading a 'life of seclusion' in a second floor room, buying only coffee, bread, pens and 'ha'porths of ink' – 'his fellow-lodgers very naturally suppose him to be an author; and rumours are current in the Dials, that he writes poems for Mr Warren.'[66] Strange as it seems, for similar small sums in 1832, it is very likely that an impecunious Dickens did the same, ironically exploiting his talent for parody, and knowledge of popular songs, to write verses for the very business which he later recalled with such revulsion.

To pro-reform members like Daniel O'Connell, the *True Sun's* combination of full debates and opinionated editorial represented a valuable service to their causes, which they were anxious to support.[67] Politically, the paper probably represented the extreme of radical opinion in the House of Commons and amongst the pre-Reform Bill electorate, but while prepared to canvass the possibility of popular uprising in support of the Paris insurrection of June 1832, both its price and limited circulation (around 3000 copies falling to 1800 after the passing of the Reform Bill), ensured that it stayed mainly in the hands of responsible householders. Even when *The Times* alienated swathes of its Radical and Whig readers in 1834, through its opposition to Owen's Grand National Consolidated Trade Union, the *True Sun* did not succeed in encroaching upon its territory.[68] Not until the Radical Unitarian preacher-turned-journalist W. J. Fox took over the editorship, well after Dickens's connection with the paper had ceased and the paper came under new management, did it enjoy a new dawn.[69]

The *True Sun's* initial stand against public executions, child labour, army flogging, the old and amended Poor Law, the campaign for stricter Sunday observance; its support for the abolition of slavery, for the reform of factory regulations and of the Court of Chancery, all in fact indicate principles closer to what we know of Dickens's own in the 1830s than the Whig paper on which he was shortly to seek an appointment. Yet its precarious finances, and the fact that Dickens's work for both it and the *Mirror of Parliament* was sessional only, meant that a more reliable income was essential. 'I am,' he wrote to Edward Stanley's private secretary in June 1833, soliciting freelance shorthand work, 'always entirely unemployed during the recess.'[70] It was during that Autumn recess, significantly, and in this context of uncertainty, that Dickens found occasion to write the first of several comic stories of suburban life which were published gratis, in a small-circulation, radically-inclined periodical called *The Monthly Magazine*.[71] Like most of his work as a shorthand copyist and all his writings as a reporter for the *Mirror* and the *True Sun*, 'A Dinner at Poplar Walk' and the four tales which followed it, were published anonymously. The confidence to establish a signature and a brand for the kind of chronicling and sketch-writing at which he excelled would not come until Dickens had secured a permanent position in the volatile newspaper trade in which he was now apprenticed.

2
Chronicling and Sketching Life (1834–36)

The years Dickens spent as reporter and sub-editor of the *Mirror of Parliament* were years in which, as he later reminisced to a certain Maria Winter, 'the qualities which have done me most good since' – earnestness, energy, giant-killing determination – 'were growing in my boyish heart.' As 'pocket Venus' Maria Beadnell, Mrs Winter had been the 'driving force' of Dickens's ambitions since 1829, for her father was a high-ranking City bank clerk, who clearly did not look kindly on a suitor from an impoverished background.[1] In November 1831 the hapless John Dickens had been gazetted, and he was to be arrested for debt for a second time in November 1834. Nevertheless, he and Barrow set to work to help Charles to something more permanent and secure than the freelance and sessional work he had been picking up. The plan was to 'puff' him for a job on the reporting staff of the *Morning Chronicle*, the most respected of the Whig dailies and the most serious rival to the ascendancy of *The Times*.

The *Chronicle*'s proprietor earlier in the century had been James Perry, the man credited with the 'invention' of modern parliamentary reporting.[2] Under William Clement, it had declined markedly, both in value and circulation, but the trio of politically-inclined businessmen who took it over in January 1833 – John Easthope, the majority shareholder; the publisher James Duncan; and the wealthy Canada trader Simon MacGillivray – realistically aimed to make it the unofficial organ of the new Whig hegemony. Easthope had himself been a Whig MP from 1826 to 1831, and aimed to deploy the paper in support of controversial measures such as the new Poor Law bill, against anticipated opposition from *The Times*.[3]

The long-serving editor, John Black, was retained but the reporting staff were to be reorganized and amplified, so on 24 July Barrow contacted Collier, the most senior of the reporters, recommending his talented nephew, and praising his abilities as a reporter, parodist, and singer of comic songs, as the last chapter outlined. Collier recorded in his diary for 27 July how he had invited the twenty-one-year old to dinner, liked him at once, and had 'little hesitation in recommending him' to Easthope, although this had little immediate effect. A later note states that Dickens 'has not been taken on the newspaper by my recommendation, however, for some more influential person, whose name I heard, had also spoken in his behalf.'[4] This was Joseph Parkes, the Radical 'brummagem attorney' and influential behind-the-scenes parliamentary agent for the Whigs,[5] to whom John Dickens, with characteristic aplomb, went on to apply in June 1834, both in person and by letter, to back up Charles's direct approach to Black:

> My Dear sir – In consequence of my Son, as I stated, having addressed a Letter to Mr Black, as I communicated to you, when I did myself the pleasure of calling on you, he had an interview with that Gentleman last Evening, but it appears he had not had any communication from you with regard to my son's application....
>
> I would not press the point, did I not know his competence in every respect for the duties he will be required to perform. His capabilities have over & over again been borne testimony to by Peers & Members, and the extraordinary facility with which he writes out, (and I would back him against any man in the Gallery in this respect) is a very valuable consideration....

Tradition also has it that Dickens's closest friend in the Gallery, Thomas Beard – who had already secured a transfer to the *Chronicle* from the *Morning Herald* – further recommended Dickens to Parkes, and so, as much by family networking as by professional merit, the appointment was finally secured in August 1834.

I

For the next two years and a half, on a basic salary of five guineas a week, Dickens was a hardworking servant of the paper, and identified himself fully with its fortunes. When, by a turn of events that would frequently recur whenever he parted company with those in positions of authority over him, relations with Easthope (nicknamed 'Blast-Hope' by his subordinates) turned sour, Dickens forcibly reminded him of the role he had carried out:

> [O]n many occasions at a sacrifice of health, rest and personal comfort, I have again and again, on important expresses in my zeal for the interests of the paper, done what was before considered impossible, and what in all probability will never be accomplished again. During the whole period of my engagement wherever there was a difficult and harassing duty to be performed – travelling at a few hours' notice hundreds of miles in the depths of winter – leaving hot and crowded rooms to write, the night through, in a close damp chaise – tearing

along, and writing the most important speeches, under every possible circumstance of disadvantage and difficulty – for that duty have I been selected.[7]

This recollection of special status accords with an oft-quoted remark of the versatile Charles Mackay, the 'Sub Editorial, paste-and-scissorsorial Craftsman of the Chronicle,' as Dickens later styled him.[8] One of Mackay's duties was to confer with Black on what kind of general work 'such as attendance at public meetings, reviews of books, or notices of new plays' the different Parliamentary reporters should be assigned during the lengthy recesses:

> Mr Black desired to spare Mr Dickens as much as possible from all work of this kind, having the highest opinion of his original genius. ... 'Any fool,' he said, in his usual broad Scotch, 'can pass judgement ... on a book or play – but "Boz" can do better things; he can create works for other people to criticize. Besides, he has never been a great reader of books or plays, and knows but little of them. ... Keep "Boz" in reserve for great occasions. He will *aye* be ready for them.'[9]

Yet Mackay's account is hard to reconcile with the evidence that Dickens clearly carried out 'a great deal of routine reporting work' for the *Chronicle*, including theatre reviewing, the latter at Black's particular recommendation.[10] Between eight and a dozen reviews – the outcome of orders at short notice to visit opening nights of London shows in 1835 and 1836 – have been identified as Dickens's work. His letters between late May and 10 September 1835, frequently endorsed between three and six o'clock in the morning, also testify to his assertion that he has been 'for months ... up all night and asleep all day,' reporting late-night sittings of Parliament.[11] The current list and nature of Dickens's known contributions to the *Chronicle*, together with numerous references in his letters to his duties, thus show that while Dickens was indeed called upon to carry out special reporting assignments, and submit original literary work (the majority of which has probably now been identified), he did so over and above much general parliamentary reporting for the paper (of which the majority has probably not been recuperated).

A judgmental generalization can also be made. As a reporter of speeches made within Parliament, Dickens remains more or less invisible, but as soon as he is employed as an extra-mural commentator, in contexts where politicians, supporters and reporters are brought together on social occasions, and where orated words – the ostensible stuff of newspaper reports – can be perceived to clash with present actualities, Dickens the journalist seems to emerge as a presence, pointing up the discontinuities between text and context, between political promise and social reality.[12]

Shortly after he joined the staff, Dickens and Thomas Beard were despatched by Black on their first 'important express' to report the preparations for, and speeches at, what journalists called a 'whacking dinner.' It was to be held in Edinburgh in honour of Earl Grey, the retiring Whig Premier now hailed as the major architect of the Reform Act. Their main report of what became known as the 'Grey Festival' reached London and was printed on 18 September, but *The Times*, with its costly new system of 'Extraordinary Expresses,' beat them by a day, and mocked the *Chronicle* editor on the 19th for labelling the Dickens and Beard report 'By Express.' Dickens's adroitness in organising expresses was to be a notable feature of his later journalistic career, traceable to this episode; so too, a fierce sense of rivalry with *The Times* that went beyond political differences.[13]

Dickens's published responses to the Edinburgh expedition are a good example of the combination of detailed observation, social commentary in a politicized milieu, and journalistic opportunism, which characterize his contributions to the *Chronicle*. The cross-fertilization of ideas and incidents with his *Monthly Magazine* work of the period is also notable, demonstrating the essential narrative uniformity of his tales and reports.[14] Five days before the long, first-person plural, report with Beard on the Festival, Dickens had filed a short, first-person singular, description of the erection on Calton hill of a Pavilion to cater for 1500 diners and many more listeners. 'I confess I do not entertain very sanguine expectations as to the accuracy of either of these calculations,' he permitted himself to comment, anticipating for some ticket-holders 'confusion and much disappointment.' More seriously, Dickens noted the irony of a 'promenade … for the benefit of the Blind Asylum, the Deaf and Dumb Institution, and the House of Refuge' which involved seating 'the poor blind-school pupils' in the warmest part of a hot enclosure while a military band played in the shade: they 'appeared very glad to be filed off from a scene in which they could take little interest, and with which their pensive, careworn faces painfully contrasted.'[15] Typically, Dickens seizes on a background detail that has caught his attention, and dwells on it rather than on the main spectacle, in such a way as to undermine the ideological framework of the performance. Moreover, Dickens's stylistic dexterity is such that, when he wants, 'he is quite able to avoid the stereotypical phrases of conventional journalism.'[16]

Dickens had started signing his *Monthly Magazine* tales 'Boz' during the first month of his *Chronicle* contract, and as the House rose on 15th August, it was soon established – perhaps at one of the daily meetings of the reporting staff 'to receive Mr Black's instructions'[17] – that he would use some of his spare time composing a series of 'Street Sketches' for the paper, under the same signature. 'Boz's' official newspaper début began on 26 September with a short, chatty paper about 'Omnibuses' in London, based on 'our daily peregrination from the top of Oxford Street' (Dickens's Bentinck street digs) 'to the Bank' (the *Chronicle's* City offices) and other personal experiences.[18] Five sketches had been published by 15 December, when, with the new session commencing in January, and a General Election in the offing, 'Boz' announced a break until the next recess:

> We have more of these imperfect sketches for [our readers'] perusal; and as we hope to have many opportunities – when the partial absence of matter of pressing and absorbing interest again enables us to occupy a column occasionally – of laying our pen-and-ink drawings before them, we postpone the further consideration of this subject until a future time.[19]

Such passages, with their deictic messaging, and their chatty asides to the reader, were naturally stripped out by Dickens when he republished his sketches in volume form in February, and again in December, of the following year. What they often show – and something that the critical history of *Sketches by Boz* has not yet fully taken into account – is the extent to which 'Boz' cultivated in the presence of *Morning Chronicle* readers the persona of an individual reporter with a wider than usual brief, who, space permitting, roves from Parliament Square, through the Great Metropolis, and out into the provinces, indulging his faculty for detecting analogies between areas of the contemporary scene normally kept discrete in newspaper columns.[20]

Three days after thus signing off his fifth 'Street' sketch, 'Boz' was back in the paper, with a satirical parody of F. W. Carové's allegorical fairytale *Das Märchen Ohne Ende*, popularized earlier in the year in Sarah Austin's English translation, *The Story Without an End*. His 'Story without a Beginning (Translated from German by Boz)' must have appealed to Black, who was himself an accomplished German translator, and, like Sarah Austin, a close friend of James and J. S. Mill.[21] Appropriately, Dickens's version begins in mid-sentence, and, applying Carové's strategy of describing experience through the eyes of a child in a flower-garden, where the flowers and insects represent different facts of Nature, he proceeds boldly to criticise the actions of the 'childish' William IV in sacking Lord Melbourne's Whig ministry, in alarm over a plan for partial disendowment of the Irish Church.[22] The dismissal was very much the topic of the hour. *The Times* had broken the news on 15 November, but it was not until 9 December that Wellington and Peel had agreed to form a Tory ministry, and the day before Dickens's attack, Peel had proclaimed his famous 'Tamworth manifesto,' promising a policy of liberal Conservatism and anti-Radical alliance.[23] In Dickens's tale, the 'noble flowers' represent the loyal subjects of the 'child' King, the 'forced' and 'bright green' flowers, his neglected and coerced Irish people, while the 'reptiles and insects' are Tories, and the 'active, hard-working bees' who are 'turned ... out of their hive' are the dismissed Whig reformers. In the final paragraph, Dickens confidently prophesies where the story will end: with misery for the King, the 'perishing' of the Tories, and the rejection of both by the people:

> But the flowers, who had been obliged to support one another when their natural protectors deserted them, turned a deaf ear to [the child's] earnest prayers; and [he] found, to his grief and sorrow, that the appeal had been made too late.[24]

This was a particularly exciting time to be working for the *Chronicle*, as the 'remarkable tergiversion' of *The Times* in agreeing to support the Peel ministry, meant that the paper won over many Whig readers of the middle-ground: 'Now,' Black is reported to have exclaimed, 'our readers will follow me anywhere I like to lead them!'[25] In the 1820s, the Scotsman had been, as Mill later recorded, 'the first journalist who carried the criticism and the spirit of reform into the details of English institutions,' in particular the operation of the courts and the unpaid magistracy. He had campaigned successfully for the right to report on-going Parliamentary enquiries, and wrote leaders across the spectrum of political affairs. All this made him something of a role model to the young Dickens, who, in spite of Black's deeply ingrained Benthamism, cherished his praise and encouragement.[26]

As a leading reporter with an established flare for witty Tory-bashing, Dickens was selected to report on violent General Election meetings in county boroughs, both in January 1835, when the Tories gained ground but no clear majority, and again in May, when Peel resigned over the Irish Church revenues question and the Whigs returned to power with a precarious coalition that would resist inherent differences until 1841. Dickens happily supported the *Chronicle*'s party line at this time, and entered fully into the spirit of its fierce rivalry with other papers. Although later to voice a near-Swiftian despair at Parliamentary hypocrisy, negligence and incompetence, Dickens seldom recalled his political reporting and special correspondent work without reliving something of its excitement and drama. In 1865 he told diners at the anniversary dinner of the Newspaper Press Fund how he had often transcribed important speeches for the waiting printers, 'writing on the palm of my hand, by the light of a dark lantern, in a post chaise and four, galloping through a wild country, all through the dead of night.' He had been, in his time, 'belated on miry by-roads, towards the small hours, in a wheelless carriage, with exhausted horses and drunken postboys, and have got back in time for publication.'[27] In 1868, he recounted to Boston friends the hectic routine on the night-road back to London, itself something of an allegory of his writing life:

> ... a bag of sovereigns on one side of his body and a bag of slips of paper on the other, writing, writing desperately all the way.... At each station a man on horseback would stand ready to seize the sheets already

prepared and ride with them to London. Often ... this work would make him deadly sick, and he would have to plunge his head out of the window to relieve himself....[28] As the station was reached, a sudden plunge into the pocket of sovereigns would pay the postboy, another behind him would render up the completed pages, and a third into the [other] pocket ... would give him the fresh paper to carry forward the inexorable, unremitting work.[29]

In between these whirlwind tours, Dickens contributed theatre reviews and accounts of visits to public amusements such as the newly-refurbished Colosseum in Regent's Park. He was also invited to develop his talents as a sketch-writer by writing 'an original sketch' for the first number of a new tri-weekly evening offshoot of the *Chronicle*, aimed, as all evening papers were, at a largely rural readership.[30] Accordingly, for an extra two guineas a week for the duration of the series, he began a series of twenty cleverly-observed 'Sketches of London,' which were published in the *Evening Chronicle* at the rate of two or three a month between January and August. Significantly, all were eventually reprinted for metropolitan readers in the morning paper – despite the pressure for space – between February and December. Subjects ranged as widely within Greater London as 'Boz' did himself as narrator, and the treatment – alternately satirical, observant, pathetic, melodramatic – shared the same mutability. The series, together with the fortuitous double exposure (as many as six papers were reprinted in April, one of which made the front page[31]) established the signature 'Boz' as a promising publishing concern, and, Forster recalled, were 'much ... talked of outside as well as in the world of newspapers.'[32] Dickens's engagement in the spring to Catherine Hogarth, eldest daughter of the *Chronicle* sub-editor who had commissioned the 'Sketches of London,' also increased his desire to find a way of setting up on his own, both as a householder and as a writer.

II

Examining the development of Dickens's *Evening Chronicle* sketches along-side his election reports is instructive. Dickens was clearly given leeway in his reporting to be not only partisan but personal, and – by contrast with the prevailing norms of the genre – to emerge indirectly as an authorial presence. His comments about the conditions experienced by reporters at the hustings are typical of this, and are particularly prominent in the long opening of his Express report, with Beard, of the nominations for the South Devon election in May:

At this period of the business there came on a tremendous shower of rain, which made the multitude fly in all directions, and which made its way through the hustings, and the temporary shelter provided for the reporters. So heavy a storm was not calculated on, nor guarded against by tarpauling; and the rain came through the hustings in water-spouts in all directions.... The storm continued with inveterate force for half an hour, by which time those on and under the hustings were completely drenched. It having then somewhat subsided, portions of the crowd returned, and the proceedings resumed; but still the drippings from the hustings were so considerable as to make that station anything but an enviable one. As to taking notes of the speeches, that was almost wholly out of the question, for as fast as any attempts were made to take notes, the torrents were nearly sure to 'swamp' them.[33]

When Dickens was again selected for the special responsibility of reporting the Norton vs. Melbourne trial of June 1836, his complaint about 'the gratuitous annoyances and ungentlemanly interruptions' experienced by Reporters from junior barristers, strikes what has rightly been judged a characteristic 'note of prickly assertion of professional dignity tinged with class resentment.'[34]

The South Devon report – considered a great coup for the *Chronicle* in its contest with *The Times*[35] – also develops, amongst much standard journalistic preamble, the analogy of the hustings as theatre or tournament, complete with spectating ladies, colour symbolism, and a hero of the hour:

No place better adapted for the purpose to which it was devoted on this occasion, than the Castle-yard, can be imagined. The Court-house extends the whole width of one end; at the opposite extremity are the entrance gate and two lodges; and on either side is a beautiful green slope, plentifully studded with trees, the graceful appearance of which adds materially to the beauty of the amphitheater we have described. Groups of people began to assemble as early as nine o'clock, ... carriages filled with ladies from time to time drove up and deposited their fair burdens at the Court-house, from the windows of which building they were enabled to see and hear what passed.

Shortly after eleven o'clock, Mr [Montague] Parker, accompanied by a body of his friends on foot and bearing banners and placards arrived; his appearance on the hustings was hailed with cheers and hisses – the latter, however, greatly predominated. Lord John Russell, attended by his friends, arrived immediately afterwards amidst tremendous cheering. His procession displayed a variety of elegant banners, on which were described, 'Be true to your King, and vote for the man of his choice' – 'Reform in Church and State' – 'Civil and Religious Liberty throughout the World' – 'The People, the source of all power.'[36]

Russell's long speech is reported verbatim over 2½ columns, as opposed to the Tory candidate's, which is summarized in the free indirect style in little more than a $1/4$ column. The drama of the event is highlighted through continuous references to the strange vehemence of the weather, and humorous attention is given, in reporting lengthy monologues, to the interruptions of other voices, represented directly or described in interpolated parentheses. Stylistically, various literary devices are deployed in the service of a politicized interpretation of the day's events.

The operation is carried out in reverse, with interesting results, in Dickens's *Evening* and *Morning Chronicle* sketches of these electioneering months, which go well beyond the simple writing up of a reporter's personal experiences (as in 'Public Dinners' and 'Early Coaches'), to offer varying degrees of satirical commentary on contemporary politics. 'The "House"' and 'Bellamy's' take *Chronicle* readers behind-the-scenes in the House of Commons, portrayed as a kind of Rotary club for eccentrics, and contributed to the nascent parliamentary sketch-writing tradition usually held to have been pioneered by James Grant.[37] The second person form of address, interchanging with the editorial 'we,' and the present tenses ('you see ... you see') buttonhole the reader, and situate him inside the building of 'the present temporary House of Commons,' where Boz acts as an irreverent guide to the proceedings, whose anxieties as a press representative (and personal weariness of what he is describing) are distinctly audible.[38] Like later Parliamentary sketch-writers, Dickens is more interested in Members' idiosyncracies – 'personal and oratorical peculiarities,' as Grant puts it – which verbatim reporting necessarily passed over, than in their principles. Indeed, more time is spent dissecting the curious political allegiances of the butler to Bellamy's kitchen than those of any MPs. Some potentially libellous assertions were removed, and the harshness of some of the descriptions softened, when the two sketches were reworked and combined for the second volume edition of *Sketches by Boz*, but along with the humour and immediacy, questions of satirical purchase remain in the revised 'Parliamentary Sketch': is Dickens not continually cashing in on the comic potential of Parliament's antiquated procedures and those who follow them, while at the same time implying that these are ripe for reform?[39]

It is in the six 'Our Parish' sketches[40] where 'Boz' comes into his own as a 'chronicler' of a comic microcosm of British social and political life that is both timely and timeless. 'Our Parish,' in its nameless municipality, is the first of his Little Britains, and the sketches derived an additional force in 1835 from coinciding with the stormy passage through the Lords of the Radically-conceived Municipal Corporations Bill. Joseph Parkes was Secretary to the Municipal Corporations Commission and a major architect of the bill, which accordingly received detailed coverage in the *Chronicle*.[41] The petty squabbles, quarrels, examples of corruption and one-upmanship in the Parish which 'Boz' reports not only rework his Doctors' Commons experiences, but also appeal wittily to the ongoing work of Commission, with its brief to 'collect information respecting the defects in ... constitution [of the several Municipal Corporations in England and Wales]' and to 'enquire also into ... the mode of electing and appointing Members and Officers of such Corporations, and into the Privileges of Freemen and other members thereof....'[42] The invitation to allegory is unmistakable, as 'Boz' remorselessly sends up his own narrative process and the whole business of partisan political reporting, in 'The Election for Beadle':

> A contest of paramount interest has just terminated; a parochial convulsion has taken place. It has been succeeded by a glorious triumph, which the country – or at least the parish – it is all the same – will long remember. We have had an election; an election for beadle. Supporters of the old beadle system have been defeated in their stronghold, and the advocates of the great new beadle principles have achieved a proud victory.[43]

As in his formal election reports for the *Chronicle*, Dickens casts the contest as 'a party contest between the ins and the outs,' and between vested interests ('the overseers ... the churchwardens ... the vestry') and those of the people ('parishioners, fearlessly asserting their undoubted rights'). The nomination speeches are reported in true 'parliamentary style,' with the speakers imitating 'the celebrated negative style adopted by great speakers,' and each stage of polling activity is described, down to the declaration of the result. 'Boz' undermines both electioneering – primarily a male activity – and social work, the business of 'The Ladies' Societies' (20 August 1835) in his 'Parish' sketches, and shows how the balance of power in local politics is subject to the dangerous 'fluctuations of public opinion.'

In December 1835, during the Kettering by-election, Dickens's criticism of Conservative corruption and intimidation at provincial elections reached its peak.[44] Setting the 'perfect order and good humour' of the Whig candidate's supporters against the 'ruffianly barbarity, and brutal violence' of the Tory supporters, Dickens describes the actions of the latter, in charging the crowd on horseback, as 'an outrage of the most disgraceful nature I ever witnessed,' and the opening of his report is dominated by an electrifying account of the deeds of a Tory parson who had barely been prevented from firing a double-barrelled pistol into the mob. Writing home to his fiancée, Dickens told Catherine that she

> will see or hear by the Chronicle of yesterday, that we had a slight flare here yesterday morning, just stopping short of a murder and riot.... I look forward to the probability of a scuffle before it is over. As the Tories are the principal party here, *I* am in no very good odour in the town, but I shall not spare them the more on that account in the descriptions of their behaviour I may forward to headquarters.[45]

His next Express, reporting the result of the first day's polling, accordingly satirized the inevitable Tory victory as a 'glorious result' for 'the most ignorant, drunken, and brutal electors in these kingdoms, who have been treated and fed, and driven up to the polls the whole day like herds of swine.' The successful Tory candidate, returning thanks for his election two days later, was reported by a different *Chronicle* reporter reacting publicly to this description, berating the paper for its 'hardihood and impudence' in thus describing 'the honest and independent electors' who had supported him: 'this was a newspaper which supported the present Government, and he supposed that the Editor must have laboured under a mistake, and meant to have said that these were the constituents of his friend Mr O'Connell [cheers].'[46]

The capacity to engage in such quick-fire cut-and-thrust during and immediately after an election was the payoff for nearly a week's preparatory work by Dickens and his colleagues at 'headquarters.' Passages of this kind, emerging out of the ostensibly objective operation of reporting speeches, were of enormous value to the *Chronicle*'s managers, who throughout Dickens's period of service were in constant, if uneasy, communication, with different ministers of the Whig administration.[47] Press historians and biographers of the protagonists record a detrimental struggle between Easthope, Parkes, and Black for control of the paper's policies during the Melbourne administration: what Dickens refers to in one letter as 'half a dozen Proprietors and agents ... pulling different ways – each for himself.'[48] Articles by or about disagreeing Whig ministers were inserted under pressure from different quarters; the demands of the Birmingham 'ultra' Radicals, mediated through Parkes, and of Utilitarian and Benthamite thinking, represented by Black, competed for space. 'There seems to be no unity of purpose, no presiding mind,' one reviewer complained; '[a]ntagonistic principles, irreconcilable opinions, jostle each other on the same page.'[49]

Amidst such tensions, Dickens, Beard, and three other reporters made bold to dispute with Easthope proposed changes in their terms of engagement, at the start of the new session of parliament in 1836. Dickens's letter of 2 February, outlining their stand, emphasized their intention to 'accept the first annual Engagement elsewhere, we can get,' if forced to sign up to unfavourable terms.[50] Dickens had more reason than hitherto to feel able to assert his independence. In September 1835 he had begun, for a guinea a time, a series of a dozen sketches called 'Scenes and Characters,' to be published not in the *Chronicle* – this despite an assurance to the paper's readers that the sketches were 'to be continued' there – but on the front page of the popular sporting journal *Bell's Life in London*. An early biographer records how Dickens left a spirited calling card for its editor, Vincent Dowling, at an oyster house opposite his Strand Office: 'Charles Dickens, Resurrectionist, In Search of a Subject.'[51] Like the bodysnatchers then in the news, Dickens too was moonlighting, hence his adoption for the *Bell's Life* sketches of a new *nom de guerre*, 'Tibbs,' though attentive readers might have recalled that this was the name of the Landlady in the first *Monthly Magazine* tale which had appeared under the 'Boz' signature.[52]

The newly-established publishing due of Chapman & Hall had also commissioned Dickens to write a sketch for the first number of their forthcoming monthly miscellany, *The Library of Fiction*. Moreover, since October, he had been in negotiations with the publisher John Macrone to publish a collection of his 'Boz' and 'Tibbs' papers in volume form, together 'with two or three new sketches, to make weight.' The famous illustrator of London scenes, George Cruikshank, had been contracted to provide woodcuts to complement Dickens's 'pen-and-ink drawings,' and the young author had been promised £100 for the copyright: enough money to marry on. The dispute with Easthope seems to have been patched up, however, and Dickens continued in the service of the paper during and after the launch of *Sketches by Boz*. *First Series*, on 8 February, and he dutifully arranged his marriage to Catherine Hogarth and brief honeymoon in Chalk, to coincide with the spring recess of Parliament (30 March–11 April).

III

In his part-amused, part-earnest, validation of the ambitions and pretensions of the masses of London parishioners *not* yet enfranchized by reform of local and national representation, 'Boz' went distinctly further than the Grey-Melbourne administration and arguably, on two issues, further than his *Chronicle* editors. At times, indeed, 'Boz' seems sufficiently distrustful of all political agendas to voice dissatisfaction both with established authorities, and with 'innovators' and 'reformers' who want to sweep away old London and its popular customs.[53] In spite of his admiration for his Editor, Dickens recalled 'how often Black and I used to quarrel about the effect of the poor-law bill,' which Black had fully supported, anticipating how 'the whigs [would] go out [of office] upon it' at the 1841 General Election, because of the unpopularity it generated.[54] The extent of the young Dickens's awareness of the Benthamite utilitarianism which informed the Poor Law Commission and the Amendment Act of 1834 has been much disputed, but the balance of opinion now supports the view that, although his published opinions approach the subject satirically and obliquely, Dickens knew – through his Parliamentary reporting rather than through formal study – the main framework of the public debate intimately, and drew on this in his writing.[55]

The other issue on which Dickens seems to have felt the *Chronicle* to be insufficiently Radical was the defence of the Sunday sports and recreations of Londoners against the Bills for the Better Observance of Sunday, championed in the Commons by Sir Andrew Agnew. Between the 'Sabbatarians' as they were known, and the mainstream press, there was little love lost.[56] Dickens very probably attended the Commons debate on the second reading of Agnew's latest and unsuccessful attempt to have his bill made law on 18 May 1835, but little space was devoted by the *Chronicle* to his report,[57] and Black's accompanying editorial was so far sympathetic to the Sabbatarians as to contemplate a fresh attempt: '[i]f we are to have Sunday legislation the subject must be committed to very different hands.'[58] Dickens's opposition was far stronger, hence his first and only major outbreak as a pamphleteer with *Sunday Under Three Heads*, an 11 000 word *tour de force* published in June 1836 by his 'new' publishers, Chapman & Hall, with four illustrations by Hablôt Knight Browne. Its tripartite structure and bluff manner recalls, perhaps deliberately, that adopted by George Cruikshank and journalist John Wight in their illustrated pamphlet *Sunday in London*, a publication which was timed to coincide with the defeat of Agnew's first presentation of his Bill, in 1833. Cruikshank and Wight had looked in turn at the way the 'Higher,' 'Middle' and 'Lower Orders' of the 'metropolitan public' behaved during each of the twenty-four hours of the Sabbath.[59] However, Dickens's attempt to envisage one actual and two possible future states in which men from different stations in life would pass their day of rest (Sunday 'As It Is,' 'As Sabbath Bills Would Make It,' 'As It Might Be') anticipates a similar kind of trinitarian operation with Scrooge's past, present and future in *A Christmas Carol*; and results in a much fiercer, more partisan attack on Agnew and his bill, in line with his comments in the original newspaper text of 'Thoughts about People.'[60] Cruikshank and Wight had conceded the bill contained 'some little good,' and although it was 'at once inefficient, partial and impractical,' Agnew himself, they opined, if he could adjust the bill in various ways and persuade the 'Higher Orders' to mend their ways, 'would be an honour to the age in which he lived.' For Dickens, however, the bill was 'an egregious specimen of legislative folly ... a piece of deliberate cruelty, and crafty injustice,' and the Baronet, a 'fanatic' displaying 'an envious, heartless, ill-conditioned dislike to seeing those whom fortune has placed below him, cheerful and happy.'[61]

Throughout this second portion of the pamphlet, Dickens adopts the rhetoric of a frustrated, impassioned leaderwriter, thundering out a broadside because 'the liberties and comforts of the people are at stake,' and marshalls arguments and, at one point, cannily-researched material from the British Museum, to this clarion call.[62] His arguments are similar in substance and in vehemence of language to those of the Bill's main opponents in the Commons, such as William Cobbett, Thomas W. Beaumont, and Edward Bulwer-Lytton.[63] The sarcastic Dedication of the pamphlet to Charles Blomfield, Bishop of London, is almost libellous in its claim not to believe that 'your Lordship' is 'at all acquainted with' the lives of ordinary people, or 'has the faintest conception' of the extent of their needs. Perhaps wisely,

Dickens adopted a third pseudonym as his signature: 'Timothy Sparks.' Yet the opening section has all the 'Boz' trademarks, including an announcement – similar to many made in his newspaper sketches – that 'there are few things from which I derive greater pleasure, than walking through ... the principal streets of London on a fine Sunday ... and watching the cheerful faces with which they are thronged.'[64] A descriptive vignette follows, cast in the present simple and continuous, as 'The Streets–Morning' and 'The Streets at Night' had been, and at times even echoing their phrasing. The infusion of a dark and melancholy pathos in the final four paragraphs again follows the pattern of several 'Boz' sketches, and the narrator stakes his claim to a public hearing on the 'truth and freedom from exaggeration' of his sketches. 'I may,' he concedes, 'have fallen short of the mark, but I have never overshot it.'

Amongst the journalists and the publishers with whom Dickens now fraternized, his authorship of this angrily demotic pamphlet must have been an open secret, and it was praised in the metropolitan and provincial press as 'a very sensible little book,' 'exceedingly well written' and distinguished by 'very cogent reasoning.'[65] Published in the same month (June 1836) as the establishment in London of the Working Men's Association, its first readers would hardly have hesitated in setting 'Timothy Sparks' down as an ultra-Radical and Chartist-in-the-making. Yet, doubtless aware that attitude and opinions are a journalist's stock-in-trade, at this juncture in his career Dickens was developing the freelancer's knack of not letting political leanings interfere with writing projects and commercial prospects. The fact, for example, that Edward Stanley had recently defected from the Whigs to the crossbenches, and then to the Tory opposition, did not hinder the young *Chronicle* reporter from exploiting their slight personal acquaintance and sending him a copy of his *Sketches*, with an sycophantic note of tribute.[66] Nor did it hinder him from accepting in the coming months two rather different propositions to 'write and edit'[67] new publications. The first of these – the *Pickwick* commission from Chapman & Hall – rather cut across the trajectory initiated by the *Sketches'* unanticipated success, and the second – the editorship of a monthly magazine for the Tory publisher, Richard Bentley – would offer him an escape route from the daily pressure of the press into the genteeler world of literary journalism. Nevertheless, Dickens never severed his connections, personal nor stylistic, with radical journalism, and although his relationship with its goals and dogmas is complex,[68] its strategies remain essential to understanding his work.

3
'Boz' As 'Editor' (1837–41)

The pleasant fiction that the papers of the Pickwick Club are 'edited' by
'Boz' from 'letters and other MS. authorities' is one that is often ignored
after the opening chapter, but an editorial tone, and the differing registers
of parliamentary reporting which 'Boz' was so adept at transposing, remain
in fact a notable feature of the early numbers of the serial. Until October
1836, the instalments interlaced with various political and parliamentary
reports for the *Chronicle*: with the shortlived 'New Series' of 'Sketches by
Boz' for the morning paper, with the anti-Sabbatarian pamphlet, two
papers for the *Library of Fiction*, and so forth. It is worth noting how closely
the early *Pickwick* numbers, with their interpolated tales, descriptive
sketches after Irving and Poole, and their self-conscious segueing of
parliamentary periphrasis into vivid street slang, replicate the miscellaneity
and juxtapositions of Dickens's already established journalistic output.
Indeed, as the opening chapter establishes, the 'Transactions of the Club'
are designed to 'bear a strong affinity to the discussions of other celebrated
bodies' and are reproduced by the editor on the grounds that 'it is always
interesting to trace a resemblance between the proceedings of great men.'
For those who recalled the famous compromise reached between Brougham
and Canning in April 1823, over an insult eventually accepted on the basis
that it was meant in a 'political' rather than a 'personal' sense,[1] the end of
the chapter makes explicit that *Pickwick* was premised as a Swiftian satire
on actual Parliamentary sayings and doings, a kind of mock *Mirror of
Parliament*:

'Mr BLOTTON (of Aldgate) rose to order.... Mr BLOTTON would only
say then, that he repelled the hon. gent.'s false and scurrilous
accusation, with profound contempt. (Great cheering.) The hon. gent.
was a humbug. (Immense confusion, and loud cries of 'Chair,' and
'Order.')....
'The CHAIRMAN was quite sure the hon. Pickwickian would withdraw
the expression he had just made use of.... The CHAIRMAN felt it his

imperative duty to demand of the honourable gentleman, whether he had used the expression which had just escaped him in a common sense.

'Mr BLOTTON had no hesitation in saying, that he had not – he had used the word in its Pickwickian sense. (Hear, hear.) He was bound to acknowledge that, personally, he entertained the highest regard and esteem for the honourable gentleman; he had merely considered him a humbug in a Pickwickian point of view. (Hear, hear.)

'Mr PICKWICK felt much gratified by the fair, candid, and full explanation of his honourable friend. He begged it to be at once understood, that his own observations had been merely intended to bear a Pickwickian construction. (Cheers.)'

The final sentence of the chapter later concedes that such verbatim mirroring of speech is an impractical form of reporting and announces that the text will proceed on the *Hansard* principle of records 'carefully collated' from different sources, and converted into 'narration in a connected form.'

It is on these terms that *Pickwick*'s engagement with the interface between rhetoric and reporting continues, after the opening number. Dickens collates, sketches and extrapolates from his own experiences as a hustings reporter in 'Some Account of Eatanswill ... and of the Election of a Member to serve [it] in Parliament ...' (August 1836), and transforms his stint in June 1836 as a court reporter at the Norton vs. Melbourne trial,[2] into a 'full and faithful report of the memorable Trial of Bardell against Pickwick' (April 1837). Later readers have voiced some dissatisfaction with Dickens's references to contemporary reality, and found his account of election malpractice 'not so much an exaggerated as a pale and euphemistic version of the contemporary scene.'[3] In a sense, such comments miss the point of Dickens's clear distancing of his new methods of chronicling from his newspaper work, and betray a lack of awareness of the parallel newspaper material. In both cases about a year had passed since the 'events' the parody ostensibly alludes to: enough time for readers to recognise the force of the satire rather than look for an immediate alignment on the satirist's part. The *Chronicle* reporter's Whig bias was unavoidable – 'an Editor's mandate is a wholesome check' the reporter had admitted[4] – but when 'Boz' becomes an editor in his own right, he is harder to place. William Maginn, reviewing for the Tory magazine *Fraser's* thus notes in August 1836 that 'Mr Pickwick was a Whig, and that was only right; but Boz is just as much a Whig as he is a giraffe.' But Maginn cannot positively label him, and Dickens himself is no more forthcoming in commenting to his publishers that 'I see honorable mention of myself, and Mr Pickwick's politics in Fraser this month. They consider Mr P. a decided Whig.'[5] Writing and editing his own monthly serial gave Dickens the freedom to sit on the fence, adjudicating between the short-term claims of political parties and legal counsel, and negotiating the tensions between matters intrinsically ephemeral and supremely enduring. The most perceptive critics of the serial focus on its sense of time and timing.[6]

Pickwick's bemusement when confronted with the violent prejudices of Eatanswill's Buffs and Blues no less than of its *Gazette* and *Independent* coincided with a growing detachment on Dickens's part from his regular *Chronicle* work. Other opportunities were opening on all sides. On 22 August, he signed an important contract with Richard Bentley to write not just one thee-volume novel, but two.[7] Ignoring his promise to continue his 'Boz' sketches for the Easthope papers, he had undertaken to write a fortnightly sketch for a new Tory weekly, *The Carlton Chronicle and National Conservative Journal*. The first sketch, 'The Hospital Patient' was grandly introduced on 6 August as 'Leaves, From an Unpublished Volume by Boz (which will be torn out, once a fortnight),' but readers had to wait six not two weeks for the second, 'Hackney Cabs and Their Drivers.' It was not published until 17 September 1836, by which time 'Boz's references to 'the approaching recess' (20 August) and the Metropolitan Hackney Carriage bill which the Commons had 'on their table at the present moment,' were distinctly out of date. The delay, and the appearance only a week later of a 'Sketches by Boz. New Series. No. 1' in the *Morning* and *Evening Chronicle*, suggests that Easthope had finally held Dickens to his *Chronicle* contract, and to his offer, made near the start of the Session, to continue his sketches 'when the Vacation commences.'[8] The four essays published between 24 September and 26 October – rightly hailed as 'four little masterpieces of the genre' – constitute Dickens's last contributions to the paper as a full-time reporter. Nine days later, he handed in his notice, eager to quit what he now characterized in his blistering parting shot at Easthope as 'a most arduous and thankless profession, as other prospects dawn upon [me],' and to exchange the role of parliamentary reporter 'for a less burdensome and more profitable employment.'[9]

It is customary to say that Dickens's experiences as a parliamentary reporter inspired him with a contempt for Parliament and party politics that lasted the rest of his life, but his position in the Gallery had given him – a debtor's son with little education – two invaluable things: a vantage point, from which to overview, with literal superiority, the conduct of public affairs, and a style (if not a wardrobe of styles), in his recreation of a moving world, at a period in English history when the public attention was transfixed by political rhetoric and its media representation. In later years, critics would not hesitate to claim a breach of privilege when the world's most popular author presumed to comment on political affairs;[10] this would be as ineffectual as the Members' calls of 'I see strangers in the Gallery!' in the years before the presence of reporters was officially approved. Dickens acquired as much if not greater power of influencing public opinion through his writings than the MPs themselves, and, as Palmerston told them, 'in political affairs' it is 'public opinion' which matters, which 'can subdue the fleshly arm of physical strength,' and which allowed those who wield it 'to exercise a sway over human affairs out of all proportion greater than belong to the power and resources of the state.'[11]

There is more to the *Chronicle* 'Boz' than clever parodying. His earnest assertion of access to a higher authority than Parliament, of the supremacy of personal knowledge of everyday people, and of face-to-face encounters, gives both an evangelical and a republican edge to his proceedings. There is his fascination with the macabre, with revenants, with both the loss of the past and the threat of its re-eruption into the present. In constructing new urban inventories and taxonomies, there is also a performative emphasis: 'Boz' showing how the lower middle classes try on the costume of class identity against a series of hastily-erected London backdrops.[12] Nevertheless, in his depiction of the extent to which all small communities and local assemblies model themselves on parliament, and replicate its pantomimic formulae – transacting, and staging business, with a view to cutting figures before an audience or in print, rather than generating action – 'Boz' returns compellingly to the primal scene of parliamentary debate.

I

Richard Bentley's offer was hard to resist: twenty pounds a month to edit a new monthly periodical of six demy octavo sheets (about 96 pages), of which one sheet (16 pages) was to be Dickens's own work, for which a further twenty guineas would be paid. With his editorial experience on the *Mirror of Parliament*, his experience of editing his own sketches and sending them for press to tight deadlines, his high reputation in newsrooms and literary circles, and a quiverful of writing projects, Dickens had all the necessary journalistic skills which Bentley required. Above all, he brought the 'Edited by "Boz"' byline which was working wonders for Chapman & Hall. Bentley and his chief clerk, Edwin Morgan, congratulated themselves on securing for their enterprise the services of the most promising young writer of the moment, and those of George Cruikshank as illustrator, 'then in his zenith.' The interaction of text and illustration in a monthly magazine (rather than a part issue) was an innovation.[13]

The abandoned title of 'The Wits' Miscellany,' though felt to be hubristic by Dickens and others, expressed what *Bentley's Miscellany* did not: that this was to be a journal predicated on humour and on the drawing power of the well-known comic writers of the day. Bentley gambled that the public were sated with parliamentary analysis and the ill-natured party warfare of existing literary journals such as *Fraser's, John Bull* and

Blackwood's; he sought to offer neutrality as a selling point. After discussions with Dickens in November and December, the latter accordingly drew up a draft Prospectus that appealed to the idea of dinner parties rather than political parties: the Miscellany would be a 'feast of the richest comic humour' provided by the 'merriest caterers of the age.'[14] In his first Editorial Address, Dickens looked to the theatre for alternative metaphors: 'scenery' would be provided by artist George Cruikshank, 'machinery' by Samuel Bentley, and the 'stage management ... confined to the humble individual with the short name, who has now the honour to address you.'[15] In his opening 'Prologue,' William Maginn, seconded from *Fraser's*, cheerfully made the eschewal of politics the defining policy of the new journal:

> In the first place, we have nothing to do with politics.... [I]s it a matter of absolute necessity that people's political opinion should be perpetually obtruded upon public notice? Is there not something more in the world to be talked about than Whig and Tory? .../
>
> > Tory and Whig in accents big,
> > May wrangle violently;
> > Their party rage shan't stain the page –
> > The neutral page of Bentley.[16]

The *Athenaeum* review of the first half-crown number agreed that a reading public bored with sallies about 'tithes, and taxes, and church reform, and municipal reform,' and with 'babble about diffusion of knowledge, mechanics' institutes, and travelling lecturers' had become instead 'mad for enjoyment – for fun and frolic,' in which field the new venture 'stands alone in its glory.'[17]

Yet, from the outset, the idea of neutral fun and frolic was one that Dickens provocatively failed to embody his own contributions to the *Miscellany*, although the 26 monthly numbers edited by him between January 1837 and February 1839 certainly contained plenty of uncontroversial matter: travel narratives from around the world; biographical sketches; papers on actors, acting and the theatre; lyric poetry; short stories and serial fiction.[18] The role which he had established for 'Boz,' as the 'chronicler' of everyday people whose lives were approached ironically through the languages of public reporting, led him straight back into a kind of sketchwriting, which, as it comically invoked parliamentary proceedings, topics of current national debate, and newspaper journalese, was hardly apolitical. Even in as *ad hoc* an item as the 'Extraordinary Gazette,' an 8-page advertising flier for the *Miscellany*, Dickens's humour played around with the formal rhetoric of government, this time with the reporting of the monarch's speech on the annual opening of parliament, presented as the 'Speech of his Mightiness on opening the Second Number of *Bentley's Miscellany*':

'MY LORDS, LADIES, AND GENTLEMEN:

'... It has been the constant aim of my policy to preserve peace in your minds, and promote merriment in your hearts; to set before you, the scenes and characters of real life in all their endless diversity ... I trust I may refer you to my Pickwickian measures, already taken and still in progress, in confirmation of this assurance.

'... I continue to receive from Foreign Powers, undeniable assurances of their disinterested regard and esteem. The free and independent States of America have done me the honour to reprint my Sketches, gratuitously; and to circulate them throughout the Possessions of the British Crown in India, without charging me anything at all.

'... I deeply lament the ferment and agitation of the public mind in Ireland, which was occasioned by the inadequate supply of the first number of this Miscellany. I deplore the outrages which were committed by an irritated and disappointed populace on the shop of the agent.... I derive the greatest satisfaction from reflecting that the promptest and most vigorous measures were instantaneously taken to repress the tumult. A large detachment of Miscellanies was levied and shipped with all possible despatch....'

NOTE OF THE REPORTER

His Mightiness incorporated with his speech on general topics some especial reference to one 'Oliver Twist.' Not distinctly understanding the allusion, we have abstained from giving it.[19]

The parody of William IV's hard line on Irish political insurrection is sublimely cheeky, but notable throughout in fact is Dickens's brazen readiness to promote in a Bentley publication all his work as 'Boz,' whether published by Bentley or not. Adding spice to the satire must have been an awareness that he might easily still have been doing the job of the parliamentary reporter whose puzzled endnote concludes the text.

In the same issue of the *Miscellany*, 'Boz' reverts to the topic as the conclusion to a make-weight essay that only semi-comically endeavoured to illustrate, with a catalogue of rather strained examples, the 'grave' theory that a 'pantomime is ... a mirror of life.' The *exempla* (pantaloons, clowns, supernumeraries of 'real' life) are defined, not by the development of a thesis, but simply by the extent of 'Boz's ingenuity, which improvises each new paragraph: 'We had scarcely laid down our pen ..., than a new branch of our subject flashed suddenly upon us. So we take it up again at once.'[20] His longest and final example, however, returns to the idea of 'the commencement of a Session of Parliament,' and 'his Majesty's most gracious speech on the opening of thereof,' which is compared to 'the clown's opening speech of "Here we are!"' 'Boz' then surveys the strengths 'at this day' of the 'cast of our political pantomime' in a series of unflattering parallels, and alludes to controversy over the relatively new practice of cabinet ministers travelling far and wide to address large public gatherings during the Parliamentary recess:

> At no former time ... have we had such astonishing tumblers.... Their extreme readiness to exhibit, indeed, has given rise to some ill-natured reflections; it having been objected that by exhibiting themselves gratuitously through the country when the theatre is closed, they reduce themselves to the level of mountebanks, and thereby tend to degrade the respectability of the profession....
>
> Night after night [in the season] will they twist and tumble about, till two, three, and four o'clock in the morning; playing the strangest antics, and giving each other the funniest slaps on the face that can possibly be imagined.... The strange noises, the confusion, the shouting and roaring, amid which all this is done, too, would put to shame the most turbulent sixpenny gallery that ever yelled through a boxing night.[21]

What Bentley, who had procured the title in 1833 of 'Publisher in Ordinary to His Majesty,' thought of this savage and contemptuous portrayal of His Majesty's Government, can only be conjectured.

II

Slight in itself, and as much of a tale as an essay, Dickens's first paper for the *Miscellany*, 'The Public Life of Mr Tulrumble, once Mayor of Mudfog,' had introduced 'Mudfog' as a typically run-down English port on a tidal river (Chatham), then spotlighted the 'town-hall, one of the finest specimens of shed architecture,' and then pinpointed Nicholas Tulrumble, a simple councillor who becomes conceited and corrupt on being elected Mayor. While still a councillor, Tulrumble is introduced as one of 'the sage men of Mudfog' who 'settle at what hour of the night the public-houses shall be closed, ... and other great political questions' in a Town Hall, whose lights burning after midnight

> warn the inhabitants of the town that its little body of legislators, like a larger and better-known body of the same genius, a great deal more noisy, and not a whit more profound, are patriotically dozing away in company, ... for their country's good.[22]

After his election, Tulrumble goes to the bad when he contracts 'a relish for statistics, and got philosophical;' he starts reading 'pamphlets on crime and parliamentary reports;' quotes at length from 'a large book with a blue cover, and ... from the Middlesex magistrates' during debate; and eventually persuades the corporation to refuse a music licence to the 'Jolly Boatmen.' These are all topical hits, not only against traditional targets like the magistracy and the House of Commons, but also now against the kind of 'philosophical' (Dickensian code for Benthamite) reforming zeal which many Whigs, and the *Chronicle* under Black, Parkes, and Easthope supported. In one recent reading, the action of the story is defined as 'the provincial repeating of a metropolitan staging of the symbols of political power, and a small carnivalesque inversion of the dignity and honour of that staging.'[23]

The municipal corporation of Mudfog is both an enlarged version of the 'Parish,' and a smaller-scale model of the greater metropolis, with its fog, mud, river, and its muddled and obfuscating leaders, which Dickens would construct in *Bleak House, Little Dorrit* and *Our Mutual Friend*. It was also more immediately significant to *Miscellany* readers as the nucleus around which 'Boz' began to build his main serial contribution to the magazine, later republished as *Oliver Twist*. 'The Public Life of Mr Tulrumble' had concluded with a repetition of the same pretence at editorial rather than authorial involvement that opened *Pickwick*, in 'Boz's laid-back comment that '[t]his is the first time we have published any of our gleanings from this particular source. Perhaps, at some future period, we may venture to open the chronicles of Mudfog.'[24] But Dickens was hard-pressed to fulfil his monthly page quota for Bentley, and readers had only to wait for the second number to read more 'gleanings.' This was the paper called 'Oliver Twist; or, The parish boy's progress,' set in the same town, and zooming in on another well-known municipal institution: 'Among other public buildings in the town of Mudfog, it boasts of one which is common to most towns, great or small: to wit, a workhouse....' The paper ended by promising a 'sequel,' but Dickens hesitated publicly 'to hint, just yet, whether the life of Oliver Twist will be a long or a short piece of biography.' Privately, he had already indicated to Bentley that he believed 'Oliver Twist ... will make a feature in the work, and be very popular,' but the scathing satire against the spirit and execution of the Poor Laws old and new which featured in the opening instalments can hardly have pleased those of Bentley's readers who were fed up with politics and 'mad for enjoyment.'[25] Intentionally or not, these episodes coincided with vigorous protests in *The Times* against the new law during the hard winter months of 1837–38, and with violent anti-Poor Law demonstrations in the manufacturing districts of Yorkshire and Lancashire.[26] Richard 'Ingoldsby' Barham, Bentley's lifelong friend and one of the journal's more conservative contributors, complained of 'a sort of Radicalish tone' about the serial in April 1837, which he anticipated that Bentley, as a 'loyal' Tory, would soon remedy. Dickens himself called the first instalment a 'glance at the new Poor Law Bill' in a letter to Beard, and it is hard not to suspect him of using his new platform in the *Miscellany* to carry on the argument he had engaged in with his *Morning Chronicle* superiors, who were among a minority of London journalists committed to supporting the new legislation.[27]

Recent commentators have thus commented on the 'polemical air' and 'overtly propagandist elements' in the serial; on the way 'a determination to respond to contemporary issues shaped Dickens's writing plans,' and on the 'shock value' of its incongruity with its magazine context, 'for Dickens was never so keen on eschewing politics as Bentley was.'[28] What has not been made so clear is the pivotal importance to Dickens's writing career of his acrimonious renegotiation of his various contracts with Bentley in the late summer of 1837, and the consequent establishment on Dickens's part of a new kind of writing and publication process that figured newspaper and magazine journalism, together with the novel, in the same textual continuum.

Part of the problem was editorial control. Bentley had attempted to exploit his right to veto the insertion of articles in order to alter the make-up of the September number of the *Miscellany*, and for this 'violation' and 'gross insult' Dickens penned a brisk letter of resignation.[29] The new agreement of 28 September clarified that henceforth Bentley and Dickens should arrange the contents between them, but gave Bentley the additional 'power ... of originating 3 Articles in every number.' But, as well as raising Dickens's monthly salary to £30, the new agreement of 28 September established that the serial now known as 'Oliver Twist' (the politically-sensitive subtitle had been dropped in March) would count *both* towards Dickens's obligation to furnish 16 pages of original material for each issue, *and* as the first of the two three-volume novels that Dickens had promised to write for Bentley back in August 1836. In other words, the same letterpress, suitably revised and repackaged (as the sketches had been), fulfilled two different functions, appealed to the conventions of two different genres – and generated two different paycheques.

Until this latest dispute was resolved, Dickens had put the writing of the serial on hold, deciding as early as 30 August that 'there will be no Oliver Twist' in October. When he resumed his pen, shortly after the signing of the new agreement, it was with a wholly new perspective on the destiny of the work, and he signalled publicly the 'conversion' of the serial from an essentially journalistic 'progress' with a political flavour, into a tortuously-plotted novel, at the start of the second chapter of the November instalment:

> It is the custom on the stage: in all good, murderous melodramas: to present the tragic and the comic scenes, in as regular alternation, as the layers of red and white in a side of streaky, well-cured bacon.... / Such changes appear absurd: but they are by no means unnatural. / As sudden shiftings of scene, and rapid changes of time and place, are not only sanctioned in books by long usage, but are by many considered as the

great art of authorship ... this brief introduction to the present [chapter] may be deemed unnecessary. But I have set it in its place because I am anxious to disclaim at once the desire to tantalise my readers by leaving young Oliver Twist in situations of doubt and difficulty.... My sole desire is to proceed straight through this history with all convenient despatch.... Indeed, there is so much to do, that I have no room for digressions ... and I merely make this one in order to set myself quite right with the reader, between whom and the historian it is essentially necessary that perfect faith should be kept.[30]

Often quoted (in their revised and shortened form) in studies of the novels because they seem to constitute Dickens's first statement of a theory of dramatic fiction, these opening paragraphs show Dickens changing genres in midstream in a spectacular manner. In place of the spoof editor-cum-biographer, commenting archly and ironically on the failures of Government social policy, Dickens substitutes an authoritative narrator, an 'historian,' conscious of literary tradition, and theorising in the first-person singular the relation between art and nature, and between authors and readers, in the magisterial manner of Henry Fielding.

Coming when and why it did, this is a key moment in Dickens, but it did not mean that he had abandoned satirical journalism in the *Miscellany*. The October 1837 issue, although it ran without 'Oliver,' carried instead the first of two lengthy 'Mudfog'-inspired papers, purporting to offer full reports of the meetings of 'The Mudfog Association for the Advancement of Everything.' As readers would quickly recognise, the Mudfog Association – whose quack professors meet twice a year to present their ludicrous theories, and for 'balls, and *soirées*, and suppers, and great mutual complimentations' – was a parody of the annual meeting of the British Association for the Advancement of Science, one of several published in popular periodicals since the Association's establishment in 1831.[31] Both papers were timed to coincide with the widespread press coverage of the British Association's meetings in Liverpool (September 1837) and Newcastle (20 August–15 September 1838), and many of the items in 'Boz's bogus reports have identifiable sources in papers read there, and critique their socio-political as much as their scientific implications.[32]

At their best, the papers transcend their immediate relationship with topical particularities as Swift's satire in *Gulliver's Travels* on the Transactions of the Royal Society had done a century before, but they also succeed on quite another level: as a mockery of the conventions of newspaper reporting itself. Like Fielding's gleeful exposure of the impossibility of real-time epistolary narration in *Shamela*, Dickens sends up the self-congratulatory way in which Editors presented their 'exclusive' and 'expressed' reports, and the breathless way in which their Special Correspondents presented, and updated at ever-decreasing intervals, their banal speculations. Some of the early despatches in the first 'Report,' in which the Correspondent comments extensively and fatuously on the availability of accommodation in Mudfog come very close to the style of the *Morning Chronicle*'s special (Dickens's successor), who had reported from Liverpool on 11 September how:

> [t]he town fills rapidly with company, and the number of strangers who have been promenading the streets of Liverpool, and inspecting the various objects of attraction, is considerable. The principal inns are full, and even private lodgings, owing to ingress of company, are becoming scarce.

Dickens had himself specialized in organising 'expresses,' and been just such a special correspondent for the *Chronicle* at society events ('Re-opening of the Colosseum') and 'whacking dinners' ('The Grey Festival'), but had done so as an anonymous writer, not as 'Boz.' Doubtless this gave an extra relish to these insider's lampoons of what he had described to Easthope as the reporter's 'arduous and thankless profession.'

III

Just as John Easthope became 'Blast-Hope' for Dickens in his bid to improve his prospects, so Richard Bentley became the 'Brigand of Burlington Street,' another villain in the melodrama of Dickens's early career, ultimately thwarted by oppressed Virtue. Dickens's contracts with Bentley 'keep me down with an iron hand,' he wrote in January 1839 to Forster, his informal literary adviser, helping him now, as posthumously, become an Author. Not only was Dickens galled by the fact that his labours were 'enriching everybody connected with them but myself' but Bentley's increased editorial powers and the monthly meetings with him to 'arrange' the contents of the *Miscellany*, were proving a trial. As Robert Patten observes, by December 1837 Dickens was 'uncharacteristically' resigned merely to forwarding his opinion to Bentley, and letting him '[o]rder the Miscellany just as you please.'[33] Although his recommendations were heeded far oftener than not, Dickens's control over the articles inserted did not strictly extend beyond the original terms of their agreement, namely to 'give his judgement upon their eligibility' for use. When the final rupture came, just over a year later, Dickens undertook to announce in the magazine 'in the pleasantest manner in which he can possibly state it, the termination of his present connexion with it.'[34]

Dickens's farewell address as Editor cleverly avoided saying anything pleasant about his relationship with Bentley, by apostrophising the *Miscellany* in a deceptively ingenuous 'Familiar Epistle From a Parent to a Child Aged Two Years and Two Months.' His first child, Charles Culliford

Boz Dickens, had been born in the same month that 'Boz' had begun his Editorship, and the opening of the epistle expands humourously on the experience of fatherhood, while indirectly drawing attention to his own hard work and success as editor, and perhaps also his new sense of himself as author:

> My Child
>   To recount with what trouble I have brought you up ... how late and often I have sat up at night working for you ... – to dwell on the anxiety and tenderness with which I have (as far as I possessed the power) inspected and chosen your food; to dilate on the steadiness with which I have prevented your annoying any company by talking politics ... is beside my present purpose, though I cannot but contemplate your fair appearance – your robust health and unimpeded circulation ... without the liveliest satisfaction and delight.[35]

The trope makes 'Boz' personally responsible for this prodigy, and while many of the early reviews praised his role as editor and contributor, it is in fact hard to isolate the extent to which his involvement influenced the magazine's prosperity. As Kathryn Chittick has shown, the majority of the early contributors were already Bentley authors, assembled not so much in a voluntary team or club as into a 'publishing stable,' a 'grab-bag of quondam literary celebrities that Bentley simply transferred from his booklist to his Miscellany.'[36] Yet Dickens was clearly successful in melding their work into an attractive monthly offering, and in promoting some sense of fraternity among the contributors, if only by assuming the role himself, during their get-togethers, of 'a quiet, modest fellow.'[37]

Sales under Dickens's editorship were undoubtedly high, earning him a bonus for exceeding 6000 copies on several occasions, and topping 7500 at his resignation.[38] He had initially been successful in imposing his own 'Radicalish' stamp on the journal without making it tediously political, and, in the months following the death of his beloved sister-in-law Mary Hogarth, even introduced a melancholy, if not Gothic element, that also ran counter to Bentley's desire for unadulterated humour. Gradually, however, the latter's desire to push 'commodities, not opinions,' of which serial fiction was the most profitable, 'elbowed out the traditional notion of a monthly periodical as a flexible commentator on contemporary affairs.'[39] In handing over the care of his 'child' to his friend Harrison Ainsworth, Dickens musters some enthusiasm, but, in observing that no 'conveyance of your property [will] be required,' bluntly complains that 'you have always been literally "Bentley's" Miscellany and never mine,' a complaint Ainsworth later repeated on his own account.[40]

This public statement of the source of his resignation is the real heart of the Epistle, but 'Boz' distances it from his opening sally by a typical hybrid of lament and eulogium on the theme of change, embodied in the transition from horse-drawn to steam-powered locomotion, and the decline of the mail-coach guard. This permits a complex concluding analogy, in which the future of the periodical and that of the railways are fused into a metaphor of modern progress, achieved regardless of party politics:

> And if I might compare you, my child, to an engine; (not a Tory engine, nor a Whig engine, but a brisk and rapid locomotive;) your friends and patrons to passengers; and he who now stands towards you *in loco parentis* [i.e. Ainsworth] as the skilful engineer and supervisor of the whole, I would humbly crave leave to postpone the departure of the train on its new and auspicious course ... while, with hat in hand, I approach side by side with the friend who travelled with me on the old road, and presume to solicit favour and kindness in behalf of him and his new charge....[41]

Touching as this appears, Dickens had no intention of being overtaken by events as the 'driver of the old Manchester mail' had been, nor of pausing long as a 'skilful engineer and supervisor' of journals and serials. He had a daunting accumulation of writing projects in hand, several, including the continuation of *Nicholas Nickleby*, with the 'Best of Booksellers,' Chapman & Hall, and he had already commenced contributing 'serious' book and theatre reviews to *The Examiner*. But, for the first time since the start of the decade, he was out of full-time journalism. To celebrate his new-found freedom, he rented a cottage in Petersham, Surrey, and took his family and a plentiful supply of books there at the beginning of the summer, to write, and contemplate his next move.

IV

The opening paragraphs of the Preface to the first collected edition of *Nicholas Nickleby* not surprisingly show a writer caught between the competing demands of literature (to be timeless, imaginative, judicious) and journalism (to be timely, accurate, spontaneous). The closing paragraphs, with their approving quotation from one of Henry Mackenzie's *Lounger* papers, display a distinct leaning towards the latter:

> With such feelings and such hopes [for affectionate indulgence] the periodical essayist, the Author of these pages, now lays them before the reader in a completed form, flattering himself ... that on the first of next month they may miss his company ... and think of the papers which ... they have read, as the correspondence of one who wished their happiness, and contributed to their amusement.

Here, the feelings of the 'Author' of the completed work are made secondary to, and seen to derive from, the more spontaneous and interactive sentiments of the periodical essayist and his reader, as they have developed over time. It was exactly this kind of relationship,[42] built on the new kind of publishing contract he felt able to negotiate, that Dickens hoped to cultivate with his next journalistic venture.

The proposal for the lavishly illustrated, threepenny weekly magazine that became known as *Master Humphrey's Clock* was the product of some nostalgic reading and reflection during Dickens's summer sabbatical in Petersham. Dated 14 July 1839, it is the first of a series of creative outlines for founding a periodical, which, however much their realization differed from or fell short of their aims, say much about Dickens's creative vision as an editor and journalist. It was to be, as advertisements in the closing numbers of *Nickleby* proclaimed, 'A New Work on an entirely new plan' but its newness was based, in Dickens's mind, on the revival of the distinctly retro idea of 'a little club or knot of characters' (sedentary rather than peripatetic as Pickwick had been), exchanging stories and anecdotes. Augustan periodicals (Addison and Steele's *Spectator*, and *Tatler* papers, and Goldsmith's *Bee*) are referred to for the general plan of the work, but 'it would be far more popular both in the subjects of which it treats and in its mode of treating them.' A series of papers about London past, present and future, entitled 'The Relaxations of Gog and Magog' would provide an 'inexhaustible field of fun, raillery and interest,' when divided up into tales like *The Arabian Nights*. Another series, likened to *Gulliver's Travels* and Goldsmith's pseudo-oriental *Citizen of the World* letters, are to be 'satirical papers purporting to be translated from some Savage Chronicles,' continuing John Black's mission to monitor the sayings and doings of British magistrates, 'and never to leave those worthies alone.' A further series is to be written on the road in Ireland or America, 'something after the plan of Washington Irving's *Alhambra*,' assuming Chapman & Hall are prepared to underwrite the expenses 'if I undertake my Travels.' The proposal has been commented on extensively by critics seeking the sources of Dickens's imagination, emphasising his debt to childhood reading, or exploring the curious narrative disjunctures between the plan and Dickens's execution of it.[43] For the moment, what is significant is that in terms of publishing genre, Dickens writes not of the serial novel, but of contributions 'throw[n] ... into sketches, essays, tales, adventures, letters from imaginary correspondents;' and in terms of authorship, he envisages 'assistance of course, ... chosen solely by me.'

What Dickens had in mind was, literally, his own *Miscellany*. More unified than Bentley's by the intricate machinery of the club, it would nevertheless be up-to-date in its attacks 'on the various foibles of the day as they arise,' and better able 'to take advantage of all passing events' through weekly rather than monthly publication. In addition to 'discontinu[ing] the writing of a long story with all its strain on his fancy,' as Forster records, Dickens hoped 'to shorten and vary the length of the stories written by himself, and perhaps ultimately to retain all the profits of a continuous publication without necessarily himself contributing every line' – an ambition not to be realised until 1850. Most importantly, in working with the liberal and heretofore compliant Chapman & Hall, Dickens would exorcise the evil spirit of Bentley, as 'the contents of every number' would be 'as much under my own control, and subject to as little interference, as those of a number of *Pickwick* or *Nickleby*.'[44] On paper, the proposal sounds remarkably like the satirical illustrated threepenny weekly which his friends Mark Lemon, Douglas Jerrold and others founded almost exactly a year later: *Punch or the London Charivari.*

Of the very favourable terms contained in the agreement finally signed in March 1840, Forster remarks that they were 'drawn up in contemplation of a mere miscellany miscellany of detached papers or essays, and in which no mention of any story appeared.'[45] The 'mere' is Forster's retrospective bias, given the rise of the novel to literary pre-eminence by 1870 and the corresponding decline of the essay; the emphasis on the absence of 'story' anticipates that *The Old Curiosity Shop* and *Barnaby Rudge* were to be the real successes of the venture, not the detached papers. By the standards of 1840, however, Dickens was decidedly moving up in the world of literary journalism by ceasing to be a mere writer of parts, and becoming the editor of his own magazine, with a weekly salary of £50 and profitshare projected for the next five years. Sales of the opening number of the *Clock* on 4 April were phenomenal, but dropped back quite quickly, prompting Dickens to announce formally in the ninth number that, contrary to the tenor of the advertisements, the magazine would contain no contributions from other writers than himself.[46] He had already written to Thomas Beard – still in thrall to Easthope at the *Chronicle* – to say that the sub-editor's job that he had hoped to give him 'vanishes into air' because it was clear that for the project to succeed 'I must write it *all*.' Also vanishing into air was his hope of some respite in the frequency and quantity of creative writing which his contracts required. Not until the eleventh number, however, did he consider converting his varied contributions to the magazine, into a single longer feature – just as he had done with *Oliver* in the *Miscellany* – telling Forster that he would let his story about the Curiosity Shop 'run on now for four whole numbers together, to give it a fair chance.'

In the event, it ran on for 35 weeks together, and was succeeded (after a single, though telling, intervention from 'Master Humphrey'), by the 42 weekly numbers of *Barnaby Rudge*, the historical tale about the Gordon Riots in London, which Dickens had postponed writing for so long. In his Preface to the first Cheap Edition of the *Shop* (September 1848), Dickens looked back on how the 'detached papers' of the *Clock*, as originally constructed, 'became one of the lost books of the earth,' and how the various introductions, essays, tales, and bridging passages were cancelled from the volume editions of the two long stories:

> [L]ike the unfinished tale of the windy night and the notary in [Laurence Sterne's] 'The Sentimental Journey,' they became the property of the trunk-maker and the butterman. I was especially unwilling, I confess, to enrich these respectable trades with the opening paper of the abandoned design, in which Master Humphrey describes himself and his manner of life.

Sterne's tale was abandoned by design, however. Dickens's detached essays and tales, like the 'Stray Chapters' in the *Miscellany*, were lost because they formed part of no series of republishable papers: had become, as one modern critic puts it, the 'prosthesis of the novel, little Nell's wooden leg'[47] – and perhaps because Dickens knew they fell well below not only his, but the public's expectations. The 'Giant Chronicles' were unceremoniously dismissed as 'nonsense' by the *Monthly Review* for May 1840, and Magog's tale in No. 1 as 'the veriest abortion in the shape of an endeavour to create interest ... that ever was perpetrated.' The intended raillery and fun, and commentary on 'foibles of the day,' take the form of heavy-handed comic descriptions, ponderous jokes, and jibes in the form of 'Correspondence' at 'gentlemanly' manners and forward society 'ladies.' The surreal return of Mr Pickwick in Nos. 2 and 3 as a candidate for a seat in Master Humphrey's club, and of Tony and Sam Weller to form a 'below-stairs' club along with the housekeeper and barber ('Mr. Weller's Watch') may be a playful experiment in literary resurrectionism, but it is hard to read their ghastly banter without agreeing that their presence is due to the temptation of 'box-office appeal,' and that, dead on their legs, they have been 'killed by context.'[48] 'Spirits,' Dickens had written to his publishers during the writing of his first Club papers, 'are not to be forced up to Pickwick point, every day,' but with 'Master Humphrey' as editor/narrator rather than the versatile 'Boz,' they seemed forcibly depressed, every day. The prevailing mood of the *Clock* – variously described as elegiac, meditative, quietist, mournful or semi-mournful[49] – cannot accommodate the Pickwickian, in either its satirical or its actively benevolent sense, and instead of the topical zest of *Punch* the style of the humour is more reminiscent of Thomas Hood's whimsical and grotesquely illustrated *Comic Annuals*, the last of which Dickens had reviewed for the *Examiner* not long since.[50]

Yet the parts of the 'opening paper of the abandoned design' and of Master Humphrey's later lucubrations in which his role as the journal's eidolon is developed, have distinct resonance with Dickens's later journalistic personae, who are often self-deprecating, or depicted as marginal in some way, apparently sidelined by the railroad of Victorian progress. Although introduced as a 'deformed' and 'crippled' creature, Master Humphrey, in defiance of his disability, reveals himself as an avid pedestrian, and a lover of night walks in the city, which

> afford[ ] me greater opportunity of speculating on the characters and occupations of those who fill the streets. The glare and hurry of broad noon are not adapted to idle pursuits like mine; a glimpse of passing faces caught by the light of a street lamp, or a shop window, is often better for my purpose than their full revelation in the daylight....[51]

Like Walter Benjamin's flâneur, and Dickens's own 'Uncommercial Traveller,' Humphrey's 'purpose' is ambivalent – is it philanthropy, detection, voyeurism, or surveillance? – and his halting progress as idler and man of the crowd echoes with the footsteps of forerunners and pursuers.[52] When his voice resumes the *Clock* in No. 45, after the *Shop* has run its course and clumsy explanations for the narrative shifts have been proffered, he seeks an appropriate introduction for *Barnaby Rudge*, as a 'tale where London's face by night is darkly seen.' This takes the form of an astonishingly rich and suggestive account of a visit to the clock tower of St Paul's, apostrophized as 'The Heart of London,' and a panoramic vision of the sleeping city, in an essay poised inchoately between investigative journalism, imaginative sketch, and allegory; between the recent past and the historic present:

> I groped my way into Turret which [the Clock] occupies, and saw before me, in a kind of loft, ... a complicated crowd of wheels and chains in iron and brass....
>
> It is night. Calm and unmoved amidst the scenes that darkness favours, the great heart of London throbs in its giant breast. Wealth and beggary, vice and virtue, guilt and innocence, repletion and the direst hunger, all treading on each other and crowded together, are gathered round it. Draw but a little circle above the clustering house-tops, and you shall have within its space, everything with its opposite extreme and contradiction, close beside....
>
> Heart of London, there is a moral in thy every stroke! as I look on at thy indomitable workings, which neither death, nor press of life, nor grief, nor gladness out of doors will influence one jot, I seem to hear a voice within thee which sinks into my heart, bidding me, as I elbow my way among the crowd, have some thought for the meanest wretch that passes, and being a man, to turn away with scorn and pride from none that bear a human shape.[53]

The final paragraph, with its Romantic allusions,[54] magically returns the crippled Master Humphrey to the streets from his view over and through the house-tops, suggesting that Dickens has a more characteristic analogy in mind, with the lame devil Asmodeus of Le Sage's *Le Diable Boîteux*, whom Dickens and contemporaries refigured in their journalism as a partly benevolent, partly mischievous spirit, eloquent of journalistic curiosity and prurience.[55] For all their weaknesses, and despite the manifest failure of *Master Humphrey's Clock* as a journalistic enterprise, the detached papers evidence an underlying preoccupation with vantage points, both for characters and the narrative act itself, whereby the ascent above the particularity and din of London's streets offers, or appears to seek, omniscience or semi-omniscience, and access to a spiritual and atemporal perspective on human affairs. Dickens's urban journalism thereafter, at its best, is enriched by the attempt, literally, the *essai*, to find stations from which to envisage and comprehend the cryptic city, with its ancient vaults and spires, Monuments, statues, and sunken burying grounds.[56]

4
Travelling, Skirmishing and Sharp-shooting (1841–44)

In the summer of 1841, in the midst of a severe agricultural and commercial depression, and as *Barnaby Rudge* rolled on from its Scott-like beginnings towards its Carlylean conclusion, Lord Melbourne's weak administration tottered. The new-look Conservatives under Peel, together with the group who had crossed the house in the so-called 'Derby Dilly' (the Whig defectors Stanley, Graham, Richmond and others) combined forces with the ultra-Radicals for whom Melbourne's cautious, aristocratic Whiggery had been too little, too late. Posterity has long since pardoned Peel and vindicated his equivocations – by 1870 Forster could claim 'we were [ignorant] how much wiser than his party the statesman then at the head of it was' – but in 1841 his involvement in the repressive measures of 1819 had not been forgotten by the public or press, nor had his initial opposition to Catholic Emancipation and Parliamentary Reform. His efforts to rebrand the Tories as a party of enlightened Conservatism made him appear shifty and deceitful, and he was loathed by Liberals, who equally feared a return to the reactionary politics of a previous era or the usurping of their own position as the party of moderate reform. Until the end of Peel's administration in June 1846, Dickens's talents as a journalist, and support as a popular public figure, were repeatedly sought after by different opposition movements and pressure groups.

In October 1842, Thomas Macaulay confided to MacVey Napier, editor of the great Whig quarterly *Edinburgh Review*, his desire to see Dickens 'inrolled in our blue and yellow corps, where he may do excellent service as a skirmisher and sharp-shooter.'[1] The description suits Dickens the journalist well in the early 1840s, a period in which, had he been a man of even modest private fortune, he could easily have imitated Macaulay's chosen manner of influencing public opinion, via a seat in Parliament and regular, well-paid contributions to a prestigious journal like the *Edinburgh Review*. Instead, dependent on his pen as any mercenary on his sword, and eschewing any particular outlet or format for his activism, he conducted a kind of one-man guerrilla warfare against the return of the bad old Tory days. No longer in regular contact with parliament and the courts, he instead relied on his excellent contacts in the press and his scrutiny of a range of daily papers for the sources of a variety of characteristic pieces of second-wave journalism.

I

In June 1840, he broke off from the writing of Chapter 15 of the *Shop* at Broadstairs ('a description of getting gradually out of town, and passing through neighbourhoods of distinct and various characters') to write to his old editor John Black at the *Morning Chronicle*, proposing 'to the public mind, a few questions which have been suggested to me in the reports of the late trial' of the notorious murderer François Courvoisier. Dickens stressed he would '*very much like*' to see the letter in the Tuesday issue of the paper. There, under the headline 'The License of Counsel,' it duly appeared.[2] The debate over capital punishment, publicly or privately executed, was one to which Dickens contributed frequently in the 1840s, in a series of powerful articles couched as Letters to the editors of various influential newspapers. Along with a mob of 40 000, he later went to see Courvoisier hung, shortly after his return from Broadstairs, on 6 July, and, like Thackeray, would write about the psycho-social effects of the experience, both in fictional and non-fictional terms. For the time being, he restricted himself to a strongly-worded critique of the behaviour of Courvoisier's defence counsel, Charles Phillips, for insulting the Police, insulting and bullying female witnesses, and for predicting damnation for the jury if they returned a guilty verdict. In a second letter, responding to a defence of Phillips's conduct from a correspondent signing himself 'Templar,' Dickens turns his rhetorical questions into an explicit challenge to the legal profession, asserting that 'counsel ... abominably and shamefully abuse the licence they enjoy' and thereby become 'not a public protection, but a public nuisance.' For various reasons, he was constrained to disguise his authorship of both letters under the pseudonym 'Manlius.'[3]

Immediately following Lord Melbourne's resignation in the midst of anti-Poor Law demonstrations and Commons defeat over the Corn Law controversy, Dickens declined – with convincing reluctance – an invitation from a group of Reading Liberals to stand for the borough in the forthcoming election alongside his learned friend, the copyright campaigner Thomas Noon Talfourd. '[M]y principles and inclinations would lead me to aspire to the distinction you invite me to seek, were there any chance of success,' he declared. Intimidation, bribery, corruption, and electoral apathy among the disheartened Liberal voters, all on a scale reminiscent of 1835, seem to have ensured the result Dickens anticipated, but his political sympathies and appetite for journalistic pugilism were roused.[4] From Broadstairs on

8 August, as the Tories prepared for office, he negotiated with Napier about the writing of a thirty-page article for the *Edinburgh*, based on the first report of the Children's Employment Commission, examining conditions in mines and collieries, due to be laid before the House during the new Session, along with a bill for reform championed by the evangelical reformer Lord Ashley. The findings were known to be sensational, but the change of ministry made the bill's prospects doubtful. The subject, Napier anticipated, 'will be more *descriptive* than speculative, and will, under your graphic pen, make a far more interesting Paper than anything of a theoretical nature.'[5]

Only the day before, the *Examiner* had published the first of a series of 'rhyming squibs' in which Dickens eagerly resumed the Tory-bashing of 1834–35, this time in tolerable verse. The first of these was a 'New Version' of Purday's popular song 'The Fine Old English Gentleman,' with the ironic refrain '… the fine old English Tory times;/Soon may they come again!' Its inspiration was the report of a Tory peer at a recent dinner in Gloucestershire who had toasted 'the return of the good old English times, when the nobleman afforded advice to his tenants, and identified himself with them.' A rendering of Purday's song had followed the speech. The description of the bad old days which Dickens heaps up in the first six of the poem's eight stanzas begins along the same lines ('the days of that old gentleman who had that old estate;' 'fine old English penalties and fine old English pains' &c.) but by verse six the satire is specifically directed at Lord Liverpool's regime during the Napoleonic wars, when the brothers Leigh and John Hunt, co-founders of *The Examiner*, had been imprisoned for a libel on the Prince Regent:

> Those were the days for taxes, and for war's infernal din;
> For scarcity of bread, that fine old dowagers might win;
> For shutting men of letters up, through iron bars to grin,
> Because they didn't think the Prince was altogether thin,
> > In the fine old English Tory times, &c.

Forster surreptitiously omitted this verse in reprinting the poem in the *Life*, despite claiming to give the poem 'entire' as it 'had no touch of personal satire in it, and [Dickens] would for that reason, have least objected to its revival.' He thus suppresses the obvious fact that personal satire was something at which his subject could excel. As Dickens himself later told Douglas Jerrold, there was nothing in his parody 'but wrath: but that's wholesome.'[6]

The other two squibs, of which only a few of the more anodyne verses were reprinted in the *Life*, illustrate this well. 'The Quack Doctor's Proclamation' (14 August) ridiculed Peel's continued support in a recent address at Tamworth for a sliding-scale of duty on corn, as opposed to the

total abolition demanded by the Anti-Corn Law League and the low fixed
duty advocated by the Whigs:

> Homëopathy too, he has practised for ages;
> (You'll find his prescriptions in Luke Hansard's pages)
> Just giving his patient when maddened by pain, –
> Of Reform the ten thousandth part of a grain.

Each verse ends with a refrain typical of the comic songs Dickens had
learned and performed as a child, once again bringing parliament and the
politicians down to the level of street ballads and consumer advertizing:

> He has only to add he's the real Doctor Flam,
> All others being purely fictitious and sham;
> The house is a large one, tall, slated, and white,
> With a lobby; and lights in the passage at night.
> > Tol de rol:
> > Diddle doll:
> > Tol de rol, de dol,
> > Diddle doll:
> > Tol de roll doll.[7]

The lengthy 'Subjects for Painters (after Peter Pindar)' had three verses
roundly abusing the ultra-reactionary MP for Lincoln, Colonel Sibthorp
(an old target, first shot at in 'The House'), and figuring Peel again in
verse nine as 'Sir Joseph Surface, fawning cap in hand,' handing in his
Honours list to the young Victoria.[8] The tenth verse conjured up an
imaginary Hogarthian canvas, ironically juxtaposing the recent Tory
election tactics of sympathising with supporters of the physical-force
Chartists transported by the Melbourne government after their insurrection, with the more barbarous punishments meted out to conspirators
under Tory rule:

> Limn, Sirs, the highest Lady in the land,
> When Joseph Surface, fawning cap in hand,
> Delivers in his list of patriot mortals;
> Those gentlemen of honour, faith, and truth,
> Who, foul mouth'd spat upon her maiden youth,
> And dog-like did defile her palace portals.
>
> Paint me the Tories, full of grief and woe,
> Weeping (to voters) over Frost and Co.,[9]
> Their suffering, erring, much-enduring brothers.
> And in the back-ground don't forget to pack,

Each grinning ghastly from its bloody sack,
The heads of Thistlewood, Despard,[10] and others.

'I doubt,' Forster wrote of these little known sallies, 'if he ever enjoyed anything more than the power of thus taking part occasionally, unknown to outsiders, in the sharp conflict the press was raging.' Enclosing the final poem on 13 August, Dickens makes a rare statement of political allegiance, rarer still in his association of 'truth' with an established party creed: 'By Jove how radical I am getting! I wax stronger in the true principles every day.' He put it down to the proximity of 'the sea,' an image he had turned to in the instalment of *Barnaby Rudge* for that week, describing the 'mob,' 'as difficult to follow to its various sources as the sea itself ... the ocean is not more fickle and uncertain, more terrible when roused.'[11] The Press picked up the subliminal message: 'We suspect, from the manner in which "Boz" takes the field against the "No Popery" people ..., that he intends a "liberal" colouring to the circumstances of the time. If so, ... he must offend many. In a work of fiction, we desire no *insinuation of politics.*'[12] But read in the context of his *Examiner* squibs, the novel's latter stages do nevertheless seem to present, in fearful and pessimistic terms, the unholy alliance between the reactionary Tories (John Willett is a county magistrate; Sir John Chester a Tory MP) and the violent ultra-Radicals (led by agent provocateur Gashford, disinherited troublemaker Hugh, and madmen, Barnaby and Lord George) which had brought Peel back to power.

The promised article on Lord Ashley's Mines and Collieries bill failed to materialise for the *Edinburgh Review* – a fistula operation in the Autumn and preparations for a recently-conceived expedition to America intervened – but Dickens's hatred of the new administration ('people whom, politically, I despise and abhor') and desire to publish on the subject did not abate.[13] Before his journey he had been sent confidential copies of the Commission's report by its chairman, Southwood Smith, and on his return, in early July 1842, he carefully checked the newspaper coverage of the debates on the bill which had taken place in his absence. By 25 July, an article was ready, but instead of sending it to Napier (the next *Review* would not appear till October), it was again directed to his old admirer Black at the *Chronicle*, whose continual support of the bill Ashley himself recognized as 'most effective.' It was published on the very morning of the Lords' debate on the Mines and Collieries bill, and, as it was widely expected that 'the tender mercies of the Colliery Lords' would 'so distort and maim' the bill as to make it unrecognisable, the article's swingeing sarcasm could not have come at a more crucial moment.[14]

Although heavily amended, the bill passed the Lords a week later, and when its principal opponent there, the Tory Marquess of Londonderry, indicated that he was preparing a public letter to Ashley as a riposte, Dickens engaged to review it in the *Chronicle*. The resulting 2-column leader was a savage attack, not of the points made in Londonderry's pamphlet (which had mostly been made before in the Lords' debate, and dealt with in Dickens's previous, detailed contribution), but on the Marquess himself, for

> one of the most charming and graceful characteristics of this remarkable production is that it has no one thought, or argument, or line of reasoning, in its whole compass, but is entirely devoted to the display of its noble author's exquisite taste and extreme felicity of expression.[15]

Dickens pauses at this point to make a pointed reflection on his former employment in the Gallery, noting how the authoring of pamphlets instead of speechifying

> cannot be too strongly commended. It is at once an economy of the public time; an encouragement to the printing, publishing and paper trade; and an interesting exhibition of the orator in his own proper dress, undisguised by any of those shreds of style and grammar in which Parliamentary reporters love to deck him out; to the great detriment and injury of such a nobleman of nature as the most noble the Marquess of Londonderry.

It was a common claim, illustrative of Victorian doubts about the derivation of authority, that unknown journalists were responsible for much of the eloquence and power in the printed speeches of the country's acknowledged leaders, which were 'shortened one hundred, and improved two hundred per cent, by passing through the alembic of [the] gallery.'[16] Dickens's *Chronicle* work had to be 'sub rosâ' on account of a compromised situation with first Easthope and now Napier. His latest review had been signed merely 'B,' scarcely capitalising on his public persona. Nevertheless, the wrath and invective in these occasional papers was quite out of character for 'Boz,' and suggest that Dickens was not above exploiting the use of such aliases. When Black was abruptly dismissed from the *Chronicle* editorship in May, to make way for Andrew Doyle (Easthope's son-in-law), Dickens turned back to Fonblanque's *Examiner*, in which such licence is also noticeable. His reading of the blue books of the Children's Employment Commission (the second report, dealing with Factories, had been published in March 1843 and left him 'stricken') led Dickens to parody the style of such publications, at the height of the Pusey controversy and the beginnings of the 'Oxford Movement.' Duly entitled 'Report of the Commissioners Appointed to Inquire into the Condition of the Persons Variously Engaged in the University of Oxford,' the parody was fictitiously signed by the four principal commissioners, and submitted that the ignorance testified by children employed in Mines and Factories was in its way less shocking than the learned ignorance of divines at the University of Oxford.[17] In a letter to Fonblanque that March, Dickens had confessed to Fonblanque that 'I am getting horribly bitter about Puseyism,' and, fearing that the latter's policies were too favourable to the Tories, jokingly offered to take over the paper: 'leave [*The Examiner*] to me, and I'll be your Shadow; undoubtedly faint; but warranted fierce.'[18]

Less than a year after Black's departure, Dickens entered into negotiations with the new *Chronicle* editor, for a series of regular contributions, in the form of occasional leaders or 'a letter a week' from abroad, 'under any signature I chose, with such scraps of descriptions and impressions as suggested themselves.' Doyle reported Easthope prepared to 'pay *anything* ... for letters from Italy,' but Dickens felt it would be unseemly to 'make any bargain ... or haggle like a pedlar' over the figures mooted of ten guineas per article or twenty guineas a week, especially with a man like Easthope ('... such a damned screw,' he complained to his lawyer, that it was impossible to hold him to anything): '"I'll write a leader now and then, and leave him, in June, to send me a cheque for the whole."'[19]

The cause to which Easthope seems to have wished to recruit Dickens at any price was the movement for repeal of the Corn Laws, the issue around which opposition to Peel's administration was crystallizing, following a series of poor harvests across Britain and Ireland. In the event, only one leader was published – a heavily ironic *reductio ad absurdum* titled 'The Agricultural Interest' (9 March 1844), in which the Government, following its successful indictment of Daniel O'Connell, is invited to indict 'the whole manufacturing interest of the country, for a conspiracy against the agricultural interest.' Dickens polarizes contemporary politics into the forces of progress (typified by engine-drivers, policemen, doctors) and those of reaction (stage-coachmen, night watchmen, professors of the law) and, while pretending to defend the latter, the former are now identified clearly with Liberal policy, not, as in the 'Familiar Epistle,' with something separate from party politics.

A similar satirical espousal of an exaggerated Tory perspective underwrites the fun in the article Dickens volunteered for the May 1844 number of Thomas Hood's new monthly magazine. The paper is cast in the form of 'A Threatening Letter to Thomas Hood' from yet another fine old English Gentleman of diehard principles.[20] *Hood's Magazine* had, like *Bentley's Miscellany*, pledged itself to 'a total abstinence from politics.' Dickens's offering (signed 'By Favor of Charles Dickens'), though lighter in touch than his newspaper articles of the period, is still tinged with bitterness, particularly when he refers to a recent sentence of death passed by a 'glorious' judge on a 'revolutionary' seamstress who, on being robbed of her earnings, had attempted to drown herself and her infant child.[21]

As though his political views were a kind of chronic disease that broke out periodically, Forster comments of Dickens at this time that 'the old radical leanings were again rather strong in him.' His readiness to find a 'vent' for them by writing in the *Chronicle* might suggest that he comes closer in the early 1840s to his old paper's positions on a range of issues than he did during his employment there. In fact, since 1839 and the more so since the Whigs had dispersed into opposition, the *Chronicle* had 'turned half against' its former ministerial patrons, and was 'floating down the Radical stream' in the direction of Dickens's position.[22] He, meanwhile, continued to seek new ways of awakening the public to a sense of their social responsibilities and their implication in the doom which inactivity would involve. His reading of the report on child employment in factories, although far from convincing him that Government enforcement of the Ten Hours proposal was necessary, had made him think in 1843 of 'bringing out, a very cheap pamphlet, called "An Appeal to the People of England, on Behalf of the Poor Man's Child."' This scheme was at once replaced with another plan, by which he predicted to Southwood Smith, by 'the end of the year ... you will certainly feel that a Sledge hammer has come down with twenty times the force – twenty thousand times the force – I could exert by following out my first idea.'[23] It has reasonably been assumed that Dickens contemplates here a pamphlet timed to coincide with the Christmas season, and is cultivating the germ of the idea that, fictionally treated, becomes the *Christmas Carol* – a kind of 'Christmas under Three Heads,' with its terrifying vision in Stave III of Man's neglected children, Ignorance and Want. Indeed, both the *Carol* and *The Chimes* (1844) share the 'wholesome wrath' of Dickens's squibs, leaders and letters of the early 1840s, and, like them, are deeply imbued with a sense of journalistic mission.

II

The dream of breaking away from England, of emigrating to 'Van Diemen's Land' or 'a new colony,' but at the same time writing from there letters and 'scraps of descriptions and impressions' which in some published form would help finance the expedition, was one Dickens realized twice in the early 1840s. He and Catherine toured parts of America for four and a half months from late January to late June 1842, and, like many middle-class Victorian couples in the era between Grand Tourism and mass tourism, took up residence with their entourage in Italy for a year, from July 1844 to June 1845.[24] The resulting travel books, *American Notes* and *Pictures from Italy*, despite being published first as volumes without a complete previous serialization in the periodical press, can usefully be considered as part of his journalistic output, partly because the starting point for both trips/narratives came from magazine and newspaper-related projects, partly because the resulting texts were largely worked up from Dickens's own, wonderfully detailed travelling letters, journalized on the road to Forster, Macready, Maclise, Fonblanque and other carefully selected friends.

In the case of *American Notes*, the rapidly-observed sketches of life and manners thus derived, also jostle with essayistic treatments of social themes (the Eastern Penitentiary in Chapter 6, Slavery in Chapter 17), and with paratextual material in which media representation, the press, and the wild frontier between literature and journalism are all uncomfortably foregrounded. The full title, *American Notes for General Circulation*, together with the motto which Forster advised Dickens to suppress,[25] indicate the way in which, on his return to Britain, Dickens sought to re-organise his profoundly unsettling American experiences into a proudly principled stand against the piracy of the American press, and the licentiousness of its journalists.

Before commencing, he confessed to Forster 'a perplexingly divided and subdivided duty, in the matter of the book of travels' he had undertaken to write, and tried in an introductory chapter (also cancelled at Forster's suggestion) to explain what the book would *not* contain: statistical accounts, gossip about individuals, nor 'a grain of any political ingredient,' nor any account of his personal reception and treatment (topics which make the original letters home compelling reading). Commentators have noted reasonably that, read out of the context of its writing and reception, the book seems uncontroversial enough, if not actually, as Macaulay pronounced it, 'frivolous and dull.' Yet, while not containing a grain of political ingredient, it was nevertheless ingrained in the politics of Anglo-American relations in the 1840s, and the state of quarrel which periodical reviewers on both sides, and various Tory travel writers, had succeeded in fomenting in the previous decade. '[R]elatively slight as the book is,' K. J. Fielding comments, 'probably no other work of Dickens was received with such expectant stirring. It was news rather than literature.'[26]

During the prelude to and early stages of his tour, Dickens was fêted as a visitor likely to be politically sympathetic with American republicanism and egalitarianism, a homespun hero 'with no other nobility about him than the universal title of simple and glorious manhood,' and one who would bring on 'the English revolution (speed the hour!) far more effectively than any of the open assaults of Radicalism or Chartism.' Dickens wrote, in Carlylean terms, of the hero worship which attended the man-of-letters: no 'King or Emperor upon the Earth' was 'so cheered, and followed by crowds, ... and waited on.'[27] But from the moment he mingled criticism with his lavish praise, as he did at the Boston banquet in his honour on 1 February, and subsequently in many passages in the *Notes*, the grand love affair between the young man and the 'republic of his imagination' turned sour. Critical post-mortems have pointed variously to deep-seated anxieties and obsessional elements in Dickens's psyche which the trip catalysed into a trauma as powerful in its way as the Blacking factory episode;[28] to his inexperience and shortcomings as a traveller dealing with cultural difference; to the unrepresentative and artificial vision of the only 'America' Dickens was permitted to see;[29] to his perceived inability to comprehend

American frontier civilization as a 'process' rather than a 'product.'[30] As a result, readings of *American Notes* have increasingly stressed its dystopic movement as a travel narrative built on the limited European paradigm of a Dantean descent into the underworld, and figured Dickens as a (post-) colonial traveller – like Conrad's Marlowe or Forster's Miss Quested – who has nightmare visions in an alien landscape.[31]

However, in Dickens's travel letters the shift in tone and style occurs much earlier than such readings of the travel book might imply: not on his journey south west into the frontier states of Indiana, Illinois and Missouri, but while he was confined with a cold to his New York Hotel in mid-February, and able to read newspaper reports of his progress to date. The attacks he read in 'scores' of newspapers 'shocked and disgusted' him, he wrote to the mayor of Boston, by 'imputing motives to me, the very suggestion of which turns my blood to gall' and attacking him 'in such terms of vagabond scurrility as they would denounce no murderer with.' He concludes with the confession that 'the scorn and indignation I have felt under this unmanly and ungenerous treatment has been to me an amount of agony such as I never experienced since my birth.'[32] It was enough to change a man's politics. He 'whispered' to Forster on the 24th his fear 'for a radical coming here, unless he is a radical on principle, by reason and reflection, and from a sense of right. I fear that if he were anything else he would return home a Tory....' The implication, clearly, is that Dickens felt his own sense of principled radicalism challenged but not overcome by his growing disappointment in what he considered 'the failure of [this country's] example to the earth.'[33]

The outrages of the American press were as much to blame as their politicians, and although the 'New York' chapter of *American Notes* is perforce silent about the 'agony' Dickens experienced at the 'unmanly and ungenerous treatment' meted to him in papers like *The New York Herald*, Dickens nevertheless breaks off from his animated account of the city, to figure the press, through a kaleidoscope of tropes, as Swiftian Yahoos who have perverted the amusements of the people:

What are the fifty newspapers, which those precocious urchins are bawling down the street ... what are they but amusements? Not vapid waterish amusements, but good strong stuff; dealing in round abuse and blackguard names; pulling off the roofs of private houses, as the Halting Devil did in Spain; pimping and pandering for all degrees of vicious taste, and gorging with coined lies the most voracious maw; imputing to every man in public life the coarsest and vilest motives; scaring away from the stabbed and prostrate body politic, every Samaritan of clear conscience and good deeds; and setting on, with yell and whistle and clapping of foul hands, the vilest vermin and worst birds of prey. – No amusements!

Aside from its recurring interest in Asmodeus as journalistic archetype, this angry indictment of American newspapers, reinforced in later chapters and taken into a new dimension in *Martin Chuzzlewit*, should be set alongside an almost equally vehement outburst against British journalists in the August of the Tory election victory.[34] Dickens readily denounces the part the press plays in unprincipled personal attacks and party politicking, yet continues to engage with its processes, just as he had done with British parliamentary procedure in the 1830s. The text and various prefaces of *American Notes* steer a perilous path through the 'journalistic mud' that the mayor of Boston, his friend Jonathan Chapman, warned him was being 'flung at him since his departure,' and occasionally flings it back in earnest, both in support for the campaign for international copyright[35] and as part of articulating a broader concern with media corruption of standards in American public life.

In this respect, *American Notes* is significantly *about* the invasive power of the press, and reveals something of the anxiety Dickens sensed about the perilous instability of the generic boundaries erected between 'literature' and 'journalism,' described to Henry Austin in these terms:

> Is it not a horrible thing ... that every vile, blackguard, and detestable newspaper, – so filthy and so bestial that no honest man would admit one into his house, for a water-closet door-mat – should be able to publish ... [books, the authors of which do not reap one farthing from their issue], side by side, cheek by jowl, with the coarsest and most obscene companions, with which they *must* become connected in course of time, in people's minds? Is it tolerable that besides being robbed and rifled, an author should be *forced* to appear in any form – in any vulgar dress – in any atrocious company – that he should have no choice of his audience – no control over his own distorted text...?

In this bizarre retelling of *Oliver Twist*, the author's innocent and pure text is kidnapped, circulated amongst foul companions, and, by free association between the newspaper columns, corrupted and criminalized.[36] Dickens overlooks conveniently that all his 'books' had hitherto achieved their reputations as newspaper or magazine series, which had also been widely excerpted in the press: the osmotic exchange of text from journalism to literature which Dickens oversaw so successfully through his publishing arrangements in Britain, could be reversed by unseen forces in America.

Dickens's granting of the name 'Eden' to the forlorn outpost of progress on the Mississippi in which Martin sinks his small capital (*Martin Chuzzlewit* chap. 21 et seq.) underlines the fact that Dickens came to view his radical ideal republic as a Fallen World, just as susceptible of improvement and in need of timely chastisement as the Old World he knew. Thus, 'Boz' could apply his London methods of research and writing-up to the great American metropolis, and portray it as an earthly city, a city of dirt and death and animal refuse, devoid of heavenly promise. The witty analogy between the 'pig about town' and the human population, where the former is portrayed as an experienced but wholly self-centred flâneur, 'turning up the news and small talk of the city in the shape of cabbage stalks and offal,' functions variously as a preparation for the coming assault on the city's journalists, a sideswipe at brutish Republican attitudes, and a way of stressing that mud is once again the native element of the city dweller.[37]

Indeed, Dickens feels stylistically safer as soon as he is able to make explicit comparisons between New York and London and allude to his own demarcated territory as a sketcher, mentioning 'one quarter [of the city], commonly called the *Five Points*, which, in respect of filth and wretchedness, may be safely backed against Seven Dials.' The verb projects as agent someone familiar with Seven Dials but unfamiliar with New York, considering a bet on which city has the worst slums, and there is much in Dickens's overall account of the American East that implicitly or explicitly, ingenuously or ironically, calls on British readers to see how their society and their government compares to the American way.[38] In two respects only (but for Dickens, important ones) the latter outshone its monarchical elders: 'National Education ... and its care for poor children.'[39] As with his earlier 'Visit to Newgate' sketch, the tours of inspection of factories, schools, asylums, workhouses are undertaken 'in an amateur capacity,' but the sense of an Old World double shadows, if not blurs, the resulting narratives. Furthermore, while a visit to Newgate was, for most London readers in 1836, a novelty, and centred around a carceral community which for obvious reasons would neither read his account of it, nor answer back, Dickens's chosen destinations in America had, with few exceptions, been selected before by British writers, and his judgements could be tried and found wanting by those on whom they were pronounced.

A recent defence of *American Notes* has been constructed on the basis that it 'is better understood in light of the conventions associated with [the] new journalism' of the late 20th century in its experimental merging of individual fantasy with impassive reporting, and that it anticipates the development of a post-modern genre.[40] The major difficulties readers have experienced with the book, however, can in fact be viewed as instances not of new but of bad journalism, in the sense that it consists of an insufficiently original 'angle,' which skirts key issues, simplifies and exaggerates incidental ones, and overprotects its sources. In the aftermath of publication, Dickens 'stands by his story,' repeating the standard journalistic claim for the 'truth' of his allegations, rather than offering an artist's defence of his vision.[41] But possibly the greatest journalistic error in a volume destined for an immediate and large readership, and one which Forster as sub-editor was unable to correct, is its 'perplexingly divided' sense of its target audience. At times, the reader is assumed to be a British armchair traveller; at times the irony is intended for *laissez aller* British government officials; at times, wrath is directed at the American press; variously, genial compliments and stern reprovals are delivered to the American reader for some national characteristic or mannerism. Scrutiny of the 'New York' chapter reveals an embarrassment of narrative strategies for reader-projection, including first-person plural invitation ('Shall we ... sally forth ... and mingle with the stream?'), second-person apostrophes and imperatives ('Irishmen both! You might know them ... by their long-tailed blue coats;' 'Ascend these pitch dark stairs ... and grope your way with me into this wolfish den'); third person 'omniscient' and semi-omniscient narration ('The great promenade ... as most people know, is Broadway'); and first-person singular, subjective reporting ('The terrible crowd with which these halls and galleries were filled, so shocked me, that I abridged my stay'). Dickens's difficulty in seeking out a 'fit audience though few' is tellingly expressed by his addressing the Dedication of the 1842 volume not to a single individual, but to a group which, almost with each new line, becomes a more limited subset of itself:

> I DEDICATE THIS BOOK TO / THOSE FRIENDS OF MINE / IN AMERICA / who, giving me a welcome I must ever / gratefully and proudly remember, / left my judgment / FREE; / and who, loving their country, can bear / the truth, when it is told good / humouredly, and in a / kind spirit.

Dickens's 'travelling letters' – effectively the first draft of *American Notes* – possess a much clearer sense of their addressees. They build up 'epistolary intimacy,' they are confident in their techniques, and are – correspondingly – freer from this weakness.[42]

The American chapters of *Chuzzlewit* – effectively a rewrite of the second half of *American Notes* – afforded Dickens the opportunity to correct his journalistic error, by allowing preoccupation with the medium (the fictional priorities of design, image, theme and character) to prevail over proselytising and rapport-building. By removing and filtering his experiences through the perspective of the selfish young Martin, there was a chance to reflect and 'see his limited self seeing America': a feat surely possible for a writer who later claimed to be 'accustomed to view myself as curiously as if I were another man.'[43] Yet the *Chuzzlewit* account of the Far West is a gleeful and savagely comic distillation of the worst traits of raw republicanism, in which Martin looks on with bemused tolerance as interacting caricatures are cut loose from any mooring in a conventionally-established reality, revealing 'a problematic tension between realism and self-enclosed fiction which is fundamental' to Dickens's work.[44] This, more than the awkward reticences of *American Notes*, is new journalism: Dickens's fear and loathing in an embryonic mid-West Las Vegas, caused not by a premonition of what is to come, but the worry that 'downward popular tendencies' in the American character will prevent anything coming at all. Twenty years on, with the Civil War raging on the other side of the Atlantic, Dickens felt his verdicts as a young man from the old country had been fully vindicated, both in their substance, and in their confident appeal to mature judgement. To Jonathan Chapman he had predicted recognition of his services 'in the slow fullness of time;' in the final paragraph of the *Notes* he assured readers 'I can bide my time;' republishing in 1862 its criticisms of the House of Representatives and the press, he sought 'confirmation' of their accuracy. Concerning no other of his journalistic writings does Dickens so consciously – and, one is tempted to add, for all the wrong reasons – claim for himself the role of special correspondent for posterity.

5
Launching *The Daily News* (1845–46)

Dickens's predicament as he foresaw the close of the *Chuzzlewit* serial was serious: the publishing depression continued, sales were disappointing, money was still owing to Chapman & Hall. His thoughts returned once more to the idea of a miscellany, the establishment of a periodical in which he would share much greater and more permanent profits than those available to an author of individual books. The printers Bradbury and Evans, to whom he was secretly planning to transfer his publishing affairs, were keen to build on their success as publishers of *Punch*. But, he told Forster in November 1843, he was 'afraid of a magazine – just now.' The time and chances of success were not right, and Dickens was also tired, and 'afraid of putting myself before the town as writing tooth and nail for bread, headlong, after the close of a book taking so much out of one as *Chuzzlewit*.' His main fear of any project was of being *'forced* (as in the *Clock*) to put myself into it, in my old shape.' The elusive editorial cum managerial role he sought was proving hard to pin down, and the only alternative was escape: 'to some place which I know beforehand to be CHEAP,' and to 'enlarge my stock of description and observation by seeing countries new to me.'[1]

I

Grand thoughts of running a newspaper had been in his head immediately on his return from America, when he wrote two remarkable letters to the elderly Whig doyenne, Lady Holland, proposing himself as the very man to take over the recently-defunct *Courier* newspaper.[2] The plan is remarkable for revealing that, however much emphasis he and contemporaries would later place on the principle of press freedom from political collusion, in 1842 he saw no obstacle to requesting both 'countenance' and 'direct pecuniary assistance' from the Whig party and the Reform Club as the *sine qua non* of proceeding. Dickens's impulsive but not altogether Bottom-like presentation of his credentials to Lady Holland is also significant, bearing in mind the scepticism with which commentators have on the whole viewed his later involvement with *The Daily News*:

> I need scarcely say, that if I threw my small person into the breach, and wrote for the paper (literary articles as well as political) I could command immediate attention; while the influence I have with Booksellers and Authors would give me a better chance of stamping it with a new character, and securing it, after a reasonable trial, good advertisements, than almost any other man could possess.[3]

Lady Holland was instructed to 'ascertain the sentiments' of Melbourne and Lord Lansdowne; for his part, Dickens was prepared to tackle E. J. Stanley, and 'one or two others' in his confidence that he 'could establish an organ for the party which would do good service.' The answers – negative – came back quickly enough, and in writing to thank Lady Holland for her trouble, Dickens complained of a characteristic lack of boldness among the Liberal leaders. Conscious that Lady Holland knew him only as the 'Boz' of *Nickleby* and later writings, he then expatiated on his journalistic background in a simile that again forges links between the press and the railways, before indicating, with appropriate nods to satirical and essayistic traditions, how his breeding lent itself to instinctive media savvy:

> The notion of this newspaper was bred in me by my old training – I was as well acquainted with the management of one, some years ago, as an Engineer is, with a Steam engine. And I always feel when I take up a paper now (which is not often) that the subjects which all the writers leave unhandled (except Fonblanque, who is another Swift) are exactly the questions which interest the people, and concern their business and bosoms most.[4]

Without a newspaper or magazine at his disposal, Dickens was an engine driver without a locomotive.

II

When Italy was finally settled on as the country in which Dickens would combine virtuous economies with regular leader or letter-writing for the *Chronicle*, Dickens and Forster summoned Bradbury and Evans to a 'council' of war. Chapman and Hall's 'mismanaging' of the expenses of publishing *A Christmas Carol* had finally convinced Dickens that their happy relationship was irredeemably 'past and over.' The meeting was held, and in it, Forster proleptically recalled, 'lay the germ of another newspaper enterprise he permitted himself to engage in twelve months later, to which he would have done more wisely to have … answered No.'

This was an expression on Bradbury and Evans's part of their willingness to establish a new paper or periodical, with Dickens at the helm. Later discussions clarified that whatever form the 'Magazine or Journal' was to take, it would commence, Dickens suggested, 'within six months ... after the expiration of my year's retirement': far enough in the future for the publishing climate to have improved, and (more importantly) after his long continental rest. Within hours of the last number of *Chuzzlewit* reaching the bookstalls, and with a no-strings advance of £2800 from Bradbury and Evans to clear debts and cover expenses, he and his family set off for Genoa. While Dickens had vague notions for a new serial story, and a second Christmas book was scheduled for later in the year, the newspaper project was the backbone of his plans for when he returned.[5]

Dickens's first letter to Forster on his reoccupation of the house at Devonshire Terrace in July 1845 accordingly contained a detailed creative outline for 'the periodical,' now projected as a very affordable $1\frac{1}{2}$d. weekly, partly reprinting (as most did) 'select' matter from other journals, but containing original book and theatre reviews, judgements on all passing events, and, most importantly, an attempt to distil from the fictional specificities of *A Christmas Carol* and *The Chimes* the essence of their radical political stance, and their apotheosis of the family hearth as the nucleus of social stability. Dickens no longer thinks in terms of an old-fashioned, reclusive, self-centred club, but of an eidolon and a prospectus that would seek an entrée into every house in the country:

> I would call it, sir, – / THE CRICKET / A cheerful creature that chirrups on the Hearth. / [Goldsmith's] *Natural History.* / ... I would come out, sir, with a prospectus on the subject of the Cricket that should put everybody in a good temper, and make such a dash at people's fenders and arm-chairs as hasn't been made for many a long day. I could approach them in a different mode under this name ... . I would at once sit down upon their very hobs; and take a personal; and confidential position with them which should separate me, instantly, from all other periodicals ... . And I would chirp, chirp, chirp away in every number until I chirped it up to – well, you shall say how many hundred thousand![6]

The motto retains an appeal to eighteenth-century literary tradition without giving it any political alignment, but the metaphor of editorial approach as an insect entering into every home – like a fly-on-the-wall – and of a hundred thousand people dashing to their armchairs to listen its confidential emissions seems a prescient anticipation of broadcasting. Beneath the whimsical presentation, Dickens was clear about the real function of such access to the living rooms of the nation, and expected Forster to 'know exactly how I should use such a lever, and how much power I should find in it.' Forster's response, typically, involved a muting of what was radical in the plan, a modification 'to involve less absolute personal identification with Dickens,' partly intended to save him from a commitment to too much writing in the new journal, but also perhaps to reflect Forster's more conventional notion of the ideal, abstract form which journalistic discourse should take.[7]

Further discussions about *The Cricket* were forestalled before the end of the month, however, by 'another new notion' from Bradbury and Evans which 'perfectly amazed' Dickens. This was the proposition that he lend his name and aid to no less a mission than the launching of a brand new morning newspaper of Liberal and independent principles, and for which they had already secured capital: '*down and ready*, fifty Thousand Pounds!' This was the kind of backing that Dickens had hoped for to set *The Courier* back on its feet, and he seems to have agreed at once, albeit provisionally, to play a prominent role in the project, which promised the consummation of many of his previous plans. Since the demise of the short-lived *Constitutional* no new morning paper had appeared to serve the Liberal vanguard of the old Whig party, committed to administrative reform and the controlled forwarding of the interests of the labouring and manufacturing classes. In particular, no major London paper had as yet declared itself in favour of the immediate repeal of the protective duties on corn, the clarion call since 1838 of the Manchester-based Anti-Corn Law League, which had mobilized overwhelming support among the unenfranchized up and down the country. The reduction of the Stamp Duty on newspapers in 1836 from fourpence to a penny per copy meant that a properly established paper, sold at the right price to this potentially huge constituency of supporters, had a real chance of making an impact, and a great deal of money. Within hours, Dickens wrote to Forster that the idea for *The Cricket* – now referred to as 'our abandoned little weekly' – could be refigured as a Christmas Book, by 'making the Cricket a little household god,' providing choric commentary on the story of a single family. The powerful idea for the weekly *Cricket* thus split into two distinct but imaginatively related projects for the remainder of 1845: the writing of *The Cricket on the Hearth*, and the whirlwind arrangements for setting up *The Daily News*.

III

Forster describes Dickens from this point as 'swept away by [the] larger scheme, in its extent and danger more suitable to the wild and hazardous enterprises of that prodigious year [1845] of excitement and disaster,' a comment characteristic of his cursory treatment of the episode in the *Life*, as a 'tremendous adventure' of which Dickens was certainly not the hero.[8] Like almost all testimony from the protagonists in the drama, Forster's needs to be adjusted in light of his personal implication, and supplemented by evidence not unearthed until long after Dickens's death. The achievements of the paper itself under Dickens's editorship, and of his own contributions, also need canvassing before its rightful place in his career as a journalist can be seen.

Dickens was effectively headhunted as editor for the new paper which Bradbury's young friend from Derbyshire, the horticulturalist, railway investor, and entrepreneur Joseph Paxton had contemplated founding for some time. Back in February 1845, while up in London to discuss it with the firm, Paxton had written home that 'the newspaper don't look so well now' but soaring railway stocks in anticipation of the passing of new Railway Acts in the Autumn and the introduction of standard gauge, meant that by the late summer the prospects were excellent.[9] Paxton (who, Dickens initially boasted, 'has command of every railway influence in England and abroad except the Great Western'), Bradbury and Evans had agreed to put up much of the capital, but, importantly for Dickens, one other 'large shareholder is to come in; and that is to be a house which has the power of bringing a whole volley of advertisements to bear upon the paper always.'[10] None of the backers had the hands-on experience of newspaper and high-circulation magazine journalism which Dickens brought to the team, nor the range of press and political contacts. And it was not as though there were any other journalist in London who had, in living memory, experience of founding a morning paper on the scale of the *Times*, *Chronicle*, *Herald* or *Post*. Almost more importantly, in terms of publicity, none had the instant name-recognition and 'star' quality as a friend of reform that Dickens had: 'sought by everybody, known by everybody and loved by everybody,' W. J. Fox's daughter enthused, '[a] more attractive and engrossing personality could not exist, and the mere glamour of his name flung itself over the whole paper like a mantle.'[11]

Just before formally accepting the job of overall Literary Editor on 3 November, for double the salary Bradbury and Evans proposed (an exceptional £2000[12]) and a share in the paper's profits to be decided when more was known about the total capitalization, Dickens wrote Forster a complex justification of his move, presenting it as an act of private sacrifice to the greater public need, that nevertheless allowed for the possibility of sudden withdrawal:

> I think I descry in these times greater stimulants to such an effort; greater chance of some fair recognition of it; greater means of persevering in it, or retiring from it unscathed by any weapon one should care for; than at any other period. And most of all I have, sometimes, that possibility of failing health or fading popularity before me, which beckons me to such a venture when it comes within my reach.

With this curiously detached attitude – like Shakespeare's Brutus deliberating in his garden – Dickens wrote to Bradbury and Evans consenting to become 'the head and leading principle of the thing.' This would involve writing frequently in the paper 'from day to day' and publishing there his series of 'Italian Letters,' and 'my constantly exercising an active and vigilant superintendence over the whole Machine': the coveted engine-driver's role.

Already, much preparatory research had been carried out. An employee of Bradbury & Evans recalled being 'in attendance on Charles Dickens' at 90 Fleet Street, Whitefriars, 'some months before the Daily News saw light,'[13] where Dickens was also provided with a model secretary and chief sub-editor in the shape of W. H. Wills. One of the first matters disputed, back in early August, related to the overall costs of running the 'Foreign Department' of a major daily paper. Setting up this Department was, given the lead-time required for recruiting agents overseas, a priority. '*Determined* to be right,' Dickens wrote to Thomas Beard for estimates, asking how much more *The Morning Herald* (to which Beard had transferred in 1844) spent on its *de luxe* coverage than Easthope did at *The Morning Chronicle*.[14] Dickens's experience of the costs involved in organising expresses was that they were extensive, and that liberality in dealing with expense claims was essential. '[W]hat gentlemen they were to serve, in such things, at the old *Morning Chronicle*!' he reminisced to Forster at one point, 'Great or small it did not matter.'[15] An abiding impression of Dickens's involvement in the setting up of the paper, indeed, was that Liberal politics and liberal business arrangements were to go hand-in-hand: an admirable policy, though admittedly easier to implement with other people's money.[16] The same obsession with organization and quality is observable during these Autumn months in Dickens's hyperactive and inspired superintendence of amateur theatricals, performed to packed houses on 20 September and 15 November, about which Forster is as complimentary as he is negative about the newspaper preparations. But the two projects inevitably overlapped. 'More than once' the cast assembled 'in the back part of the ground floor of No 90 to "run through their parts."'[17]

In between these performances, in mid-October, Dickens visited Paxton at Chatsworth to learn more of the 'paper scheme' and the financial details settled with Bradbury and Evans, and, having determined to 'take the plunge,' he at once began 'trying to engage the best people, left and right.' He also continued detailed planning for the transmission of foreign news from the subcontinent; being 'particularly anxious to shine in reference to India.'[18] His object was to have as many of the operational plans and editorial and reporting staff lined up before any public announcement of the paper appeared. To which end, Paxton's 'loose, and flurried way of proceeding' in 'prematurely broach[ing]' their plans to potential backers was, Dickens told Bradbury and Evans on 28 October, highly injurious. Yet Dickens himself was by now informing his close friends privately of 'these great Newspaper arrangements,' and, attracted by news of high salaries, journalists were lining up to join the new venture:

> The secession from the established papers to [the offices in] Bouverie Street was large; every inducement was held out to critics, leader-writers, and reporters; and to retain their best men the *Morning Chronicle*, the *Standard*, the *Morning Herald*, the *Morning Post*, and other journals had to make a distinct advance in rate of pay.[19]

The *Chronicle* lost, amongst many others, Eyre Evans Crowe, its leader writer on foreign affairs, assistant editor George Hogarth, and the radical economist Thomas Hodgskin, the last a loss which Dickens reported on 1 December as 'likely to drive Easthope (when he knows it) raving mad.' Clearly, there were old scores still to settle.

Given that the new paper, in its timing and ethos, was predicated on the 'railway mania' of 1845, it was fitting that its existence should be threatened on the day Dickens formally accepted the post of Editor, by news of the spectacular bankruptcy of a major City stockbroker dealing in railway shares, affecting both Paxton and the third shareholder. At once, Dickens prepared to withdraw unscathed, conceiving that the paper '*cannot be.*' Within 'the little world of newspapers' he knew so well, the loss of the 'prestige, and vague impression of success which surrounded the idea' meant that carrying on would be futile, he told Bradbury and Evans. It would be impossible to get the first-rate staff needed for the different departments of the paper, and 'the dread of this Venture among the other papers (which was very great) is ... gone, past all restoration.'[20] All of which led Dickens to conclude that 'I cannot connect myself with it as I originally intended' and that if the publishers felt obliged to continue (their investment in machinery and financial commitment to the new staff were huge) 'it would end in your Ruin.' Already, he had penned a gracious memo intended for the redundant reporters: to say how 'seriously and bitterly surprised' he was by the news, but that the losses to the backers '(of whom I was never one to the value of a farthing)' made the paper impossible.[21]

Given the finality of all this, it has seemed surprising that on 14 November Dickens should resume engaging staff and detailed editorial preparations, as though nothing had happened. His reasons for changing his mind are not known: but he needed the salary, and given Bradbury and Evans's resolute determination to continue,[22] Paxton's confidence that new backers could be found, and the willingness of all three to address the still unresolved matter of share options, it must have seemed that returning were tedious as go o'er. The backers went ahead with a 'Memorandum of Agreement' on 17 November, amplified into a Deed of Co-partnership on 21 January 1846, which shows that while the capital investment remained at the original £50 000, it was now to be split amongst nine[23] rather than three shareholders, and that the net profits of the paper were to be divided into 125 shares, of which ten 'literary shares' were to be Dickens's in view of his services as 'first Editor of the said paper.' This was an option equivalent to subscribing £4000 of the original capital: worth considerably more than a farthing. The wording (*first* Editor) also suggests some recognition by the partners that while Dickens's continued help in the start-up and launch of the paper was assumed, the chances of his being a long-term connection with it were small.

Thus persuaded, having built up a head of steam, and with *The Cricket on the Hearth* at last despatched to the compositors, Dickens's own momentum impelled him forward on the new tracks again, which now led regularly to the ramshackle *Daily News* offices off Fleet Street, where

> [t]he ceaseless noise of the presses ... produced a busy hum, whilst in the foggy atmosphere one could see flitting, like ghosts, the forms of men in paper caps and dirty shirt-sleeves, wetting paper, padding frames, presiding at the delivery or withdrawal of sheets that slid in and out of monstrous machines in all kinds of movement, back and forward – sliding, revolving and jumping ... .'[24]

He re-engaged the staff who were in limbo, and, with Forster's help,[25] continued to appoint first-rate writers without too much embarrassment, drafted a Prospectus (now lost), and by 1 December, he was able to report to Paxton that he was 'regularly in harness now; and we are getting on vigorously, and steadily.' He travelled to Liverpool, Manchester and other manufacturing towns – the power-base of the Anti-Corn Law League – for several days, engaging key correspondents and reporters. By 11 December, he was informing job-seekers that there were no vacancies, 'a very large Establishment having been formed for the New Paper in very one of its working departments.'[26]

This was no exaggeration. It included three sub-editors, a secretary, six or seven leader writers, seventeen parliamentary reporters co-ordinated by a manager, a foreign editor and nine European correspondents or agents; a colonial editor and sixteen or so overseas correspondents or agents; sixteen or more provincial correspondents in the principal ports, cities and strategic bases of the British mainland; reporters to cover the twenty-plus London courts and the fourteen Metropolitan Police courts; three City and Commercial editors and various reporters; a Theatrical and Musical Editor, a Court Circular and a Sporting Reporter. 'Yea, even the miscalled penny-a-liner was there,' W. H. Russell recalled. This represented a newsgathering staff of some seventy to a hundred, a weekly wagebill of approaching £600 and overall expenses of over £1000.[27]

Friends and acquaintances gossiped and worried about this latest undertaking of 'Boz the universal,' alternately questioning and admiring his fitness for the task. Elizabeth Barrett doubted he had, for all his gifts, the '*breadth* of mind.' The perennially glum Macready had long regarded Dickens's involvement 'with a sort of dismay.' Henry Reeve, walking home with Charles Dilke from a dinner at which Dickens, Forster and Crowe had expatiated on the project, guessed that his companion's expertise would later 'be called upon to remedy the mischief done by Dickens's genius to the new paper.' Forster himself, nettled that his advice was not being heeded and that 'he, Forster, was useless to Dickens as a counsel,' told Macready that 'Dickens was not qualified for the situation of director.' Yet further afield, the editor of *The English Gentleman* rejoiced at the symbolic value of Dickens's leadership:

> The whole Press owes much to Mr Dickens ... for this practical recognition of its respectability and importance. Henceforth, instead of shrinking from any supposed connection with a profession which certain nervous dunderheads of the aristocracy, both of rank and wealth, are permitted to treat with contumely, we shall find conductors of newspapers and their corps of contributors only too proud to avow themselves of the same calling as the admirable Boz.... [W]e rejoice sincerely at Mr Dickens's adhesion to the Press....

For its part, *The Times* refused to print an announcement of the new venture, and responded on 27 December with a 'savage' and 'remorseless' review of *The Cricket on the Hearth*, determined, Macready thought, 'to disable [its] antagonist] by striking to maim or kill him if he can.' Dickens's imaging of the rivalry was no less sanguinary: 'it is war to the knife, now, with the Times' he wrote to Paxton, 'and if they don't repent the day that ever we started in the field against them, my name is not CHARLES DICKENS / And I rather think it is.'[28]

There was more to the approaching battle than the reputation of a single champion, however. The political as well as financial climate was dangerously volatile, and a worried Prince Albert recorded in his diary that 'Revolution might have been the consequence of it.'[29] Lord John Russell, the Liberal leader with whom Dickens was by now on close personal terms, had declared his support for immediate repeal of the Corn Laws in late November, and was widely expected to form a new administration in early December, when Delane of *The Times* spectacularly finessed Peel's announcement of a plan for progressive reduction of protective duties, which split his support in the House, and forced his early resignation.[30] Had Russell been able then to agree a cabinet, the *Daily News* would have commenced publication with a strong line of communication to the new Liberal government, and a natural advantage over all of its rivals. As things stood, with Peel still in power and pledged to repeal in some shape or other, Dickens decided that the paper could only prove itself on the speed and comprehensiveness of its expresses, and publication day was fixed for 21 January, the week before Peel's eagerly anticipated policy statement to the reconvened House.

In spite of his misgivings, a formidable writing force was assembled to work on the opening issues, but looking around him in the ensuing campaign, Dickens might have been forgiven for thinking himself still rehearsing for *Every Man in His Humour*, or, more curiously, still a rookie journalist surrounded by the friends and patrons from earlier phases of his career. Of the various leader writers, Fonblanque, Jerrold, Forster and W. J. Fox were by now personally well known to him. Dickens had worked alongside the chief of the sub-editors, John Hill Powell, on the *Morning* and *Evening Chronicle* in the 1830s. The Rome correspondent was Francis Mahoney, with whom Dickens had dealt as editor of *Bentley's Miscellany*; the Boston correspondent was his great American friend C. C. Felton; Emile de la Rue, his former neighbour at Genoa, was roped in to operate a courier service for the Italian mails. His close friend the Countess of Blessington provided court and society gossip, under the suggestive gallic headline of 'On Dits.' His father-in-law George Hogarth, employed as 'Theatrical and Musical Editor' for five guineas a week, sent Sidney Laman Blanchard and Blanchard Jerrold, the sons of his friends, out on theatre-reviewing trips, as he himself had been despatched by Hogarth to sketch, ten years before. His most useful adviser for months during the preparation of the newsgathering service, and execution of expresses, was his old team-mate from the Gallery, Thomas Beard. More bizarrely, the correspondent recommended by Dickens for an arduous year's reporting and newsgathering in India was his elderly but still enterprising uncle, shorthand-tutor and former editor, John Henry Barrow, laid off from *The Morning Herald* and desperate for work. Most bizarrely of all, perhaps, the man employed to manage the troop of Parliamentary and Legal reporters, their terms and conditions, co-ordinate their activities, and liaise with MPs and ministers over transcripts of their speeches, was his own father.

The later Micawberization of John Dickens has undoubtedly led commentators to deprecate the wisdom of the appointment unfairly; in confusing his role with that of the overall business manager of a paper, some have compounded the injustice.[31] While there were doubtless hidden psychological accounts to be settled in their relationship, in many respects, the sinecure was sensible enough. John Dickens's several years' service on Barrow's *Mirror of Parliament* were essentially similar in their responsibilities to his new position, which, despite the high staff turnover on the paper, he held until his death in 1851. The young foreign correspondent Joseph Crowe recalled him not unadmiringly during these years, sitting sweatily as 'chairman' in the pandemonium of the newsroom, 'looking carefully to the regular marking and orderly despatch to the printers of the numerous manuscripts thrown off at lightning speed by the men of the gallery.'

Although 'never given to much locomotion' – unlike his son – his 'enviable stamina' in making a rapid railroad journey to Plymouth and Exeter and back with express copies of Peel's speech in the sixth edition of the paper, was eulogized in the *Western Times*.[32] Dickens himself proudly claimed that there was 'not a more zealous, disinterested or useful gentleman attached to the paper': a positive assessment of his father's professionalism amplified both in his 'autobiographical fragment' of the following year, and by an obituary in *The Gentleman's Magazine*, praising John Dickens's efficiency and 'thorough business habits.'[33]

IV

The week before the start, Dickens was busy with preparations to use the influence of the 'Railway King' George Hudson, on the Eastern Counties line, to secure a Special Engine to express copy from an Anti-Corn Law meeting in Norwich. Unable to sleep, he dozed and dreamed 'of first numbers till my head swims.' At the point of greatest apparent commitment, with the launch in his sights, he could articulate his plans to a distant friend: '[t]he new calling shall not long supersede the old one. I should be glad to establish the Paper well, if I could. My share of it would then be a fine property.'[34] For the time being, however, the second statement was all that mattered, and the same day, an entire dummy issue of the new paper was composed and printed, using the brand new founts specially cast for the *Daily News* by Thorowgood & Besley. This was a technical rather than a dress rehearsal; the few surviving copies are riddled with typographical errors and misreadings, but Bradbury & Evans's printers, under Hicks's direction, had never used the expensive steam-driven presses before. At a launch party a few days previously, one of the machines had been christened 'Perseverance,' and a bottle of wine 'sacrificed' against it. Dickens may even have thought of the name.

Most of the text of the dummy issue was collated under the appropriate headings from cuttings from other papers, but, ever a master of the personal touch, Dickens composed a comic leader specially for the occasion, and gave out advance copy for the first of his series of Italian letters. The leader was a spoof report of the trial of 'a person named *Jones*' concocted for the amusement of all the staff, who in the weeks leading up to the launch had observed the master builder of that name who, Dickens writes, 'had been suborned by certain other miscreants not in custody, to procure the completion, at any cost or sacrifice, of certain premises, in course of erection in Whitefriars, for purposes of the most despicable and atrocious nature' (Building work on the new printing office had been completed at breakneck speed, and Jones is accordingly 'indicted' for the 'murder' of his workforce.) The Italian letter contained still more intimate details, intended for Dickens's own wife and family, who are nameless in all of the later, published versions of the letter, but who here are named one after another – 'Kate,' 'Georgina,' 'Charley,' 'Mamie,' 'Katey,' 'Walter' and the 'angelic baby' – in the passage which describes them descending from their coach at the Hotel de l'Ecu d'Or.[35]

Catherine Dickens dutifully preserved her copy of the real first edition of the paper; 'brought home by Charles,' she wrote on a corner of the cover, 'at two o'clock in the morning, January 21st.' The date is correct but the time wrong: at six, Dickens was still at the office, dashing off a note to tell Forster that they had been at press for three-quarters of an hour, and thus were out 'before *The Times*.' There was, W. H. Russell recorded, 'a wild rush for the first number' followed by a ray of hope which 'at once lighted up the gloom of Printing House Square' and other newsrooms when rival editors realized that it was 'ill-printed on bad paper, and "badly made up," and, despite the brilliant picture from Italy by Dickens, ... a fiasco.' Damning as this verdict is, blame strictly lay not with Dickens as editor of the Literary Department, but Bradbury and Evans as managers of the print force. 'They,' Joseph Paxton wrote to his wife, 'had engaged an incompetent printer and all our efforts was {sic} nearly being floored at four O clock this morning and it was only by exertion almost superhuman that it was got out at all.'[36]

Scrutiny of the first issue suggests that fiasco is an overstatement. There was much on which Dickens and his staff could congratulate themselves, not least in the establishment, at the height of the terrible Irish Famine, of a powerful London voice for the hitherto unrepresented free trade agitation embodied by the National Anti-Corn Law League, described in W. J. Fox's leader as '[the] most significant movement of our times.' Three of the four leaders in fact dealt with the pros and cons of repeal, prompting Elizabeth Barrett to complain of a 'mere newspaper support of the "League,"' although she noted shrewdly that there were 'enough advertisements to promise a long future.'[37] Dickens's own opening address (looked over no doubt by Forster) set forth the grand principles of the paper, devoting 'a few words to ourselves and the course which lies before us' before 'proceeding on our way.' The principles it claimed were those of 'Progress and Improvement': first, education, next civil and religious liberties, then 'equal legislation' for rich and poor alike, in the aspiration of creating not exactly a classless society in Jeffersonian terms, but one in which essential differences between social groups are at least reconciled by broad recognition of the interdependence between them. The politics of reform and moderation the address preaches are not strikingly original, but are consistent in essence – though shorn of the imaginative presentation – with Dickens's other real or projected journal manifestos. More characteristic of Dickens in style and substance is the expression of the paper's mission to 'elevate the character of the Public Press' and to help 'purge' it of its 'disposition to

sordid attacks *upon itself,* which only prevails in England and America.'
There is nothing, Dickens argues,

> in the editorial plural that justifies a gentleman, or body of gentlemen,
> in discarding a gentleman's forbearance and responsibility, and venting
> ungenerous spleen against a rival, by a perversion of a great power....
> The stamp on newspapers is not like the stamp on Universal Medicine-
> Bottles, which licenses anything, however false and monstrous; and we
> are sure this misuse of it ... not only offends and repels like-minded men
> ..., but naturally (though unjustly) involves the whole Press, as a pursuit
> or profession, ... and places all who are associated with it at a great
> disadvantage.[38]

Elsewhere in the eight-page issue, a page was devoted to the report of the
previous night's debate at Norwich between Cobden and his protectionist
opponent despatched at 10 p.m. by 'Special Express', and to that of a 'Great
Metropolitan Meeting to Petition for the Repeal of the Corn Laws;' a page
ditto to Railway News, and another to general news and a long article on
music by George Hogarth. A lyric by Charles Mackay ('The Wants of the
People') and Dickens's 'brilliant' letter from Italy, printed on page 6,
provided the only form of fanciful, poetic relief in an otherwise factual and
unremittingly sober publication.

Sales of the first issue, Paxton reported, were 'above 10 000 copies over
the counter': a flying start for a new paper, but a long way off *The Times*'s
25 000, and only just sufficient, at a cover price of 5d., to cover weekly
expenses, after deduction of the penny stamp duty. By day two, the technical difficulties had been addressed, producing a 'very striking improvement,' Fox noted, but the 'reading' (press correction) was still bad, the
paper 'none too good,' the paragraphing erratic, and (most seriously in
Fox's view) the reporting off-target.[39] Nevertheless, Dickens pronounced it
'Capital,' having 'sat at the Stone' where the compositors imposed the
columns of type 'and made it up myself.' To preempt criticism of the day
before's errors, he faked a witty letter to himself as Editor from 'Your
Constant Reader' complaining of them, and replied to it reassuringly.[40]

By the following week, everything was ready for the 'Extraordinary
Express' to relay the contents of Peel's policy speech on the Corn Laws to
the nation. Dickens aimed to have it sent 'to every town on every line in
England' by special engines. Peel finished his speech after two o'clock in
the morning, and at five, one contemporary recalled, the *Daily News* was
on sale in Bouverie Street; 'at eight o'clock it had reached Bristol and
Liverpool ... at midday it was in Scotland, and at ten the following
morning in Paris.'[41] Twenty-one years after being beaten down from
Edinburgh by the *Times* post-chaise express, Dickens had got his revenge,
by railway. Over the next two weeks, he worked in tandem with Beard and

Edward Baldwin, the *Morning Herald* proprietor, to set up 'all possible *retrenchments*' (cost-sharing on foreign and domestic expresses) to consolidate the advantage. Yet beating *The Times* to the newsstand or onto the 6.15 from Euston to the North was one thing; surpassing its range and authority as a morning newspaper was another. Macready felt *The Times* to be so clearly superior on 30 January that he was 'in despair for the result of *The Daily News*.'[42]

As Editor, Dickens could perhaps be accused of putting speed of delivery before content. Yet, in the absence of confidential intimations from ministers of the kind which Delane and even John Black were accustomed to receive, it is hard to see how superior intelligence could be conveyed to the public. John Dickens's fulsome letter to Peel, requesting, on his Editor's behalf, an advance ' "pull"' of his 'very important speech' the day before its delivery was politely answered, the day after, with a refusal.[43] With this acknowledged handicap – complaining 'how difficult it *is* to make anything out at a Newspaper Office' – Dickens settled down to his editorial work. The surviving correspondence shows him to have had a fair grasp of his responsibilities, attempting to second-guess the direction of political events, and guide the paper's response to them. He confidently touches up political leaders, adding, for example, a passage to W. J. Fox's leader of 23 January, venturing to predict that Peel's future policy would remain

> as it has ever been, vacillating, hesitating, and weak; with here a bold suggestion of advance, and there a timid provision for retreat; marring its lame and late concessions to justice, stern necessity, and truth. But this is auguring from the past. May we have to read him ... to new purpose in a brighter future!

It was a 'pretty safe' prediction to make 'about such a Customer,' he told Fox, which at the same time reserved '(like the good Vicar of Wakefield) a means of coming out creditably.'[44] However, given that twenty-six of the sixty-four editorials published under his formal editorship dealt in detail with the operation of the Corn Laws and the philosophy of the League, Dickens does not feel himself qualified to lay down strong lines. A certain hesitancy obtains in his dealings with those senior staff and leader-writers who were not well known to him. His effort to arbitrate in a row between sub-editor Thomas Hodgskin and financial leader-writer John Towne Danson is tactful and pleasant, and indicates a desire for consistency in the paper's policies, but evinces little of the powerful controlling spirit which he invests elsewhere in his anticipatory descriptions of editorial power. He is, he admits, 'not learned in the minute details' of the theories over which his employees had clashed.

Years later, Danson elaborated on this lack in a lengthy MS memoir of their relations, in which he complains that if Dickens had 'been fit for, &

had he done, his duty fully, I shd. have seen more of him. But my department was the Economic & financial; and of Political Economy ... he knew
nothing.' In spite of his sincere desire to be 'effective' in what he did,
Danson felt that Dickens should have been able to guide or correct him,
and in this respect 'he was, & felt himself to be, very weak ... and my
presence always roused and intensified his uneasiness.'[45]

Dickens's uneasiness could have been caused, however, by his finding
Danson, as Fox seems to have done, 'a stupid man of figures and statistics
... who is worse than nobody.' A letter written on the day of his resignation
shows him in fact quite severely correcting Danson for attacking Peel's
repeal proposals too violently in a leader that had gone to press on a
Sunday night, when it was Dickens's custom not to go to the office to read
proofs:

> [Y]our leader ... has no warrant in anything that had previously been
> written in the subject in the *Daily News*.... [A]ll the writers of Leading
> articles here, have admitted that there is great good in Sir Robert Peel's
> plan.... To say that we "cannot approve of its general scope *or* of its
> details," and that it is "miserably unsuited to the occasion, and paltry in
> the extreme," is to out-Herod Herod, most violently, and to stand quite
> alone by yourself and apart from the paper.[46]

Peel was thus not always the villain.[47]

Adjudicating between the differing claims of his heterogeneous team of
leader writers cannot have been an easy task for Dickens. They consisted of
financial journalists and diehard Free Traders, as well as those who, like
him, were satirists rather than statisticians, and who had also learned their
trade on less 'gentlemanly' publications than the one he and Forster now
aimed to establish in the *Daily News*. He must have felt uncomfortable in
seeming to sanction the unshakeable belief in the providence of political
economy projected by the paper's editorial columns, although some of the
positions adopted (such as the paper's strong opposition to Lord Ashley's
bill to limit factory shifts to ten hours) underline that Dickens was by no
means so opposed to certain Benthamite principles as modern readers have
expected.[48] More certainly, mutual recriminations and back-biting accusations of incompetence among the senior writing staff suggest an underlying unease about the paper's early performance, a reaction to its failure to
live up to great collective expectations. Forster's 'nobody could be a worse
editor than Dickens' can be set beside Fox's comment on Forster's unfitness
'to be at the head of anything political and popular' or his disappointment
that, for all Dickens's pride in his familiarity with the mighty engine of the
press, he 'broke down in the mechanical business' of the paper: 'to my
great vexation, as he has really a better morale for editorship than
Forster.'[49]

Beside these anxious insiders' insights, W. H. Russell's widely-quoted verdict on Dickens's editorial performance needs to be heavily qualified by an appreciation of his considerable distance from the frontline:

> Dickens was not a good editor; he was the best reporter in London, and as a journalist he was nothing more. He had no political instincts or knowledge, and was ignorant of and indifferent to what are called 'Foreign Affairs'; indeed, he told me himself that he never thought about them till the Revolution of 1848.... Dickens, having all the tools at his hand to turn out a splendid newspaper, failed even to exhibit moderate carpentry.[50]

Dickens had of course strong political instincts (though they did not lend themselves to compliant analysis of political intrigue and 'business') and, in his American and European travels, had developed an interest in foreign affairs during the early 1840s that extended to the establishment of the newspaper's successful foreign department.[51] Moderate carpentry was exactly what the early numbers of the *Daily News* did exhibit, along with flashes of journalistic brilliance in Dickens's own contributions, which continued for several weeks after he had resigned as editor.

V

The resignation, when it came, was hardly unexpected, nor perhaps was the manner of it. Dickens's belief in the 'gentlemanly' conduct desirable in an Editor meant he eschewed blaming colleagues in the Literary Department for the failures and half-successes of the paper, but turned, as was his wont, the full force of his disappointment on the managers. He voiced on 30 January a general concern that the paper's 'Railway policy' (articulated by the Railway Editor, William Scott Russell, but influenced by Paxton and the railway advertisers) was biased and 'threatening to taint it,' then swiftly homed in on a supposed snub to his authority, in the form of a suggestion from Bradbury and Evans that John Hill Powell was unfit for the role of sub-editor. Known for his 'excitable temperament' Powell had been sacked from the *Chronicle* in the 1830s for unpunctuality, but Dickens now stood by him, and demanded to know with whom his managers had consulted in forming their opinion. 'I shall leave the Paper immediately, if you do not give me this information' he threatened, adding that he would probably leave it anyway if they did: 'it would be natural in any man ... to consider this disrespectful, and quite unendurable.' This despite the fact that the Deed of Co-Partnership signed nine days before stated that Bradbury and Evans had the right 'to engage appoint and remove the Editor Sub-editors Contributors ... and all other persons.'[52]

The speed, finality, and extent of the over-reaction present a condensed repetition of Dickens's quarrel with Bentley over editorial control, with the variation here that Dickens had already rehearsed his exit, made all the easier now that his ambition of launching the paper was accomplished. To Forster he confided what must long have been obvious as his only alternative: 'quitting the paper and going abroad again to write a new book.' Sales had been as low as 4000 since the paper's inception, and, understandably worried by mounting losses, Bradbury had started cutting back in the counting house, in a manner that added fuel to Dickens's fire. 'He seems to have become possessed of the idea that everybody receiving a salary in return for his services, is his natural enemy' he wrote at the end of February. Editorial orders and expenses had been countermanded or refused; Bradbury had been disrespectful to John Dickens, and therefore to his son: 'in the worst times of Sir John Easthope, I never saw anything approaching Mr Bradbury.'

Dickens's interest in *The Daily News* becoming 'a fine property' meant, however, that his departure could not be precipitate. Although his 'Literary Shares' in net profits were unlikely be worth anything in the short term, the paper paid him his salary, and for his contributions, until the end of April.[53] He continued his editorial functions until 12 February, handing over to the not-unprepared Forster, the first of a 'series of editors, transient and embarrassed phantoms [who] flitted across the stage,' as Paxton's biographer records. To different correspondents, Dickens presented his motives for leaving and degree of separation from the paper in different lights, but his fullest and in some ways most clear-headed assessment is given in a letter to de la Rue:

> I am again a gentleman. I have handed over the Editing of the Paper ... to Forster; and am contemplating a New Book.... The Daily News is a great success – expences at first, most enormous of course. It is very much respected by the good men of both parties ..., by reason of its forbearance and sense of responsibility. But I am not quite trustful in, or quite satisfied with, some of the people concerned in its mechanical and business management, which is a very important part of such an undertaking. Therefore, I confine myself to writing, which is much more agreeable.[54]

Dickens had long sought to combat the prejudice that a newspaperman was a 'thorough-going blackguard' rather than a gentleman,[55] and it is a measure of his frustration with the interference of managerial and corporate interests on the paper that he is prepared to voice it here, even half in jest. In the ensuing months he became as anxious for Forster to escape from the 'daily nooses' of Bouverie Street quarrels, as he had formerly been to involve him. 'God knows,' he reflected in October, hearing of Forster's resignation, 'there has been small comfort for either of us in the D.N.'s nine months.'[56]

VI

Dickens's known contributions to the paper after the opening issue consist of two poems on Corn Law-related themes ('The British Lion' and 'The Hymn of the Wiltshire Labourers'), the eight Italian 'Travelling Letters,' a leading article on the nascent Ragged School movement ('Crime and Education'), five leaders cast as 'Letters on Social Questions' dealing with the capital punishment debate, and continued intermittently until 16 March, at which point in the tortuous discussions of the paper's future, he withdrew his support even as a contributor.

The first poem is a satirical squib, signed 'Catnach' after the publisher of low ballads and broadsheets, which mocks the decline of Protectionist spirit in the Lords in terms of the decline of a British circus lion, unsuccessfully paraded and stirred up by his principal keeper. Its apparently defective scansion is referable to Dickens's habit of 'setting' his squibs to some well known melody or other, in this case Holcroft's 'Great Sea Snake;' also characteristic is the use of Cockneyisms like 'wery bold' and the comic refrain:

> Oh, p'raps you may have heard, and if not I'll sing
> Of the British Lion free,
> That was constantly a-going for to make a spring
> Upon his en-e-me;
> But who, being rather groggy at the knees,
> Broke down, always, before;
> And generally gave a feeble wheeze
> Instead of a loud roar.
>> Right toor rol, loor rol, fee faw fum,
>> The British Lion bold!
>> That was always a-going for to do great things,
>> And was always being 'sold'![57]

The second poem, described by one impatient biographer as 'an infliction in verse' but which impressed Lord John Russell,[58] is a declamatory piece of Christian socialism inspired by reports of an illiterate Wiltshire woman, Lucy Simkins, whose rough eloquence at open-air meetings of the distressed rural poor, had attracted press attention. Dickens speaks for her and the other Wiltshire labourers in the artificial language of the church hymnal, but manages to capture something of the suppressed menace of such meetings in the veiled threats to 'Lords and Gentry':

> The GOD, who with his finger drew
> The Judgement coming on,
> Write, for these men, what must ensue,
> Ere many years be gone!

Oh GOD whose bow is in the sky,
Let them not brave and dare,
Until they look (too late) on high,
And see An Arrow there![59]

The poem presents a complex series of displacements: Dickens, the public
wordsmith, putting into the mouths of the starving workpeople the words
of a prayer which asks God to intervene politically on their behalf with
'Lords and Gentry' whose resistance to pity (and, by implication, repeal) is
likened to a wall, 'stern, obdurate and high.' The symbolic actions which
God is asked to perform in each verse – to strike, look down, teach, write,
and remind – are all ones which the newspaper itself, and Dickens in his
editorial role, undertook to carry out.

At times of civil unrest, Dickens unfailingly looked in his journalism to
the magistracy and judiciary to adapt their use of discretionary powers to
the political climate, and to consider the wider effect which their remarks
to juries might produce. Two high profile murder trials during February
1846 led him to articulate his strong views on capital punishment in a
series of powerful articles signed and 'authenticated,' the paper announced,
'as all communications from the same hand will be, by the writer's distinguished name.' The subject was one which had attracted him as a journalist
since 'A Visit to Newgate,' and which, since the witnessing of Courvoisier's
death and the writing of *Barnaby Rudge*, had fascinated him as a matter of
individual and group psychology. There is much more to his response to
the phenomenon of the scaffold than a simple 'scapegoating' of the crowd,
and his descriptions of its 'ribaldry, debauchery, levity, drunkenness, and
flaunting vice,' though striking, occupy a mere three paragraphs in the
second article.[60] Once again, it was a topic on which he had promised to
write for the *Edinburgh Review*. In the Autumn he had got as far as detailing
his approach in a letter to Napier, and discussing length and deadlines but
instead of the lengthy treatise which that would have entailed, drafted
instead these five pithy essays under the heading 'Letters on Social
Questions' which look at the death penalty and the social effects of public
hanging from a variety of angles.[61] On this issue, if not on questions of
political economy, Dickens demonstrated the confidence to lead public
opinion, in the sense of arguing and substantiating a clear view on a
subject that provoked fierce and confused debate.

This is partly a question of knowledge. Over the series – nowhere
currently in print[62] – no fewer than seven recent and thirteen historic trials
and executions are mentioned as reference points; extracts are given from
six books and pamphlets on the topic; quotations are made from parliamentary returns, speeches, numerous judges, while references to *Macbeth*,
More's *Utopia*, Goldsmith's *Bee*, and Hogarth's engravings add an imaginative dimension. In the second article, where Dickens uses the phrase

'attraction of repulsion' for the first time, he appears to lean heavily, though apparently unconsciously, on Hazlitt's insights into the dangerous fascination felt by some for 'objects of terror,' like the gibbet.[63] Each of the five letters deals in some depth with a different aspect of the conceptual and practical arguments for and against the death penalty, and the series culminates in Dickens's advocacy of 'the total abolition of the Punishment of Death, as a general principle, for the advantage of society, for the prevention of crime, and without the least reference to, or tenderness for any individual malefactor whomsoever.'[64]

Dickens's closing summary of his reasons for advocating total abolition in fact mixes matters of principle with utilitarian benefits and emotional reflexes: 'in most cases,' he goes on, 'my feeling towards the culprit is very strongly and violently the reverse' of tenderness. An ambivalence, and a keeping in play of both (authoritarian) hostility and (liberal) empathy without finally settling where each should be directed, is already present in these letters, as it had been in *Rudge*, and the practical problems of crime prevention and what to do with convicted murderers are clearly at odds with the 'general principle' laid down that executions are not a Christian law. But Dickens entitled his *Daily News* leaders 'Letters on Social Questions' because they continually attempt to demonstrate the negative impact of capital punishment not on the individual to be punished but on the society for whom the punishment supposedly acts as a deterrent. In terms of the social advantages to be derived from either reform, the difference between total abolition (not achieved in Britain until 1965) and the introduction of private executions (eventually achieved in 1868) was, for Dickens, slight. His later pursuit of the lesser objective has been taken as evidence of a hardening in his penological views, but in fact reveals a pragmatic desire to support a campaign which had some chance of short-term success. The hardness was there from the start.[65]

The intellectual *cul de sacs* involved in handling complex social questions in the columns of a daily newspaper, were fewer in number when education rather than capital punishment was the topic of debate. In 'Crime and Education,' Dickens contextualises the theoretical issues by subjoining to his analysis a colourful account 'of a visit of my own to a Ragged School,' in a stylistic development that allows 'Charles Dickens' as present-tense leader-writer to merge into 'Boz' as past-tense reporter, thus negotiating the tension between the theoretical and the graphic which Napier had anticipated in Dickens's journalism.[66]

The 'Ragged School' movement, assisted by the London City Mission and the foundation of a 'Ragged School Union,' had been gathering momentum in some of the worst London slums since 1843, and Dickens had taken an early interest in its progress and enlisted the support of millionaire philanthropist Miss Coutts (for whom he acted as unofficial almoner). He had carefully researched material on the schools' progress for yet another

Edinburgh Review article that failed to materialise, and corresponded with Samuel R. Starey, the so-called 'godfather of Ragged Schools,' about trying to bring the schools to the attention of the government. Alongside various 'distinguished individuals' (prominent evangelical clergymen and titled gentry), Dickens was by 1845 the only journalist and man of letters who had befriended the movement.[67]

His article of 4 February 1843, published together with the paper's full report of a public lecture on the schools, was hailed as a propaganda coup by the Ragged School Union, one of whose workers recalled in 1850 how 'the struggling efforts of a few individuals were brought into a striking and brilliant light' by 'those simple but touching columns in the *Daily News*, in which he showed the world a glimpse of these children of misery, and of what was being done for them.'[68] At the close of the paper, Dickens reflects that he 'might easily have given [these remarks] another form,' as indeed, in describing Scrooge's encounter with the neglected city children, Want and Ignorance, in *A Christmas Carol*, he already had. The relationship between fiction and journalism is such, he feels, that those who enjoy the former may be persuaded to read the latter, through knowing the author of both to be the same: 'I address this letter to you in the hope that some few readers in whom I have awakened an interest, as a writer of fiction, may be … attracted to the subject, who might otherwise, unintentionally, pass it over.'[69]

VII

Read in the context of the columns of *The Daily News*, Dickens's travelling letters take on a somewhat different function from that which similar text performs as the opening to *Pictures from Italy*. Dickens's opening Address for the newspaper figured the launch of the paper as the commencement of a journey in tune with the 'advancing spirit of the time': the first 'Travelling Letter' complements the figure by describing the commencement of a liberating journey undertaken by a tolerant, non-Sabbatarian English family 'starting for Italy on a Sunday morning': the second progress being an allegory of the first, an endorsement of the 'doctrine of nationalities' which the *Daily News* would preach in its foreign coverage for much of the nineteenth century.[70]

In order to give *Daily News* readers a greater sense of the contemporaneity of their travelling correspondent, Dickens brought the date of the journey forward to summer 1845 (in all editions of the travel book, it is given, accurately, as 1844). The complex opening sentence plays with generic expectations about beginnings and viewpoints, invoking but casting off the inappropriately literary opening of a historical novel in the style of a Scott or Bulwer, which situates the narrator-as-observer on some lookout-point distant in space and time,[71] and quickly reassures the reader that they are setting out on a thoroughly modern journey in a modern journal, where observation is close range, and part of a communicative cultural exchange:

> It was on a fine Sunday morning in the Midsummer time and weather of eighteen hundred and forty-four, my good friend, when – don't be alarmed; not when two travellers might have been observed slowly making their way over that picturesque and broken ground by which the first chapter of a 'Middle Aged' novel is usually attained; but when an English travelling-carriage of considerable proportions, fresh from the shady halls of the Pantechnicon near Belgrave-square, London, was observed (by a very small French soldier; for I saw him look at it) to issue from the gate of the Hôtel Meurice in the Rue Rivoli at Paris.[72]

The second letter, published three days later, also carried a significant political charge in its unashamedly Jacobinical justification of the slaughter of priests in Avignon at the height of the French Revolution: a 'much better' abuse of power, Dickens observes, than the blasphemy of the medieval church authorities, for the revolutionaries acted

> in the name of Liberty – their liberty; an earth-born creature, nursed in the black mud of the Bastille moats and dungeons.... But the Inquisition used it in the name of Heaven. / ... The light in the doleful vaults was typical of the light that has streamed in, on all persecution in God's name, but which is not yet at its noon![73]

The implication that the corruption of religious despotism was yet to be swept aside by the advance of national progress was wholly in tune with the *Daily News* position on papal affairs,[74] and this was the note on which Dickens eventually ended the text added to the newspaper letters to complete *Pictures from Italy*. His travels, after all, had been to 'fair Genoa' in Charles Albert's liberally-inclined Kingdom of Sardinia-Piedmont, with only brief excursions into the states and kingdoms controlled by the Pope, imperial Austria, and the Bourbons, where the change of atmosphere is noted disapprovingly in the ensuing accounts.[75] Later writings show he became interested in the case of at least one 'political offender' during his travels.[76] The itinerary itself was thus indicative of an ideology, added to which, Dickens's characteristic interest in scenes of past violence – graveyards, crypts, tombs, murder scenes and scaffolds – allows for plenty of politically-inflected commentary in his reports. The prefatory address ('The Reader's Passport') added to *Pictures from Italy* eschews 'any grave examination into the government or misgovernment of any portion of the country,' but Dickens's examination of its graves and churches performs the task as tellingly.[77]

'The Readers Passport' closes with a light-hearted attempt to define an ideal reader for the book, but beneath the Sternean humour lies the same anxiety about audience and reception detectable in the dedication and cancelled opening chapter of *American Notes*. In the newspaper letters, Dickens has fewer doubts about his audience, who, whether they were of the class which could contemplate a foreign sojourn or not, could all be presumed, as *Daily News* readers, in favour of broad 'Religious Liberty' – the kind of male readers who would have appreciated his swipe at female intellectuals and joking approval (omitted from the volume edition) of devout Italian women wearing blue 'for a year or two' to please the Madonna: 'upon the whole, I think I like them nearly as well as some "Blue ladies" in England.'[78] Dickens's own mockery of Roman Catholic shows and ceremonies hardly seems ecumenical, but he had grown up with the Whig strategy, during the emancipation debates of the late 1820s, of laughing Protestant readers out of more violent bigotry, a tactic brilliantly pioneered by Sydney Smith in the *Edinburgh Review*.[79] Even so, Dickens rightly anticipated that some *Daily News* readers might confuse his relentlessly facetious accounts of the 'ridiculous or offensive' in Catholic ceremonies, his comic emphasis on the performative (and hence implicitly worthless) aspect of ritual, with an attack on the essentials of their faith. A satirical description in the sixth travelling letter of roadside shrines near Genoa, with money-boxes 'for the benefit of the souls in Purgatory' was carefully footnoted, to prevent such 'misunderstanding,' while an account of a teenage girl taking the veil in the seventh, was discreetly cut from the volume edition.[80]

The signed 'travelling letters' were an innovation in newspaper journalism, one of a number credited to Dickens's *Daily News*.[81] As incorporated into *Pictures from Italy* they are much less remarkable, however, and come to share the travel book's difficulties in and anxieties about, marking out new terrain. More salient in volume form, are the discontinuities in the traveller's persona, a flexible and at times troubled entity built up from the successive revisions of personal letters to different readers, who does not always handle the change from grave to gay with the assurance of the London-based 'Boz,' as early reviewers noted.[82] The projection in many passages of a bluff, sceptical monologist, determined not to be taken in by the gimcrack shows displayed in the corrupted context of Catholic churches and decaying aristocratic palaces, lays Dickens unavoidably open to the charge of iconoclasm, even allowing for the displaced burden of suppressed political and religious criticism which freights his strictures on Italian art.[83] Dickens's field of vision is too broad to frame religious art within purely aesthetic parameters. In his recollection of the interior of the Cathedral and crypt at Parma in 'Travellings Letters. No VIII,' the crowd of beggars – symptomatic of the present-day corruption of the Italian body politic and the atavism of the Church – makes Dickens project the same morbid confusion back into the sixteenth century of Correggio's frescoes, and distorts his vision. The realities of the secular and mysteries of the spiritual world are alike reduced into the fragments of a surgeon's nightmare.[84]

The complexities and ambivalences of the persona introduced through the 'Travelling Letters' and developed in the material added to complete *Pictures from Italy* are worth noting, because the figure of the traveller and the rhetorical strategies of the *récit de voyage* recur in much of Dickens's later journalism, including many of the better-known essays in *Household Words* and *All The Year Round*. There, as a later chapter will explore, Dickens finds ways of consciously negotiating the tourist/anti-tourist dichotomy,[85] of investing the travel metaphor not just with European but with local-global cultural significance, and of rediscovering the latter's power as satire and its correlation with the writing process.

Not the least of the travel book's reformulations and suppressions of experience is contained in the final paragraph of the 'Reader's Passport,' where all the time and energy it had taken to establish, launch, and leave the *Daily News* is imploded into 'a brief mistake I made, not long ago, in disturbing the old relations between myself and my readers, and departing for a moment from my old pursuits.' This manner of describing the 'tremendous adventure' of the previous six months shows Dickens admitting publicly to an error of judgement – an uncharacteristic move – but the admission is adroit PR as much as a genuine indication of regret. Dickens was now gambling everything on a return to serial fiction, and needed to distance himself publicly from newspapers for a space, and more particularly from Bradbury & Evans, the Newspaper publishers, in order to make 'the board ... quite clear and clean for the playing out of a very great stake.'[86] Accordingly, he concentrated his energies on the fictional world of *Dombey and Son*, and published no journal articles for nearly two years. Yet nothing shows Dickens's continuing journalistic ambitions more clearly than his resumption, that November, of serious discussions with Forster about the establishment of a 'sort of *Spectator*' magazine, 'very cheap and pretty frequent,' mooted as though the *Daily News* had never, with much travail, been born into the world. 'It would be a great thing,' he innocently confided to the man who had only just resigned as his replacement Editor, 'to found something.'[87]

6
Reviewing *The Examiner* (1848–49)

The fivepenny Sunday weekly which Leigh Hunt founded and edited until 1821 still occupied a distinctive niche in the newspaper world of the 1840s. Its early outspoken republicanism (which had warned the youthful Dickens of the 'existence of a terrible banditti, called "The Radicals," whose principles were that the Prince Regent wore stays, and that nobody had a right to any salary, and that the army and navy ought to be put down') had given way to an intellectual radical tradition on Albany Fonblanque's installation as editor-cum-manager in 1830, while its excellent, independent coverage of drama and literature remained a selling point amongst well-to-do Whig and Liberal readers throughout the country.[1] As much a review as a political print, for most of its life only three to four of the sixteen pages of *The Examiner* contained original matter, the rest being supplied from cuttings and digests of the week's news. As Fonblanque aged and mellowed, and following Forster's official appointment as Editor in November 1847, it steered a slow but firm course towards respectability and the political centre-ground, without breaking openly with Benthamite thought. Whilst growing ever more critical of the working class aspirations represented by Chartism and the Ten Hours movement, the paper during Forster's ten-year editorship gave unqualified support to the new Liberal prime minister Lord John Russell and the 'best-conditioned middle class in the world,' advocating what Carlyle considered the essentially conservative 'theory of human affairs prevalent in fashionable Whig circles.' 'Gradually but inexorably,' Forster's biographer affirms, '*The Examiner* became the unashamed defender of those who bought it;' 'Podsnap ... tends to lurk behind [his] editorial chair.'[2]

The shift of position was itself representative of Victorian Radicalism in the lull between the parliamentary reform campaigns, however, and through the late 40s and 50s *The Examiner* maintained its circulation at a respectable 4400 to 4900 per issue, as well as its particular reputation for strong writing. A 'terse, polished, educated style,' was required of contributors, one new recruit recalled in 1850, 'with a quick fancy, store of illustration, [and a] vein of fun and earnestness at heart.'[3] All of this Dickens could and did provide in the thirty papers he is reckoned to have published in its columns between February 1848 and December 1849. These constitute his most sustained appearance in its pages as one of a small number of leader writers and reviewers.[4]

I

As earlier chapters have indicated, Dickens had submitted during the previous decade occasional theatre and book reviews, various angry satires in prose and verse, and an announcement about International Copyright, but his only piece of news reporting in the paper had been a collaborative effort with Fonblanque and possibly also Forster, written the day after Queen Victoria's coronation, but never hitherto reprinted. The leader is indicative both of the *Examiner's* continuing distrust of the pomp and circumstance of royalty (commenting from Westminster Abbey on the 'strange differences of the sorts of monarchs crowned within those walls, even to the so recent lavish and luxurious Fop, and homely mannered Sailor – all thus ending with a girl!') and of Fonblanque's initial estimation of Dickens's capabilities as a journalist: the latter's brief merely being to provide 'a few lines about the [coronation] fair' for Londoners, in Hyde Park.[5] The result is a truncated 'Boz' sketch with republican overtones, similar to those animating *Sunday under Three Heads*, and foregrounding the interest in, and defence of, popular entertainment which are a constant in Dickens's journalism:

> ... we must not omit a word on the holiday of the common people, after noticing this holiday of princes. The fair in Hyde Park – which covered some fifty acres of ground – swarmed with an eager, busy crowd from morning till night. There were booths of all kinds and sizes, from Richardson's Theatre, which is always the largest, to the canvas residences of the giants, which are always the smallest; and exhibitions of all sorts, from tragedy to tumbling....
>
> This part of the amusements of the people, on the occasion of the Coronation, is very particularly worthy of notice, not only as being a very pleasant and agreeable scene, but as affording a strong and additional proof ... that the many are at least as capable of decent enjoyment as the few. There were no thimblerig men, who are plentiful at race-courses, as at Epsom, where only *gold* can be staked; no gambling tents, roulette tables, hazard booths, or dice shops. There was beer drinking, no doubt, such beer drinking as Hogarth has embodied in his happy, hearty picture, and there were faces as jovial as ever he could paint. These may be, and are, sore sights to the bleared eyes of bigotry and gloom, but to all right-thinking men who possess any sympathy

with, or regard for, those whom fortune has placed beneath them, they will afford long and lasting ground of pleasurable recollection....[6]

The characteristic synecdoche of 'bleared eyes of bigotry and gloom' canvasses all those puritanical forces of the establishment (the Sir Andrew Agnews and teetotal fanatics) which would do away with social drinking amongst the industrious multitudes; the ambivalent gap between 'all right-thinking men' and a working class whose ranks have either always or only recently, been escaped, has a personal and professional significance for Dickens, his co-authors, and readers.

II

The articles of 1848–49 seem to range much more widely across the field of contemporary news and public affairs. Given that all were probably offered to the paper gratis, the range of subjects can also be taken as representative of Dickens's personal interests, mediated through Forster's hints and suggestions: five of Dickens's reviews were of work by their personal friends and acquaintances (Cruikshank, Leech, Jerrold, Macready and Lemon). With Lord John Russell and the Liberals in office, however, Dickens steers clear of topics which would necessitate judgement on the performance of a government he by-and-large supported. On the main political issues of the day – Europe in turmoil, Irish insurrection, the success of the Ten Hours movement, the failure of Chartism – he is silent, focussing instead on social, legal and sanitary matters, and trimming his naturally exuberant and facetious style to the paper's requirements. As an anonymous contributor to Forster's *Examiner*, and taking Fonblanque as his stylistic model, Dickens works a more sober vein of forensic and satirical paper.

An urgent concern with the twin issues of crime and education, evident in his leaders on 'Social Questions' for the *Daily News*, comes through strongly. In many cases the essays are founded on official reports, the daily press accounts of current events, and other newspaper articles: on information already in the public domain, which Dickens wishes to publicise, interpret or criticise. Public interest in the murder trial of J. B. Rush in the spring of 1849, for example, coincided with no fewer than four articles probably by Dickens, dealing once again with the conviction and sentencing of criminals.[7] The volume and frequency of Dicken's contributions on penological topics (no fewer than eleven articles in the late 1840s, and numerous essays in his journals from 1850 onwards) indicates a consistent, if complex, journalistic commitment: one which holds in creative tension both the ideological conflict between the utilitarian 'less-eligibility' principle and sympathetic fascination with individual criminal psychology, and the ethical pull between recommending conceptually-based attitudes towards discipline and punishment, and those based emotively around reactions to

recent events. Restrospectively, critics can complain that Dicken's engagement seems opportunistic, following in the wake of sensational trials and
executions, that his interest in such issues is not consistent, but 'fitful and
immediate.'[8] Monitoring events as they unfold however, Dickens provides a
valid justification of this common journalistic practice. Firstly, in the articles
themselves, individual trials are seldom considered without reference back
to appropriate legal and historical authorities, and to the more permanent
aspects of the debate. Secondly, as Dickens had explained in the first of his
Daily News leaders on the effects of public hanging, 'the importance of the
question is very strongly presented to the public mind' in the wake of
specific cases: 'no better occasion can be seized for reviving [the] discussion
than when such circumstances are generally remembered.'[9] Public opinion
has to be aroused before it can be swayed.

Dickens seizes appropriate occasions to revive discussion of other
perennial issues relating to crime and education, in seven further *Examiner*
articles, only four of which are collected. 'Ignorance and Crime' (22 April
1848) shows Dickens interpreting the recently published Government
statistics on arrests and convictions made by the Metropolitan Police for
the years 1831 to 1847, in order to extract 'much useful evidence in
reference to the alliance of crime with ignorance.' This supports his call for
'schools ... deep as the lowest depths of Society, ... leaving none of its dregs
untouched.'[10] Yet the government-subsidized National Schools, run by the
Church of England, were failing manifestly in their duty, Dickens argues in
'Ignorance and its Victims' (29 April 1848). Quoting a recent press report
from the trial of a fortune-teller who had duped a credulous servant girl
into parting with money and clothes, Dickens expostulates at the mild
attitude taken by the magistrate to the obvious failure of the servant's
catechism-based education:

> if the complainant had left the Kensington National School with a
> religious belief that the moon was an immense agglomeration of green
> cheese and the whole solar system so many myriads of small stiltons,
> the result of her 'education' need not have been more surprising to
> the good magistrate. ... This is one of the effects of teaching by rote
> certain pet abstractions, most weary of acquirement and of doubtful
> service when acquired confusedly, and leaving plain, interesting, solid
> knowledge quite out of the question.[11]

Whereas pupils with a perfunctory acquaintance with the Church
Catechism were nevertheless capable of acts of almost comical ignorance,
those children without such acquaintance, however intelligent, were
considered incapable of giving evidence before a judge or magistrate,
according to English law. This was leading to the iniquitous denial of
justice to the poorest and most helpless members of society, which Dickens

alludes to in 'A Truly British Judge!' and which *The Examiner* attacks directly in 'The Central Criminal Court,' 'The Exclusion of Evidence,' and 'An Edifying Examination.' These papers are probably by Dickens in collaboration with Fonblanque or Forster, the three writers forming 'a team who influenced each other strongly.'[12] The argument is enlivened by a semi-dramatized presentation of absurd courtroom dialogue, towards which Dickens had been tending in his earlier sketches of English law in 'Doctors' Commons,' and the trial scene from *Pickwick Papers.* The present-tense verbatim exchanges are simultaneously more lively and telling than the periphrasis of reported speech, and lead on to trenchant satirical commentary. In general format and in specific details the articles point the way to the combination of dialogue and forensic oratory voiced through the third-person narrator of *Bleak House,* and the encounter between Jo and the Law.

'Judicial Special Pleading' offers further evidence of Dickens's determination in these *Examiner* articles to emulate John Black and his own plans for *Master Humphrey's Clock,* by 'keep[ing] a special look-out ... in town and country' for any notably ignorant or prejudiced pronouncements by the magistracy and judiciary. Yet although the prose of this and other articles looks big and sounds fierce, its implications by no means overstep the *Examiner*'s increasingly moderate line. Following the high-publicity trials of Chartist leaders in London and the provinces following the third and final rejection of the People's Charter in April 1848, there was plenty of scope for arguing (as modern historians do) that judges had 'jettison[ed] ... any element of judicial impartiality,' but in this leader (23 December 1848), Dickens has no qualms assuming that the 'physical-force' supporters of Chartism were genuine offenders and 'enemies of the common weal.'[13] In censuring Sir Edward Alderson (the same judge roundly attacked for excluding a child's evidence in a case of abuse in 'The Central Criminal Court') for his conduct of trials at Chester, Dickens makes no complaint about the sentencing and instead takes him to task for introducing by way of an analogy, an inaccurate interpretation of the causes of the French Revolution. In the course of exposing the 'nonsense' of Alderson's remarks, and demolishing his 'proof' with telling references to Steele's *Tatler,* and Carlyle's and Thiers's recent histories, Dickens has much to say about the French Revolution – characterized as 'a struggle for social recognition and existence' rather than 'a mere struggle for "political rights"' – but avoids saying anything direct about contemporary Chartism. Yet the implication is clear: that unlike the French, the British uprisings *are* merely political, and, in so far as they are promoted by 'active and mischievous agents,' dangerous. When Dickens had written in October 1840 of Nell and her grandfather fearfully witnessing the Chartists' torchlight processions, and of 'maddened men,' urged on by their leaders, 'rush[ing] forth on errands of terror and destruction' (*MHC,* No. 29), the presentation is suitably lurid and distorted. Yet in both serial fiction and weekly journalism, Dickens presents the same point of principle, and does so obliquely: the social deprivation fuelling Chartist discontent needs reforming, not the political superstructure of 'the whole system which rules and restrains.'[14]

Similar concerns underlie a further series of sober Dickens essays in *The Examiner* – the four articles which deal with the deeds, trial and acquittal of the notorious Tooting 'baby farmer,' Monsieur Drouet. The verbal irony, echoing Swift and Voltaire, which at first represents Mr Drouet in 'The Paradise at Tooting' (20 January 1849) as a 'golden farmer,' and his Parish-funded establishment for pauper children as 'the best of all possible farms,' gradually gives way to the harsh truth behind an epidemic which cost many lives:

> The cholera ... broke out in Mr Drouet's farm for children, because it was brutally conducted, vilely kept, preposterously inspected, dishonestly defended, a disgrace to a Christian community, and a stain upon a civilized land.[15]

In a case where known individuals are so clearly to blame (Mr Drouet, the Poor Law Inspector, and the Clerk of the Holborn Union Board of governors are singled out for graduating degrees of condemnation), satire ceases to be the strongest means of attack. Instead, Dickens focuses in 'The Tooting Farm' (27 January) on the importance of the case being 'rigidly dealt with on it own merits' when Mr Drouet passes for judgement to the Central Criminal Court, on a charge of manslaughter. This is because of what Dickens characterises as the 'vague disposition to smooth over the things that be, which sometimes creeps into the most important English proceedings' – a governmental bias exerted through its appointments to the judiciary, which Dickens believed to be dangerous, given the social unrest still being fomented by Chartist agents. Thus he repeats his former argument from 'Judicial Special Pleading,' in calling for a verdict that would educate the 'poor working men' of England 'in the conviction that the State is unfeignedly mindful of them, and truly anxious to redress their tangible and obvious wrongs':

> Let the debtor and creditor account between the governors and the governed be kept in a fair, bold hand, that all may read, and the governed will soon read it for themselves, and dispense with the interpreters who are paid by chartist clubs.[16]

Drouet's subsequent acquittal by the obviously partial Baron Platt on a verdict of 'not proven,' produces a restrained response from Dickens, however. In his final article on the case ('The Verdict for Drouet,' 21 April), he displays surprising patience with the law itself, even though it has allowed a guilty man to walk free, presumably because to question it would swiftly lead to the justification of civil unrest such as the campaign of the 'physical-force' Chartists. He is thus content to accept 'the peculiarity' of the result on the basis that a moral, if not a legal victory had been won, through the extent of public notice which the trial had attracted. Recent reviewers have described 'The Paradise at Tooting' as a 'masterpiece of invective,' 'the most splendid journalistic offensive,'[17] yet it is hard to avoid concluding that the sum of his attacks in the *Examiner* on legal bias and prejudice is rather less radical than its parts.

III

Of the remaining five news articles contributed or probably contributed by Dickens to the *Examiner*, 'Court Ceremonies' (15 December 1849) and 'The Chinese Junk' (24 June 1848) are of more than passing interest.[18] The first notices with approval the late Queen Dowager's request for her 'mortal remains to be carried to the grave without any pomp or state;' Dickens takes the opportunity here to express his strong dislike of extravagant state funerals, and of 'the preposterous constraints and forms that set a mark upon the English Court among the nations of Europe.' This dislike is not confined merely to court ceremonies. Dickens links it here to all ceremonies under direction of the Lord Chamberlain's office. In several later essays in *Household Words*, the out-dated pageantry and feasting of the Lord Mayor's office come under attack, and English funeral traditions are continually portrayed in Dickens's journals as the result of shameless jobbery in the undertaking profession, and social pretension amongst the paying public.[19] In the tradition of the British Essayists, Dickens seems to reserve his sharpest satire for censoring the manners and mores of the nation.

'The Chinese Junk' seems at first sight unlike Dickens's other *Examiner* essays, being a piece of colourful first-hand reporting. The object of the piece is to describe a visit to the 'Keying,' the first Chinese vessel to reach England, which had been put on display along with its oriental crew to the public at its moorings in the East India Docks, in April 1848. By the time Dickens's account was published on 24 June, the junk had become a popular attraction, inspected by Royalty and reported in the illustrated press, hence, on closer inspection, Dickens's account takes on some aspects of editorial commentary. His ideas are framed in the narrative context of a magical, space-shrinking, railway flight to and from the scene:

The shortest road to the Celestial Empire is by the Blackwall railway. You may take a ticket, through and back, for a matter of eighteen pence. With every carriage that is cast off on the road at Stepney, Limehouse, Poplar, West India docks – thousands of miles of space are cast off too, the flying dream of tiles and chimney-pots, backs of squalid houses, frowzy pieces of waste ground, narrow courts and streets, swamps, ditches, masts of ships, gardens of dock-weed, and unwholesome little bowers of scarlet beans, whirls away in half a score of minutes. Nothing is left but China.[20]

The ability of the railway to expose hidden territory to the traveller, to forge unexpected connections, like a metaphysical conceit, between previously discrete areas of both physical and cultural landscapes was something the narrator of the seventh number of *Dombey and Son* (April 1847) had digressed to explore.[21] Here, building on the exaggerated contrast between East and West accentuated by this trope, and reproducing both factual details and stereotyped attitudes towards Chinese culture and religion gleaned from the brochure he had bought on board,[22] Dickens develops a self-conscious orientalism that initially ridicules the apparent stasis of Chinese technology and narrowness of outlook (paragraphs 2–6), embodied in their 'doctrine of finality.' But in the midst of developing a line of thought by no means unrepresentative of the attitude of Forster's *Examiner* to other cultures, or of his own journals in the 1850s and 60s,[23] Dickens is impelled to reject the implication that national institutions have achieved a state of perfection, and the satire veers round 180 degrees to point back at the Oxford Movement in the Church of England. The argumentation of the essay and the narration of the visit reach their natural conclusion together: 'There is matter for reflection aboard the Keying to last the voyage home to England again.' The exercise is in some ways a blueprint for the reports of the 'Uncommercial Traveller' in the 1860s, which often show a similar synchronic development of thought and motion, set against a similar London topography.

Dickens's handful of review essays written for *The Examiner* under Forster's editorship complement his news journalism, singling out books, plays and public amusements that strike him as signs of the times. The most substantial is the paper known as 'The Niger Expedition,' properly a review of Captain W. Allen and T. R. H. Thomson's *Narrative of the Expedition sent by Her Majesty's Government to the River Niger in 1841.* Dickens was a voracious consumer of narratives of African travel, and a Mungo Park enthusiast,[24] but his enthusiasm did not extend beyond the heroic attempts to explore and chart the Niger's course to include the later efforts of the Colonial Office and evangelical missionaries to promote up-river trade and convert the heathen. In his review, he looks immediately beyond the question of the book's quality, to present an informed but strongly-worded critique of the aims and methods of the Exeter Hall-inspired 'Society for the Extinction of the Slave Trade and for the Civilization of Africa' which had promoted the expedition, summarising the reasons for the failure of its grandiose aims as 'British credulity' combined with the African 'climate, ... falsehood, and deceit.' On the absurdity of the concept of signing anti-slave trade treaties, the expedition's principle *raison d'être*, Dickens pours particular scorn, albeit without perceiving what has become clear to West African historians in retrospect: that the inevitable failure of the treaties led on to the suppression by force of the overseas slave trade, and provided 'an indispensable prelude to the British occupation of Nigeria.'[25]

Moving from the particular to the general, Dickens justifies his interpretation of the narrative with ironic commentary on a selection of lengthy extracts, before articulating his opposition to the waste of life and energy, and neglect of primary duties shown by the prioritising of evangelical foreign missions over the 'work at home.' The result is an essay which, according to Humphry House, was 'remarkable' even in 1941 'for its vigour, eloquence, and even, in places, enlightenment.' Modern readers are scarcely likely to be comfortable with Dickens's assumptions about European racial superiority, however, and his lament for the loss of 'the useful lives of scholars, students, mariners and officers – more precious than a wilderness of Africans,' although the accuracy of his pessimism as to the likely perpetuation of inequality into the foreseeable future has been confirmed:

> The history of this Expedition is the history of the Past, in reference to the heated visions of philanthropists for the railroad Christianization of Africa and the Abolition of the Slave trade. ... Between the civilized European and the barbarous African there is a great gulf set. ... In the mighty revolutions of the wheel of time, some change in this regard may come about ... To change the customs even of civilized and educated men, and impress them with new ideas, is – we have good reason to know it – a most difficult and slow proceeding; but to do this by ignorant and savage races, is a work which, like the progressive changes of the globe itself, requires a stretch of years that dazzles in the looking at.... There is a broad, dark sea between the Strand in London, and the Niger, where those rings are not yet shining, and through all that space they must appear, before the last one breaks upon the shore of Africa. Gently and imperceptibly the widening circle of enlightenment must stretch and stretch, from man to man, ... until there is a girdle round the earth; but no convulsive effort, or far off aim, can make the last great outer circle first, and then come home at leisure to trace the inner one.[26]

The ripple and light imagery, use of feminising words like 'gently,' 'girdle,' even the ideologically-burdened term 'enlightenment' itself, combine to make this one of the most lyrical of Dickens's explicit pronouncements on empire,[27] but do not, by any means, guarantee the enlightenment of its outlook, in which Dickens is already rehearsing the racist rhetoric that fulminates in the ghastly comedy of 'The Noble Savage,'[28] and through which even the strongest of Victorian anti-imperialist critiques was articulated. In contrasting a group of Sierra Leonean 'Krumen' tribespeople ('a faithful, cheerful, active, affectionate, race ... the only hopeful human agents ... for aid in working out the gradual raising up of Africa') with the deceitful character of 'King Obi' {sic} and his Ibo people ('formed, essentially, in the inscrutable wisdom of God, by the soil they work on and the air they breathe'), and despite some apparent efforts to find out more 'about the Blacks as a species' before writing the article, Dickens falls prey to a Conradian oversimplification of West African anthropology.

In *American Notes*, both African slaves and native American Indians had been sorrowfully apostrophized as 'simple' peoples brutalized by their experience of white abuse of power, and likely to be eradicated by the 'new possessors of the land,'[29] but the sympathy had been relativistically generated in context of Dickens's remarkable revulsion at Southern republicanism. In later journalism, there is a tendency to reduce the ethnic diversity of the African peoples to one of only two paradigms: the good-natured, grown-up child who is the victim of exploitation and violence, and the treacherous, irredeemable barbarian, who violates and exploits. The portrayal of Mrs Jellyby in *Bleak House*, and her wild schemes for 'cultivating coffee and educating the natives of Borrioboolah Gha, on the left bank of the Niger,' gives fictional specificity to Dickens's general target in the *Examiner* review, famously encapsulated in the journalistic catch-phrase 'telescopic philanthropy.' The Dickensian humanity displayed towards the neglected Jellyby children needs to be offset by recognition of the telescopic misanthropy of the article which focused its operation. Like the uncertainly Liberal narrator of *A Passage to India*, Dickens's social inclusiveness does not possess infinite gradations; does not indeed, stretch far beyond the confines of a civilized Europe: 'perhaps it is futile for men to initiate their own unity, they do but widen the gulfs between them by the attempt ... . We must exclude someone from our gathering, or we shall be left with nothing.'[30]

The urgency of the 'home mission' is emphasized by Dickens in two further review essays which consider the physical and moral causes of drunkenness, and its cures – there being, in Forster's words, 'no subject on which through his whole life he felt more strongly than this.'[31] Dickens registers first a 'gentle protest' at George Cruikshank's second series of plates advocating Total Abstinence principles, *The Drunkard's Children: A Sequel to The Bottle*. (*Examiner*, 8 July 1848). Cruikshank, in his opinion, had failed in his responsibility to present the government's sins of omission as well as the sins of the alcoholic: 'drunkenness, as a national horror' being 'the effect of many causes.' By way of contrast, he analyses the virtues of 'Gin Lane,' an engraving by Hogarth who, unlike Cruikshank, 'was never contented with beginning at the effect' in devising his compositions. In the process, Charles Lamb's views on the engraving are referred to, taken from an essay in *The Reflector* of 1811: 'the reader must be impressed,' one critic argues, 'not only with Dickens's seeing all there is to see, but with his ability to interpret what there is not to see.'[32] The same could be said of Dickens's art criticism in his formal panegyric on *The Rising Generation*, John Leech's series of sketches republished from *Punch*, in which he comments that there 'is no reason why the farmer's daughter in the old [Gillray] caricature who is squalling at the harpsichord ... should be squab and hideous: the satire on the manners of her education ... would be just as good if she were pretty.' Dickens much prefers Leech's 'pretty woman' figure, because she is 'not only a pleasanter object in our portfolio, but [w]e care more about what does become her, and does not become her.' This is to prove the point that Leech is the 'first English caricaturist ... who had considered beauty as being perfectly compatible with art,' before arguing that Leech's sketches of 'growing boys' as well as 'grown women,' are simultaneously artistically perfect, and true to nature ('We recognized the legs of the philosopher who considers Shakespeare an over-rated man, dangling over the side of an omnibus last Tuesday'). The reciprocal assimilation of Forster's mature literary and artistic aesthetic is noticeable in the peroration:

> [Mr Leech] has a becoming sense of responsibility and self-restraint: he delights in pleasant things; he imparts some pleasant air of his own to things not pleasant in themselves; he is suggestive and full of matter, and he is always improving. Into the tone, as well as into the execution of what he does, he has brought a certain elegance which is altogether new, without involving any compromise of what is true.[33]

Forster had recently praised Bulwer's *King Arthur* in the paper in almost identical terms, and in Volume 3 of the *Life* would later celebrate the symbiosis of the 'real' and the 'ideal' modes of treatment in Dickens's own art.[34]

Returning to the theme of drunkenness, and the 'wrong conclusions' drawn by advocates of teetotalism 'from premises that are to a certain extent right,' Dickens argues in 'Demoralization and Total Abstinence' (*Examiner*, 27 October 1849) that despite his radical scepticism of the effectiveness of Parliamentary legislation, some kind of remedy at a national level is required to combat 'a national horror.' The article is perhaps Dickens's most accomplished leader for the *Examiner*, opening with the keynote observation that characteristic of modern life is its maintenance of 'a large class of minds apparently unable to distinguish between use and abuse.' Hawkishly, this is applied to the thinking behind the recent Peace Congresses organized in Paris, which were advocating total abstinence from war 'at a time when a deplorable reaction towards tyranny is visible throughout Europe, and when it is, of all times, most important for the hopes of the world that a free country, abhorrent of the detestable cruelties practised by absolute government, should be in a bold and strong position.' Turning from the international arena to the domestic issue of drunkenness and the 'Extent and Causes of Juvenile Depravity' as outlined in a recent pamphlet by Thomas Beggs, Secretary of the National Temperance Association, Dickens urges the case first that drunkenness is as much the consequence as the cause of the wretched condition of the urban poor, 'and that it prevails in the low depths of society, as an evil of vast extent, because those evils have been too long unfathomed and unsunned.' Beggs's remedy – for the middle classes to 'dash down the cup' and 'banish the social glass' – now seems in consequence wholly inadequate and illogical.

Given that a cholera epidemic had killed over 16 500 Londoners in the four months since mid-June, Dickens's alternative emphasis on improving sanitation, housing, water supply and the provision of non-denominational schools for poor people's children, strikes home. Proceeding next to demonstrate, with merciless humour, the inaccuracy and injustice of a number of related positions maintained by Beggs and the Abolitionists, the article considers the fatuity of administering the Pledge in prison, and the naivety of Temperance researchers who point to question-naire results connecting drink and a life of crime, allowing Dickens to indulge in a characteristic *Examiner* reductio ad absurdum:

> If a notion arose that the wearing of brass buttons led to crime, and [the prisoners] were questioned to elucidate that point, we should have such answers as, 'I was happy till I wore brass buttons,' 'Brass buttons did it,' 'Buttons is the cause of my being here,' all down the columns of a grave return.

Dickens's assault is expertly planned and executed, culminating in the appropriation to his own cause of one of Beggs's own case histories, concerning a Glamorganshire factory complex where the workers were cleanly housed, their children educated, and two well-regulated public houses catered for moderate drinking habits. Drunkenness amongst the 4500 employees was there almost unknown. It is this kind of scheme 'on a great scale,' which the Government must imitate, Dickens concludes, 'or there is no hope left in us.'[35]

Perhaps, with his insistence on 'a fleet and an army' to support bold diplomacy, his call for abolition of the Window Tax, and massive state investment in new housing and schools for the poor, Dickens anticipates unrealistic levels of government expenditure at a time when revenue streams such as income tax, reintroduced in 1842, were running low. Yet there is no doubt of the article's consummate artistry in effecting the task in hand. Brice and Fielding, republishing it for the first time in 1981, justly introduce it as 'a plea for detachment, common-sense, a reasonable use of statistics, the larger view, and perhaps the clearest and the most complete statement of his social philosophy that he was to write outside his fiction.'[36] The final qualification, however, is unnecessary. Dickens's fiction is a vast and heterogeneous body from which one would have to extrapolate, infer, and interpret at length to arrive at a statement of social philosophy as succinct. Dickens was enough of a Benthamite to doubt the propriety and efficacy of state interference in many areas of national life, but not where drunkenness and its parent issues of public health, sanitation, housing, and education, were concerned.

IV

Two lengthy reviews of 1848 give some indication of Dickens's interest in both natural and supernatural 'science.' His remarks on Catherine Crowe's *The Night Side of Nature* evince a working knowledge of both contemporary and historical theories on the spirit world, and psychic phenomena. References are made to Addison, Johnson and Fielding's opinions, and to DeFoe's little-known *History of the Black Art*. Some familiarity is shown with the theories of Hegel and other 'German writers of undoubted ability.' Throughout, Dickens displays a lively scepticism, backed up by intelligent analysis of the kinds of structural weakness common to many tales of the supernatural:

> It is the peculiarity of almost all ghost stories, as contradistinguished from all other kinds of narratives purporting to be true, to depend, as ghost stories, on some one link in the chain of evidence, and that supposing that link to be destructible, the whole supernatural character is gone. ... In history, in biography, in voyages and travels, this peculiarity does not, and cannot, obtain....[37]

In 'The Poetry of Science' (9 December 1848), scepticism of the supernatural is complemented by a positive faith in recent scientific explanations of natural phenomena, as collected and described in a new publication by Robert Hunt. Dickens's remarks are prefaced by the significant comment that the book, although dealing with highly specialized material, is likely to find a wide readership thanks to Robert Chambers's anonymously-published *Vestiges of the Natural History of Creation* (1844), which had advanced a pre-Darwinian evolutionary theory called 'Progressive Development' and 'created a reading public – not exclusively scientific or philosophical – to whom such publications may hopefully be addressed.' In so doing, Dickens hazards, 'the author of that remarkable and much-abused book has not rendered his least important service to his own time.' Dickens later knew the well-kept secret of Chambers's authorship, but his defence of *Vestiges* in 1848 and of the right of the non-specialist to speculate based on 'knowledge of certain geological facts' point to the important conclusion that 'Dickens was a decided [God-fearing] evolutionist about a dozen years before *The Origin of Species*.'[38] In later journalism, Dickens himself indulges openly in speculations based, albeit humourously, on his assumption that fossil remains have exploded the orthodox scriptural chronology of the earth – Inspector Field of the Detective Police, on duty in the British Museum, recognises 'the Ichthyosaurus as a familiar acquaintance, and wonder[s], perhaps, how detectives did it in the days before the Flood.'[39] Dickens greatly approves Hunt's rational demystification of the physical wonders, which for him, offered truths no less imaginative than the superstitions which they displaced, and often more beautiful because divinely rather than humanly inspired:

> To show that the facts of science are at least as full of poetry, as the most poetical fancies ever founded on imperfect observation ... [t]o show that Science ... instead of binding us, as some would have it, in stern utilitarian chains, when she has freed us from a harmless superstition, offers to our contemplation something better and more beautiful, something which, rightly considered, is more elevating to the soul, nobler and more stimulating to the soaring fancy; is a sound, wise and wholesome object.

His praise of Hunt's ideals here echoes his praise of Macready's acting, Maclise and Leech's drawings, and is notably similar to his own aesthetic standard of 'the romance of everyday life,' shortly to be raised in the 'Preliminary Word' to *Household Words* in 1850.

Dickens's work in the *Examiner* during the two years preceding the successful establishment of his own periodical was of great importance in the development not only of a line of attack on the social evils of the day, but also of set of positive principles and ideals to be encouraged amongst Liberal readers. This despite the formal and stylistic conventions imposed by the paper, which restricted him mainly to serious, argumentative articles and review essays, all spoken through the detached mouthpiece of the editorial 'We,' or impersonal constructions. 'In contributing to the *Examiner*,' Brice and Fielding suggest, Dickens 'learned to be a journalist rather than a reporter,' and used the experience 'as a try-out or training ground for *Household Words*.'[40] Although this somewhat telescopes Dickens's apprenticeship in journalism, which had had its own 'progressive development' over fifteen years, notably concentrated during his association with the *Daily News*, it is true to say that the articles of 1848–49 'helped shape his style as well as his thought,' and gave him invaluable experience of leader-writing for an influential weekly. Weekly rather than daily, indeed, was the right periodicity for Dickens the journalist, as it was for Forster,[41] and suited his methods of research, composition, and satirical fancy.

7
Editing Life: Dickens and *Household Words* (1850–59)

Attempts at describing a periodical are stupid, it might be argued, *pace* George Eliot, for

> who can all at once describe a periodical? Even when it is presented to us we only begin that knowledge of its appearance which must be completed by innumerable impressions under different circumstances. We recognize the alphabet; we are not sure of the language.[1]

Between March 1850 and his death in July 1870, Dickens was responsible as editor for 1061 issues of *Household Words* and its look-alike successor, *All the Year Round*: for over 23 million words of original letterpress, and well over 6000 articles, poems and installments of serial fiction. More than 380 different writers (around ninety of them women) contributed to *Household Words*. A range of challenges thus faces the reader who would draw conclusions from this diversity of raw material, or attempt to evaluate the periodicals or their editor's performance in the increasingly crowded weekly magazine marketplace of the 1850s and 60s.

The critic of Dickens's journals has, however, some advantages over those researching the as yet unmapped reaches of the Victorian periodical press. Complete runs survive. Tables of contents and contributor lists (in the case of *Household Words*, annotated and complete with payments to contributors, reprinted from the original Office Book) have been published. Estimated circulation figures are available, and the bi-annual profits from 1850 to October 1867 are known. Dickens's detailed advice to contributors, discussion of general and specific editorial principles, and above all, the bulk of his day-to-day correspondence with his sub-editor, W. H. Wills, are all preserved in volumes six to twelve of the magnificent 'Pilgrim' edition of his letters. The journals were a popular success and Dickens's international fame made them a talking point, so there is a wealth of contemporary critical opinion recording their impact, together with various valuable surveys in modern editions and reference works.[2] Yet a central problem remains to be negotiated, which is the difficulty of establishing the extent to which the journals, taken as a whole or randomly sampled, may reliably be taken to represent Dickens's own views and opinions. There is no simple answer, and the orthodox assumption that Dickens's actual editorial and artistic control was such that 'every article published had to bear the stamp of Charles Dickens'[3] leads to unwarranted conclusions, and needs scrutiny. What is clear, nevertheless, is that Dickens's desire for such control – thwarted in his dealings with Richard Bentley, and lost in the trammels of the *Daily News* – was strong, even if the published results fell frequently short of his ideal. Underlying the practical measures he took to achieve it was an elaborate vision of how a multi-authored journal might project a powerful single identity into the public sphere, to access and influence the minds of a mass readership.

I

Reminding Forster, in November 1846, of his continuing ambition to 'found' a journal, Dickens had stressed that it needed to be 'something with a marked and distinct and obvious difference, in its design, from any other existing periodical.' After the 'prodigious success' of his gamble on a return to serial fiction with *Dombey & Son* and the opening numbers of *David Copperfield*, and having publicly distanced himself from the Press for nearly four years (even if continuing to write anonymously for *The Examiner*), Dickens was ready, in July 1849, to articulate what Forster called his 'floating fancy for a weekly periodical which was still and always present in his mind.'[4] This began with a promise to Bradbury & Evans to get into 'such harness one of these days, please God, in connexion with that long-deferred- but-never-sufficiently-to-be-considered-and-never-to-be approached-though-not yet-planned-or-named Periodical as shall carry us to Chambers-like profits at a hand gallop.'[5] Profits, speed, and locomotion are characteristically linked together in this heavily-articulated phrase, but as yet no name or marked design difference had been conceived. By 7 October, he had envisaged a way to bind all the possible contents together and establish a character for the journal, as he wrote excitedly to Forster:

> I want to suppose a certain SHADOW, which may go into any place, by sunlight, moonlight, starlight, firelight, candlelight, and be in all homes, and all nooks and corners, and be supposed to be cognisant of everything, and go everywhere, without the least difficulty. Which may be in the Theatre, the Palace, the House of Commons, the Prisons, the Unions, the Churches, on the Railroad, on the Sea, abroad and at home, a kind of semi-omniscient, omnipresent, intangible creature....[6]

Dickens had once offered to be Fonblanque's shadow, but here the journalistic eidolon occupies not only the editorial chair, but 'all nooks and corners' of the modern world. The idea of omniscience has been discussed recently as 'an appropriate narrative model for the age that developed statistical science, producing vast quantities of information attributable to impersonal agencies rather than to individuals,' but 'semi-omniscience' has seemed problematic.[7] For Dickens, however, to attribute omniscience to the Shadow as well as omnipresence would trespass too nearly on his broadly Unitarian concept of God: an assumption of Authority beyond what even he expected of popular journalism. Nevertheless, such supernatural qualities clearly invest the Shadow, as a metaphor for mass readership, with potentially less benign powers than those possessed by the Cricket on the family hearth, whose 'confidential position' with readers had been the unique design feature of Dickens's earlier projection. With its unimpeded circulation and penetration of public and private spaces in search of copy, the Shadow threatens to undermine any such separation of spheres, and spare no-one. Elsewhere in his writing Dickens's complex inter-association of light and shade indicates that he does not automatically equate shadow with approaching doom,[8] but it is hard not to read his expression of its 'unthought-of Power' of surveillance as an uncomfortable foreshadowing of an Orwellian future:

> I want [The Shadow] to issue warnings from time to time, that he is going to fall on such and such a subject; or to expose such and such a piece of humbug; or that he may be expected shortly in such and such a place. ... I want him to loom as a fanciful thing all over London; and to get up a general notion of "What will the Shadow say about this, I wonder? What will the Shadow say about that?" ... I think the importance of the idea is, that once stated on paper, there is no difficulty in keeping it up. That it presents an odd insubstantial, whimsical, new thing, a sort of previously unthought-of Power going about. ... [T]he Thing at everybody's elbow and in everybody's footsteps. At the window, by the fire, in the street, in the house, from infancy to old age, everyone's inseparable companion.... Now do you make anything out of this?

'... I could not make anything out of it,' Forster later commented in the *Life*, as though replying to Dickens's anxious question: 'anything out of it that had a quite feasible look.' Nevertheless, he continued, 'hardly anything more characteristic survives him,' in all the 'range and scope of his own exhaustless land of invention and marvel.'[9] The plan and its fate clarify the important truth that in Dickensian journalism, 'fancy' is as much a medium of audience approach or a communicative strategy, as a body of fixed principles or an intellectual process.

On Forster's advice, the foregrounding of the 'Shadow' in the developing design of the new periodical was subsequently avoided, and, although it remained a working title for a few weeks, Dickens was left with a more mundane but widely marketable set of components for a new periodical: 'a weekly journal, price ... two-pence, matter in part original, part selected,' with the additional provision of 'a little good poetry' whenever possible.[10] Replacing its animistic concentration of satirical possibilities and journalistic curiosity into a single figure, impersonal statements about social mission and social purpose begin to be privileged in most descriptions of the new journal, for which bills and press advertisements started to appear around Christmas 1849.[11] By January 1850, a business plan and contracts were drawn up. Although Dickens's annual salary of £500 would not be princely, he was to own one half of the business and receive a share of profits in proportion, as well as payment for his own articles. Bradbury & Evans, responsible for the commercial department of a kind of publishing which Dickens knew this time they could manage well, agreed to a mere quarter share. Forster and an Assistant Editor – still to be appointed – were to own one eighth each. The team were able to begin writing personally to solicit contributions from prominent writers, both male and female, who had shown a social conscience and an interest in writing for a broad readership. One of the first letters went to Mrs Gaskell: 'I should set a value on your help, which your modesty can hardly imagine,' Dickens wrote suggestively. 'Every paper will be published without any signature,' he continued, trying to put the vexed question of anonymity in a positive light, 'and all will seem to express the general mind and purpose of the Journal, which is, the raising up of those that are down, and the general improvement of our social condition.'[12]

With the launch date now announced for Saturday 30 March, a lavish advertising campaign underway in major towns in Britain and Ireland, an 'exceedingly pretty' bow-windowed office-cum-apartment being fitted up to Dickens's specifications at 16 Wellington Street North, Covent-Garden,[13] a name for the new journal and an Assistant Editor were now urgently needed. Forster claims credit for suggesting the name of William Henry Wills, the staff writer for *Punch* who had been Dickens's assistant on the *Daily News* in 1846, and with whom Dickens had established an excellent working relationship. He was promptly engaged at an annual salary of £416. The choosing of the title was a more pressing challenge that occupied Dickens for several weeks. In an age of anonymous authorship, it was standard practice for any popular writer whose name had achieved marketable value to contemplate an eponymous periodical (*Leigh Hunt's London Journal, Hood's Own, Ainsworth's Magazine, Eliza Cook's Journal*, and so on) so the 'egocentricity' of toying with the title and by-line '*CHARLES DICKENS. A Weekly Journal ..., CONDUCTED BY HIMSELF* is more apparent than real.[14] But Dickens wanted both a title and a related motto. Of the nearly thirty prototypes considered, some (*The Lever, The Forge, The*

Crucible, The Anvil of Time) stressed the naked power he hoped to wield with the journal, but a similar number stressed the word 'Home' or 'Household' (*The Household Voice, Household Guest, Household Face, Home-Music*), suggesting the hearth-loving cricket but going one better than *The Spectator* in terms of social inclusiveness, by embracing domestic servants as well as the bourgeois female readership that Addison and Steele had courted in their 4th number.[15] The chosen vehicle was finally revealed 'as the profoundest secret and most mighty mystery' in a letter to Miss Coutts of 4 February: '"*Household Words*" *conducted by Charles Dickens*' with this quotation adapted from Shakespeare's *Henry V*, "Familiar in their mouths as Household Words." ' That Dickens's name did actually feature in the 'full' title of the periodical would later prove significant.

The motto, which was to appear on the front page of every issue throughout the journal's lifetime, invokes Henry's famous speech before the battle of Agincourt, as he rouses his dispirited and hugely outnumbered troops to great deeds. It supplies a conflicting, masculine frame of reference to the domestic and feminine overtones of the title, in which death-defying valour and ambition for fame and social advancement are upper-most. Just as the groundlings of Shakespeare's time were to be roused by the speech's anti-hierarchical concept of social betterment through military service, so Dickens might expect his readers to be inspired by its radical vision of social upward-mobility and self-improvement. And for him and his small band of fellow writers seeking personal prosperity and public reforms through their works, this indeed was 'the raising up of those that are down and the general improvement of our social condition.' The uncomfortable marriage of imagery had been present in *The Battle of Life*, the Christmas Book of 1846, with its Christian themes of domestic renunci-ation and forgiveness curiously overlaid on the palimpsest of an Anglo-French battlefield 'with the corn and grass growing over the slain.' It is as though Dickens were celebrating and thus exposing two conflicting para-digms for man's duty in society: on the one hand, studiously turning from the outside world and seeking fulfilment through idealized family pleasures, and on the other, taking on the world competitively, battling onwards and upwards in his chosen profession. One might even suggest that the clash prophetically 'expose[d] the limitations of the domestic ideal.'[16] Dickens was to be so intimately involved with *Household Words* for the next ten years that the periodical, however anonymous, apparently impersonal, and detached, still shows the multiple fault lines and stress points in its Conductor's outlook.

II

On the appointed day *Household Words* was finally ready to come before an expectant public and form what *The Leader* called 'the gossip of every reunion.'[17] Judging by modern design standards, it is amazing that something so typographically and visually drab, could ever have provoked a stir. Apart from tables, only one full-page illustration was ever included.[18] Its two columns of tiny Roman type, smaller than today's 9-point, boxed and ruled with a central division and a horizontal ruler below the running head, exactly followed the layout established nearly twenty years before by *Chambers's Edinburgh Journal*, the only difference being that *Household Words* offered 24 slightly smaller pages for 2d., rather than 16 pages for 1½d. This despite the fact that in other areas of house style, Dickens felt that adopting a practice which *Chambers's* favoured would be 'decidedly objectionable on that account. There is nothing I am more desirous to avoid than imitation.' In April 1844, he had dismissed this successful competitor as 'that somewhat cast-iron and utilitarian publication (as congenial to me, generally, as the brown paper packages in which Ironmongers keep nails).'[19] At the time, however, its Assistant Editor was none other than W. H. Wills, who held the job for three years, was married to the Chambers's sister, Janet, and who wrote frequently for the magazine both then and in 1849.[20] *Chambers's* was thus more than simply 'the direct inspiration for *Household Words*,' it was the successful staple product which Dickens deliberately ensured he could match, week in week out, and use as a marker by which to gauge the superiority, in imaginative appeal and journalistic impact, of his own offering.[21] In reminding Wills in November 1853 that 'KEEP "HOUSEHOLD WORDS" IMAGINATIVE! is the solemn and continual Conductorial injunction,' Dickens was reminding him of the key brand difference between the rival periodicals, both of which his sub-editor knew intimately.

Aside from *Chambers's*, there was in the marketplace a range of more or less worthy and didactic weeklies priced at 1½d. or 1d., which offered their serial fiction on the 'spoonful of sugar' principal – of these, *Howitt's Journal* was probably the closest rival to *Household Words* in literary quality[22] – as well as a raft of London-based magazines replicating the luridly illustrated serial fiction of the 'penny dreadfuls,' in tandem with incendiary political editorial and 'red cap' republicanism by the likes of Edward Lloyd and G. W. M. Reynolds.[23] At 2d., *Household Words* was already staking a claim to the superior end of the market, seeking to rise above the 'Saturday trash' which the Select Committee on Public Libraries felt characterized the mass of the cheap weekly press. In terms of readership, this meant excluding circulations like that of *Chambers's*: 'chiefly among shopkeepers, not among those dependent upon weekly wages; not certainly among any portion of the working classes earning less than 16s. a week.'[24] But by being exclusive within the sector, Dickens of course hoped to persuade the aspiring and more discriminating working class reader to trade up, as well as to interest the more affluent consumers of literature and *belles lettres* to take *Household Words* in addition to their usual press diet. Accordingly, Dickens adapts the normally bland paternalism and anodyne imagery of the opening leader of such a journal to situate *Household Words* boldly with respect both to the 'utilitarian' and the 'degrading' classes of rival magazine:

> Some tillers of the field into which we now come, have been before us, and some are here whose high usefulness we readily acknowledge, and whose company it is an honour to join. But, there are others here – Bastards of the Mountain, draggled fringe on the Red Cap, Panders to the basest passions of the lowest natures – whose existence is a national reproach. And these, we should consider it our highest service to displace.[25]

An opening sale reported at 100 000, settling down to an estimated average weekly circulation of about 38 000 (various contemporaries placed it at nearer 60 000)[26] justified Dickens's confident prediction on 12 April that the magazine would 'become a *good* property.' In addition to the Editor's salary, after one year of trading he received a personal profit share of over £850 pounds, rising to a high of more than £1100 in the third year, and for the remainder of his life, the profits from his journals would 'cushion the sharp fluctuations in his income' from serial fiction. Just as importantly, however, Dickens rejoiced that *Household Words* was 'playing havoc with the villainous literature.' As the latter's leading promoter, Reynolds was further attacked in the *Household Narrative* (see below) as a 'person notorious for his attempts to degrade the working men of England by circulating among them books of a debasing tendency,' provoking a reply in *Reynolds's Newspaper* addressed to 'that lickspittle hanger-on to the skirts of Aristocracy's robe – 'Charles Dickens, Esq.' – originally a dinnerless penny-a-liner on the *Morning Chronicle*.'[27] Thus, from the 'red cap' perspective of the radical pro-Chartist press, could Dickens's journalistic career and class affiliation now be viewed.

The contents of the opening number were nothing if not respectable, both in provenance and literary craftsmanship. After Dickens's 'Preliminary Word,' came the first episode of 'Lizzie Leigh,' Mrs Gaskell's three-part Manchester tale of a fallen woman and her family that Dickens had buttered many parsnips to secure, then a well-researched and imaginatively presented article about mail-sorting technology by Wills and Dickens ('Valentine's Day at the Post-office'[28]), a dramatic blank verse 'parable' on religious presumption by Leigh Hunt ('Abraham and the Fire-Worshipper'), a keynote report by Dickens on standards of popular entertainment in London ('The Amusements of the People'[29]), a translation by George Hogarth of a supernatural 'Incident in the Life of Mademoiselle Clairon,' a poetic apostrophe to 'The Wayside Well' by the young Irish poet William Allingham, an article compiled by Dickens and Caroline Chisolm, encouraging working class emigration to Australia through the provision of no-interest loans ('A Bundle of Emigrants' Letters'), and, finally, a pair of makeweight items reprinted from other sources (the only occasion *Household Words* made use of 'selected' material). It was not so much the variety of what was being offered cheaply to a mass readership that marked *Household Words* out – contents lists of the magazine's many competitors reveal broadly similar coverage – but the polish of its original contributions in poetry and prose fiction, combined with first-hand documentary and field research in the sourcing of its non-fictional articles, and the imaginative colouring which Dickens tried to ensure was cast over their presentation.

The alloy of fact and fancy in the journal's make-up was something which the 'Preliminary Word' indicated in a few paragraphs of aspiring essay:

> We seek to bring into innumerable homes, from the stirring world around us, the knowledge of many social wonders, good and evil....
>
> No mere utilitarian spirit, no iron binding of the mind to grim realities, will give a harsh tone to our *Household Words*. In the bosoms of the young and old, of the well-to-do and of the poor, we would tenderly cherish that light of Fancy which is inherent in the human breast ... . To show all, that in all familiar things, ... there is Romance enough if we will find it out: – to teach the hardest workers at this whirling wheel of toil, that their lot is not necessarily a moody and brutal fact, excluded from the sympathies and graces of imagination, to bring the greater and the lesser in degree, together upon that wide field, and mutually dispose them to a better acquaintance and a kinder understanding – is one main object of our *Household Words*.[30]

The essential ideas which animated previous attempts to sketch out plans for a periodical, which surfaced in the muted paragraphs of his opening leader for the *Daily News*, and which are the prime motive behind his polemical novels of the 1850s, are all present here. Whereas Master Humphrey and his friends had been creatures in whom the 'spirit of romance is not yet quenched, ... content to ramble through the world in a pleasant dream, rather than ever awaken again to its harsh realities' and who 'beguile [their] days with ... fancies,' these same concepts are now realigned by a more active and vigorous journalistic voice, to stress an increased positivism and realism, which can be enhanced, but never substituted, by romantic fancy.

III

Aside from the comforting evidence of high sales, praise for *Household Words* was lavish from Dickens's well-heeled friends and acquaintances, indicating that its mission to bring the 'greater in degree' to a better understanding of the things which mattered to the poor, was certainly being fulfilled. Looking back 'after a tolerably wide experience of such matters,' Edmund Yates considered the early numbers to be 'perfect models of what a magazine intended for general reading should be,' partly for the range of writing talent, and partly for the contributions of Dickens himself, who was 'never better than in his concentrated essays.' And despite his characteristic hyperbole, W. S. Landor's declaration in the *Athenaeum* of 1854 that more 'pure pleasure' and 'useful knowledge' had been transmitted by *Household Words* than by any other publication 'since the invention of letters,' must have given particular pleasure. 'If the Public are not satisfied,' Dickens had congratulated himself and Bradbury on looking at the proof of his first issue, 'I don't know what they would have. *I* never read such a Number of anything else.'[31] Not all voices were unanimous in praise, however, and there was a residual doubt hanging over from Dickens's *Daily News* connection concerning his ability to manage the enterprise.[32] Just as Dickens's serial fiction came under fire in the monthly and quarterly reviews for perceived faults in style and intellect, so some readers of the quality press disliked the tone of the new journal. Henry Morley, a university-educated doctor and schoolteacher recorded in letters of 5 and 7 April 1850 how

> I don't care very much for *Household Words....*
> [Dickens] has not sound literary taste; his own genius, brilliant as it is, appears often in a dress which shows he has more heart and wit than critical refinement. So I much doubt that he is the right man to edit a journal of literary mark, though it would be full of warm and human sympathies, and contain first-rate writing from his own pen.

Morley's response indicates an initial misconception of Dickens's priority, which was to raise the quality of the cheap press rather than establish a journal 'of literary mark.' He had ample opportunity to correct it, when, following a change of career in June 1851, he became a researcher and staff writer on *Household Words* at Dickens's invitation, and a leader-writer for *The Examiner*, at John Forster's. In fact, Morley became the most prolific of the journal's many contributors, publishing in it over 300 more pages than Dickens did himself, including 59 leading articles and 18 leaders in collaboration with other writers, and acting 'as a sort of deputy lieutenant' to Wills. He clearly found adapting to the requirements of popular journalism difficult, writing after completion of his second article that 'the journal does not seem my element ... the readers are an undiscriminating mass to whom I'm not accustomed to imagine myself speaking,' but accepting that the 'witty satire and a laughing style' characteristic of the *Household Words* leaders 'arrest attention.'[33] At his Editor's instigation, Morley dealt with many, if not all, of the controversial issues of the 1850s, which Dickens himself also handled – factory legislation and working conditions, housing and hygiene, public health, the cholera, education, prison discipline and reform work, criminal trials, the Great Exhibition – and had a significant influence on the magazine's overall achievement.

The way in which Dickens undertook to train his principal writer in the exigencies of writing for a mass readership is thus significant, and indicative of a keen sense of correlation between grace of house style and effectiveness in the battle with the blackguard press for readers. Beginning with a mild reprimand to Morley for 'not giving sufficient consideration to some of your papers in *Household Words*,' Dickens explains how

> [t]he indispensable necessity of varying the manner of narration as much as possible, and investing it with some little grace or other, would be very evident to you if you knew as well as I do how severe the struggle is to get the publication down into the masses of readers, and to displace the prodigious heaps of nonsense, which suffocate their better sense. I know of such 'perilous stuff' at present, produced at a cost about equal to the intrinsic worth of its literature, and circulating six times the amount of *Household Words*.

Dickens talks to Morley in physician's language, but corrects the impression that the journal's readers are to be thought of as constitutionally deficient:

> My confidence in the ability of such people to receive and relish a good thing, is so far from being the least shaken by this knowledge that I only feel the more strongly that the good thing must be done at its best. ... [I]t is not enough to see a thing and go home and describe it, but ... the necessity is, for ever upon us of patiently considering *how* to describe it, so as to give it some fanciful attraction or some new air. I have kept back the gold-refining paper, because it is exactly like a hundred other papers we might shake in a drawer together; merely shewing the reader what is to be seen as the Peep-Show man does.

While generally preferring the 'graphic' to the 'theoretical' in journalistic discourse, to adopt Macvey Napier's polarization, Dickens clearly emphasises through the 'Peep-Show' simile (references to Peep Shows in his writing are surprisingly negative[34]) that he believes 'straightforward' documentary or quasi-photographic realism insufficient to maintain readership for informative journalism. The reporter's art lies in stylization and the mode of address: the reformer must needs become a mannerist.

In the event, Dickens rewrote the paper in question (based on a visit to Brown & Wingrove's Smelting Works at 30–31 Wood Street) as a collaborative leader which he called 'Discovery of a Treasure near Cheapside,' adding an introduction and conclusion which transform Morley's bald account of the company's processing of priceless raw materials, into the story of a dreamer's descent into a metropolitan Aladdin's Cave, couched in allusions to Grimm's fairytales, classical mythology, *Gulliver's Travels, Candide,* and his imaginative touchstone, *The Arabian Nights.*[35] The conversion of 'The Shadow's' raw research findings on social, industrial and cultural matters into stories embroidered by Scheherezade proves to be a key editorial process. As elsewhere in his writings, Dickens's re-fashioning of *The Arabian Nights* as a redemptive mythology for modern Britain is worthy of Blake. Even in such editorial interpolations and revisions, a recent critic has noted, Dickens 'was aiming for nothing less than an absolute engagement with the processes of the world around him: the way it was run, its goings-on, its falling into decay and final ends.'[36]

The accusation that *Household Words* was mannered was to become one of the most frequent accusations levelled at the publication by reviewers and contributors alike. The progressive Tory weekly, *The Press,* looking back on the journal's nine year history, complained of the negative influence Dickens had had on his fellow writers, that the 'mannerism which a single great genius finds it difficult to sustain ... was certain to become ere long unbearable in the hands of his professed imitators.'[37] In the same month, the *Examiner* too commented on how 'the mannerism that ... crept into *Household Words* arose very naturally, but all mannerism is a defect.'[38] For her part, Mrs Gaskell simply called the style of periodical 'Dickensy.' Even the young Percy Fitzgerald, who owed his writing career to the journal and idolized Dickens, reminisced that

> [o]ne result of his extraordinary influence was – he seemed, indeed, a sort of literary Gladstone – that all his followers and 'merry men' felt bound to copy ... all his forms and 'turns' and blemishes, ... with the result of wearying and disgusting the readers. It is difficult now to understand the tricks that were played with this strained and exaggerated sham 'Dickensese.'[39]

To an extent, however, such responses merely reflected the downside of having a strong and well-defined brand.

IV

Roughly a third of the journal's eighteen bi-yearly volumes (the form in which it commonly survives) consists of original poetry and fiction. Most leading articles, however, and another rough third of its pages, are dedicated to a form of political agitation on social issues, researched and written for the most part by Dickens and a small group of staff writers.

Some commentators have worried that the agitation is irresponsible or insufficiently involved with the 'actual debate' going forward in parliament,[40] but if Dickens's journalism of the 1850s reveals anything of his political attitudes, it is his increasingly vehement, radically democratic belief that Britain's governing institutions had stagnated and corrupted to the extent that her people needed literally, to re-form them, and re-direct their activities for the welfare of the majority. British local and national assemblies, his leading articles proclaim, were self-serving cliques which smoke-screened or ignored the most urgent issues, and exemplified how *not* to do it. *Household Words* gave Dickens the platform and the power to bypass such slow-moving traffic and work directly and independently on public opinion. 'Our Honorable Friend' and 'Our Vestry' (consecutive leaders published during the summer recess after the General Election of 1852) state the case with lighthearted comedy. A much angrier humour dominates the sequence of articles published in the wake of the Crimean War in 1855, when Dickens 'believed that the gloomy silence into which the country fell, was by far the darkest aspect in which a great people had been exhibited for very many years.' His articles break the silence with virtuoso passages of verbal irony, and 'savage and Zoological roaring.'[41]

The remaining third of *Household Words* consists of informative articles on an encyclopaedic range of subjects, though for the most part eschewing the encyclopaedic or polemical style. These covered popular science (medicine, physics, chemistry, astronomy, geology), popular entertainment, natural resources, financial affairs, agriculture, natural history, national biography, trade, inventions, life in the colonies, ancient history, fashion, domestic economy, and so forth. In its coverage of these areas, *Household Words* aims to help its readers keep pace with progress 'in this summer dawn of time,' but does so in continuous dialogue with tradition, at times reflecting the uncertain hierarchy of the 'past and present' binary so prevalent in Victorian thinking.

Dickens's shadow in the opening numbers of the journal was ubiquitous, and not just because during its first year he wrote or co-authored fifty articles of the 137 he wrote for its pages all told (not including the thirty-nine instalments of *A Child's History of England*, twenty of *Hard Times* and seventeen Christmas stories). He and Wills took painstaking care re-writing, adapting, and otherwise 'touching up' material by other contributors, working away at the proofs until, Dickens said, they looked like an 'inky fishing net.' On one article of Wills's describing a midnight visit to the Bow Street police station, he sat revising the manuscript 'nine hours without stirring,' possibly aware that the *Household Words* accounts of the work of the detective police (of which this was the first example) would pioneer a distinct new genre of modern, forensic literature.[42] Such investigations – like the visit to the 'treasury' in Cheapside, and a whole range of other research trips performed and written up by Dickens and his staff –

concentrated on both demystifying and re-mystifying, through fanciful and quasi-magical narrative, modern institutional, bureaucratic and industrial practices which affected the general reader, but which were faceless and intangible. Through stylization and metaphorical ingenuity, *Household Words* engaged modernity and modern issues in a way that offered to make them manageable by re-configuring their operation in familiar poetic or rhetorical terms.

As far as his solo contributions were concerned, Dickens supplied leaders for the journal which either distilled from recent events a single or multiple issues to comment upon, or which were designed to balance the overall feel of a given number in accordance with his interpretation of the national mood. The balancing was an aspect of editorial strategy that he took very seriously, frequently crafting papers expressly intended to act as a corrective to what he felt would be an overly dull, or overly flippant issue, without them. He thus unsentimentally explains the genesis of 'A Child's Dream of a Star,' a brief essay about the deaths of little children steeped in the pre-Victorian sentimental tradition:

> ... [H]ere's man for you! – They sent me today the proposed No. 2 in a list of articles. The amazing undersigned feels a little uncomfortable at a want of Household tenderness in it. So he puts away Copperfield, at which he has been working like a Steam Engine – writes (he thinks) exactly the kind of thing to supply the deficiency – and sends it off, by this post, to Forster! What an amazing man!

A few years later, as British and French troops fought alongside each other during the fierce initial assaults of the Crimean campaign, Dickens ordered Wills to postpone G. A. Sala's comic article on French military dandyism, as it came 'painfully upon the Battle Field accounts in the *Times*; ... I would rather say nothing about France unless I had plenty to say about its gallantry and spirit.' The next leading article to be printed on a French theme was 'Our French Watering Place,' Dickens's handsome tribute to Boulogne, the beauty of its fisherwomen and chivalry of its citizenry, who are proud to billet troops for free. In its conclusion, Dickens is careful to praise the 'long and constant fusion of the two great nations there, [which] has taught each to like the other, and to learn from the other.'[43] He viewed his leader-writing in *Household Words* in context of the journal's overall response, and that of the press in general, to the national scene.

The other contributors to *Household Words* responded ambivalently to Dickens's decision to maintain the practice of anonymous publication, which was coming to be viewed as an important corollary of the contemporary debate over press freedom and responsibility. Other journals of similar pretensions, such as *Howitt's Magazine* and *Douglas Jerrold's*

Shilling Magazine (a monthly), already published authors' names or initials. Writing in the *Daily News*, Dickens himself had, in the newspaper's own words, 'authenticated' all his major contributions 'with the distinguished writer's name,' as part of his efforts to elevate the character of the press. Why then prevent other writers from doing the same in *Household Words*? Douglas Jerrold, declining his friend's invitation to contribute, quipped that, with Dickens's name on every page, the journal would in fact be 'mononymous.' Others who did become contributors agreed with G. A. Sala and John Hollingshead's recollections that Dickens was 'always credited' with the 'good things' in his magazine as a result of the practice, which retarded the career development of promising young writers, particularly if they agreed to write articles jointly with Dickens. Even a distant onlooker such as Elizabeth Barrett Browning could see that such collaboration 'must be highly unsatisfactory' to the younger author, 'as Dickens's name would swallow up every sort of minor reputation in the shadow of its path.' From the publication of 'Lizzie Leigh' onwards, there is evidence of such misattribution, but Dickens believed the process could work in two directions. On hearing the grounds of Wilkie Collins's objection to the offer of a year's engagement to write for *Household Words* in 1856, he tartly observed to Wills that 'such a confusion of authorship ... would be a far greater service than dis-service to him. This I clearly see.'[44]

Yet anonymity at last gave Dickens the chance to run a periodical without being '*forced* (as in the *Clock*) to put myself into it, in my old shape,' without having 'to write it *all*.' In his initial approach to Mrs Gaskell, Dickens had stressed a less selfish motive. Anonymity would allow all the contents to 'seem to express the general mind and purpose of the journal,' in the same way that his original idea of the journal as the 'Shadow' would have fused together and given cumulative power to the work of different writers, as well as himself, all sharing the disguise afforded by the figure. Furthermore, in his initial approaches to other contributors, Dickens made clear his intention 'to give established writers the power of reclaiming their papers' and republishing them 'after a certain time,' without the proprietors laying claim to any share in the copyright. This was an important concession, extended in the event to unknown as well as established writers, and of the thirty-four who can be identified as 'corps' writers for the journal, twenty-six took advantage of the launch pad thus provided. The house policy on anonymity was later changed, however, when Dickens felt that a writer's famous name in conjunction with a long serial work would help maintain circulation. He allowed Mrs Gaskell's *North and South* to be identified as 'by the author of *Mary Barton*' and Collins's *The Dead Secret* to be advertised in the journal under its author's name – privileges hitherto reserved for his own serial contributions, *A Child's History of England*, and *Hard Times*.

V

The 'corps' *Household Words* contributors were a varied group who between them wrote some 78 per cent of the journal over its nine-year life. Apart from Wills, only three others (Morley, Collins and R. H. Horne) held official engagements on the staff at any stage. Several (Gaskell, the Howitts, Charles Knight, Eliza Lynn, Harriet Martineau, Harriet Parr, James White) were famous authors of the day, sufficiently dedicated to the causes *Household Words* espoused to lend their voices. Some were versatile journalists who had worked under Dickens on the *Daily News* (Dudley Costello, Frederick Knight Hunt, Sidney Blanchard, Blanchard Jerrold) or had relevant professional experience on which they could draw (Costello in the army, Hunt and Morley as doctors, James Hannay in the Navy). Some were recruited for their expertise in specific areas that Dickens wished to cover (Samuel Sidney on emigration, John Capper and John Lang on Sri Lankan and Indian life, the *Times* Naples correspondent, H. G. Wreford, on Italian affairs, E. Grenville Murray on continental manners, Walter Thornbury for sketches of Southern Spain), or targeted the journal with a specialist area in mind (Hollingshead, on political economy and commercial matters). Others submitted verse of some distinction (Adelaide Procter, George Meredith, William Allingham), though many of the poems in the journal bear out Mary Russell Mitford's comment that the Dickens 'did not know good verse from bad.' Others submitted unsolicited papers of the bright and breezy kind which Dickens liked, or showed aptitude for general work following recommendations from friends, and joined the 'band' of 'Dickens's Young Men,' as they became known, for whom their 'Master' devised journalistic topics and tasks (Sala, William Moy Thomas, Percy Fitzgerald).

In sending Sala to St Petersburg in search of copy after the Russian war, Dickens in fact secured something of a scoop in magazine journalism. Foreign correspondents as factual reporters had long been a feature of the daily press, but Dickens's varied deployment in his magazines of 'Specials' as writers of sketches of travel, life and manners in Russia, Turkey, Paris, Rome, Naples, and Cologne, was a distinct innovation. Sala's 'Journey Due North' was serialized in twenty-two instalments in *Household Words*, and despite its mildly deviant obsessions with 'bugs, boots and beatings,' created a stir amongst readers, and a name for its author.[45]

Of the remaining, occasional contributors – over 350 of them – the majority wrote for the journal only once, with the rest publishing between two and twenty items. Some of these were friends of Dickens and his circle, some (like Leigh Hunt, Elizabeth Barrett Browning, W. H. Russell, Edward Bulwer Lytton) were celebrated for their work outside the journal, but most were, and remained, unknown. The hopeful attempts of such 'Voluntary Correspondents' to appeal to the Editor, sending him their unpublishable work or that of 'gifted friends,' or leaving manuscripts at the office 'rolled up in paper like a whitey-brown bolster,' are mercilessly caricatured in Dickens's share of a joint article with Morley called 'H. W.' Dickens frequently satirized in print what occupied elsewhere his serious attentions. Morley noted in November 1851 how 'Dickens reads every letter sent to him, and not a note to the office is pooh-poohed; every suggestion that may lead to good, however overlaid with the ridiculous, is earnestly accepted and attended to.' There is probably some truth in the statistic that in 'the last year, we read 900 manuscripts, of which eleven were available for this journal, after being entirely re-written.'[46]

'H. W.' dealt both with the editorial process of selection and the technical process of printing, but was silent about one major reason why so many aspiring authors sent their work. *Household Words* paid amply and (no small virtue in a Victorian magazine) promptly: a guinea for a 2-column page of prose, double or more for poetry, and by arrangement for serial fiction. Dickens and Wills played good cop, bad cop in negotiations with contributors over payment, it being Wills's initial target to keep the cost of contributions down to £16 per issue.[47] For the most part contributors were more than satisfied. Mrs Gaskell stared in disbelief at the £20 she received for 'Lizzie Leigh' and wondered if she were 'swindling them.' Sala and Morley both worried that they earned their *Household Words* wages too easily.[48]

VI

Evidence of Dickens's abiding commitment to his periodicals is everywhere to be found in his correspondence with his sub-editor. Nearly 450 surviving letters written between 1850 and his death in 1870 suggest that Dickens wrote more frequently to Wills than to any other correspondent in this period, and every aspect of *Household Words* and *All the Year Round* is discussed in them. There is little doubt that he was, even if not consistently so, an extremely hands-on editor, and extremely exacting. Wills's share in the editorial process should not be underestimated, however. From the date of his engagement, he took an active part in the pre-publication planning for *Household Words*, submitting a list of possible topics for articles, many of which were made use of, and suggesting ways of treatment. He was efficient, well-read, with a precise if pedantic writing style, and combined a liking for 'correcting manuscript' with a 'love of detail, which he liked to clothe in picturesque shape,' making him 'an admirable writer as well as editor of papers, in Dickens's weeklies.'[49]

Although the articles of agreement for the periodicals always specified him as sub-editor, Wills was commonly referred to by contemporaries as 'editor,' one of 'the editors,' 'acting editor,' 'working editor,' 'co-editor' and so forth.[50] Dickens's letters to him are businesslike and friendly, but could be peremptory, autocratic, and dismissive of the decisions of a man who, Dickens exaggerated to friends, had 'not the ghost of an idea in the imaginative way' and 'no genius': being 'in literary matters, sufficiently commonplace to represent a very large proportion of ... readers.'[51] A few months after the launch, Dickens ordered him 'in future [not to] touch my articles without first consulting me' and followed up with this comment on Wills's suggestion for the title of a joint article: 'I don't think there could be a worse one within the range of human understanding.' Wills's reply, by return of post, stoutly defended his action ('a matter of mechanical convenience,' as well as good journalistic practice) and his title, modestly claiming for it 'a *locus* within that pale....' On this, and other occasions, Wills's alterations were allowed to stand.[52]

The five published letters from Wills to Dickens on business matters indicate a similar combination of professional firmness, and humorous tact. The most detailed of these concerns one of Dickens's frequent outbursts about the heaviness and lack of 'elegance of fancy' in *Household Words*. Reading through back numbers in mid-October 1851, Dickens had complained how '[t]hey lapse too much into a dreary, arithmetical ... dustyness that is powerfully depressing.' Considering he had been absent from London for nearly five months, calling at the Wellington Street Office only intermittently during a long residence at Broadstairs, a reason for the shortcoming might have suggested itself. Wills's reply is a clear, if flattering, appeal for more editorial involvement:

> Elegance of fancy cannot be thrown broadcast over such an acreage of letter-press; although ... it can be *sprinkled* over its pages. If you could regularly see and go over each sheet before it is put to press there would be a very thick sprinkling of the excellence in which you say *Household Words* is deficient.... I was delighted with your proposal of coming from Broadstairs every Wednesday, to give a finishing touch.... I should go on with more confidence because with less uncertainty. ... [A]lthough I have good reason to suppose from the latitude of confidence you give me, that my notions square with your own generally, yet I cannot ... be *always* right; and it would lift a great weight of responsibility from me if everything which passes into the columns of *Household Words* had the systematic benefit of another judgment before publication.[53]

The reply also makes clear that Wills enjoyed a certain amount of autonomy, that articles had gone to press which Dickens had not seen in proof, and that the orthodox view of Dickens's editorial omnipresence – his putting 'himself, his thoughts, feelings, and inspirations, into each column,' as Percy Fitzgerald once claimed – is suspect.

Dickens's complaints and pleas concerning the dullness or poor making-up of recent issues are evidence of his perfectionism but also therefore of a kind of negligence inevitable in an Editor who travelled as far and as frequently from his desk as Dickens. Writing from Boulogne in late September 1854, for example, during a severe outbreak of Asiatic cholera that had killed thousands of Londoners, he declared himself 'shocked and ashamed' to see that the next two numbers of the journal had nothing to say about it, and enclosed a swingeing address 'To Working Men' on the subject of sanitation reform, which Wills managed to insert as the leader for 7 October.[54] On the one hand, it is a striking example of energetic intervention and desire for balance; on the other, of lack of editorial foresight. The epidemic had been raging since the summer. In this, as in other areas of its response to public events, *Household Words* was not pre-emotive, and followed in the wake of the daily press.

Wills's request for more supervision meant that from 1852 a mid-week conference was instituted,[55] when Dickens was within reach of the office, and when he was abroad, this was replaced by a weekly postal exchange of one or more packets of proofs, manuscripts, and number plans, of which Wills usually produced the initial draft. Even then, material was published which did not satisfy Dickens's sometimes conflicting demands for lightness, brightness, accuracy and topicality. Nor did Wills easily learn to separate Dickens's bluster about the 'awfulness' of the magazine from criticism of his own work for it. 'The last published No. ... is – not to mince the matter – frightfully bad,' the latter wrote from Paris in April 1856, 'No idea in it, no purpose, no appropriateness to or about anything, a mere hash-up of the most indifferent magazine papers at a chance medley.' Wills's hurt reply produced no apology: 'you take it too personally.... I have a way ... of expressing myself in a strong manner. I beg Sub to brighten up.'[56] But the central problem remained, that for all Wills's conscientiousness and efficiency, Dickens's energy and creativity, it was difficult for an Absentee Editor to keep his lands under constant watch.

The 'young men' apprenticed in the Dickens school of journalism, and staff writers such as Collins, Horne and Morley were relatively easy to monitor. Dickens's rejection and subsequent revision of the latter's draft paper 'A Doctor of Morals' might seem the last word on the subject of editorial control –

> 'A Doctor of Morals' *impossible of insertion as it stands* ... with all the difficult parts of the question blinked, and many statements utterly at variance with what I am known to have written.... The article ... must have these points [concerning strict prison discipline] in it; otherwise I am not only compromising opinions I am known to hold, but the journal itself is playing fast and loose, in a ridiculous way.[57]

Yet it is clear from the pages of the journal, and from the incessant and often very funny critiques Dickens makes of contributions, that in spite of much intervention, Dickens often failed to make his 'corps' writers write either what or how he desired. 'The problem with the notion that Dickens exercised strict control over his journals,' one recent study has argued, 'and [with] his biographers' focus on "fancy" is that they sometimes seem almost unaware of the need for it and the gap between what he wanted and what actually happened.'[58] It was not just that established writers liked to go their own way: Leigh Hunt writing in the manner of Skimpole ('I couldn't write it more like him'), Eliza Lynn getting 'so near the sexual side of things as to be a little dangerous' in a family journal, Mrs Gaskell's liking for stories in which protagonists die or fall over, or both ('I wish to Heaven, her people would keep a little firmer on their legs!').[59] They sometimes held opposing views on controversial issues, and here the anonymity of articles in the journal had serious implications.

VII

A significant case is that of Harriet Martineau, and investigation of the differences leading to her 'secession' from the regular writing team naturally involves some broader consideration of the policies of the journals Dickens edited, their consistency, and their approximation or otherwise to the positions Dickens seems to espouse in other media or genres.[60] *Household Words* and *All the Year Round* were distinctly unusual among the cheap high-circulation family weeklies in presuming to shape public opinion on political matters at all. With a staff tiny in comparison with that he had hired for the *Daily News*, Dickens tackled an ambitious range of issues, many of them controversial and requiring more time and resources to master fully than his establishment could spare. This is the commonest of journalistic dilemmas, however, and superficial and flippant as some of its political articles may seem,[61] the 'eye-witness' and interview-based reporting techniques that *Household Words* pioneered allowed it to straddle very successfully the boundaries between news commentary and recreative literature. On that shifting faultline Dickens's journalism had always built its daring superstructures, with corresponding perils for the critic.

When first invited to contribute to *Household Words*, Martineau was in her late forties and something of an anomaly in Victorian letters: a woman journalist from the provinces who wrote on political economy, travel, and spiritual matters, as well as didactic short stories and novels, celebrated for nearly two decades as 'a national instructress.' In 1838, Dickens's Radical 'Political Young Gentleman' had given 'all the young ladies to understand that Miss Martineau is the greatest woman that ever lived.'[62] Her comforting *Illustrations of Political Economy* in the 1830s had made her a household name amongst the manufacturing classes, and it was perhaps her popularity amongst this sector of his target audience more than her ultra-Benthamite politics that Dickens recalled, in inviting her to become a contributor. Nevertheless, in 1850 she and Dickens were sufficiently united by their American experiences, their opposition to American slavery, and above all by a Liberal faith in progress, to make her a welcome collaborator. Her series of twenty articles of 1851–52, explaining modern manufacturing processes from around Britain, with copious references to their 'magic,' 'artistry,' 'mystery' and 'ingenuity,' seem perfect illustrations of Dickens's stated aims in 'A Preliminary Word.' Martineau was deaf, however, and had no sense of smell; thus, it has been suggested, 'much unpleasantness may have escaped her notice' on her factory visits. She was also the daughter of a ruined factory owner, and her articles demonstrate 'some of the assumptions of the class and world of Bounderby and Gradgrind' which 'strikingly ... conflict with Dickens's editorial views.'[63] Her unrelenting positivism about the social benefits of new technology and working patterns (she was adapting Comte's *Cours de Philosophie Positive* for its first English publication while she wrote her *Household Words* papers) seems first to have struck Dickens in October 1854, when he noted to Wills how she seemed 'grimly bent upon the enlightenment of mankind' – an agent now of the 'iron binding of the mind to grim realities' which he had promised *Household Words* would *not* espouse.[64] It is strange that he had not anticipated such a divergence.

But Dickens himself had become much less of a positivist since 1850, and, during the recent Tory and re-shuffled coalition administrations, much more convinced of the evils of *laissez faire* political economy, and the self-interested, toadying and tuft-hunting incompetence of Britain's middle and governing classes. He had altered his view that all strikes were necessarily wrong and ill-conducted, after a research trip to Preston in January, and had just finished serializing *Hard Times* in the journal, with its angry assault on prevailing industrial conditions and attitudes. In particular, Morley and he were in the process of championing in *Household Words* the need for better enforcement of those sections of the 1844 Factory Act which required owners to fence their machinery safely, and it was over these articles[65] that Martineau and the journal came publicly to blows.

Household Words highlighted cases of death and mutilation which had resulted from the factory owners' non-compliance. In her libellous pamphlet on *The Factory Controversy* (1855) Martineau predictably took the Benthamite/Bounderby line that any state intervention in factory regulation was 'meddling' interference with natural laws, and that 'if the charge [of fencing] is thrown upon the employers of industry, they will retire from occupations intolerably burdensome.' Less predictably, she rounded on Dickens, whom she accused at great length, and by name, of the kind of

> unscrupulous statement, insolence, arrogance and cant, to which the door is opened when meddling legislation is accorded to the pseudo-philanthropy which is one of the disgraces of our times.[66]

The journal had also been criticized for publishing 'trash' by the recently-formed National Association of Factory Occupiers, a group of owners combining expressly to pay the cost of fines imposed on any of their number for not fencing their machinery according to the law. It was the selfsame Association which published Martineau's pamphlet, paying her 100 guineas for it. Dickens and Morley eventually replied with a temperate but impeccably-researched refutation, entitled 'Our Wicked Mis-statements,' which clarifies the impact which their 'wide publication of the illegal position of the recusant mill-owners' had had, and reveals quite how wide a gulf separated Martineau from Morley and Dickens in their attitudes to the industrial scene. To Dickens she was now, 'what I always knew her to be ... a Humbug.'[67] Yet all had written on factory matters in *Household Words* under the same anonymous editorial 'We.'

Such fissures do not necessarily result in the journals 'playing fast and loose, in a ridiculous way' – but they do further underline the danger of assuming that it is possible to establish Dickens's views on a given question from those announced anonymously in his journals. While there is no doubt that the informed reader can detect many of Dickens's strongest convictions, principles and prejudices recurring like patterns through the pages of *Household Words*, shared, echoed by, or interpolated into the work of colleagues, it is equally clear that the following editorial announcement printed in *All the Year Round* is unreliable: 'THE STATEMENTS AND OPINIONS OF THIS JOURNAL GENERALLY, ARE, OF COURSE, TO BE RECEIVED AS THE STATEMENTS AND OPINIONS OF ITS CONDUCTOR.'[68] It is perhaps truer of Dickens than of other Victorian magazine editors, and certainly indicates the level of editorial consistency he aimed for, but, like 'elegance of fancy,' editorial consistency was something that could at most be 'thickly sprinkled' rather than broadcast.

VIII

Convictions, principles, and prejudices can look deceptively similar in print. Harriet Martineau seems wrong and Dickens right over their factory controversy, but in her *Autobiography*, published shortly before the contretemps, she mentions two other grounds for questioning the editorial policies of *Household Words* which will seem much sounder to modern readers: its anti-Catholicism, and its anti-feminism.[69] Dickens's opposition to Catholicism had been strengthened since writing *Pictures from Italy* by residence in Switzerland in 1846, where he had attributed differences in prosperity, progress, and public health in the adjacent cantons of Vaud and the Valais, to the negative effects of the Catholic Church and 'priestcraft' in the latter. He had observed similar differences constantly, he told Forster, 'since I first came abroad,' and had misgivings 'that the religion of Ireland lies as deep at the root of all its sorrows, even as English misgovernment and Tory villainy.'[70] Dickens's hostility to Catholicism had more to do with what he perceived as its socio-political and aesthetic accompaniments than with serious theological disagreement, and his grounds of complaint against the Oxford Movement and Puseyism were more to do with the distraction their disputes caused from earnest missionary and apostolic work among the poor than the nature of disputed points of doctrine and observance. His own crudely satirical or grandly rhetorical remarks in *Household Words* leaders on papal aggression and the damaging irrelevance of theological controversies make these points clear in a suitably stylized and forceful manner.[71]

So much could be seen as conviction, but Martineau relates how a tale submitted to the journal, based on the life story of an admirable Jesuit missionary, was rejected by Dickens and Wills on the clearly-repeated grounds that 'they would never publish any thing, fact or fiction, which gave a favourable view of any one under the influence of the Catholic faith.' Furthermore, Martineau adds, *Household Words* was not just an 'anti-Catholic publication' but 'anti-Catholic on the sly,' because in it Dickens happily published fictions in which individual Catholics were seen to be corrupt and wicked. These included Wilkie Collins's 'The Yellow Mask,' and Mrs Craik's 'A Ghost Story' but Martineau might equally have cited Dickens's horrified treatment, in instalments of the all-too puerile *Child's History of England*, of the nation's relapse into Popery during the reigns of Mary and James II.[72] An Irish journalist wrote to Dickens to complain that the periodical's attitude was preventing Roman Catholic readers from enjoying or profiting from it, but did not receive the kind of answer 'which might have been looked for from one of so large sympathies.' Indeed, the claim of a reviewer of *Little Dorrit* a few years later, that Dickens most deserved comparison with Shakespeare for his 'universal sympathy' and the way he 'soars above all considerations of sect, above all narrow isolations of creed,' is over-stretched as a description of the editor and leader-writer of *Household Words*. Content to support Unitarian positions and those of the Broad Church movement within Anglicanism, Dickens the journalist was never above attacks on the two extremes of the Low to High Church spectrum, and on the social, political, and cultural forms of Catholicism.[73]

Martineau likewise took exception to Dickens's articles in *Household Words* on 'Woman's position,' articles in which, she claimed,

> he ignored the fact that nineteen-twentieths of the women of England earn their bread, and in which he prescribes the function of Women, viz., to dress well and look pretty, as an adornment to the homes of men.[74]

The claim vigorously oversimplifies the response of *Household Words* to the Woman Question, but is certainly recognizable as a description of the essentialist and patriarchal assumptions Dickens himself made about the 'natural' roles of men and women. The anti-feminism of his only sustained engagement with the subject, a leader called 'Sucking Pigs' (8 November 1851) is notable. Although claiming not to wish to 'enter upon the great question of the Rights of Women,' the narrator continues, by a deft *occupatio*, with the 'personal' admission that the thought of his wife 'Julia' entering public life would disturb him, and prompt the following lecture:

> 'Apple of our eye, we freely admit your inalienable right to step out of your domestic path into any phase of public appearance that pleases you best, but we doubt the wisdom of the sally. Should we love our Julia ... better, if she were a Member of Parliament, a Parochial Guardian, a High Sheriff, a Grand Juror, or a woman distinguished for her able conduct in the chair? Do we not on the contrary, rather seek in the society of our Julia a haven of refuge from [such men]? Is not the home-voice of our Julia as the song of a bird, after considerable bow-wowing out of doors?'

Despite pouring scorn elsewhere in his journalism on the performance and windy rhetoric of such (exclusively male) public officers, Dickens's narrator is clearly threatened by the notion that such jobs might conceivably be as well or better done, by women. The same prejudice against women usurping male roles is revealed even in obscure passages of the *Child's History of England*, where the historian exclaims how much happier Joan of Arc's life would have been if she had ignored the call to arms, 'and had gone home ... and had been a good man's wife, and had heard no stranger voices than the voices of little children!'[75]

The remainder of Dickens's detailed retelling of the peasant girl's story emphasized her betrayal and cruel treatment at the hands of an array of national authorities and institutions – the crown, clergy, and courts – and he concludes his account by praising her statue in Rouen, referring ironically *en passant* to 'some statues of modern times ... which commemorate less constancy, less earnestness, smaller claims upon the world's attention, and much greater imposters.' Constancy and earnestness are key Dickensian virtues, which, even as he revolves the historical subject, Dickens weighs against imposture and the persecution of women in the present. For concomitant with the satirical treatment of Bloomerism, and the exaltation of the female 'Angel in the House' and 'Angel of Death' ideals, ran a protective strain of discourse in Dickens's journals, which gave space to the question of the Law's failure to protect married women, and its insensitive treatment of them.[76] *Household Words* strongly supported the Matrimonial Causes and the Married Women's Property Bills in the late 50s and 60s.[77] Dickens had not forgotten the humiliating treatment in court of Lady Caroline Norton, nor of the bullied female witnesses at Courvoisier's trial. When his philanthropic friend and guide Miss Coutts found herself successively dragged through the courts by a blackmailing imposter, all his manly indignation and scorn was poured into a leader ironically singling out this flagrant case of 'oppression and ill-treatment of Women' as one of the 'Things that Cannot Be Done' under splendid English Law. Equally tellingly, the 'sad epic' of Caroline Norton's marriage and the Law's denial of her right to remarry, to her own earnings or to custody of her children, was dramatically retold in *Household Words* while new legislation was being framed from the findings of the Royal Commission on Divorce. In case the need for reform to the law escaped readers' attention, the roles were reversed in the very same number of the journal, which opened with the tenth chapter of *Hard Times*, in which Stephen Blackpool's 'disabled, drunken' and shamefully ruined wife – from whom English law cannot grant him an affordable divorce – makes her unwelcome return.[78]

Household Words did not merely deal with the extremes of the Woman Question. Many of its papers discussed ordinary women's working lives: in manufacturing, crafts and the arts, as seamstresses, governesses, charity workers, shop assistants, teachers, actresses, and (albeit obliquely) prostitutes.[79] Martineau's complaint that in his articles Dickens 'ignored the fact that nineteen-twentieths of the women of England earn their bread' is inaccurate of the journal as a whole, and faintly obtuse, for she records that its immediate provocation was a proposal from Wills that she contribute a series of papers 'on the Employments of Women.' It also seems likely that the article which most aroused her indignation at Dickens's sexism in *Household Words* was the astonishingly reactionary 'Rights and Wrongs of Women' – not by Dickens at all, but another professional female journalist, Eliza Lynn. Yet undeniably, the domestic ideal which, at first sight, *Household Words* seems to encourage, is continually undercut by the 'battle of life' and struggle between the sexes, inscribed both in the journal's motto and in many articles in its pages.

IX

Two other periodical publications developed as spin-offs from *Household Words*. These were the *Household Narrative of Current Events*, a twopenny monthly retrospect of national, international news, and other information, published from April 1850 to December 1855 (including numbers for January–March 1850), and the short-lived *Household Almanac*, a fourpenny calendar and factual guide to annual, seasonal domestic and national affairs, devised and first compiled by Henry Morley for the year 1856, but discontinued in 1857.

Both publications aimed to extend the scope of the main journal in new directions, making the suite of publications a complete, cheap and widely available compendium to the life of the times. An advertisement for the *Narrative* called it 'a complete and carefully-digested ANNUAL REGISTER,' indicating Dickens's hope that in its bound volume form it would emulate Burke and Dodsley's famous *Annual Register ... [of] History, Politicks, and Literature,* which he himself found so useful as a reference work for his journalism and historical fiction.[80] Dickens's front-page announcement of the new venture reminded readers of 'the intimate connexion between the facts and realities of the time, and the means by which we aim, in *Household Words,* to soften what is hard in them, to exalt what is held in little consideration, and to show the latent hope there is in what may seem unpromising.' The *Narrative* would thereby be another means 'to bear the world's rough cast events to the anvil of courageous duty, and there beat them into shape.' If the Victorian reporter is often figured as Asmodeus, the strange compound metaphor here casts the Victorian editor as Vulcan.[81]

The *Narrative*'s nine subdivisional headings – 'Parliament and Politics,' 'Law and Crime,' 'Accident and Disaster,' 'Social, Sanitary and Municipal Progress,' 'Obituaries, Colonies and Dependencies,' 'Foreign Events,' 'Commercial Record,' 'Stocks and Shares,' and 'Emigration Figures' – clearly signalled a continuation of the special interest shown by *Household Words* in all these topics, presented in a more regimented, heavily factual and statistical format. To the extent that it provided the kind of corroborative detail and data on which the parent magazine based its arguments and reform campaigns, the *Narrative* acted as a guarantor of the integrity of opinion in *Household Words.* However, parts of the *Narrative* unmistakably maintain the ideological slant of the magazine, in particular its opinion-driven leading articles on 'Parliament and Politics,' attributed to John Forster.[82] Forster, indeed, for several years received an annual income of over £200 from his eighth share, for which it seems reasonable to assume that he was expected to do more than simply publicise the journal by excerpting its articles in *The Examiner.*[83] Only six *Household Words* articles by him are recorded in the Office Book between 1850 and 1853, and there is certainly a Forsterian gravitas about some of the *Narrative's* pronouncements, which seem beyond the scope of the 'good old simple-minded man' (Dickens's father-in-law, George Hogarth), whom Morley recalled had the routine job of 'compound[ing] the news of the household narrative out of the papers.' Wills also helped with the publication, taking what he called 'the labouring oar,' in its production, rather than 'a higher berth.'[84] It was Dickens himself, however, who orchestrated the dual coverage of important events in the two publications. After the death and extravagant State Funeral of the Duke of Wellington, for example, he reserved space in the columns of *Household Words* for his own objections, and in those of the September and November *Narratives* for leaders on Wellington's character, Chancellor Disraeli's Parliamentary panegyric (the 'bad taste' of which was predictably contrasted with the 'sincere and deep expression' of sorrow shown in the streets by working people), and factual resumés of the career of 'England's greatest general.'[85]

The *Household Narrative* became briefly significant for Dickens studies in the 1940s when a pioneering critic indicated how it could be mined as a source for 'originals,' incidents and other clues about the crafting of Dickens's fiction, but it has remained in this and other respects, as another scholar agreed in 1961, 'specially relevant and little explored.'[86] The reason for the *Narrative*'s discontinuation after the December 1855 number is unclear, but apart from the obvious suggestion that it was not paying, may be connected with Forster's retirement that Christmas as editor of the *Examiner*, and from full-time journalism. Two months later, he also relinquished his eighth share in *Household Words*, having continued to receive profits until 30 September of the previous year.[87] In letters to Dickens on his Italian bachelor jaunt of 1853, Forster had complained of W. H. Wills 'as not consulting him enough' in the management of the periodical during Dickens's absence, and was 'evidently very sore on that connexion.' The marked coolness which developed between the two rival advisers and assistants may have strengthened his resolve to cut all ties with the journal. The relinquished share was made over to Dickens, who in turn gifted half of it – though the terms were never satisfactorily defined – to Wills.[88]

One of Forster's last services was the insertion in *The Examiner* of 8 December of a puff for the forthcoming *Household Words Almanac for 1856*, welcomed as an antidote to the kind of almanac which has 'hitherto been allowed to encourage superstition in the dwellings of the poor.' As Dickens's own editorial announcement of the *Almanac* in *Household Words* made clear, although the reader would find in its 24 pages 'a number of remarkable predictions,' they were ones which had all been 'falsified by the result, inculcating the wisdom of not too venturously binding down the Future.' Likewise, for those inclined to preach up the Past, there was attached to the Calendar, 'a Chronicle of Progress, enabling the reader to compare the times in which he lives, with the times of a hundred years ago.' Illuminated with decorative woodcuts, the *Almanac* also set out the natural as opposed to the supernatural

> laws that maintain ... the Earth, in its appointed place among the stars, and regulate the winds and waters; the principles on which the preservation of our health and cheerfulness mainly depends; the times of the development of the several kinds of trees and flowers, and when the melody of the various sorts of birds is first awakened....[89]

Unlike the *Narrative*'s expressly linear march through time, the *Almanac* emphasized the cyclical nature of life. Though Dickens had little directly to do with its composition, Morley was by now well placed to convey his Editor's earnest preoccupation with sanitation and hygiene, and imbue the 'Remarkable Predictions' with the heavy '*Examiner*' style of irony Dickens regularly adopted for describing the opponents of reform. Though he did his best to sound like Dickens, the venture was not a success. Something was missing, as Dickens later noted: 'The Almanac ought to have done more. It is a pity (I observe now) that my name is nowhere upon it.'[90]

Even before *Household Words* began publication, Dickens had 'foreign arrangements' for simultaneous publication abroad in hand, and although these fell through the great entrepreneurial German publisher Baron von Tauchnitz soon purchased the right to reprint the bi-annual volumes of the journal in his *Collection of British Authors.*[91] Given Dickens's editorial mission to displace villainous publications, it is perhaps surprising that no evidence has come to light of plans to franchise *Household Words* in America, with its vast and fast-growing reading public, badly served, in his opinion, by its press. The main difficulty in the way of any such expansion was the continuing lack of copyright protection in America for British authors, whose work could be legally republished there by any firm willing to undertake the gamble. Unauthorized sales of *Dombey and Son* in America are said to have topped 175 000.[92] Dickens's loss was American publishers' gain. A competitive market developed for *Household Words*, which was freely pirated by Angell, Engel & Howitt and a string of other New York houses, as an undated weekly periodical, priced at 6 cents or $2 annually, as a monthly, and in bi-yearly volumes.[93] There are no *pictures* in it,' the jejune Ezra Barker of McElrath & Barker wrote to Dickens, explaining why the circulation of their pirated edition – '5000 copies weekly & monthly included' by March, 1854 – was lower than it should be. He offered to make secret plans to overreach his senior partner, and undertake the official publication of *Household Words* himself. Writing to Bradbury & Evans, P. D. Orvis blamed over-pricing for the low circulation, citing his own firm's success with an authorized American reprint of *Chambers's Journal*, which they had 'got ... up to 8 to 10 000 copies' in four months, although 'it has not as many claims by far as *Household Words*.' Dickens and his partners declined to pursue any of these offers. Apart from such glimpses, the fate of Dickens's *Household Words* in America is still – unlike its successor's – 'almost absolutely dark.'[94]

X

From the outset, the conducting of *Household Words* required a level of energy, concentration, creative drive, and planning that would have sufficed any ordinary editor for a full-time job. The sub-editing alone was enough to occupy Wills's time: his 'whole life' was 'completely ... bound up in *Household Words*,' he lamented, when Dickens firmly vetoed his accepting an undemanding part-time editorship elsewhere.[95] But Dickens himself freely combined his journalism in the 1850s with the writing of *David Copperfield, Bleak House,* the *Child's History, Hard Times,* and *Little Dorrit,* the first of the Public Reading tours, and a bewildering array of public and private commitments. In 1855 he memorably described the magazine as that 'great humming-top *Household Words*, which is always going round with the weeks and murmuring 'Attend to me!'[96] There were human voices in Dickens's life which must occasionally have murmured 'Attend to me!' – Catherine's, perhaps, or any of their nine surviving children's – but at home too the battle of life was undercutting the domestic ideal. Letters of these later years show Dickens casting himself in the role of lone warrior, soldiering on in life's battle – 'we must all be brave, as good soldiers are, and when the fast-thinning ranks look bare, ... close up solidly and march on' – increasingly conscious of 'one happiness I have missed in life, and one friend and companion I have never made.' There is evidence of friction, unhappiness, dissatisfaction with Catherine verging on revulsion, and frustration that neither their incompatibility as a couple nor her 'indescribable lassitude of character' were grounds for divorce.[97]

Dickens had concluded his first leader in *Household Words* with an allegory of the editorial undertaking, which told how the 'adventurer in the old fairy story, climbing towards the summit of a steep eminence on which the object of his search was stationed, was surrounded by a roar of voices, crying to him ... to turn back. All the voices *we* hear, cry Go on!' After years of trying to accommodate romance and realities at home no less than in the journal, in December 1857 Dickens oddly rewrote the allegory in a letter to Lavinia Watson:

> I wish I had been born in the days of Ogres and Dragon-guarded Castles. I wish an Ogre with seven heads ... had taken the princess whom I adore – you have no idea how intensely I love her! – to his stronghold on top of a high series of Mountains.... Nothing would suit me half so well this day, as climbing after her, sword in hand....[98]

In the letter, the story is immediately followed by another, that of the extraordinary emotional release he had found 'all last summer' in publicly performing the part of Richard Wardour in the climax of Wilkie Collins's arctic melodrama *The Frozen Deep*. The juxtaposition is important. With the added knowledge that during the August performances in Manchester, Dickens met and fell in love with Ellen Ternan, the young professional actress with whom he was to conduct a secret, and in many ways mysterious, affair for the rest of his life, it becomes easy to recognize the identity of the Princess, and the almost-confession in the second version of the fairy story. Almost-confession because Dickens had no intention of supplying his correspondent with the key to the allegory. But the temptation to allegorise went well beyond the confines of private correspondence, and the editorial adventure and love adventure were already being pursued together, logically enough, in full public view of the readers of *Household Words*.

It was not simply that Dickens's latest remarks in the magazine about divorce laws seem to take on, in retrospect, an uncomfortable application to his own case.[99] After a twelve-month period in which he had contributed only three solo articles, his overdue return to its pages throughout October 1857 was entirely dedicated to 'The Lazy Tour of Two Idle Apprentices,' a five-part meta-fictional account co-written with Wilkie Collins, of his flight in September from the family home to Cumberland in pursuit of the eighteen-year-old Ellen, who was booked to appear in a Yorkshire theatre.[100] He and Collins appear as 'Francis Goodchild' and 'Thomas Idle' respectively, and the former shares Dickens's restless energy, and 'is always in love with somebody.' Naturally there was a mountain for the adventurer to climb – Carrick Fell, 'a gloomy old mountain 1500 feet high' which Dickens had read up about in a picturesque travel guide before leaving London – and a series of obstacles to be overcome before the damsel could be discovered. The narrative of the climb and the obstacles occupies the first four installments, the last of which presents, in the inset tale of the 'Bride's Chamber,' a nightmarish confusion of Dickens's feelings about Catherine and the new object of his affections. The 'fair, flaxen-haired' Bride's name is Ellen and she is persecuted by a nameless 'He' who is old enough to be her father, but she is also a girl with 'no character, no purpose ... a weak, credulous, incapable helpless nothing,' whom the wicked Husband longs to be rid of:

[T]he poor fool's constant song [was]: 'I beg your pardon,' and 'Forgive me!'
   She was not worth hating; he felt nothing but contempt for her. But, she had long been in the way, and he had long been weary, and the work was near its end, and had to be worked out.

Eventually, by willing her constantly to die, the husband rids himself of his imbecilic wife. The air of utter unreality and lack of specifics in the tale are striking, but also reminiscent of Dickens's allegorical style in 'The Story Without a Beginning,' or 'A Child's Dream of a Star' – and while no obvious key is supplied within the frame narrative, if one is sought in the context of Dickens's otherwise unspeakable desires, then the 'Bride's Chamber' is indeed what Dickens told Miss Coutts, a 'bit of Diablerie.'
   The last instalment of the 'Lazy Tour' was for many years thought to be Collins's work alone – a piece of subterfuge on Forster's part – but Dickens's letters to Wills and others show him to be responsible for the section describing race week and theatre crowds at Doncaster, where the object of Francis Goodchild's longing makes her appearance at last:

'O little lilac gloves! And O winning little bonnet, making in conjunc-tion with her golden hair quite a Glory in the sunlight round the pretty head, why anything in the world but you and me! ... Arab drums, powerful of old to summon the Genii in the desert, sound of yourselves and raise a troop for me in the desert of my heart, which shall so enchant this dusty barouche ..., that I, within it, loving the little lilac gloves, the winning little bonnet, and the dear unknown wearer with the golden hair, may wait by her side for ever...!'

Another almost-confession, doubly disguised, but Dickens can scarcely be said to have taken pains to disguise the journalistic trademarks which marked the leader out as his: the fanciful mode of approach, the *Arabian Nights* allusions, the serio-comic treatment of the amusements of the people.

Critics have expressed amazement at this kind of 'strange – and exceedingly dangerous impulsion' of Dickens's 'to share with his readers his most personal raptures and longings'[101] but his genius and his journalism were so essentially communicative in spirit, that it is perhaps not surprising to find *Household Words* used as the medium. In happier times, he had often used the shelter of anonymity the journal proffered as an opportunity for partial self-exposure in various familiar essays. 'All through in this secret crypt of his,' a regular contributor recalled, 'he found pleasure in putting on record little incidents of his own life, family sufferings and feelings, and thus giving them a permanence.'[102]

The formal separation in May 1858 of Dickens and his wife, and the splitting up of his household, naturally made familiar essay-writing for *Household Words* inappropriate, but, when Dickens became aware of slanderous rumours circulated by the Hogarth family (he thought) and others, concerning his relationship with Ellen Ternan, and with his sister-in-law Georgina, he opted for complete self-exposure in the journal as a response. This involved publishing a lengthy signed statement of his absolute innocence, headed 'Personal,' as the leading article for the issue dated 12 June, and arranging for the mighty *Times* – whose editor, John T. Delane, had advised Dickens to go ahead with the announcement – to pre-publish the declaration. This stepping out from the shadow, even if there had been no grounds whatsoever for the rumours, was a highly questionable decision. Had another contributor to *Household Words* made the request, Dickens would have refused to print. As things stand, and given that modern readers suspect, as Delane clearly did not, the reality of Dickens's passionate platonic attachment to Ellen Ternan, and that he had circulated disguised declarations of love for her in previous leaders for the journal, Dickens stands charged of both hypocrisy and abuse of editorial privilege. His only defence, commentators agree, is that he valued what he had recently described as the 'peculiar' and 'personal (I may almost say affectionate) relations which subsist between me and the public' higher than any he had yet established in professional or private life.[103]

XI

Although *Household Words* carried on for nearly a year and two complete volumes after the publication of 'Personal,' Dickens decided for complex reasons that it too had to die. During the painful negotiations over the separation, Frederick Evans and Mark Lemon, as close family friends, had acted on Catherine's behalf, and were her co-trustees in the Deed of Separation. But in their respective professional capacities, as publisher and editor of *Punch*, Dickens expected them to reprint there his 'Personal' declaration, in which he had appealed, as a journalist who had 'ever been unaffectedly true to our common calling' to all his 'brethren' in the press, for help to spread the word. National and provincial papers alike had responded to the call,[104] but when Lemon and Evans failed to do so – it not occurring to them, they later explained, to publish 'statements on a domestic and painful subject in the inappropriate columns of a comic miscellany' – Dickens was outraged, and resolved to dismiss Bradbury and Evans as his publishers, buy up their share in *Household Words*, and have it printed elsewhere. Dickens's icy tone in a letter to Evans in late July ('I have been forced to include you in [the] class ... [of] those who have been false to [my] name'), suggests that he must also have felt Evans supported Catherine too strongly, if not actually believed or fuelled the rumours.[105]

For much of the Autumn Dickens was occupied with his first, wildly successful, tour of 85 Public Readings, but on his return to London in November, he moved swiftly to dissolve the partnership, transfer publication, and – when Bradbury and Evans refused to sell either their share in the property or in the copyright to the journal's name – close the journal down, and immediately found another. Bradbury and Evans contested his right to act unilaterally, citing the original Articles of Agreement which, 'in consideration of the mutual trust and confidence' of all the signatories, had, among other things, bound the proprietors to seek arbitration over disputes. When they filed a Bill of Complaint in Chancery to prevent him from distributing 'upwards of half a million Copies' of a Prospectus announcing that the journal would be discontinued, and claiming their legal costs, Dickens found English Law surprisingly un-asinine and Chancery a model of efficiency. The Master of the Rolls heard the case within a week, and endorsed the legal opinion Dickens had been given, that the Partnership could be dissolved 'at the Will of any of [the partners] without the consent of the others, and at a moment's notice.' Also upheld by the Master of the Rolls was the defence's contention that the full title of the publication was '*Household Words Conducted by Charles Dickens*' and that anyone continuing it would have to make clear that the 'light' of Dickens's name did not 'still shine upon the work.'[106] Gambling that this would be the outcome, he and W. H. Wills had a series of arrangements in hand to terminate *Household Words* at the end of its nineteenth half-year volume, and publish a new magazine for themselves.

The last number of *Household Words*, dated 28 May 1859, appeared four weeks after the start of Dickens's final adventure in popular journalism, *All the Year Round*. In spite of, or perhaps because of, all the scandal and the gossip, sales had remained as high during its last six months as at any time in the last six years, and for the weeks when it was published side by side with *All the Year Round*, circulation seems to have stayed steady at little under 35 000 copies.[107] The number began with a 2-column leader by Dickens, reminding readers that the new publication was a true reincarnation of the old in appearance and values, but also crowing over its better circulation, which 'trebles that now relinquished in *Household Words*.' To use the enemy's compositors, ink and presses to coolly promote his own breakaway venture was the ultimate demonstration of control. To add insult to injury, in the Chancery auction of the partnership property, some sharp bidding tactics allowed Dickens's agent to buy up the 400 000 copies of printed stock and the stereo plates (sold on at a tidy profit to Chapman & Hall) plus the right to the name, all at a very affordable price.[108] Easthope, Bentley, and – twice, now – the 'fools' Bradbury and Evans had been worsted in their efforts to shackle Dickens's editorial freedom: which he had finally gained by *tour de force*, by becoming a magazine publisher and proprietor himself. That such active participation in the power struggles that make press history more like a branch of military than cultural studies, should, in aesthetic and popular terms, make Dickens a better and more successful journalist seems unfair. Yet the last proper leader Dickens contributed to *Household Words* stood at the head of an innovative 'New Year's Number' for 1859, which he had somehow found the time to devise and orchestrate, amidst the tumult. It comprises a series of reflections, by turns comic, wry, personal and cosmopolitan, on New Years' Days at home and abroad. Its detail, scope, and remarkable 'richness and serenity' have been commented on, and the way in which it 'looks forward to his very finest journalistic writings,' which are to be found in the columns of *All the Year Round*, along with *A Tale of Two Cities* and *Great Expectations*.[109] Out of the ashes of *Household Words* and Dickens's burnt-out marriage, the new periodical rose like a phoenix.

8
Publishing and Recalling Life: *All the Year Round* (1859–70)

At the age of forty-six – a time of life when many choose or are forced to plateau – Dickens embarked on two demanding new ventures, as a public reader of his own works, and as a publisher. Neither is strictly the province of a study of his work as a journalist, but in so far as both departures impacted on *All the Year Round* and all three pursuits were facets of the same media phenomenon, they deserve some attention. The working patterns Dickens and Wills had established for making up the weekly numbers of *Household Words* were stretched to the limit by his reading tours, which would take him to venues across mainland Britain, Ireland, France and the United States. A new creative rhythm was needed for writing journalism no less than fiction, for as he told his old friend De Cerjat in 1867, 'When I read I *don't* write. I only edit, and have the proof sheets sent to me for that purpose.'[1] He relied more than ever on Wills to manage all aspects of the Commercial Department and much of the Literary work from London,[2] but the increased correspondence his absences brought on shows no slacking of vigorous and detailed interest in editorial matters – he had not won outright control of his journal in order to hand it over to a subsidiary. The incessant travel which the tours involved – symptomatic of Dickens's inner restlessness – contributed to various self-projections as a traveller, 'the British Wanderer' as he styled himself,[3] or, more significantly, 'The Uncommercial Traveller,' under which polyvalent guise he wrote the thirty-six articles for *All the Year Round* which mark the climax of his career as a journal essayist. His actual or reported circulation through hundreds of towns and cities where his periodical and books were on sale, actively boosted their circulation. Articulate working-class characters, first created for the Extra Christmas Numbers of *All the Year Round*, were converted into some of Dickens's most popular readings, and their voices shared the platform with him, at a time when franchise reform and increased voting rights for British artisans were topics of national debate. The readings, too, carried a political charge.[4]

As his own publisher in a boom decade for the industry, when the last of the remaining 'Taxes on Knowledge' was repealed and competition grew cut-throat amongst the magazines,[5] Dickens made several policy changes which affected the contents, preparation and distribution of *All the Year Round*. The most far-reaching of these was the decision to permanently 'reserv[e] the first place in these pages for a continuous original work of fiction' – a change announced as *A Tale of Two Cities* finished its run, and Wilkie Collins's *The Woman in White* began. Dickens's synoptic leading articles, the cutting edge of *Household Words* and its reforming agenda, made way for historical and 'sensation' fiction. *All the Year Round*, no less than the *Examiner* or *Punch*, indexed the wider decline of radicalism in the 1860s.[6] In any case, the new overseas readerships which Dickens was securing for the magazine, and the associated stress in its pages on international affairs and outlooks, meant perhaps that leaders on the ins-and-outs of domestic politics (which Dickens had always likened to the workings of 'Our Parish') were inappropriately parochial. Innovative arrangements for simultaneous publication in New York meant – for a time, at least – bedding each issue down much earlier, to allow time to ship the plates across the Atlantic, and a corresponding loss of topicality.

The changes of direction and emphasis in *All the Year Round* which resulted from these new ventures were thus not always planned or desired. At times, indeed, it seems that Dickens's desire for omni-presence across a range of media, leads instead to a series of unpredictable disappearances and reappearances from view from individual platforms.[7] It is certainly true that after 1863, the frequency of Dickens's contributions to *All the Year Round* declines dramatically. All this was complicated by his need to genuinely 'vanish into space,' in order to spend time with the now invisible Ellen Ternan, living discreetly with her mother and sisters in the house in Ampthill Square which Dickens had (almost certainly) leased on their behalf.[8] Nevertheless, after eighteen months in the field, J. M. Emerson, the authorized American publisher of *All the Year Round*, was able to announce to readers that the magazine they were reading 'has now the largest circulation of any similar publication in the world.' His numerical estimate that, including authorized and unauthorized excerptions from the journal, its serialisation of *Great Expectations* 'will find in this country alone more than three million readers' reads more like a 20th-century TV rating than a mid-Victorian circulation figure.[9] Individual readers, too, registered its sensational popularity. The actress Ellen Terry recorded in her autobiography that during her Paris engagement of 1866, *All the Year Round* was 'the thing that made me homesick for London' –

> The excitement in the 'sixties' over each new Dickens can be understood only by people who experienced it at that time. Boys used to sell [it] in the streets, and they were often pursued by an eager crowd, for all the world as if they were carrying news of the 'latest winner.'[10]

I

All the Year Round had been publishing successfully for four months before the new 'Articles of Agreement' were ready for signing. They were based on those for *Household Words*, with terms adapted to make them refer to Dickens and Wills only. The former now owned three-quarters of the business and received an Editor's salary of £504; the latter, one quarter, and a salary of £420. But Wills lost as well as gained under the new arrangements. In addition to continuing as sub-editor, he was now responsible, as Bradbury and Evans had been, for the general management of the 'Commercial Department.' Yet the wording used stressed that Wills's authority here was only delegated to him from Dickens, who had the power to overturn any of his decisions. One of the legal advisers commenting on the agreement thought its success depended 'so much upon the personal character, exertions, and relations of the promoters' that it would be better 'to confine the partnership articles to a definition of the interests of the two parties.' This did not happen, and Wills's interests were never properly defined. Although he 'owned' in theory a quarter of the business, this only meant sharing in that proportion in its profits or losses during his employment. If he retired, the Articles made clear, he would only retain an eighth. Dickens had even suggested, during the drafting stages, that if Wills retired his whole share should be 'subject to a new distribution.'[11] There is no evidence, furthermore, that he had felt obliged to pay Wills his share of the proceeds from the sale of *Household Words* stock to Chapman & Hall. In incorporating the old journal's name into that of *All the Year Round*, and then insisting point blank that the new 'Title is *mine*' (a point on which the Articles are explicit) Dickens had also swallowed Wills's three-sixteenths share in the *Household Words* copyright. Yet the latter's suggestion that his interest be recognized was met with a cold rebuff; his even raising the matter, Dickens told Ouvry (his solicitor and go-between in the dispute) 'leaves an impression in my mind, as to Wills, which is new and disagreeable.' Indeed, he wrote, the 'strict law of the thing between Wills and me never entered my head.'[12] That it should have entered Wills's, given his partner's track record of wilful and autocratic conduct, is hardly surprising.

A name for the new periodical was essential before Dickens could begin to advertise the discontinuance of *Household Words*. He and Collins between them seem to have come up with the required title and motto towards the end of January 1859. Forster records Dickens's perfectly serious suggestion of '*Household Harmony*,' along with his nettled response to the obvious objection that this was hardly a 'happy comment' on the whole saga that had led to the need for a new title: 'I am afraid we must not be too particular about the possibility of personal reference and applications: otherwise it is manifest that I can never write another book.' The new motto, 'The story of our lives from year to year,' was adapted from

Othello's lines explaining how Desdemona's father listened raptly to him tell 'the story of my life' (Act 1 scene 3). 'All the Year Round' itself seems to have been Collins's scribbled addendum to a list of Dickens's suggestions.[13]

Curiously, another of their joint ideas, *Once A-Week*, was identical to that used by Bradbury and Evans for the new magazine that they felt stung into starting themselves, from 5 July 1859, to replace *Household Words*. Pusillanimous exchanges between Dickens and Wills about the poor prospects of this rival venture, and the impending bankruptcy of Bradbury and Evans, appear to have been wishful thinking, however.[14] It ran for years, and – with a circulation rising from 22 000 in its first six months, to an estimated 60 000 in 1865, falling to 40 000 by 1870 – performed as well as *Household Words* might have been expected to do.[15] Perhaps more worrying for Dickens and Wills was the prospect of wholesale defections from their 'corps' writing staff. Charles Knight, considering Bradbury and Evans 'as perfectly blameless,' contributed to the early numbers, and George Meredith at once identified himself with its interests, regarding Dickens and *All the Year Round* as 'the enemy.' The redoubtable Harriet Martineau returned to magazine journalism as a frequent contributor to *Once a Week*, specifically because 'Dickens's conduct to Bradbury and Evans ... roused my indignation.' Eliza Lynn was invited to write for *Once a Week*, but only after some soul-searching, stayed loyal to Dickens. Will's letter of 3 November 1859 to a possible contributor puts a positive gloss on the situation, in claiming that 'not *one* of our friends ... who wrote most in *Household Words* ... but who has either written, or offered to write for *All the Year Round*.' Other sought-after authors such as Charles Reade, G. H. Lewes, George Borrow and Tennyson (paid £100 for his first poem, and £2000 a year for his contributions) all signed up to *Once a Week's* generous terms. Thomas Hughes, 'disgusted with Dickens and his set,' promised to try his hand. In the wake of the *Household Words* debacle, and gossip about Dickens's handling of the separation from Catherine, the Edinburgh manager of *Blackwood's* summed up a strong current of feeling against Dickens in press and publishing circles, in a passing reference to 'that fallen angel, C. D.'[16]

The fallen angel, meanwhile, had been busy removing pandemonium – in the shape of the publishing office – to new, more spacious headquarters a few doors away from the old, at 11 Wellington Street North (re-numbered 26 Wellington Street in April 1860). Once again, rooms above the office, five of them, were fitted up into a 'temporary Town Tent' for Dickens when overnighting in London, 'as comfortable, cheerful, and private as anything of the kind can possibly be,' he told his daughter Mamie in September 1860. A visitor to the Office in 1867, however, commented on the 'exceptionally plain' facilities and somewhat Scrooge-like provision for employees: 'not a square yard of carpet of any kind ... or a single article of furniture' apart from a table and two cane chairs.'[17] From here, Wills and

Dickens masterminded an extensive and eye-catching advertising campaign to launch the new title. As well as press announcements, 240 000 handbills were distributed nationally by W. H. Smith, along with 'double demy' posters and six-foot 'placards on a rich golden orange ground with black and red lettering' posted on hoardings and blank walls, in all the major railway terminals and the London stations, with smaller posters sent to agencies for display in railway carriages and circulating on 130 London omnibuses. Similar campaigns were used to promote the serial novels running in the journal, at 'enormous' cost, one grateful author recalled, 'but everything was done magnificently at the office.'[18] Dickens clearly knew where his budget priorities lay.

Sales of the early issues of *All the Year Round* 'exceed[ed] the most sanguine expectations' – 120 000 of the first number 'settling down to a steady current sale of 100, 000,' Wills wrote to an overseas agent on 19 May 1859.[19] Dickens introduced a variety of new regular features in the early issues, determined to ensure a good start. These included 17 celebratory 'Trade Songs' by the popular poet 'Barry Cornwall,' a series of reports of topical peculiarities by 'Our Eye-Witness' ('an observant gentleman, who goes about with his eyes and ears open, who notes everything that comes in his way'),[20] a series of critical articles on the state of criminal and common law,[21] and a hard-hitting 'Occasional Register' of satirical announcements, similar to 'Supposing!' in *Household Words*. Dickens collaborated on the last two series. The following six paragraphs (never previously republished) were among his fourteen known contributions to the 'Occasional Register,' the brevity of the format registering the occasional lapses in Dickens's Liberalism in a particularly stark manner:

WANTED

VERY PARTICULARLY; the chief engineer of the steam-ship Bogota, who ordered a man to be roasted to death at a furnace. Which order was obeyed, under circumstances of brutality ... so abominable, that the earth can hardly be expected to produce grains and fruits after their several kinds while the said engineer remains unhanged upon it.

THE REASON WHY London Aldermanic justice ... sentenced a ruffian, for a series of perfectly unprovoked assaults of a most violent description, beginning with a respectable young woman and ending with the police in general, to one month's imprisonment only. The attention of Alderman Mechi is invited.

THE PHILANTHROPISTS who are so benevolent as to open the public-houses, free of expense, at election time. Also, the Samaritans who pay arrears of rent for people, at about the same time.

A FEW IDEAS for the walls of the Royal Academy. One hundred cart-loads of fancy dresses, dolls, and old furniture may be taken in exchange....

FOUND

ALWAYS. An immense flock of gulls to believe in preposterous advertisements.

MISSING

ON ALL OCCASIONS, the man who is responsible for anything done ill in the public service. He will particularly oblige by coming forward.[22]

He also made careful additions to Wilkie Collins's article in the first issue, wrote up a characteristic anti-Teetotalism paper (based on a research trip to Rothamsted in Hertfordshire to inspect a model working man's club) on 'The Poor Man and His Beer,' and otherwise coaxed and chivvied contributors old and new into delivering their strongest performance. Long queues formed outside the *All the Year Round* Office to buy the new number, of which 20 000 copies were sold in little over twenty-four hours.[23]

II

There is no doubt however, that the major selling point of *All the Year Round* in its early days was the serialisation of *A Tale of Two Cities* over the thirty-one weeks from 30 April to 26 November 1859. The extent to which the advent of serial fiction in Dickens's journal changed it into an outlet for recreational literature and lessened its relevance as a vehicle of a contemporary analysis and commentary, needs examination, though the placing, where Dickens is concerned, of those categories into binary opposition clearly begs a number of questions. The themes of re-creation, and resurrection, are fundamental to the *Tale*, and in selecting the course of the French Revolution as the current through which his characters must make their way, Dickens had chosen what was, for Victorian commentators, very much the defining political lesson of recent history. At a time when Britain was again preparing to defend her interests from French expansionist ambitions,[24] the plot enforced consideration of what had become, in the work of Macaulay and Carlyle, two competing views of historical shaping, the progressive line of development, versus the cyclical and prophetic. More subtle in its implications and Carlylean in argument, the *Tale* provided the same kind of echoes of the footsteps of the national scene that the *Child's History* had done in *Household Words*. His experiments with the *Narrative* and *Almanac* no less than the title 'All the Year Round,' suggests Dickens's apprehension as an editor of the relevance to readers of both kinds of patterning.

The completed novel was coolly and, in one case, savagely reviewed by critics in the monthlies and quarterlies, but a much more 'enthusiastic response ... in the popular weekly press' to its effects during serialisation has been noted.[25] Its opening instalment was pirated in more than one newspaper, as an encouragement to readers.[26] As with *Hard Times*, the weekly instalments had to be kept short (an average of $9\frac{1}{2}$ columns per issue) to leave room for other items in the journal, and – in direct contradiction of the Jamesian stereotype of the Victorian novel as loose and baggy – required a rigorous economy of style and 'incessant condensation,' causing Dickens, as he told Carlyle, 'the utmost misery by being presented in the "tea-spoon-full" form.' Weekly serialization, as a recent analyst has emphasised, also encouraged the development of three specific features: a 'striking opening to the work as a whole ... the episodic integrity of the individual number; and "climax and curtain" endings to instalments.'[27] Yet the combination of condensation and serialisation seems to have helped propel readers into a fast-moving current of narrative, in which Dickens's stated aim of telling a *'picturesque* story, rising in every chapter with characters ... whom the story itself should express ... pounding the characters out in its own mortar, and beating their interests out of them' applies as much to its historiographical as its storytelling technique. A fortnight before the close of serialisation, the *Illustrated London News* commented that *All the Year Round's* popularity

> is attributed to the very obvious circumstance of the issue of Mr Dickens's 'Tale of Two Cities' ... which probably carried most of its readers along with it. In the form in which it has been produced ... it has the effect of keeping up the desire to ascertain what it is all about through every successive number.[28]

Beyond simple effects of suspense, however, it can be argued that publication in short but frequent instalments artfully complemented the narrative pattern of the frequent journeys and rests undertaken in the novel by its representative 'ordinary' Englishman, Jarvis Lorry, with whom readers naturally identified on his introduction as 'the passenger, booked by this history,' who is 'on the coach-step, getting in.' The constitutionally moderate Lorry, and the reader of the serialised novel, are both forced to step onto the juggernaut of history, with its relentless forward motion, and must make the most of any pauses to glimpse its trajectory, as, vividly recalled to the responsibilities of living in history, they are drawn successively along the golden thread of its narrative and the track of the revolutionary storm. For the final flight by coach from Paris, Dickens not only adopts the present simple but the first person plural – a pattern common both to editorial narration, and to the descriptions of modern continental travel which Dickens had experimented with in *The Daily News* but also in journalistic papers like 'A Flight' (30 August 1851), where 'we' are taken to Paris by the new S. E. R. 'special express.'[29] Although the chronology projects readers backwards into the past, their identification with the characters' experience of the actuality of travel and their attempts to predict the future of individual lives, however determined the general fate, brings everything forward into the immediacy and uncertainty of the present. This includes the *Tale*'s cautionary moral, where the rhetoric mixes Biblical and *Arabian Nights* metaphors to describe the onward-rolling wheels of the tumbrils, and merge the cyclical with the linear pattern of historiography:

> Sow the same seed of rapacious licence and oppression ever again, and it will surely yield the same fruit according to its kind. Six tumbrils roll along the street. Change these back again to what they were, thou powerful enchanter, Time, and they shall be seen to be the carriages of absolute monarchs, the equipages of feudal nobles, the toilettes of flaming Jezabels ... . No; the great magician who majestically works out the appointed order of the Creator, never reverses his transformations. 'If thou be changed into this shape by the will of God,' say the seers to the enchanted in the wise Arabian stories, 'then remain so! ... ' Changeless and hopeless, the tumbrils roll along.[30]

In certain respects, therefore, the prioritising of serial fiction over non-fictional articles in the first year of *All the Year Round*'s publication did not necessarily involve a wholesale abandonment of socio-political analysis. Dickens and Wilkie Collins, mutually influencing each other in their novelistic as much as their journalistic aesthetic, seem in broad agreement that the two should – must – overlap. But a shift in balance must be recognised, especially noticeable where two serials themselves overlapped, through design or necessity, or when the inability of other novelists to condense their episodes as skilfully as Dickens made their instalments over-length. In addition to running for a month longer than planned, for example, *The Woman in White* swallowed in each of its last three instalments nearly twenty of the forty-eight available columns of the journal. When its successor, Charles Lever's diffuse and garrulous *A Day's Ride: A Life's Romance* failed to take a hold with readers, and sales flopped alarmingly, Dickens ran his own *Great Expectations* in parallel with Lever's serial for nearly four months.[31] As a result of such expedients, essays and non-fictional articles were inevitably displaced – the average number of items per issue in Dickens's journals falls from about eight in *Household Words* to about six in *All the Year Round*. Dickens held out, however, against running three serials concurrently, explaining to Sheridan Le Fanu that 'the public have a natural tendency, having more than two serial stories to bear in mind at once, to jumble them all together, and do justice to none of them.'[32]

During negotiations to serialise Bulwer-Lytton's 'elixir vitae' novel *A Strange Story* (*All the Year Round*, August 1861–March 1862) Dickens proudly told his noble friend that 'there is no publisher whatsoever associated with *All the Year Round*' and that therefore 'implicit reliance may be placed in the Journal's proceedings.' Research into those proceedings in the early years has suggested that 'Dickens presided over something like a truly novel-publishing venture, that *All the Year Round* offered, for a while at least, a glimpse of the ideal in publisher-novelist relationships.'[33] Studies of successive serials in the journal, and their influence on *Great Expectations*, have also indicated how the various authors, observing the different plots under construction week on week, consciously or unconsciously sought to rival or better each other's work through creative ripostes and thematic revaluations.[34] But there was of course a publisher associated with the venture, Dickens himself, and ideal relationships were formed only when popular authors felt *he* could be implicitly relied upon, and only when he was able to offer them a sufficient recompense for the widely-recognised difficulties of writing quality fiction for the cheap weekly press. George Eliot considered Dickens's repeated invitations to write for *All the Year Round* carefully, but ultimately declined – and was later able to negotiate the princely sum of £7000 for monthly serialisation of *Romola* in the upmarket *Cornhill Magazine*. The debate over Dickens's liberality as a paymaster supports the conclusion that he held, with little of the flexibility shown by contemporaries, 'to the average standard of his time.' As Hollingshead neatly observed, 'political economy, if it governed nothing else in Wellington Street, certainly governed the business conduct of the journal.'[35]

Lytton's *Strange Story* was followed by Collin's sensation novel *No Name* (15 March 1862–17 Jan 1863), Gaskell's novella *A Dark Night's Work* (24 January–21 March 1863) – 'not good enough' for the *Cornhill*, she told its publisher, but 'might be good enough' for Dickens's journal – and Reade's *Very Hard Cash* (28 March–26 December 1863). After this, with the exception of Wilkie Collins's *The Moonstone*, the names of the serials and even the authors become, to 21st century readers, obscure and uncanonical: Henry T. Spicer, G. A. Sala, Percy Fitzgerald, Amelia Edwards, Charles Allston Collins, Edmund Yates, Frances Trollope, and Rosa Mullholland. In their day, however, they were by no means nonentities. Sala and Yates were already acquiring fame as journalists, for whom the crossover to 'Literature,' following the trail blazed by Dickens and Thackeray, was a natural one. Their serials, a one recent study has contended, were redolent of a 'pervasive and knowledgeable Bohemianism' that would have struck readers as 'an integral part of the mythology of modern journalism,' and, veering between what their mutual friend, M. E. Braddon, called the 'Balzac morbid-anatomy school' of fiction and the 'down right sensational,' sailed close to the wind in their depiction of 'fast' heroines, and the vices of city life.[36] Nevertheless, with the required dose of warmth and melodrama that Dickens's editorship seems to have exacted, their serials took the circulation of *All the Year Round* higher than ever before, and kept it there. It has reasonably been claimed that, apart from Eliot, Thackeray and Anthony Trollope (who would eventually become a contributor in 1878, and whose brother and mother were both 'regulars') Dickens 'employed all the leading novelists of his age' to write for his journal. With the possible exception of Smith and the *Cornhill, All the Year Round* 'brought out more good novels than any comparable house' in the 1860s.[37]

III

A particular attraction for authors serialising their work in *All the Year Round* was Dickens's unrivalled position as publisher and editor to give them exposure in America, and ensure that they received additional payment for it. This was due to the complex series of arrangements Dickens and Wills entered into with American agents and publishers for the sale of foreign 'rights'[38] in the journal, and the strong business relationships which Dickens himself was pioneering, in arranging first for *A Tale of Two Cities,* and then *Great Expectations,* to be published (rather than pirated) by American houses. Initially, Dickens sold one year's rights for simultaneous American publication to Thomas C. Evans, an entrepreneurial agent and man-of-letters, who negotiated with various publishers to find the highest bidder, and eventually sold the contract on to Emerson & Co. of New York. The handsome sum agreed with this 'American ambassador,' to be remitted in two payments by 1 May and 1 November, was £1000 – about 60% of the whole annual profits in the last years of *Household Words.*[39] The arrangements involved shipping copies of the stereotype plates used for the British edition at least two weeks before the nominal (Saturday) date of publication,[40] and thus having the contents of each number written, proofed, corrected, and made-up, a week to ten days earlier than those of *Household Words* had been. After only a couple of issues, Evans was asking for a further week's advance, but Dickens refused. As Wills explained, 'We are already under great disadvantage in being forestalled with subjects; and, if we were to grasp even a single additional hair of Time's forelock in making our numbers ready, he would leave us too far behind him when we appear to the public.'[41]

Emerson & Co. initially sold the journal for 5 cents or $2.50 a year, and after only three issues, announced to readers that the 'large circulation ... already attained' would enable them to publish 'each week in elegant tinted covers' and arrange 'for its occasional embellishment with superb steel and copperplate engravings.'[42] One of the main attractions of the deal was that it gave Evans and Emerson exclusive access to the instalments of *A Tale of Two Cities,* and its value to them was naturally lessened when on 1 April, for a further £1000, Dickens contracted to furnish *Harper's Magazine* with advance sheets and the right to republish the 31 instalments of the *Tale* one week after their appearance in *All the Year Round.*[43] Even though Evans was to be paid a total of £550 by way of recompense, and was reassured that if *Harper's* published 'before the specified time' they would forfeit their supply of advance sheets, he complained in July of an understandable drop in *All the Year Round*'s sales.[44] When he then defaulted on the November payment, Dickens was able to terminate their contract, and negotiate separate agreements direct with both Emerson & Co. and Harper Brothers. Emerson agreed to pay $200 plus production and shipping costs to receive a month's supply of plates at a time, and to publish *All the Year Round* as a 25 cent monthly, from January 1860. Variations in exchange rate affected what was actually gained, but after 16 months' trading Wills concluded that the arrangement was 'rather a good thing netting from £600 to £700 a year.' Harper's, meanwhile, paid £250 annually to receive, via their London agent, early sheets of the publication two weeks before its nominal (Saturday) publication date, from which they were entitled to publish in their weekly papers any items from *All the Year Round*, apart from serial stories of longer than three months' duration.[45] These, they contracted for separately with the author, paying Lever £125 for *A Day's Ride*, Lytton £300 for *A Strange Story*, and Dickens himself £1000 for *Great Expectations*.

The disruptions to printing and international shipping before and during the Civil War complicated life for the American editions of *All the Year Round*. The date stamp disappears from Emerson's monthly parts from January 1861 onwards, and their standing guarantee for synchronised release with London was modified on 17 November 1861, to claim publication 'nearly simultaneously in the old and the new world.' In January 1863, Harper Brothers reported themselves unable to continue paying for advance sheets of *All the Year Round*, but Wills, in recognition of their 'liberality ... to ourselves and to our novelists,' offered to continue supplying them gratis, but to do so one week not two before publication. Dickens, from Paris, approved the decision, adding that hitherto the financial gain had not been worth the loss of topicality: 'the perpetual sliding away of temporary subjects at which I could dash with great effect, is a *great* loss.'[46] From this point, therefore, the long lead-time and other drawbacks associated with the American editions notable in 1859, were considerably reduced, while significant improvements in the speed and reliability of transatlantic crossings also cut the margin needed for the monthly shipping of plates, and its intermittent impact on the timeliness of the journalism. Though the income fluctuated, it was significant not only in itself but as an indicator that a substantial American market value now existed for British periodicals and British authors.

IV

Both in Britain and America, the most popular single issues of *All the Year Round* remained, as with *Household Words*, the annual Extra Christmas Numbers.[47] These, Forster considered, had the highest circulation of any of

Dickens's serial or periodical writings. References in Christmas-time letters of the 1860s rejoice in steadily-growing UK sales reports of 191 000 (*Somebody's Luggage*), 220 000 (*Mrs Lirriper's Lodgings*), 250 000 (*Dr Marigold's Prescriptions*), 265 000 (*Mugby Junction*), and ultimately reaching, Forster records, 'before he died, to nearly three hundred thousand' (*No Thoroughfare*). With understandable enthusiasm, Dickens continued the innovative work of writing collaborative fiction with up to five other writers in a single number, though the effort of orchestrating the contributions reduced him, he told Lewes in late November 1859, to 'a state of temporary insanity.'[48]

That year's project, *A Haunted House*, carried on to an unusual extent a journalistic campaign that Dickens had been pursuing elsewhere in his journal, namely the debunking of American-style Spiritualism, and the exposure of fraudulent claims about supernatural occurrences. William Howitt had become an ardent believer in ghosts and séances ('a kind of arch rapper among the rappers,' Dickens called him) and objected to articles published in *All the Year Round* which had explained various ghosts away. When he republished in *The Spiritual Magazine*, without consulting Dickens, their exchange of letters on the subject, Dickens devised the format of the Christmas Number as a humorous riposte, encouraging his five co-writers to project characters whose 'ghosts' – as the frame-narrator concludes – turn out to be nothing 'more disagreeable than our own imaginations and remembrances.'[49] Howitt's version of their disagreement – articulated in his *History of the Supernatural* – makes the valuable point, however, that Dickens had 'played with spiritualism as a cat with a mouse; it has a wonderful fascination for him' and that his position was somewhat perverse, given that 'he has of late years, in his periodicals, been alternately attacking spiritualism, and giving you the most accredited instances of it.' The attacks, and the imaginative engagement, can be critically appraised on their own terms.[50] Alternatively, as one recent study has demonstrated, they can be viewed as part of the broader response of Dickens's journals to modern science and technology: a process which suggests the justness of Howitt's objection.[51] On another level again, it should be noted that the emphasis in Dickens's own solo tale, 'The Ghost in Master B.'s Room,' on memories of youth, and a sense of adult loss ('Ah me, ... No other ghost has haunted the boy's room, ... than the ghost of my own childhood, the ghost of my own innocence, the ghost of my own airy belief') is one which recurs with haunting persistence in the narrative voices which Dickens projects in the early 1860, both in the 'The Uncommercial Traveller' series and in *Great Expectations*.[52]

V

The perceived diminution of domestic political and social commentary in *All the Year Round* has been attributed to the discovery that 'American readers were put off by too much "local" ... controversial matter.' The main reason for the diminution, however, was the displacement by serial fiction, which was only the most obvious of a number of changes of editorial emphasis. As well as the increased interest in matters spiritual, there was, in fact, a marked increase in the number of articles on international affairs, though not, specifically, on American affairs.[53] Concessions to a new transatlantic readership are perhaps only detectable in such slight touches as Dickens's adding geographical markers unnecessary for British readers into his self-introduction as the 'Uncommercial Traveller':

> [N]o house of public entertainment in the United Kingdom greatly cares for my opinion of its brandy or its sherry.... I am always wandering here and there from my rooms in Covent-garden, London – now about the city streets: now, about the country bye-roads....[54]

American readers were indirectly canvassed, however, in the numerous articles Dickens published between 1865 and 1867 about the origins and dangers of the Irish Fenian movement ('this absurd society'), which he knew drew heavily on American Irish support, and recruited disaffected Civil War veterans into its ranks. The discussion of the topic was one he prudently vetoed in *All the Year Round* during his six-month reading tour of America in 1867–8, fearing that the Fenians in America 'would be glad to damage a conspicuous Englishman' – particularly, it may be supposed, the publisher and editor of a journal with huge transatlantic sales that had continually criticised the movement.[55]

The foreign news that most filled the journal's pages, particularly in the early volumes, concerned Italy. Like most of the Liberal press, *All the Year Round* gave full support to the movement for Italian Unification, encouraging its readers in a variety of ways to understand the reasons behind what Dickens himself melodramatically described as the 'rising of the Italian people from under their unutterable wrongs ... after the long long night of oppression that has darkened their beautiful country.' Over thirty articles on Italian themes had already appeared in the journal by this date, including the flippant reports filed from Rome by 'Special Correspondent' Percy Fitzgerald, a Roman Catholic lawyer-turned-penman who later worried 'that it was not exactly reverent to apply the free and easy *All the Year Round* methods to the city of the Holy See, and that I gave too much freedom to my *frondeur* pen.'[56] Although Dickens intended to make the journal less openly anti-Catholic in sentiment than *Household Words* – an article on medieval simony was carefully qualified to 'guard our readers against attributing to the well-educated Roman Catholic of our own day, faults that ... were as much faults of a period in the age of society as of a creed,' while Tom Trollope's criticism of Pope Pius IX was moderated 'with a view to the English Catholics' – the underlying bigotry of the stance remained consistent with *Household Words* and Dickens's *Daily News*.[57] Fledgling nationalist movements in other regions of Europe where monarchic, imperial or religious oppression held sway were also supported. Poland, whose independence Dickens's friend the late Dudley Coutts Stuart had championed, was the subject of a series of articles in 1863, in the wake of recent Russian incursions and atrocities. Life in the cities of Turkey, Britain's unlikely ally against the Russians, was also explored in the numerous travel sketches by special correspondent Walter Thornbury.

Thornbury's penchant for lurid and sensational detail – what Dickens described to Wills as his 'coffin-relish' – was exploited in a long series of articles they projected on historical and biographical subjects, which formed together a further category of non-fictional articles to which distinctly more space was given in *All the Year Round* than in its predecessor.[58] Elsewhere, the journal maintained *Household Words's* post-Crimea scrutiny of the condition of the British army and navy, their strategic resources, installations, accommodation and training,[59] and, maintaining generous coverage of commercial and consumer affairs, presented a wide-ranging debate about public and private finance, fraud and forgery.[60] A range of open-ended articles on natural history summarised and discussed intelligently the relative virtues of evolutionary theory from de Maillet, Lamarck, through *Vestiges*, down to Richard Owen and Darwin's opposing arguments of the early 1860s, viewed respectfully as admirable but incomplete attempts to solve 'the mystery of creation.'[61] It carried, however, notably fewer articles on emigration, education, industry and science, travel and the arts, though these subjects were by no means ignored. In many cases, topics had simply become passé, and in others, Dickens and his writers had simply exhausted the avenues of approach and appeals for reform that made for strong copy.

Readers had no complaints, to judge by circulation figures, of *All the Year Round*'s commitment to social reform, and doubtless interpreted its editorial selection in the wider context of the general waxing and waning of media interest. Regular writers, however, who had experienced the excitement of *Household Words* journalistic campaigns, complained that the new journal was 'never so heartily relished,' even that its title had a '*pragmatical flavour.*' 'All the H.W. contributors regretted the merging of *Household Words* in *All the Year Round*,' Hollingshead recalled in 1900. 'It was not the same journal, although we had the same chief.' *All the Year Round* was 'less personal' and offered 'less of the one prevailing tone.' The claims of *The Examiner*'s review of the first bi-annual volume, partisan no doubt, nevertheless contradict some of these charges:

> One large source of the popularity of this journal ... is the fact that ... it has a distinct sound of its own, and speaks its mind out fearlessly.... In turning over the six hundred pages of the ... volume ..., many will for

the first time distinctly see how various are the topics of strong social interest which have been already discussed in the new journal, with full knowledge and from special points of observation. ... The depth and reality of its great central purpose is the surest safeguard against affectation, and to this the journal owes that strongly defined individuality which gives it life.[62]

The extent to which 'personality' and 'individuality' were detected in the journal was of course an indication of Dickens's success in casting his shadow over all his contributors' work, and sprinkling consistency of opinion and fanciful approach. The perceived 'deterioration' in the journal is probably therefore a simple function of his gradual disappearance, from 1863 onwards, from its pages. That the journal should thereafter appear more anonymous is natural enough, given that neither the Office Book or 'Office Set' of journal has survived, and the authorship of three-quarters of the non-fictional items in the journal remains unknown.

VI

Dickens was quite aware that anonymity went hand-in-hand with sales-boosting speculation about authorship, yet in the case of himself and his most illustrious contributors, the advantages of signature hand-in-hand with selective advertising were too great to ignore. Anticipating his likely public reading commitments, and private reasons for travelling incognito hither and yon, Dickens made in early 1860 a remarkable virtue of necessity in his decision to advertise his authorship of a series of travelling essays in *All the Year Round*. Wilkie Collins's ongoing serial was proving a resounding success, but the Christmas launch of the lavishly-produced *Cornhill Magazine*, directly threatened the monthly parts of *All the Year Round* and the most affluent and influential portion of its subscribers. Thackeray was its editor, and his manifesto for the magazine had launched a veiled attack on Dickens's mission as a journalist, in the approved negative manner. He did not pretend as an Editor, he said, to be

a great reformer, philosopher and wise-acre, about to expound prodigious doctrines and truths until now unrevealed, to guide and direct the peoples, to pull down the existing order of things, to edify new social or political structures, and to ... set the Thames on Fire.[63]

Instead, he aimed to 'amuse and interest' (rather than teach), by encouraging as contributors 'pleasant and instructed gentlemen and ladies,' and as readers, those 'glad to be addressed by well-educated men-and-women.' Classist, certainly, but the double stress on education also looks like a hit at Dickens and his streetwise but distinctly under-educated staff, Edmund

Yates among them, whose journalistic practice (during the Garrick Club controversy) Thackeray had branded as 'intolerable in a society of gentlemen.'[64]

The opening number of the *Cornhill* sold nearly half a million, and had closed with the first of a series of witty, and ostentatiously 'literary' essays, billed as 'Roundabout Papers. No. 1,' in which Thackeray reached out to readers in the warm and intimate terms which had been Dickens's calling card in *Household Words* and the Prefaces to his novels in volume form.[65] A response was needed urgently in *All the Year Round*. In early January, Dickens told Collins he was contemplating a series of 'gossiping papers' but instead devised the quirky alter ego of 'The Uncommercial Traveller' as the preamble to a paper already drafted, about a recent shipwreck off the Welsh coast.[66] Partly an extension of positive ideas about the professional 'commis voyageur' as a new heroic type for the age, partly a rejection of the extremist economic theory dominating political debate over the Commercial Treaty signed by Cobden and Chevalier on 20 January,[67] the persona required for its projection a certain literary distancing that allowed Dickens to pay homage to the Augustan and Romantic periodical essayists and sketchers whom he had read, and loved, since childhood. The narrator's incessant travelling and compulsive observation made him a latter-day 'Spectator,' while his 'idle manner' and whimsical dedication to his 'day's no-business' marked him out as the modern counterpart of Mackenzie's 'Lounger,' Johnson's 'Idler,' and Lamb's 'Elia.' His Covent-garden base and magisterial sifting of city refuse recalled that of Fielding's *Covent Garden Journal*, while his country and antiquarian travels emulated Cobbett's *Rural Rides*, and (in its awareness of describing Britain for an American audience) Irving's *Sketchbook*.[68]

By advertising the 'Uncommercial Traveller' in *All the Year Round* as 'A Series of Occasional Journeys, by Charles Dickens' and announcing after the publication of each when the next would appear (one, two or three weeks ahead), Dickens promoted a new and labour-free form of serialisation, adapted to his semi-nomadic lifestyle in the 1860s, encouraging the illusion that the public journal was his traveller's journal. The first series of papers, consisting of sixteen items, ran from January 28 1860 until October 13; a second series of thirteen papers was published between May and August 1863 – articles in both these series appearing untitled under the heading 'The Uncommercial Traveller' – and a final series of six papers, timed to coincide with the beginning of an improved 'New Series' of *All the Year Round*, appeared under the signature 'New Uncommercial Samples. By Charles Dickens,' and began on 5 December 1868. An angry single article, called 'The Ruffian. By The Uncommercial Traveller' but eschewing the humorous restraint characteristic of the persona, preceded the final series on 10 October 1868. Dickens himself collected and republished the first two series in single editions. Along with *Sketches by Boz* and an eclectic selection of *Household Words* papers unimaginatively released as *Reprinted Pieces* in 1858, these were the only collections of his own journalism that Dickens authorised.

The distancing instrinsic to travel narrative and to the appeal to literary tradition encouraged some backward journeying for Dickens's narrator into a re-imagined 'private' past that was as much generic pre-Victorian child-hood idyll as genuine autobiography.[69] It restores an ambivalent dialogue between conservative nostalgia and radical progressivism that had been facetiously handled in the 'Boz' sketches and other early journalism, such as the 'Threatening Letter' (see Chapter 4). Here, however, the nostalgia, and perhaps also the conservatism, are given a romantic, personal intensity:

> Ah! who was I to quarrel with [Dullborough] town for being changed to me, when I myself had come back, so changed, to it! All my early read-ings and early imaginations dated from this place, and I took them away so full of innocent construction and guileless belief, and I brought them back so worn and torn, so much the wiser and so much the worse![70]

Wiser but worse is not Dickens's usual gloss on returning to the present from the past, but where the lost world of youthful illusion is concerned, it is the prevailing conclusion, and is often bound up – as in the papers later titled 'Dullborough Town,' 'Travelling Abroad,' 'City of London Churches,' 'City of the Absent' and 'An Old Stage-Coaching House' – with a recogni-tion of physical decay in once-thriving areas of public life that have been superseded by modernity.[71] 'Uncommercialism,' with its critique of 'whole-sale' and impersonal theories of human nature such as utilitarianism and political economy and its recommendation of 'retail' values and face-to-face confrontation, appears to embrace both reactionary and Utopian alternatives to liberal modernity.

One recent study, indeed, sees signs in this later journalism that Dickens has abandoned his earlier celebration of the social 'improvisation' he detected amongst London's marginalized, depreciated and criminalized classes, and has begun 'to develop strategies of journalistic authority' and to organise the elements of national life 'in a controlled, reformist rhetoric.' The process requires the repression of the traveller's vagabond self, his denial of any sense of recognition that those who have wilfully excluded themselves from the benefits of the Liberal reform programme (ruffians, workhouse refractories, begging-letter writers, rag-clad vagrants, unrepentant prostitutes) might represent, linguistically or subconsciously, his own doubles.[72] The selective emphasis here on control, regulation, exclusion and repression denotes the pervasive influence of Foucauld and the psycho-biographical tendency in modern critical approaches. It has also been common for twentieth-century critics to find the articles startlingly macabre, in line with the invariable 'late Dickens = Dark Dickens' equation.[73]

Not the least interesting feature of Dickens's 'occasional journeys' as the 'Uncommercial Traveller' is the residual doubt in many cases over whether a 'real' journey is signified, and the play that is instigated between textual, mental and physical displacement. The central strategy of 'Travelling Abroad' takes the idea of the armchair explorer that Dickens had amusingly explored through the character of Mr Booley in *Household Words*, and applies it to his own persona, a fictive process which allows for a wistful retrospect of the family expedition to Genoa, and the uncanny exchange between the narrator and his own 'queer' younger self on the road to Gadshill.[74] Other essays hint at analogies between writing, reading and (time-)travelling that go well beyond the fanciful, consistent with the presentation of the Uncommercial Traveller throughout the collection as a literary representation of the author's self-image which is given public life and mobility only through travel narratives, specially adapted for periodical publication. In the case of 'Great Tasmania's Cargo,' the complexity of the reporting style is further compounded by doubts about the status of the Traveller's account. If Pangloss is invented, then why not also the Traveller's presence, and his 'interviewing' of the soldiers and medical officers? The circumstantial details in his report had all been made public in the *Times* and *Manchester Guardian* accounts of the Inquest. External evidence cannot prove one way or the other if the 'out of town' engagement Dickens refers to in the last fortnight of March took him to Liverpool or not. As well as assimilating approaches from the great eighteenth-century essayists and satirists into his journalistic practice, Dickens was not above imitating the skilful fabrications of the great eighteenth-century travel liar, Daniel Defoe.[75]

VII

'If there were only another Wills,' Thackeray is said to have exclaimed before the *Cornhill* launch, 'my fortune would be made.' From March 1868, when Wills was permanently invalided from his duties after a severe hunting accident, Dickens was to discover the extent to which his *All the Year Round* fortunes were dependent on his sub-editor, Business Manager, partner, and general 'factotum.' During his final six-month American Reading Tour (November 1867 to April 1868) when there was no possibility of exchanging packets of proofs, Dickens had reposed all his 'confidence and trust now and ever' in Wills's judgement in the corrections, proofing and make-up of the weekly numbers, commenting only in retrospect on their contents and appearance. After receiving four or five perfectly good issues, all he could suggest was that in 'making up A. Y. R.' Wills 'try to bring the matter closer down to the last page of the No.' Clearly, Wills was coping well enough with the Editor's role. Conversely, on Dickens's return from America, with Wills 'banished into Sussex for perfect rest' he found 'all the business and money details of the journal' devolve upon him, and complained of having to 'get them up, for I have never had experience of them.' Percy Fitzgerald, bringing the manuscript of *A Fatal Zero* down to Wellington Street in October 1868, was struck 'by the sort of helpless, weary air with which he sat – solitary in his office – having for a time to attend personally to all sorts of trifling details.' For help with the sub-editing, he seconded the ever-reliable Henry Morley from his UCL professorship, on a summer vacation contract until the end of October. Wills wrote to congratulate Morley on the results: 'the numbers appear to me to be better than ever they were in my time.'[76]

There are no financial records for *All the Year Round* after October 1867, so it is not possible to test Wills's self-deprecatory evaluation against the May–October profits, but what is clear from Dickens's correspondence is that in spite of the extra burden he managed to master the fine detail of the Commercial Department and to put into action longstanding plans to commence a 'New Series' of the journal from 5 December. The twentieth bi-annual volume was on the point of completion – 'the noontide volume of *All the Year Round*' as it was optimistically described, suggesting that Dickens saw his circadian cycle as 'Conductor' only half complete – and new subscribers were in danger of being put off by the length of the set to be collected. The idea was also, readers were told, to put in place 'some desirable improvements in respect of type, paper, and size of page' and bring the distinctly old-fashioned look of the journal up to date. A larger, clearer font was used for serial fiction and for the 'New Uncommercial Samples' series, and – despite Dickens's general reluctance to experiment with graphic design where his journals were concerned – a new illustrated masthead, with flowers and fruit in the four corners representing the cycle of the seasons, replaced the old, bare capitals.[77]

Thursdays were reinstated as the Chief's 'Office Day.' A shorthand clerk employed there for 18 months at around this time, claimed that Dickens dictated 'most' of his *All the Year Round* articles and short stories to him, recalling his employer as an 'insatiable cigarette smoker' who 'when dictating to me always had a cigarette in his mouth,' and who changed his shirt collar several times through the day and was always combing his hair, even during dictation.

> He used to come into his office … at about eight o'clock in the morning and begin dictating. He would walk up and down the floor several times after dictating a sentence or a paragraph, and ask me to read it … in nine cases out of ten, order me to strike out certain words and insert others. He was generally. tired out at eleven o'clock, and went down to his club in the Strand. A very singular thing was, he never dictated the closing paragraphs of his story. He always finished it himself. I used to look in the paper for it, and find that he had changed it very greatly from what he had dictated to me.[78]

Some of the account's embellishments seem rather of the 'weal cutlets and dog-fighting' variety, but not the emphasis on the care Dickens took and the effort now involved in journalistic composition. Various manuscripts of the 'New Uncommercial Samples' have been preserved (in Dickens's hand rather than in that of the 'ammanuesis'), and most show the heavy correction and interpolations typical of his later years.[79]

As Morley's temporary contract drew to a close, Dickens made two final decisions regarding the future of his journal. The first recognised that, however strongly the public had come to associate his name with the Christmas season and the mixed sentiments of generosity, celebration and regret which it inspired, there was really nothing further that he could offer them within the format of the 'Extra Christmas Number.' Chesterton was to hail Dickens as the 'great Wizard of the Christmas ghosts' whose followers 'have a strange sense that he is really inexhaustible,' but as far as devising further stage machinery for presenting Christmas stories was concerned, Dickens confessed his exhaustion.[80] From a magazine owner's viewpoint, moreover, the labour and production costs did not justify the profits. A sale of even 300 000 of the 4d. number grossed only £5000, of which he might clear 'a thousand or even fifteen hundred pounds' at most, for all his editorial work, and for supplying between twelve and 24 000 words of his own writing.[81] This compared unfavourably to the rates he could now negotiate from American magazines for the advance sheets of short stories, and the boost to regular UK profits that could be engineered through well-advertised 'simultaneous' publication of the same tales at home. During the early winter months of 1868, Dickens serialised 'A Holiday Romance' and 'George Silverman's Explanation' in *All the Year Round*, and in Ticknor & Fields's Boston periodicals, *Our Young Folks*, and *The Atlantic Monthly* – about 24 500 words in total – for which he received £2000 in addition to the increased home sales. When further compared with the profits to be made from Public Readings of works already written, the death knell for the remarkable fusion of occasional journalism and communal storytelling which the 'Extra Numbers' had represented, tolled even louder. Over the Christmas season 1868–69 he contented himself with advertising his authorship of a few of the 'New Uncommercial Samples' and delivering a 'Farewell Series' of UK readings. By 1869–70, the 'Farewell London Readings' occupied his energies entirely, and he made no further appearances on any journalistic stage.

The second decision was to place his inexperienced eldest son, Charlie, in Wills's job, as general manager and sub-editor – a move which must have reminded him at some level of his own start in journalism, through the nepotism of his Uncle Barrow, or of the way he had once gathered father, family and friends around him for the launch of the *Daily News*. Charlie began at the start of November 1868, and proved himself, his father thought, 'a very good man of business,' and by July of the following year was evincing 'considerable aptitude in sub-editing work.' The same letter described in terms of understandable envy the freshness of John Thadeus Delane, editor of the *Times* since 1841, who 'looks as if he had never seen a Printing office, and had never been out of bed after midnight.'[82] On Dickens, by contrast, twenty years of editorial work had taken their toll. Photographs show all too clearly the lines impressed by the printing office lifestyle. He was ready to hand over the reins.[83] This was formally done, with almost prescient swiftness, in the weeks before his death on 9 June 1870. In a codicil to his Will made six days before his final seizure, he signed away to Charlie all the powers and authority which he had spent a lifetime in popular journalism seeking to acquire – climbing periodical mountains and battling with 'Blast-hopes,' brigands, fools, and blackguards to carry off and defend his prize, the fairest circulation figures of them all. Into the competent but not overly-gifted hands of his son he gave 'all my share and interest in the weekly journal called *All the Year Round*.'[84] With its predecessor *Household Words*, for two decades it had offered – both in round unvarnished terms, and bound in chains of Dickensian magic – cleverly parcelled and personalized accounts of battles, sieges, fortunes, moving accidents, slavery, Cannibals, stories of escape, endurance and travellers' history, childhood recollections, pilgrimages, interspersed throughout with household and domestic affairs – and created for hundreds of thousands of Victorian periodical readers 'the story of our lives from year to year.'

9
Dickens the Journalist: Models, Modes and Media

'He was a great novelist,' G. K. Chesterton wrote in a brief introduction to Dickens's *Reprinted Pieces* from *Household Words*, 'but he was also ... a good journalist, and a good man. It is often necessary for a good journalist to write bad literature. It is sometimes the first duty of a good man to write it.' As usual, Chesterton flaunts his talent for Wildean paradox, omitting only to add 'That is all' after his climax. From the dualist perspective of aesthetically-demarcated high and popular cultures, it may have been possible to view good journalism and 'bad literature' as compatible judgements, but modern readers, accustomed to reading in the broader church of cultural studies, may want the matrix of quality, style,[1] and medium to be probed a little further. One way to consider the problem of Dickens's style is to recall the career in journalism which the last eight chapters have endeavoured to trace, and consider the many different formats of journalism and journalistic discourse which such a career imposed: starting with the periphrasis and 'unnecessary detail' of penny-a-line items in the *British Press*, verbatim transcriptions of parliamentary speech in the *Mirror of Parliament*, selective reports of the debating along with puff verses in the *True Sun*, graduating to the descriptive 're-staging' of election contests in the *Morning Chronicle*, editorial banter in *Bentley's Miscellany*, theatre reviews in the *Examiner*, leader-writing in the *Daily News* and *The Examiner*, and so forth.

Even a partial taxonomy such as this reminds us that although journalism is often constructed as monolithic, the opponent or reflection of 'other' entities like 'Literature' or 'government,' it is of course built up from a whole array of writing and governing practices, each with their distinctive rubrics, right down to the branding distinctions between different newspapers' manner of handling the same writing genre. Dickens had an extremely varied schooling in the rubrics of journalism – broader than many of his press brethren – but as earlier chapters have shown, his exceptional career was also predicated on assimilating and converting a second-hand wardrobe of imposed press styles into a range of brand-new costumes, with a distinctly personal signature. The deployment of 'Boz' as the signature to 'Street Sketches' and then 'Sketches of London' in the *Morning* and *Evening Chronicle* reserved a window in the newspaper columns for the witty play and display of reporting techniques, mixing and clashing theatrically with city stories and street slang. Within two years, 'Boz' moved from signature to title position, and had acquired the sobriquet 'inimitable' as public recognition of this unique fusion of styles. If Dickens as a young journalist becomes 'inimitable' through imitation, it is also the case, however, that Dickens's mature journalistic style was most often discussed, and criticised, in terms of its imitability, and the countless, if inferior, imitations it gave rise to.

Important stylistic studies have been made over the years of the prose non-fiction of major Augustan and Romantic journalists: Swift, Johnson, Hazlitt and Cobbett, have all been scrutinized.[2] The key studies of Dickens's language, however, have focused overwhelmingly on his fiction, and ignored the journalism, letters and speeches.[3] G. L. Brook's classic account briefly considers 'journalese' as a class or occupational dialect capable of sub-division into categories, and gives short examples from *Nicholas Nickleby* and *Great Expectations* of 'vituperative editorial,' the 'fulsome gossip paragraph,' and the satire of journalese itself.[4] This study has shown that journalese, in its multiple forms, is far more than a dialect, and that – at least until the November 1837 number of *Oliver Twist*, and arguably, long after – it is the default language of Dickens. Robert Golding, perhaps unwisely, follows Dickens's own undervaluation of *Sketches by Boz*, in a 3-page chapter considering the volume edition as 'fictional apprenticeship' rather than as an anthology of sketches, essays and reports:

> Dickens fully realised the many weaknesses and immaturity of his first book ... in which the provocatively original goes alongside the self-consciously derivative. In respect of authorial voices, there is really no homogeneous style, but rather a complex mixture made up of the then prevalent ornate journalistic mode, with its pompous circumlocutions and a kind of high-flown literary potpourri manner full of flowery phrases, terribly heavy irony and the almost inevitable mock heroic, the whole occasionally and somewhat clumsily intermingled with legal jargon evidently picked up in his office-boy days.[5]

Shorn of its vague qualifications and perjorative adverbs, however, the passage brings out well the accomplishments of 'Boz' as 'bricoleur,' and ultimately resembles the more sympathetic account of Dickens's 'multi-functional' approach to language offered by Randolph Quirk. Quirk examines the use of 'particular locutions and systems of grammar' for purposes of individuation, typification, structural organisation and experimentation, and argues that Dickens's minor writings (examples are taken from 'The

Uncommercial Traveller' and *Mrs Lirriper's Lodgings*) show him experiment-
ing 'rather more radically and to a more sustained degree' than in his
novels, with such flexible forms as free indirect style and stream-of-
consciousness.[6] H. P. Sucksmith's wide-ranging analysis of the narrative art
of Dickens's novels applies what must surely be the key concept in the
discussion of his journalistic style: rhetoric, both as a science of composition and a function directed towards producing powerful effects on readers
and/or listeners.

Exponents of rhetoric-based approaches have felt the need to act as
apologists for its re-introduction into a critical practice still inspired by a
combination of Romantic and formalist aesthetics and the anti-authoritarian,
poststructuralist philosophy of the left. Because 'persuasion is a very special
anathema of our time,' Sucksmith too voices doubts about the word 'as a
modern critical term' before cautiously beginning to use it to illuminate the
complex effects of sympathy and irony which Dickens can be seen to build
up in his work, at manuscript and proof stage, and through subsequent
revisions.[7] Orwell had of course boldly grasped the nettle which such doubts
hesitate over, announcing in his essay on Dickens that while 'all art is propaganda ... not all propaganda is art.' The two terms here take up similar oppo-
sitional roles to literature and journalism in Chesterton's formulation. Such
epigrams and paradoxes, based around unquestioned and over-narrow
categories, can possibly be negotiated by stressing the fundamental interdependence of rhetoric and Victorian journalism, in order to offer some
concluding remarks on Dickens's style, on his influences, and influence on
other writers, and to comprehend his contribution to the powerful cross-
currents of nineteenth-century press development.

I

Dickens's direct knowledge of the writings on rhetoric of Aristotle, Cicero
or Quintilian was, it may safely be said, negligible. However, barred from
the joys of a classical education though he was, he had ample opportunity
to study the fruits of one during his five years as a reporter of parliamentary
speeches, and to compare its spoken and written results with other styles of
oratory. Sir Robert Peel stressed to students in Glasgow in 1837 that classical rhetoric was still 'of immense importance to all who aspire to conspicuous stations in any department of public or learned life.'[8] Its governing
principles survived in both Houses of Parliament, and from there perme-
ated the press, and must have influenced Dickens strongly, as the similarly
unschooled Victorian journalist, G. A. Sala, stresses in his epideictic obituary of his own 'Master':

He had listened to masters in every style of rhetoric: he had followed
Henry Brougham the Demosthenes, Shiel the Cicero, O'Connell the

Mirabeau, of their age; and albeit in dialogue and in description, the eccentricity of his humour and the quaintness of his conceits sometimes marred the purity of his fabric, and betrayed him into exaggeration and into mannerism, he was, in genuine essay, in grave and deliberate statement, and in his culminating passages of invective or eulogium, a well-nigh unrivalled master of racy, pungent, idiomatic English. In nobility of diction, strength of expression, harmonious balance of praises, and unerring correctness of construction, very many of Charles Dickens's short essays rival the grandest of Dryden's prose prefaces, and surpass the most splendid dialectical flights of Macaulay.[9]

The impact of Brougham and O'Connell has already been noted. Another example of the way this form of assimilation works may be seen in Dickens's response to Edward Stanley the future Lord Derby and so-called 'Rupert of Debate,' whose long speech on the Irish Disturbances Bill Dickens had 'taken' and reproduced in its entirety in 1833, and who was a distinguished classical scholar and translator of that 'instinctive' rhetorician, Homer. On his consolidation as Conservative Prime Minister after the July 1852 General Election, Dickens mocked him as 'the honorable member for Verbosity,' in a *Household Words* leader which parodied both his written address and speech to his constituents:

Our honorable friend has issued an address of congratulation to the Electors, which is worthy of that noble constituency, and is a very pretty piece of composition. In electing him, he says, they have covered themselves with glory, and England has been true to herself (In his preliminary address he had remarked, in a poetical quotation of great rarity, that nought could make us rue, if England to herself did prove but true.)

He might be asked, he observed in a peroration of great power, what were his principles? ... His principles were written in the countenances of the lion and the unicorn; were stamped indelibly upon the royal shield which those grand animals supported ... . His principles were, Britannia and her sea-king trident! His principles were, commercial prosperity co-existently with a perfect and profound agricultural contentment: but short of this, he would never stop. ... His principles, to sum up all in a word, were, Hearths and Altars, Labor and Capital, Crown and Sceptre, Elephant and Castle.

The *Times* leader writer excerpted this passage, and marvelled at the closeness of the imitation to the original, asking 'can jest come so near earnest, and the playful irony of a political satirist so closely resemble the ... enthusiasm of a thick and thin partisan?'[10] But Dickens had long since assimilated the available forms of *elocutio*, as they had been adapted to

British political oratory, as this passage of summary from his January 1835 report of the Suffolk West nomination of a Tory candidate, suggests:

> Mr Waddington proposed Colonel Rushbrook.... Mr Philip Bennett, jun., seconded the nomination.... [H]e had no hesitation in saying his Honorable Friend was respected and loved by all who knew him....
>
> Colonel Rushbrook then presented himself.... He ... was painfully conscious of the scantiness of his pretensions, and want of experience in, a public oration.... He should be most happy to support any measure for the improvement of institutions ... but his principle was to improve, not to destroy – to ameliorate, not to annihilate, the constitution of Church and State.... He conjured [the electors] to return such men to Parliament as would stand or fall by the constitution and by their country. He conjured them, as they revered their altars and homes, to discharge their duty faithfully, zealously, and fearlessly; and to bear in mind the words of England's immortal bard –
>
> —— 'Nought shall make us rue
> If Britain to herself do prove but true.' [loud cheers][11]

The repetition of the distinctive 'conjured' (possibly Dickens's choice) as the verb describing the speaker's manner of exhortation suits the rather one-sided response Robert Garis takes to Dickensian rhetoric, that is, as a form of 'theatrical art' or paraded illusion, designed to focus attention on the narrator/writer's skills as a 'self-exhibiting master of language.'[12] Sucksmith carefully refutes the charges, but so do the examples above, and in fact, all those many passages where Dickens is not using rhetorical strategies *in propria persona* but ironically reproducing them to emphasise the emptiness of such phatic conventions, at times even to voice similar suspicions of rhetoric-as-charlatanry, to Garis's.

Opposed to the conventional purity and 'harmonious balance' in the texture of neo-classical rhetoric, as Sala's needlessly negative qualification hints, nineteenth-century critics from the Schlegel brothers onwards had distinguished a northern European rhetorical idiom, which stressed humour, asymmetry, imaginative flight, and organic, associative structures. This is not unlike Hazlitt's definition of 'Gusto,' and a way of starting to place Dickens's journalistic style might be to say that he shared with Hazlitt a dislike of neo-classical stasis and favoured the energy of a Romantic, radical style: Boythorn's rhetoric over Sir John Chester's.[13] This is only a beginning, however: as we have seen, through Harold Skimpole, Dickens worked a devastating satire on what he saw as the irresponsibility, egotism and potential inhumanity of Romantic speech and posturing. Burke, whose 'forked and playful' style Hazlitt revered, Dickens sent up in the written and spoken styles of another 'honorable member,' Mr Gregsbury, whose 'senatorial gravity' and 'tolerable command of sentences with no meaning in them' is contrasted to the plainness of Pugstyles, his combative constituent.[14] Also, in Dickens's faithful re-composition of the turns and figures of Tory oratory it is notable that populist Shakespearean rather than remote classical allusion, has totemic value. Given the extent to which Whigs, Liberals and Tories fought uncertainly over a narrow centre ground in British politics, usurping and adopting each other's terminology no less than territory in order to make their appeal to the People, it is unlikely that a clear-cut stylistic dichotomy could be established in Dickens's politically-sensitive prose, between Augustan conservatism and Romantic radicalism

The metalanguage of rhetoric can perhaps be used to go a step further. Basic structural and syncretic techniques, such as those which feature in the speeches of 'Honorable Friends' – anaphora, parison, antithesis, clichéd metonymies – naturally feature with regularity in Dickens's prose non-fiction, but tend not to be foregrounded, unless with satirical intent. Instead – to develop J. Hillis Miller's helpful classifications in articles on *Sketches by Boz* and *A Christmas Carol* – one finds the striking use of synecdoche and newly-minted metonymies, lists and parataxis, prosopopeia, facetious paronomasia and syllepsis, both hyperbole and meiosis. In terms of an appeal to tradition, the texture is thus neither strictly neoclassical nor Romantic, neither intellectual nor seeking to ground viewpoint in an essentialist aesthetic of feeling. Instead it might be designated urban (in its appreciation of juxtapositions), ingenious (in its appreciation of the infusion of the comic spirit in inanimate objects), and Gothic folkloric (in its appreciation of puns, grotesqueries, tall tales and popular traditions). Combining these preferred forms of *elocutio* with the exigencies of the different press styles noted above, may lead to a formal description of something approximating to the narrative voice of Dickens the journalist.

If the style of journalistic writings can be described in terms of their rhetorical elocution and disposition, recent theory suggests that the reading process which influences and persuades a writer/rhetor towards adopting a particular belief requires consideration as a form of rhetorical *inventio*. Invention thus comes 'to mean more than the devising of arguments to support a point of view' and includes 'constructing the point of view itself through the consumption of others' rhetoric.'[15] The working journalist, reading, consuming, writing, all in short order, might well comprehend this practical, post-industrial concept of invention better than any classical or Romantic account of inspiration. In Dickens's case, it fits the pattern of his writing career, early and late. As a shorthand writer, he was always already a consumer of others' rhetoric, even as he reshaped their elocution. Simultaneously, as a reader in the Library of the British Museum, he was entering into constructive dialogue with other persuasive writers, living and dead, whose viewpoints he swiftly adapted to his own writing agenda. The idea that a reader can be moved and convinced by the rhetoric of a text is one Dickens evidently took for granted as a journalist, because he himself as a reader, could be so affected. Not only does he actively represent himself as a responsive audience for his own writings but in writing to others of their work, his critical approach rests not on discussing the intrinsic merits of a text, but in its ability to create emotional effects and change belief in himself as reader.[16] The nearest thing to a manual of rhetoric to be found amongst Dickens's books was Mangin's *Essays on the Sources of the Pleasures Received from Literary Compositions*.[17]

The unfashionable debate over the books which Dickens read and which influenced him could be usefully revived through reconstituting reading as a form of rhetorical invention.[18] In terms of his development as a journalist, what is worth stressing here is that the writers whom Dickens cites most frequently as models and/or influences were all journalists and satirical essayists rather than authors of fiction. The citations may be perfunctory – those references to Addison's *Spectator*, Steele's *Tatler*, Swift's *Gulliver's Travels*, and Goldsmith's *Bee* or *Citizen of the World* when Dickens needed to give Forster a 'general idea of the plan' of the periodical he dreamed of founding, or to Henry Mackenzie, when Dickens wanted to explain the reciprocal affection of the 'periodical essayist' and his readers – but the debts are real, and those acknowledged seem to fall into two main groups.[19] In one, the writers persuade readers of their social and moral purpose through projecting a fanciful narrator, whose imagined interaction with the city (for example) is as important a vehicle of the author's humanitarian position as any direct arguments pursued. Indeed, Dickens does not seem to have shared the admiration of contemporaries such as Macaulay and Forster for

> the serious papers in the *Spectator*, which I think (whether they be Steele's or Addison's) are generally as indifferent as the humour of the *Spectator* is delightful.

Of the two writers, Dickens had an unfashionable preference for Steele, 'the brilliant Essayist,' who was responsible for the papers describing the clubs of parleying London eccentrics that Dickens had tried to imitate in *Master Humphrey's Clock*.[20] Dickens responds to the persona, not necessarily in a simplistic sense, but often happily associating (or feigning to do so) attributes of projection and source, as when he introduces a friend to 'the original, kind-hearted veritable Elia' of Charles Lamb's *London Magazine* essays, or affects, on being introduced to John Wilson in Edinburgh, to take offence at finding him so different from 'Christopher North,' the 'real, actual, veritable old gentleman' of Wilson's *Blackwood's* essays.[21] In both cases, the polysyllabic 'veritable' signals Dickens's awareness that he has willingly indulged the book-lover's pathetic fallacy.

In another group of references, Dickens mentions journalists and essayists whose interests – in matters such as crime and punishment, criminal psychology, dreams, emigration, child labour – coincided with but preceded his own, and whose ideas and speculations he assimilated, and liked to reiterate in his own words. Henry Fielding and Francis Bacon are cited in this way.[22] The process is also recorded by James T. Fields, the Boston publisher who, with his wife, formed such an enthusiastic private audience for Dickens in his later years:

> There were certain books of which Dickens liked to talk during his walks. Among his especial favourite were the writings of Cobbett, De Quincey, the lectures of Moral Philosophy of Sydney Smith, and Carlyle's *French Revolution.*[23]

That Dickens's reading of Carlyle led to extensive rhetorical inventions and interventions in his prose probably needs no further reiteration here.[24] Dickens's confidence in the effective rhetorical transmission of thought and knowledge between readers and writers is summed up in the epistemic equivalences urged by his request to be allowed to dedicate *Hard Times* to Carlyle: 'it contains nothing in which you do not think with me, for no man knows your books better than I.'[25] Smith, however, is a neglected influence: an author whose jokes Dickens re-told, whose journalism he quoted, and whose *Sketches of Moral Philosophy* Dickens 'always travelled with' himself, and tried to impress on others, by leaving the book on the bedside table of his guests at Gadshill. Ridiculing the position of the opponents of reform through extravagant *reductio ad absurdum* is Smith's favoured technique, faithfully reproduced by Dickens in his Preface to the Cheap Edition of *Oliver Twist*, at the climax of which his *Edinburgh Review* essay on 'Chimney Sweepers' is quoted, and Smith himself described as 'that master of wit and terror of noodles.'[26]

Cobbett and De Quincey seem an unlikely pairing. Their vast works (from which Dickens owned extensive selections) nevertheless offer heuristics to understanding crucial aspects of Dickens's journalistic endeavours: in Cobbett's case to combining extraordinarily successful and professional popular journalism, with the self-elected roles of Scourge of Parliament and the Poor Man's Friend; in De Quincey's to essaying such disparate psychologies as those of travel, suicide, dreams, and childhood trauma. But Cobbett too was an inveterate autobiographer, strewing his reports with childhood recollections as an alternative form of political aetiology. Ackroyd's insight that Dickens was 'a man of infinite nostalgia about himself' might be revised to suggest that Dickens learned from both Cobbett and De Quincey to be a man of infinite curiosity about himself.

In the scale and variety of Cobbett's projects – his histories, dictionaries, records of parliamentary debates, the *Weekly Political Register*, his tours and reports of rural inspection, his multiple addresses and pamphlets 'to the working man' – there is an urge to systematize and simplify critiques of what is wrong with 'The System' for readers, which is as urgent and ambivalent as Dickens's need to establish a process in *Household Words* for explaining the intangible Processes of modernity. A recent defence of weaknesses identified in Cobbett since Hazlitt's appraisal – his inconsistencies, litigiousness, bigotry, polarizations along class lines – has urged what might well be applied to Dickens, that in the context of the political prose of his age, such 'faults' were adroit rhetorical strategies designed for the consumption of discrete tiers of readership, of widely different degrees of sophistication. In *Sunday under Three Heads*, Dickens imitated Cobbett's urgency and the substance of his arguments as MP for Oldham, to defend the Sunday recreations of the working man. By the 1860s, Dickens arguably responded more critically but was still engaging with Cobbett's method and moods, in such essays as 'An Old Stage-Coaching House' and 'Arcadian London.' It is hard to imagine him not warming to the wholesome wrath of Cobbett's war cries, and his idiosyncratic italicising of keywords. 'At any rate,' one new assault begins, 'here is a *humbug* to be exposed; and to expose it is a *duty*.' Like Dickens's, his improvisatory rhetoric is never coldly formal. As Hazlitt noted, in an essay Dickens probably read, Cobbett's 'argument does not stop to stagnate and muddle in his brain, but passes at once to his paper. His ideas are served up like pancakes, hot and hot.'[27]

In his passionate exposition of Hazlitt's prose style, Tom Paulin hazards the 'hunch that Hazlitt's writing exercised a profound influence on Dickens, whose account of the limits of utilitarianism closely follows his,' and who also shared with him a fascination with the criminal underworld, and Leigh Hunt as a subject for portraiture.[28] It is a promising speculation. Dickens's debt to Hazlitt's essay on 'Capital Punishments' has already been noted. Both were parliamentary reporters before they became essayists, and both had a passion for books read in childhood, and the amusements of the people. Dickens worked with Hazlitt's only son on the *Morning Chronicle*, and later employed him on the *Daily News*. Moreover, he purposefully acquired over the years no fewer than twelve different collections of Hazlitt's essays, and quotes from them twice, not in his writings but – appropriately, given Hazlitt's speculations on 'the differences between writing and speaking'[29] – in his speeches. On the first occasion, it is to repeat, at a festival of the General Theatrical Fund, Hazlitt's observation about the public's affection for actors, and the 'pleasant associations' which meeting them revives. On the second, Dickens quotes from Hazlitt's 'On the Periodical Essayists,' the paper which voices his severest criticisms of Johnson's 'mechanically' balanced neo-classical style, and praises the freshness of Steele's characters: 'what old-fashioned friends they seem; and yet I am not tired of them, like so many other friends.' On both occasions,

Dickens stresses the 'fanciful associations' and personal sense of gratitude which the individual's imaginative engagement with the arts arouses; the approving quotations express those feelings in Dickens for Hazlitt, with some sensitivity. What Paulin identifies in Hazlitt's work as 'the principle of association' – 'a type of instantaneous, subconscious, mnemonic short-cutting' which substitutes meaningful 'concrete and anecdotal' images for 'abstract' reasoning when approaching complex ideas – is crucial in Dickens's journalistic writings too, as the imagery and juxtapositions of such papers as 'Lying Awake' or 'Night Walks' testify.[30]

The only other mention of Hazlitt in Dickens comes in response to Wilkie Collins's request in 1854 for ideas to help him turn their recent jaunt to Italy into some travel sketches for *Bentley's Miscellany*. Dickens's reply encapsulates his own inventiveness in matters of journalistic composition; it relates that inventiveness to a much deeper reading of European literature (particularly travel writing and the essay) than might be expected; it argues that the way in which the knowledge of the reading is transmitted, is through rhetorical speech ('say,' 'sounding'). It also demonstrates Hazlitt's associative principle in a striking way:

> Sitting reading tonight, it comes into my head to say, that if you look into Montaigne's journey into Italy (not much known now, except to readers), you will find some passages very curious for extract. They are very well translated into sounding kind of old English, in Hazlitt's translation of Montaigne.

Dickens remembers, and associates with the language of the translation, Hazlitt's own commendations of others' speech in his final collection of essays, *The Plain Speaker*. There, 'plain speaking' is a form of rhetorical sincerity, that can be achieved in different media: the 'clear, short, pithy old English sentences' of Chatham's parliamentary speeches, or the 'fine, manly and old English' quality of Holbein's portraiture.[31] Such intertextual play is a remarkable feature of Dickens's non-fictional writings, deriving from a rhetorically interpretative approach to books and their personalities. Kenneth Burke's fanciful metaphor for such communicative intervention as the 'unending conversation' ('... you enter a parlor. You come late. Others have long preceded you, and they are engaged in a heated discussion' &c.) would have appealed to Dickens – although, in a sense, 'Boz' entered the chat room well before Burke, and left a typically irreverent response to theory in 'The Parlour Orator.'[32]

II

Hunches about the dialogue Dickens maintained with several generations of journalists, essayists and sketch-writers other than Hazlitt could have proved equally revealing. Dickens's readings of Swift, Goldsmith, Thomas Hood, and even from Leigh Hunt's numerous familiar and topographical essays, were extensive and stimulating, even though he consumed their words in volume form rather than 'hot and hot' as they came off the press. In Swift's case, Dickens felt that his spirit to a certain extent lived on in the weekly journalism of Albany Fonblanque, whose caustic style provided a model for Dickens during his *Examiner* years. Through his regular reading of the periodical press and his unflagging interest in the amusements of the people, Dickens was able to find and respond to a less canonical tradition of sketching, represented by London writers, artists and hacks whom he often 'knew' in their original forms.[33] These included Pierce Egan, John Poole, John Wight, James Grant, W. T. Moncrieff, George Cruikshank and Robert Seymour, and much of their work has recently been republished – for the first time in a century and a half – in the six volumes of *Unknown London: Early Modernist Visions of the Metropolis*. The working thesis behind the collection argues that between 1815 and 1845 'a relatively small number of authors, playwrights and illustrators, working within or on the fringes of a bohemian culture' innovatively attempted 'to grasp the complex totality of the metropolis.'[34] As the *Mirror of Parliament* had tried faithfully but failed to reflect the totality of Parliament, so such writers, and the early Dickens among them, essayed to represent the city itself, through the dramatic, graphic and literary device of a series of sketches.

Drawing opportunistically on the traditions of 'rogue literature,' 18th-century criminal biography, evangelical social science and a range of demotic forms of entertainment (cartoons, street theatre, popular melodrama), such writers certainly succeeded in temporarily uniting audiences in the post-war years. Whether one can precisely argue that as a result, 'during this period ... a break with classical modes of representation took place, and the modernisation of vision was set in motion,' is debatable, however.[35] Some, but by no means all, of the tributary currents of European modernism can be sourced to Victorian and Romantic foothills. The polyvalent and increasingly critical figure of the city spectator or flâneur, traced back by Walter Benjamin to the writing of Poe and Baudelaire, is one of the best examples – but there is little of the flâneur's cosmopolitan anxiety, self-awareness and sophistication of analysis in Egan, Poole, or Wight. Their sketches have a certain predictability, whether in the rhetorical constructions (Egan's are distinctly neo-classical) or simply in returning to their own formulae: Wight following up his successful *Mornings at Bow Street* (1824) with *More Mornings at Bow Street* (1827). What seems modernist about Dickens in comparison, is his essentially serious preoccupation with pushing and criss-crossing the boundaries of his medium, with parodying old formats, with (as he told Morley) 'varying the manner of narration as much as possible,' with finding treatments for topics that involved displacement of the narrator or narrative voice rather than an assumption of authorial omniscience. A consideration of the modes – of construction, of generic patterning – of Dickens's journalism might explain this sense of difference.

In the dozen newspapers and magazines for which he worked before founding *Household Words*, Dickens had manoeuvred, often against the prevailing norms of the publication, for the freedom to adopt unconventional modes. Aside from the required press formats already noted, he had experimented with the discursive, comic sketch, the amateur inspector's report, the moral essay or story, the miscellaneous satire on topical abuses, the poetic 'squib' or song, the character-narrator's account of himself, 'travelling letters,' and articles on urgent social questions. From 1850, full editorial control of a weekly magazine gave Dickens the scope to extend this range still further, with collaborative 'process' articles, multi-authored 'Christmas Numbers,' original investigative reporting, political spoofs, vacation sketches, and familiar essays. It is natural to condemn the mode of address adopted in 'Personal' as an experiment too far, but this ought not to obscure the remarkable variety of Dickens's overall journalistic output. Many of these formats admitted into their narrative structure the possibility of being imaginatively cast as a traveller's tale, as a monologue spoken by a fictive persona, or as a dialogue between the 'traveller' and those whom the traveller encounters and interviews. *Récit de voyage* and dialogism (in a rhetorical rather than a strictly Bakhtinian sense) are key modes.

Dickens's engagement with travel writing was so intense and his versions of it so varied that some conceptual framework for discussing it seems necessary. In the second section of his seminal essay 'Le Voyage et l'écriture,' Michel Butor proclaims what he half-humorously calls the 'Elementary considerations of a Portable Iterology' – iterology being 'a new science ... strictly tied to literature, concerned with human travel.' One of its aims is to try to formulate the 'kinship between travel and writing [that] has always been (more or less) sensed.' An iterological interpretation of *The Uncommercial Traveller*, for example, offers a way of approaching what can otherwise seem a random collection of Dickens's thoughts and notes, by emphasizing the cultural relation between each of the essays and some important kinds of Victorian journey, and suggesting how the narrator, in articulating his private travels, assumes a social and interpretative function.[36]

It is important to remember, however, that Dickens is well aware that his travels are pursued, not in a primitive state of culture and over aboriginal terrain, but begin in a supposedly 'polished state of society' and in 'the heart of the world's metropolis.'[37] Travel in the modern city involves a complex and derivative iterology of signs and interpretations to which 'elementary considerations' cannot ultimately do justice. The unsystematic dialectic of Walter Benjamin in his study of 'The Paris of the Second

Empire in Baudelaire' gives powerful expression to many of the tensions sensed in the narratives of the mid-Victorian city from which so much of its social history has been constructed. The mediating principle between these oppositions is the flâneur, 'an interpreting consciousness of the network of signs in the streets;' flânerie is the habit of observation and speculation secretly cultivated by the interpreter, whose idle and noncholant air is an affectation.[38]

In the London of Queen Victoria in Dickens, just as in Baudelaire's Paris, such an interpreter tended to belong to certain atypical social groups, each of which had a carefully concealed motive for its street-walking. Cocottes, detectives carrying out surveillance, agents provocateurs, bohemian conspirateurs, social misfits, street artistes and men of letters are all linked in Benjamin by their journey to the boulevard to abandon themselves in the crowd for reasons at once professional and personal; all assume, to disguise their intentions, the pose of the flâneur, enjoying the broad pavements, gas-lighting and arcade displays. It is no coincidence that the people whom Dickens, in his guise as the 'Uncommercial Traveller,' encounters in the street, belong exclusively to these classes: the prostitute from Charles Street, whom Mr Uncommercial Traveller has arrested for using foul language as she goes 'flaunting along the streets;' the knowing Superintendent of the Liverpool Police who exposes the traps set by pimps and landlords for unwary merchant seamen on shore-leave; guilty debtors 'with a tendency to lurk and lounge;' ruffians 'skylarking' on the Waterloo-road; tramps and beggars with fictitious tales of woe, and the 'houseless poor' who loiter furtively in doorways.[39]

Dickens clearly sensed the strangely mutual understanding between such apparently opposed social groups; one of the first points established in his account in *Household Words* of an interview with the detectives of Scotland Yard is that

> in a place of public amusement, a thief knows an officer, and an officer knows a thief ... because each recognises in the other, under all disguise, an inattention to what is going on, and a purpose that is not exactly the purpose of being entertained....[40]

If Dickens himself possessed the same faculty, it is because in the street, or in places of public amusement, or in many of the public institutions which the city came increasingly to maintain, he too entertained a purpose that was not exactly the purpose intended. His consciousness of the pressing need for the modern city to be travelled and interpreted to its own inhabitants, of the marketability of the process, reveals an ulterior motive behind his journeying, which surfaces, arguably, in the impulse to adopt some kind of disguise for the narration of his professional travels: hence 'Boz,' 'Master Humphrey' and finally, 'The Uncommercial Traveller.'

The relevance to Dickens's journalism of Benjamin's notion of flânerie rests in its concentration on the ambivalent response of the artist to the experience of traversing the modern city, seeming to draw disparate elements of Dickens's life, interests and preoccupations in the 1860s together with fugitive qualities of his narrative personae, and stressing the concealed purposes inherent in his mature writing. It should be stressed, however, that just as there are pitfalls in assuming that 'Boz's 'Sketches' provide 'a paradigm of straightforward mimetic realism,' there is a danger in reading Dickens's 'travelling essays' as paradigms of straightforward travel narrative.[41] As with any recognisable literary mode, that of voyages and travels establishes its conventions, adapts, undermines, parodies and flouts them, and Dickens is quite as conscious of them in his journalism, as he is of the traditions of the British periodical essay, and conscious of their political implications.

One of the most striking conventions is that by which the journalist describes unfamiliar terrain as 'terra incognita,' indulging what, in the literature of foreign travel may involve basic imperialist assumptions (the land may be well known to its inhabitants), but which, when displaced onto domestic journeys, involves a series of complex and potentially unstable ironies to argue the political case for the priority of the Home over the Foreign Mission.[42] During the mid-Victorian period, the implications for the civilized world of the 'terra incognita' metaphor undergo a sea-change. Rather than suggesting adventure and entertainment in what is facetiously perceived as a distant land, it begins to threaten the constitution of society, dangerously unknown and dangerously close. Concomitant with developing research in the biological sciences, geology and anthropology based on a greatly-extended pre-history and on studies of uncivilized tribes then being 'discovered' in Africa and the Americas, went a growing fear that Britain's urban poor might degenerate into something reminiscent of the prehistoric or savage state. From the early 1840s onwards, Dickens took up the matter in a fashion typical of his involvement with public affairs in general: through satirical commentary in his writing, and active engagement in private life. 'The constitution will go down, sir (nautically speaking), in the degeneration of the human species in England, and its reduction into a mighty race of savages and pigmies,' Dickens's Ancient Tory gentleman had warned in 1844, parodying the experts. By 1850, his involvement with the Metropolitan Sanitary Association, the campaign for Extramural Sepulture and the newly-formed General Board of Health demonstrated the seriousness of his private concern with all aspects of public health.[43] Increasingly, in representing his urban investigations, Dickens shows partiality for language which ambivalently identifies certain groups as a race apart, as an integral feature of an over-arching trope.

This state of affairs is given a precise dramatization in a later essay, in which the narrator meets a horde of street children near Temple Bar, who fight in the mud and 'claw' with 'wolfish gripe' over a coin he has cast to one of them, until a policeman appears and discharges his constabulary duties to the limit by driving them back into the 'wooden hoardings and barriers and ruins of demolished buildings' from which they had come:

> I looked at him, and I looked about at the disorderly traces in the mud, and I thought of ... the footprints of an extinct creature, hoary ages upon ages old, that geologists have identified on the face of a cliff; and this speculation came over me: If this mud could petrify at this moment, and could lie concealed here for ten thousand years, I wonder whether the race of men then to be our successors on the earth could, from these or any marks, by the utmost force of the human intellect ... deduce such an astounding inference as the existence of a polished state of society that bore with the public savagery of neglected children in the streets of its capital city, and was proud of its power by sea and land, and never used its power to seize and save them![44]

Such language is, as Dickens concedes, that of 'speculation': impromptu reflection and conjecture, which is represented as occurring within the temporal framework of the *récit de voyage*. It is of a piece with the narrative framework, however, in the way it freely adopts ideas and phraseology from the journalism of explorers and scientists, and the spiritual language of the foreign mission, in order to plead the case for 'seizing and saving' the neglected youth of London. The phrase neatly encapsulates what is now thought of as the inherently ambivalent blend of aggression and evangelism which characterized the imperial spirit.

If Dickens offers a less divisive social vision in his journalism, then it also is effected through the travelling mode, as his narrator passes from an impressively general, powerfully metaphorical critique of society, based on ideological grounds, to focus on minutiae: factual detail, inventories and interviews, which act as a corrective to the distorting language of the Foreign Mission. In 'A Small Star in the East' (1868), the 'Uncommercial Traveller' first represents his journey to the East of London as though it were indeed to the Orient, and comments on the condition of the 'primitive' peoples he encounters:

> The borders of Ratcliffe and Stepney, Eastward of London, ... [a] squalid maze of streets, courts, and alleys of miserable houses let out in single rooms. A wilderness of dirt, rags and hunger. A mud-desert, chiefly inhabited by a tribe from whom employment has departed, or to whom it comes but fitfully and rarely. They are not skilled mechanics in any wise. They are but labourers. Dock labourers, waterside labourers, coal porters, ballast heavers, such like hewers of wood and drawers of water. But they have come into existence, and they propagate their wretched race.[45]

The implied geographical distance and the anthropological classification together seem to forbid any expression of sympathy on the narrator's part for those he writes about. Revulsion more than pity is audible in the application of 'squalid,' 'miserable,' and 'wretched' to the streets, homes and families of the region. The allusion to the hewing of wood and drawing of water of the Hivites in service of the children of Israel (Joshua 9.27) lends the labouring of London's poor a certain symbolic value, however, and as the narrator's speculations continue it becomes apparent that the distant, unsympathetic impression created by his phrasing is to be identified more with the language of party propaganda and government planning, than with his private feelings:

> Pondering in my mind the far-seeing schemes of Thisman and Thatman, and of the public blessing called Party, for staying the degeneracy, physical and moral, of many thousands (who shall say how many?) of the English race; for devising employment useful to the community for those who want but to work and live; for equalising rates, cultivating waste lands, facilitating emigration, and, above all things, saving and utilising the oncoming generations, and thereby changing ever-growing national weakness into strength: pondering in my mind, I say, these hopeful exertions, I turned down a narrow street to look into a house or two.[46]

While the Uncommercial Traveller cannot pretend to have a 'far-seeing scheme' for solving the same problems, he can at least offer an *ad hoc* alternative, which gives the reader food for thought. In 'looking into a house or two' he restores the inhabitants of the *terra incognita* to their human rights as men and women. Their clothing and style of 'dress' is described. Their possessions are described meticulously – one room boasts 'an old gallipot or two,' 'a broken bottle,' 'broken boxes for seats,' 'rags in an open cupboard' – and also what they do not possess – 'there was no crockery, or tinware, or tub, or bucket' (358). 'I could take in all these things without appearing to notice them, and could even correct my inventory,' the narrator comments, before adding several further items, each important, such as the 'old red ragged crinoline hanging on the handle of the door,' in revealing more about the lives of those who own so little. Their speech is also recorded; many of the essays contain long stretches of dialogue, conferring a high degree of mimetic realism on the account.

Dickens experiments continuously in his journalism with modes of representing speech, conversation, dialogue and monologue, both interior and 'dramatic.' The informal interview, as distinct from the conventional forms of juridical interrogation reported in the newspapers, was not itself used as a means of presenting social investigation much before 1850, when Dickens and Henry Mayhew began to popularise it. 'Boz' never puts himself forward as an interlocutor, observing and retailing dialogue only, nor was the technique used by Dickens in *The Examiner*, though it was one he had briefly sampled in the 'New York' chapter of *American Notes*. As editor of *Household Words*, however, Dickens encouraged it as a means of reinforcing the originality and independence of the first-hand research which he and his staff writers carried out. In 'On Duty with Inspector Field' and other policing articles, one of the attractions is the stylistic aplomb with which Dickens handles two sets of interview reports at once: his own interrogation of the detectives, and theirs of their criminal suspects. After a passage of traditional dialogue set out line by line with speech marks, Dickens pares the transcript down through extensive use of unmediated direct speech, and the daring use of free indirect style, in such a way as to convey information from various different observers at once, in a fashion true to their individual idiom:

> So *you* are here, too, are you, you tall, grey, soldierly-looking, grave man, standing by the fire? – Yes, Sir. Good evening, Mr Field! – Let us see. You lived a servant to a nobleman once? – Yes, Mr Field. – And what is it you do now; I forget? – Well, Mr Field, I job about as well as I can.... Mr Field's eye rolls enjoyingly, for this man is a notorious begging-letter writer....
>
> Ten, twenty, thirty – who can count them! Men, women, children, for the most past naked, heaped upon the floor like maggots in a cheese! Ho! In that dark corner yonder! Does anybody lie there? Me Sir, Irish me, a widder, with six children. And to the right there? Me Sir and the Murphy fam'ly numbering five blessed souls. And what's this now, coiling about my foot? Another Irish me, pitifully in want of shaving, whom I have awakened from sleep – and across my other foot lies his wife – and by the shoes of Inspector Field lie their three eldest.... And why is there no one on that little mat before the sullen fire? Because O'Donovan, with wife and daughter, is not come in yet from selling Lucifers![47]

The narrative subject and sense of self, with distinguishing rhetorical markers, move seamlessly between journalist, detective, and interrogatee, preventing the journalist's tendency to dehumanise what he fears ('maggots,' 'coiling about my foot') from assuming a more privileged status than the detectives' practical enjoyment of conversation with their suspects, and the latters' ingenious and vociferous responses. The absence of what Joyce would later call 'perverted commas' ensures that when Dickens does the police in different voices, some interesting and essentially modern questions are raised about who is talking, who is being quoted, and out of what context.[48]

The discipline of projecting the self-deprecating persona of the 'Uncommercial Traveller' ensures that Dickens likewise tends to grant equality of status to interlocutors presented in his interview reports, either through unmediated direct speech, or, on one occasion, by presenting the dialogue as a script, complete with stage directions. In 'Bound for the Great Salt Lake,' Dickens has been to inspect a shipload of Mormon emigrants at the start of their voyage to America, expecting to find them good copy as a target for his campaigns against different forms of religious extremism and hypocrisy. The article is constructed, however, to dramatically convey to the reader 'the rout and overthrow of all my expectations' on discovering the Mormon families to be exceedingly well-organised, cheerful, courteous and spiritually-composed. Having established that the man he is interviewing is 'wholly ignorant of my Uncommercial individuality, and consequently of my immense Uncommercial importance,' Dickens adopts the new format, as a graphic illustration of their equal conversational footing:

UNCOMMERCIAL. These are a very fine set of people you have brought together here.
MORMON AGENT. Yes, sir, they are a *very* fine set of people.
UNCOMMERCIAL. (looking about). Indeed, I think it would be difficult to find Eight hundred people together anywhere else, and find so much beauty and so much strength and capacity for work among them.
MORMON AGENT (not looking about but looking steadily at Uncommercial). I think so. We sent out about a thousand more, yes'day, from Liverpool....
UNCOMMERCIAL. Do you get many Scotch? ... Highlanders, for instance?
MORMON AGENT. No, not Highlanders ... they've no faith.
UNCOMMERCIAL (who has been burning to get at the Prophet Joe Smith, and seems to discover an opening.) Faith in –!
MORMON AGENT (far too many for Uncommercial). Well. – In anything!

A further interview with a wily Wiltshire labourer also points up humourously the 'discomfiture' of the 'Uncommercial' in his original hidden agenda, reflections on which form the conclusion to the piece that Dickens actually writes:

I went on board [the Mormons'] ship to bear testimony against them if they deserved it, as I fully believed they would; to my great astonishment, they did not deserve it; and my predispositions and tendencies must not affect me as an honest witness.[49]

Ultimately, the stratagem works brilliantly to persuade readers of the 'Uncommercial's' reliability as people's witness, and the unimpeachability of *All the Year Round's* reporting practices.

Together with the travelling tale, the handling of complex issues through the informal interview or semi-fictive dialogue between representative positions in the debate was clearly a mode of approach which Dickens felt would help 'get the publication down into the masses of readers.' So too the satirical monologues voiced by character-narrators such as the reticent inventor 'Old John' ('A Poor Man's Tale of a Patent'), the complacent provincial councillor 'Snoady' ('Lively Turtle'), or the retiring Civil Servant, Mr Topenham ('Cheap Patriotism').[50] The conversational language and paratactic construction naturally appealed to a broader readership than the hypotaxis and polysyllabic display of conventional, deliberative rhetoric. At an early stage of his leader-writing for Dickens, Henry Morley deduced that this house style was sufficiently distinct for him to use the same material in both the *Examiner* and *Household Words*. For a series of papers in the latter on the key issue of public health he told his fiancée that he had devised the persona of

> a gossipy old lady with conceits and prejudices, giving *my* views of things, characteristic and laughable, but so put as to inculcate sanitary truths. It's the same upside-down style as in the *Examiner*, but treats of different topics, and puts them in queer, crotchety points of view, so that there's not the slightest identity of plan. Writing as an old woman, there will be no polished composition wanted – only a quizzical slip-slop....

In fact, only one 2-column article of the projected series was published, and a few months later Morley reported how 'Dickens, bother him! wants the combination paper altered from a cheerful dialogue to a grave essay.'[51]

Dickens's approach to the dialogic mode was in fact less predictable than Morley imagined, and required a highly developed if unconventional form of composition, far more complex than a simple stringing together of miscellaneous details. One of many examples, but possibly the subtlest, comes in the paper Dickens wrote after his 48-hour research trip to Preston in January 1854, during the acrimonious lock-out of 20 000 factory workers striking for the restoration of a 10 per cent wage cut they had accepted during the crisis of 1847. 'On Strike' combines elements of récit de voyage and dialogism, narrated by a railway traveller (a clear prototype of the 'Uncommercial') who confesses to his brusque travelling companion that he is going to Preston 'in my unbusinesslike manner ... to look at the strike.' Their lengthy argument over the efficacy of strict Political Economy to solve the standoff, and the workers' right to form unions, terminates when the man moves to another carriage, but gives the traveller the last word in the exchange, which contains the *narratio*, or statement of position, phrased as a hypothesis:

> Now, if it be the case that some of the highest virtues of the working people still shine through them brighter than ever in their conduct of

this mistake of theirs, perhaps the fact may reasonably suggest to me – and to others besides me – that there is some little thing wanting in the relations between them and their employers, which ... political economy ... will [not] altogether supply, and which we cannot too soon or too temperately unite in trying to find out.[52]

This suggestion is rephrased in editorial mode as a powerful call for serious arbitration ('I do not suppose that such a knotted problem as this, is to be at all untangled by a morning party at the Adelphi') in the peroration of the article, but the intervening stages of proof and *argumentatio* are achieved through Dickens surrendering the narrative to a range of other voices and formats. These include the reprinting in full of the text of one of the most recent workers' placards posted on a street corner, the lyrics of songs, and 'poetical remonstrances,' militant or otherwise. The 'worst' of these bills is quoted, '[b]ut,' the narrator observes, 'on looking at this bill again, I found that it came from Bury ... and had nothing to do with Preston.' Also included are accounts of the proceedings at three different assemblies of striking workers or strike supporters, in which Dickens pays close attention both to reproducing the speech and the body language of the actors: noting, for example, that the Preston weaver in the Chair has 'a particularly composed manner, a quiet voice, and a persuasive action of his right arm.' The most detailed account is prefaced with the comment that '[i]f the Assembly, in respect of quietness and order were put in comparison with the House of Commons, the Right Honorable the Speaker himself would decide for Preston' – a characteristic slap which also manages to pat both chairmen on the back.

Newspapers hostile to the strike action, such as the *Preston Chronicle* and the *Manchester Guardian* emphasised in their reports the 'dissension and discussion' of the proceedings on the day Dickens attended, respectively describing the strike leader Mortimer Grimshaw (Dickens's 'Gruffshaw') as a speaker who 'poured out a volley in invective' and 'poured out the vials of his wrath upon the committee and the operatives' of a neighbouring district.[53] Rather than describe an indiscriminate 'pouring' Dickens represents Gruffshaw (easily identifiable here as the model for Slackbridge in *Hard Times*) in a flow of speech which is held up and eventually dammed by more persuasive actions and voices. Again, no speech marks are used, to let the languages speak for themselves:

Then, in hot blood, up starts Gruffshaw (professional speaker) who is somehow responsible for the offending bill. O my friends but explanation is required here! O my friends but it is fit and right that you should have the dark ways of the real traducers and apostates, the real un-English stabbers, laid bare before you. My friends when this dark conspiracy first began – But here the persuasive right hand of the chairman falls gently on

Gruffshaw's shoulder. Gruffshaw stops in full boil. My friends, these are hard words of my friend Gruffshaw and this is not the business – No more it is, and once again, sir, I the delegate who said I would look after you, do move that you proceed to business! Preston has not the strong relish for personal altercation that Westminster hath. Motion seconded and carried, business passed to, Gruffshaw dumb.[54]

'Hath' makes Westminster sound archaic and, like Gruffshaw and Slackbridge's hollow-looking 'O's (an effect directed at readers not listeners), its rhetoric untrustworthy. The Chairman's closely-rendered northern brogue and the efficient, democratic procedures of the 'business' he facilitates together provide assurances of the trustworthiness of the Weavers' Assembly, which figures as one of the few positive models for a public meeting in Dickens's writings.

The processes at work in the creation of 'On Strike' – from first-hand research, through Dickens's creative engagement with, and careful representation of, the rhetoric of commentators and participants, to the elaborate composition and disposition of material – make it appear, by any standards, a thoroughly accomplished piece of reportage which also functions as a think-piece. It is surprising to recall that it was the tenor of articles like this which prompted Martineau's outburst in 1855 against Dickens as an editorial equivalent of Slackbridge: a mere 'humanity-monger' guilty of 'wilful one-sidedness' and acts of journalistic 'unfairness and untruth.'

III

Dickens's forty-year career in the media displays a remarkable combination of writing and business skills, special interests, and journalistic innovations, yet at the same time, its tensions and compromises are indicative of many of the major issues confronting the press in the period from 1830 to 1870. Its foundation was the magic art of shorthand, which took Dickens on a fast-track from common copyist to star parliamentary and election reporter during the tremendous upheavals of the Whig reform ministry. En route, he acquired essential sub-editing skills and unparalleled experience of organising extraordinary expresses, giving him an insight into the function of speed, information, and distribution as key variables in the rapidly-expanding multiverse of Victorian print, and its consumption. Side by side with routine journalistic work, he made space for his own brand of arch commentary on the amusing parallels and unjust discontinuities between the life of the people, the press, and the politicians: a kind of meta-journalism. Such was the interdisciplinarity of his approach, that even when he moved into the more genteel world of literary journalism, as editor of a supposedly non-partisan monthly, and then of his own weekly miscellany, he could turn serial fiction and short-story-writing to account, to continue satirical attacks on what he saw as the extremism of the philosophical radicals, the hardline Tories, and the seditious elements amongst the otherwise peaceful working-class movements of the day.

With the return of the Tories to power in the years from 1841 to 1846, Dickens identified himself fully with the radical wing of the Liberal opposition, and his visit to the United States in 1842 was undertaken on the strength of a political ideal to see the 'Republic of my imagination,' as well as to inspect the southern slave states, and to talk about international copyright. His experience of the 'freedoms' taken not just by an unregulated press, but by what he felt to be a wholly unprincipled sector of the American media, marked him. He voiced outrage too at the licence which anonymity seemed to encourage in the British press (despite using its protection himself, or that of false signatures, to attack a range of Tory and legal bigwigs in the *Morning Chronicle* and the *Examiner*). Dickens may have tried to convince himself that his principled radicalism and egalitarianism had not been affected, but his attitudes to press accountability and the upholding of standards in public life, had certainly changed. On his return from America, he anticipated no compromise of independence in proposing to establish an evening paper 'on the right side,' with finance and intelligence deriving from Whig grandees such as Melbourne and Lansdowne: dignity would be lent to the profession of journalism by such a connection. Dickens's opening leader for the *Daily News* as launch-editor stressed the dignity which a 'body of gentleman' engaged in producing a newspaper ought to uphold, rather than 'perverting' their great power by 'venting ungenerous spleen.' Despite the Jacobin streak in his earlier writings, Dickens's quest to raise the status of journalism through the *Daily News* was largely a question of gentrifying it.

The status of the *Daily News* as a flagship for the Anti-Corn Law League, the politics of free trade and – given its backers and advertisers – for the principle of untrammelled capitalist expansion, involved Dickens therefore in several ironies. Yet his instincts were broadly with the League as the means by which the greatest popular movement of the day could be influenced and educated, and by which the reactionary 'agricultural interest' could be put in its place. The editorship of its newspaper allowed him to address the politicians, employers and employed on the subjects he felt most strongly about, and to sketch the horizons of a liberal Europe free from tyranny. Certain aspects of the job he managed well. His setting up of the newsgathering service and recruitment of staff, were sound and far-sighted (if costly), his 'morale' for editorship strong: but the demands of daily leader-writing were physically and intellectually uncongenial. His lack of control over the commercial department annoyed him; editorial intrusions from the printers infuriated him; the shadowy influence of backers and railway interests unnerved him; the prospect of long hours of editorial work for a small share of unguaranteed profits depressed him. Worst of all, his position vis-à-vis his readers was obscured. Despite the fact that editing a popular journal was, of all the forms of public platform which Dickens contemplated, the one he most desired, he backed away from the industry, and 'printing house' connections, with something approaching distaste.

This was partly a ploy to re-establish himself as a serial novelist. It did not prevent him from undertaking a voluntary period of training as a weekly leader-writer for *The Examiner*. With a Liberal government led by Lord John Russell (the only Prime Minister whom Dickens actively admired while in office) in power until 1852, Dickens concentrated on specific cases of legal or administrative malpractice, and, for the only concentrated period in his career, on literary and theatrical reviewing. He continued to develop his own ideas of how a multi-authored journal could achieve maximum power and hold over the imagination of its readers. Since the mid-1840s, what Dickens viewed as the gutter press had been encroaching, in their cheap weekly publications, on the adjacent fields of fanciful satirical journalism and politically-aware sentimental fiction which 'Boz' had marked out as his own, and *Household Words* and *All the Year Round* were the eventual response.

Over the next twenty years Dickens established himself as, arguably, the most potent individual force – taking into consideration editors, publishers, and proprietors of periodicals and the different weights of influence of mass, bourgeois and elite readership – in weekly journalism. It was with some sense of this that Lord Northcliffe of the *Daily Mail*, at a later period of media development, hailed Dickens as 'the greatest magazine editor either of his own, or any other, age.'[55] In the last decade of his life, he expanded very successfully into publishing and 'new media,' through public readings of his own work – an innovative self-publishing technique that did away with the need for any form of printing at all. When the Readings took him back to New York in 1868, an ill and exhausted Dickens re-entered the lion's den of the American press, which proved so formative of his own attitudes to the media in the years since 1842. Somewhat to his surprise, he emerged not only unmauled, but lionized. Perhaps the zenith of his public career was the dinner held at Delmonico's in his honour by the Press Club of New York, which broke its own privacy rule, and invited over 200 representatives from over thirty newspapers from different states. Dickens's speech recalled the part which the 'wholesome training of severe newspaper work' had played in his own success, and expressed the 'loyal sympathy' he felt for the 'brotherhood' of the press, 'which, in spirit, I have never quitted.' The response from the editor and essayist George W. Curtis on behalf of the weekly press, celebrated Dickens, in all his writings, as a journalist 'commissioned by nature to see human life and the infinite play of human character, and write reports upon them.' The speech was, Dickens later said, 'the best he had ever heard.' With all due allowance for the occasion, there was substantial truth in Curtis's eulogy:

> The members of the Weekly Press ... pursue literature as a profession, and I know not where we could study the fidelity, the industry, the conscience, the care, and the enthusiasm which are essential to success ... more fitly than in the editor of *All the Year Round*. ... It is impossible to determine the limits of individual agency, but there is no doubt that among the most vigorous forces in the elevation of the character of the Weekly Press have been *Household Words* and *All the Year Round*: and since the beginning of the publication of *Household Words*, the periodical literature of England has been born again.[56]

IV

From 1850 until his death Dickens enjoyed full editorial freedom, and from 1859, complete managerial freedom, of his journals, which he shared to a limited extent with his sub-editor. The enjoyment of full freedom and the exercise of complete control are different, however. Given the extent to which he deferred to the knowledge of specialist contributors, or those whose writing he admired, and the extent of his own unavoidable absences from editorial duty, Dickens could not impose his views wholesale on everything published in the journals he 'conducted' but rather sought to give readers the impression of an individually retailed product. The give-and-take and 'furnace-like conditions' involved in the creation of composite articles, multi-authored narratives and serial fiction, meant that in some important respects the journals enjoyed 'the atmosphere of what we might call a writing workshop.'[57] Dickens had earlier associated the press with metaphors of locomotion and powerful machinery, but his Wellington Street experiences encouraged him to think in terms of a more Arts and Crafts analogy: the blacksmith, his anvil, and the sparks from the forge.

As an editor, Dickens was ultimately accountable to no-one other than his readers. Their tastes and abilities, and what they would 'relish,' he predicted with such confidence that it is ultimately hard to say whether he reflected their pre-existing requirements, or through such forcible projection, created them. In writing for *All the Year Round*, Dickens told his old Gallery colleague, Thomas Beard, to

> fancy throughout that you are doing your utmost to tell some man something in the pleasantest and most intelligent way that is natural to you – and that he is on the whole a pleasant and intelligent fellow too, though rather afraid of being bored.[58]

Dickens had many female readers too, who, although sometimes patron-
ised and addressed in parenthesis, were for the most part actively introduced to as broad a range of social and cultural activities as the male, much
as Esther Summerson is inevitably exposed to the 'true' condition of
England by the progress of *Bleak House*. While the journal was undoubtedly
sexist and patriarchal in many of its assumptions, and occasionally coy, it
did not – at least – enforce a limited vision on the responsibilities and interests which it imagined for its different classes and genders of reader.[59]

Such lack of accountability could infuriate other commentators – particularly if, like Martineau or James Fitzjames Stephen, they had a stake in the
prevailing dogma of political economy or the political establishment – but
it allowed Dickens to innovate. Stylistically, *Household Words* established a
new and immediately recognizable brand of journalism, which, its critics
realized, was providing a new paradigm for media discussion. 'We say
discussed,' an enthusiastic *Examiner* reviewer wrote of one collection of
articles from the journal,

> because when facts are so wisely selected and ingeniously put that they
> inevitably become for every intelligent hearer starting points of valuable
> trains of thought, argument and discussion may go on without
> semblance of didactic reasoning. ... Of much that it tells there would
> probably have been no adequate record but for the system established
> from the outset in the management of *Household Words*.[60]

Among other things the system involved the training of younger journalists, which Dickens undertook partly through employing Morley, R. H.
Horne, Wilkie Collins, and Andrew Halliday as staff writers based at the
office, and partly through sending these and other promising contributors
– Sala, Grenville Murray, Fitzgerald, Thornbury, Hollingshead, Yates – out
on the road to look for copy, in the same way that the daily newspapers
had traditionally sent out 'our own reporter,' and engaged foreign correspondents. He revised their work with particular care.[61] The results were
series of fresh, original but often (so the reviews complained) flippant, self-
aggrandizing and impertinent magazine sketches. Although in writing
under his own name, Dickens himself avoided anything approaching the
'personal' in terms of attacks on others, his familiar essays could be very
personal in terms of divulging private history. His 'young men' followed,
developed, and exaggerated his habits, and as recent research has argued
that they – Yates, Sala and Grenville Murray in particular – should be
credited as architects of the 'New Journalism' of the 1880s, there seems
every reason to suggest that Dickens was the Old Master of the new
school.[62] In the area only of typography and graphic design were Dickens's
journals conservative and unadventurous – but there was a limit to what
could be purchased for two pence.

In the debate raging over anonymous versus signed publication, Dickens occupied an equivocal position, to judge by his private letters.[63] He complains of vicious writers sheltering under the protection of anonymity or the editorial 'We' but promotes the concept of anonymity as a form of solidarity when soliciting contributions for his own journal. In terms of his own practice, however, Dickens seems to have viewed anonymity and signature on the one hand as simple options of house style, and on the other as stages in a writer's quest for an audience, and to be regarded much as an actor would regard their billing. He himself had acquired such celebrity by 1850 that it would have been overkill to sign articles in his own journals, which announced 'conducted by Charles Dickens' on every spread. With the development by 1860 of a market for *All the Year Round* in America, where there was more of a tradition for signature, he began signing his own papers, and persuaded his authors of serial fiction to do the same. 'It is so very important to us,' he told a doubtful Bulwer Lytton, '... to have a name – THE name.'[64]

As the most conspicuously successful journalist and literary name of his generation, it was natural that Dickens should be invited to throw his weight behind the long-running campaign to repeal the so-called 'Taxes on Knowledge.' The three taxes – excise duty on paper, a tax on advertisements, and a 'stamp' duty on newspapers which allowed them to be sent free by post – had been imposed on the press and its readers as a triple whammy since 1794. At their height, in 1815, the British government had charged 3s. 6d. per advertisement, 4d. per copy of a newspaper, and 3d. per pound weight of printing paper, and had naturally been accused by its radical critics of holding back the forces of education, progress and universal knowledge. But after amended legislation in 1833 and 1836 (which Dickens had been in Parliament to report), the three rates stood, in 1850, at 1s. 6d. per advert, 1d. per copy, and $1\frac{1}{2}$ d. per pound.[65] Even so, Charles Knight argued vociferously that the paper duty was preventing the quality cheap press, with its high-end costs, from competing with the 'pillagers of copyright books, the translators of vile French novels, the manufacturers of brutal fictions.' On his *Penny Cyclopaedia*, a flagship publication of Brougham's 'Society for the Diffusion of Useful Knowledge,' Knight had already paid £32 000 in duty since 1843, and, he claimed, could no longer afford to reprint. When he wrote in February 1850 – the month before *Household Words* took up cudgels against the blackguard literature – to present Dickens with a copy of his pamphlet *The Struggles of a Book against Excessive Taxation* and sound out his views, one might have imagined a wholly enthusiastic response. Instead, the response was heavily qualified, indicative of Dickens's relationship overall with the repealers, in what was undoubtedly the major media debate of the mid-Victorian era.[66]

The tax on paper was excessive, unjust, and unwise, Dickens agreed: but with the living conditions of the 'great mass of the people' still in need of much reform he could not 'find the heart to press for justice in this respect, before the Window duty is removed.' Without light, the people could not read or enjoy good health, a worse ill than printers and publishers had to bear, 'and the things first done in this wise must bear on mere physical existence.' *Household Words* thus gave pride of place to sanitary reform, although in his own contributions, Dickens in fact struck a blow for the repeal of paper duty some months before confronting the evils of the Window Tax.[67] Of the three, it was the tax which affected him most as a journal editor and, later, publisher, so in January 1851 he went with Knight, Robert Chambers, and a large deputation of press luminaries to Downing Street to put his case. He repeated his belief that the Window Tax was a far worse evil, but told the Chancellor, Sir Charles Wood, that he hoped both would be repealed as the Government hardly knew what the tax really cost 'in the way of immorality and degradation' because of its encouragement of cheap and 'pernicious publications.'[68]

Looking into the figures, Dickens later concluded that repeal would 'make a very large difference to … such a journal as *Household Words*' – but not sufficient to lower the cover price. But in putting 'the difference into my pocket,' he might, he thought, improve the quality of the journal a little.[69] The eventual repeal of the paper duty in October 1861 (finally agreed, after a bizarre constitutional crisis, as part of a general financial measure[70]) brought savings in production costs which, Dickens informed readers, would consequently allow him to afford the best-known authors of the day:

> The repeal of the Duty on Paper will enable us greatly to improve the quality of the material on which *All the Year Round* is printed, and there-fore to enhance the mechanical clearness and legibility of these pages. Of the Literature which we have a new encouragement to devote them, it becomes us to say no more than that we believe it would have been simply impossible, when paper was taxed, to make the present announcement … that the next number of this Journal will contain … a new romance by Sir Edward Bulwer Lytton, … [to] be succeeded by a new serial story by Mr Wilkie Collins.[71]

So good were the prospects for the industry, indeed, that Charlie Dickens, with help from Miss Coutts, was set up in the re-vitalized paper-making business, from August 1861.[72]

As *All the Year Round* carried no paid advertisements, Dickens had little reason either to rejoice or celebrate when the tax, the least lucrative to the Treasury of the three, was abolished in 1853. The stamp duty, however, was a different affair, and Dickens came to object to the purposes and effects of the three taxes being 'unfairly' and 'unnecessarily confounded.'[73] In his opening leader for the *Daily News*, he had argued – rather against the ethos of the paper – that the newspaper stamp 'is not like the stamp on Universal Medicine-Bottles, which licenses anything, however false and monstrous' – figuring it, in other words, as a badge of honour rather than a sign of trade repression. Writing in 1850 to Thomas Milner-Gibson, the Manchester MP dedicated to tabling full repeal legislation, Dickens refused to sign a petition against the stamp, articulated his feeling

> that the tax increases [newspapers'] respectability – that they have a fair return for it in postal arrangements – and that if it were taken off we might be deluged with a flood of piratical, ignorant, and blackguard papers, something like that black deluge of Printer's Ink which blights America.[74]

There are at least two personal traumas bound up with Dickens's response here – the American press attacks of 1842, and the old fear of blacking – but his attitude to the tax is clear: it is a form of justifiable regulation through fiscal policy. Exactly this kind of muted support comes through in Wills's heavily statistical article 'The Appetite for News' (1 June 1850) based on the 1849 Stamp returns, which charts slow but steady increases since 1821 in newspaper consumption and national literacy levels.[75]

At that point, Dickens could contemplate the pros and cons of the tax as a spectator, but he was soon to find himself caught up in the debate as an unwilling protagonist. Since its launch in April 1850, the *Household Narrative of Current Events* had been issued, like all monthlies, unstamped. But as it clearly contained news and as it was a relatively respectable and unthreatening exemplar of its class of publication, it was selected for prosecution in the Court of the Exchequer a few months after its first appearance. Dickens and his partners were accordingly notified of an order forbidding its publication: 'The vilest and most *intolerable* oppression!' as Forster exclaimed.[76] The *Household Words* partners ignored the ban, and waited. A year later, after prolonged litigation, Dickens fretted that no judgement had yet been given, although the trial 'attracted much attention,' and was being eagerly watched by the press and by the recently-reformed Association for Promoting the Repeal of all Taxes on Knowledge, which regarded it as an important test case – particularly as the Association (modelled on the Anti-Corn Law League, and drawing from the same power base) had succeeded in packing with its supporters the House of Commons Select Committee on Newspaper Stamps, which was taking evidence throughout 1851. By late November, with the Attorney General and Solicitor General protesting that the *Narrative* should be stamped, the Court of Exchequer judges were still divided three against one in favour of Bradbury & Evans, and judgment was finally delivered on 1 December. The judges found that since it was issued less than once every 26 days, the *Household Narrative* was a chronicle or pamphlet rather than a newspaper.

In light of 'Dickens's triumph,' the Association's doughty Secretary, Collet Dobson Collet, immediately established one of a number of copycat monthly sheets, *The Stoke-upon-Trent Monthly Narrative of Current Events, and Potteries' Advertiser* specifically to challenge the courts. 'The repeated prosecution of these sheets,' Henry Fox Bourne records, 'caused so much irritation that the authorities soon saw it would be prudent to give way.' During the sustained parliamentary agitation of 1852, the Dickens case was cited in the Commons as a key example of the law's arbitrariness and state of confusion with respect to the levying of the Taxes on Knowledge, and although a bill proposing that all monthly publications be exempt from tax floundered on the change of ministry in December 1852, it contributed to the eventual abolition in August 1853 of both the Advertisement Tax, and the Stamp Duty for monthly publications.[77]

The triumph was ironic, given Dickens's increasing support for the stamp – a 'fair tax enough,' as he observed to Macready in January 1852, 'very little in the way of individuals, not embarrassing to the public in its mode of being levied, and requiring ... the American kind of newspaper projectors' to think twice before setting up in business. Moreover, the poor man, from whose perspective Dickens tried to consider the case, was mistaken if he thought that repeal would allow several new newspapers to spring up to offer competition to the *Times*: 'not knowing the immense resources and gradually perfective machinery necessary to the production of such a journal.'[78] Dickens recalled the almost ruinous outlay and on-costs of the steam presses Bradbury and Evans had bought in for the *Daily News*, and touches here on a key factor in the changing economic structure of the nineteenth-century media.

James Curran, challenger of the central thesis of Whig press history (that press progress and the broadening of political liberties went hand in hand) has argued that in fact, even as the 'taxes on knowledge' were being abolished, 'market forces succeeded where legal repression had failed, in conscripting the press to the social order.' A sinister gloss is put on the activities and rhetoric of the repealers, who are seen as the bourgeois and patrician instruments of 'political indoctrination' and 'social control.' Against the 'ugly face of reform' are set the positive values of the 'committed radical' (unstamped) press, whose leaders are sympathetically portrayed as 'activists' rather than commercialists and ideologues.[79] In one sense, Dickens's insight that from the working man's viewpoint, the abolition of the stamp was irrelevant in face of the increasing capital investment needed for a projector to break into the mass market, exactly confirms the contours of Curran's explanation for the defeat of the free press. His 'shadow' concept of newspaper influence also had its sinister side.

Yet there is something about the characterization of the actors in Curran's version of nineteenth-century press drama that doesn't seem to fit the performance in it of Dickens and his 'brethren of the press.' Doubtless he, Knight, Chambers and the other 21 journalists and publishers who called on the Chancellor in 1851 were interested in a form of 'social control' through their publications, and were paternalistic in their attitudes to the working man. But their interest in such issues as education and public health were palpably genuine, and at least as 'committed' as that of the unstamped press, albeit less militant, and most were untiring activists of one kind or another. Their periodicals and businesses were still by-and-large small family concerns, and significantly predated the conglomeration and commercialization of the late Victorian 'massocratic' press.[80] In these respects, it is difficult to construe their journals – Knight's *Penny Magazine*, Chambers's *Edinburgh Journal* or Dickens's *Household Words*, for example – as representing a tendency to 'political indoctrination' of any worse kind than the values championed by the radical press which Curran celebrates. Press industrialization may have led to 'a progressive transfer of ownership and control of the popular press from the working class to wealthy business-men,' but if Dickens's weekly journals and their immediate rivals can be considered examples of the popular press, there was an important transitional stage during which the dominant force in print media was exerted by a number of hard-working radical editors and publishers who *themselves* became (if they were lucky) wealthy businessmen.[81] At the point of repeal of the 'Taxes on Knowledge,' in other words, the members of both the radical, unstamped and the Liberal, stamped press were still equally valuable participants in the bourgeois public sphere. Like the historical dating of the emergence of European modernism, the degeneration from an active, participatory form of liberal market capitalism to the politically-demotivating consumerism of state-sponsored capitalism (to put the debate in Habermassian terms) cannot be indefinitely pushed back into the nineteenth-century.[82] Even if the 1850s and 60s saw the beginning of the decline, Dickens's ambivalent relationship with the campaign for the Repeal of the Taxes on Knowledge, his uncertainties concerning it, mark out his independence from any institutionalizing political or media agenda.

10

Special Correspondence: Reading Dickens's Journalism

'I am of the streets, and streety' proclaimed Sala, in one of his reports from St. Petersburg for *Household Words*. Dickens himself was streety, if not streetier, but as Bagehot sensed (and Butor would agree), there is a connection between streets and newspapers: and Dickens was a man of newspapers, and newspapery – even when he played at travelling, acting, or being an Author. His account, as David Copperfield, of the discovery of his calling ('nature and accident … made me an author, I pursued my vocation with confidence') is bald and unconvincing in ratio to its lack of corroborative details. The proposal, the streets, the notes and memoranda, the blue ink and manuscript paper, the galley proofs, consultation, revision and correction, columns of newsprint, onto the news-stand, bookstall or shelf, and out into the streets again: these were the ancillary movements of the Dickens creative process and product, periodically repeated and renewed. Everything discussed in this study, apart from *American Notes*, passed through it. There is, and always has been, something faintly anomalous about the critic poring over *Pickwick Papers* or *Bleak House* in a handsomely-bound hardback, and trying to assess Dickens in that lumpish form without that vital dramatic unity of time which his original periodical readers instinctively appreciated, because he accompanied them as an observant outside-passenger on their journey forward through the nineteenth century. Perhaps Dickens's claim to artistic excellence lay most in his spectacular straddling, like a literary Ducrow, of two distinct art forms simultaneously: the novel as weekly or monthly periodical, and as monolithic opus. In the latter silent form, the later novels have stayed still long enough for critics to take their full measure. It has been hard to do the same for Dickens's journalism.

The preservation of journalism provokes a debate similar to that over the Elgin marbles: on the one hand, to collect journalism in volume form is to rescue it from its perishable, ephemeral publishing medium – on the other, to appreciate it fully, one would wish to restore it to, and approach it in, the context for which it was designed. The four weighty volumes of

Michael Slater's *Uniform Edition of Dickens' Journalism* have rescued, preserved, and canonised the majority of his newspaper and magazine writings, and now a critic has written a heavy book about them, in which Dickens's development and methods are examined, his themes, preoccupations and influences discussed, his major tropes identified, and his career in journalism mapped out. Although I have attempted to restore Dickens's journalism to, and approach it in, its original context, using authentic materials (extracts from his writings, and writing about his writings), my contextual rendering of the periodical press of the day has been largely an artificial reconstruction, sketchy, incomplete, and doubtless inaccurate. It would have been preferable, for example, to quote more spontaneous responses to the writing from Dickens's contemporaries, from magazine readers and reviewers experiencing his journalism in the right place and at the right moment, rather than to indulge in critical speculations 150 years after the fact. It would have been matching like with like. But because most of the journalism was published anonymously, and given the convention of Victorian reviewers only noticing volumes, there was possibly not much more (written) critical debate than has been documented above.

Dickens's newspapery and streety affinities offer an alternative. The four volumes of the Dent edition, published two years apart in 1994, 1996, 1998 and 2000, formed a sort of periodical in themselves, and received such remarkably broad and detailed press coverage – over sixty substantial reviews, many of them a half or full broadsheet page – that Dickens the journalist returned to his own medium. In that form, he has enjoyed a public reception more positive than ever he did as a novelist in his own lifetime, perhaps than he did on that memorable night at Delmonico's, with assorted writers[1] hailing his work as 'stunning,' 'superb,' 'searing,' 'savage,' 'scintillating,' 'prodigious,' 'full of surprises,' 'as brilliant as anything in the novels,' 'as dazzling as any of his fiction,' his 'finest prose,' 'outstanding' &c. The last of four reviews in the (modern) *Spectator* signs off on a note of wondrous envy, and the grand assertion that there 'has never been a greater novelist than Dickens, and it seems entirely unfair that he should so unarguably, so effortlessly, have acquired the mantle of the greatest journalist along the way.'[2] The superlatives are questionable, as is the idea that Dickens's striving for editorial and journalistic perfection was effortless, but the recognition of the parity of genres is essentially accurate and long overdue. Just as in the mid-1830s, through the widespread excerpting of 'Boz's' magazine and newspaper sketches, Dickens received sufficient exposure for *Pickwick* to take off, so for about six years his journalism came before readers and reviewers in nearly the right medium and temporal framework to create a reputation.

Nearly, but not quite right – the difference are instructive. As we have seen, Dickens wrote his leaders with the balance of a whole number of

Household Words in mind, adapting them to his sense of the national mood and of variety within the journal: to read several in succession in a collected volume of his essays, severed from their magazine context, has a distorting effect. Thus Alethea Hayter finds 'A Child's Dream of a Star' 'a pretty enough allegory,' another leader 'ponderously sarcastic,' and comments:

> Such journalism tickles the palate when it is first published in a newspaper, but it is apt to taste rancid or stodgy when served up again as part of a complete meal. One can think of columnists and sketch-writers today of whom this remains true, though it does not detract from the force, often salutary, of the original impact ... . His constant use of what he called the 'emphatic, homely English phrase of humbug' to damn as hypocritical any institution, custom or group of people which he did not personally relish sometimes tastes to the reader like an over-salted ragout, savoury but rather corrosive.[3]

This acknowledges the effect of the change in form of consumption, but assumes – in line with the usual hierarchy of 'literary' forms – that volume form represents the better, balanced diet, whereas of course it is the magazine or newspaper. This was the selling-point of the Victorian idea of a miscellany. Satire itself (Latin, satura/ae, a dish filled with different kinds of fruit) presupposed a medley, a farrago of themes or targets to suit a varied palate.

Another difference: despite the similarity of publishing medium, newspaper reviews of journalism 150 years old will also, and with Dickens in particular, be burdened with all the changes in the author's reputation in the intervening years. In the twentieth century, outside academia, Dickens's reputation has morphed through adaptation and transposition into other media – film, radio, television, theatre, newspaper gossip surrounding Dickensian biography and the Ternan affair – until latterly, the term Dickensian itself has taken on a life (or rather multiple lives) of its own, as a polyvalent term for describing different facets of modernity's engagement with the nineteenth century. Adjectivally, it can equally qualify run-down dwellings, weather in towns, injustice, escapism, hypocrisy, sentiment, jollity, excess, or tradition, and in most cases, intensify these as well. The Dickensian can 'accommodate a variety of viewpoints,' a historian of the Victorian legacy notes, 'the cheerful, gloomy, sinister and satirical all co-exist, though never in any pattern than can be easily predicted.'[4]

The delayed reviews of Dickens's journalism are shot through with such apparent contradictions, and bear witness to a century and a half's imposition of multiple profiles on the palimpsest of his public image (the beginning of which process Dickens complained bitterly even during his lifetime[5]). Hayter's appreciative summing-up transfers to the journalism the perceived multifariousness of the writer:

> After all the carping, what wonderful journalistic work Dickens pro-duced in the ... years covered by this volume; what marvels of close argument and true concern for misery, what lively descriptions, mimicry, telling absurdities of anecdote and illustration, inexhaustible invention of fantastic turns of speech, and sheer good fun.[6]

Various interesting forms of polarization occur, however, as reviewers strive to make sense of complexities which have been preserved, but compounded further, by compilation.

One common thread is the urge to try to 'fix' Dickens's politics in contemporary terms. The Dent edition (1994–2000) bridged the end of a Tory era of power and the beginning of a long-awaited reform ministry, with which, by the end of its first term, the press had become disillusioned. The opportunities for topical parallel with Britain 1830–35 and beyond, were too good to miss, hence the strapline to *The Independent*'s review of December 1996: 'Who would get the Great Inimitable's vote in a 1997 General Election? John Sutherland thinks New Labour has it.'[7] But writing of the same volume of journalism, Alan Massie notes in the *Daily Telegraph* that Dickens's attitudes to crime and criminals came in part from 'an awareness of the savagery within himself' which 'prompted the outbursts of harshness on a scale which makes the present Home Secretary [the Tory Michael Howard] appear a bleeding-heart liberal.' Not content with out-Howarding Howard, Dickens (so *Scotland on Sunday*'s review of the 1998 Dent volume observes) presciently voices Old Labour's critique of the New: 'well before talk of the Nanny State, we find [Dickens's version of] govern-ment treating the public as "a Great Baby, to be coaxed and chucked under the chin at elections ... and stood in the corner on Sundays, and taken out to stare at the Queen's coach on holidays ..."'[8] Dickens's satire on the parish authorities' reluctance to disclose official documents in 'The Election for Beadle' meanwhile, was greeted by Paul Foot with the comment 'Messrs Rifkind, Clarke, and Lilley could hardly improve on that.'[9]

Of course, no current schema or label neatly contains Dickens's politics, and this is as much the result of inconsistencies which the sheer range of the portfolio Dickens assumed as a political and social commentator brought upon him, as of the inadequacies of the sliding-scale paradigm of Left, Centre, and Right to cope with the reversals and transformations of the last century and a half. Nor is using the descriptors available to nineteenth-century commentators much more helpful. In 1832, for example, Benthamite politicians were radicals, and came from the (self-) educated middle, or patrician classes, although they interested themselves, statistically if nothing else, in the working classes and labouring poor. But we have come to associate radicalism generally with subversion and subversion with socialism, ergo (incorrectly) to assume radical and left-wing to be equivalent: whereas modern (Thatcherite) right-wing policies and 19th-century radical (free market) politics are much closer akin. Hence John Gross in the *Sunday Telegraph* has to note how Dickens's 'radicalism, sharp and very funny when it goes into attack, is diffuse when it comes to suggesting remedies, but certainly stops well short of advocating revolution.' As almost every chapter of this study has shown, Dickens's journalistic brand of radicalism was so particular and specialised in many ways, that the term in itself becomes misleading unless further distinguished: was it philosophical-radicalism, working-class-radicalism, sentimental-radicalism? In his journalism Dickens continuously made his opposition clear to what he saw as the dangerous extremes in the first two permutations, but if one is left with the last (Bagehot's perjorative coinage), the irrational modern dislike of the term 'sentimental' prevents it from placing a useful emphasis on the synthesis of thought and emotion which Dickens brought to his journalistic positions. 'Humanitarian-radicalism' might come closer to a label, given the essential humanism of Dickens's interpretation of Christianity, and the close-range Wordsworthian focus he brings to his reporting: writing accounts of encounters rather than trying to square the incomplete circle of his own theoretical positions in light of each new event.

Not surprisingly, perceptive reviewers move on from the process of trying to post Dickens into a set of political pigeonholes that seem to have been designed by Escher, and look for explanations of the dynamic tensions in his journalism in his own fictional creations, or in psychoanalytic terms. John Mortimer in *The Spectator* reiterates the now familiar twentieth-century 'uncanny' recognition of Dickens in Scrooge as well as his nephew, to explain why Dickens is so harsh on offenders in 'Pet Prisoners' and 'The Begging-Letter Writer.'[10] John Carey in the *Sunday Times* admires the 'freewheeling tone' of the 'Uncommercial Traveller' pieces, but constructs his valuable review on the premise that

> the articles in this volume are written by two people, both called Charles Dickens. The first is an eminent Victorian, battling for social justice and slum-clearance, and thunderous in his denunciation of vice and crime. The other Dickens, shadowing the first, is a grotesque fantasist with a demonic sense of humour. The eminent Victorian tirelessly inspects hospitals for the working classes, schools for the working classes, self-supporting cooking depots for the working classes, and applauds their cleanliness, their brisk and cheerful attendants, and the forest of hands that shoots into the air in response to every question in mental arithmetic.

The shadow Dickens tags along on these outings, but the things he notices are less dignified. He is facetious about the dim-wittedness of the paupers, about the comic charade that has to be gone through to persuade the illiterate ones to try to write their names, about the way the elderly female inmates of the Wapping Workhouse constantly seem to be munching 'like a sort of poor old cows.'[11]

The division between ego and alter-ego, pompous inspector and subversive doppelgänger, is an illuminating one: as though Dickens were constantly accompanied in his walks by the Dickens he might have been, 'a little robber or a little vagabond,' as he bitterly recalled to Forster, 'for any care that was taken' of him in the Blacking factory days. The division is also reminiscent of Dickens and his 'shadow' concept of media influence: the observer accompanied by the creative artist, already noting and devising the fanciful manner of narration which will mark out his work from the prosaic 'graphic' methods of the peep-show reporter. In the journal which specialises in reviewing nineteenth-century journalism, *Victorian Periodicals Review*, Lillian Nayder offers a telling reminder that the 'other' Dickens is a writer who, in articles like 'the Noble Savage' and 'Sucking Pigs,' is capable of 'disturb[ing] modern readers':

> While very little is gained by simply labelling Dickens a racist or a misogynist, we need to recognize 'the other Dickens' for what he is, and consider how those *Household Words* articles we are likely to find offensive can be used to reveal the *function* of Dickens's troubling views: his use of racism or sexism to unify Englishmen, for instance, and to quell working-class resentment.[12]

Like most dualisms, however, the Dickens/'other Dickens' account of his journalism cries out for synthesis. Later in his review, for example, Carey suggests that as a result of his too-obvious pride in 'England's military triumphs' – detected in the article called 'Chatham Dockyard' – a '20th-century Dickens would be unthinkable.' This is justified on the basis that the Eminent Victorian was a man of long-gone imperial times – but this is to ignore the enduring appeal of shadow-Dickens, who is there too in 'Chatham Dockyard,' the boy who loved to hang around harbours and pick up tall stories from the yard (like the macabre tale of 'Chips,' re-told in 'Nurse's Stories'). In a review of an earlier Dent volume, Carey offers an alternative explanation, which argues that Dickens's journalism still seems remarkably relevant in a modern context, despite its occasional harshness:

> We think we know better. But the interest of this splendidly-edited volume, containing much that will be new even to devotees of our greatest English novelist, lies not just in its historical vividness, its range and its writing (better than anyone else's that will be published this

Christmas), but in its persistent engagement with social problems that we are still – or again – having to face.[13]

Appreciation of this strange permanence or sense of repetition runs through many of the press reviews. 'The book is rich in treasures,' *The Scotsman* writes of Volume 3, 'Dickens sounds off in it about all the things dearest to his heart' (government incompetence, parliamentary sleaze, homelessness), but 'since none of these social ills have been exactly cured 150 years later, his voice might yet be heeded.'[14]

My badly-xeroxed copy of the above review makes the last word look like 'needed' – a reminder, if any were required, of why the Dent edition's rescuing of Dickens's journalism from bad Library microfilm and photo-copies of crumbling newspapers and journals was so important. But, in the tone of these reviews of Dickens's journalism, there is indeed an underlying sense that his views – whether we agree with them or not – are needed, to help us make sense, or to understand the nonsense, of our milieu. Such a sense, as I hope this study has shown, has more to do with the manner of delivery of Dickens's opinions, than their substance, though that too, in so far as it captures our own mood swings, remains relevant. From the outset Dickens the journalist established a way of engaging with, talking about and around, probing, exposing, praising, condemning, frequently laughing at, aspects of modern living that was very new in its day, but which is still recognisably 'our' way of exchanging views about the world.

There is then, a special relevance to reading Dickens's journalism, a special relationship or correspondence that obtains where his journalism is concerned perhaps more than any other writer's. This is not to make a judgment of literary quality, still less of individual greatness. Neither kinds of judgment indeed are required (nor indeed are fully appropriate for the medium) in order to make the claim – now that we have become the posterity which Bagehot anticipated – that complete with his inconsisten-cies, and all the kaleidoscope of gem-like flaws and virtues which this study has attempted to illuminate in motion, Dickens the journalist describes our world like the special correspondent – for modernity.

Notes

Introduction

1. Carlton's *Charles Dickens, Shorthand Writer* deals only with his apprentice days, Chittick's invaluable *Dickens and the 1830s* does not follow his journalistic career beyond *Bentley's*; Stone (*Uncollected*), Lohrli and Oppenlander's introductions offer focused surveys of CD's methods as editor of *HW* or *AYR* exclusively; in terms of general articles, Kent and Matz offer affable jog-trots over the territory, while Adam Roberts is more incisive but brief; Carlton's dozen or so short papers in the *Dickensian* are a mine of well-researched information, to which I am much indebted.
2. *D1* ix.
3. See Bibliography.
4. De Vries and Grillo.
5. *D4* 436–46.
6. *Charles Dickens* 80.
7. See Pykett (discussing interdisciplinarity, poststructuralism and Barthes' views on 'Text') and Beetham, 'Towards a Theory of the Periodical as a Publishing Genre' in Brake et al., eds, *Investigating* 9–16, 19–32.
8. See Hartley 33–34 ('Journalism is *the* sense-making practice of modernity' *et seq.*); Campbell 'Journalistic Discourses and Constructions of Modern Knowledge' in Brake et al., eds, *Nineteenth-Century Media* 40–53; Campbell, 'On Perceptions of Journalism,' in Campbell ed., *Journalism, Literature and Modernity*.
9. Williams 69–76.
10. 'Charles Dickens,' *National Review* 7 (October 1858), 458–86, repr. Hollington, ed. *Critical Assessments* 1.171.
11. *HW*, 1 August 1857; *D3* 413–9.

Chapter 1

1. Paul Johnson 986, Wiener, *Unstamped* cited in Schlicke, ed. 409; stamp duty was reduced to 1d. per copy in 1836 (see chap. 9 below).
2. See Cook 5–6 for details of the dinner given to Barnes by Lyndhurst as informal ratification of the conditions Barnes had imposed on the Tories on their unexpected return to office, in return for his paper's support.
3. In 1833, the Commons sat for 142 days, or 1270 hours; 8 years before, in 1826, it sat for a mere 64 days, or 457 hours (statistics from Sir Robert Inglis's statement to the House at the close of the 1833 session, *MP* 1833 4.4044.)
4. See Chittick, *1830s* chap. 1 and 'Parliamentary Reporting' 151–6.
5. Jerdan 1.88; see also Hall 1.112; Robson 12–13&n quotes a reporters' petition to the Lords of May 1849, summarizing the 6 main qualifications required for the post.
6. For parliamentary reporting, the status of journalists and the legislative agenda in the 1830s see Chittick as above, Aspinall 'Reporting' & 'Social,' Graham Mott, chap. 3.

7. Hall 1:111, repeated 2.155.
8. 2 January 1826, 4b; 24 June 1826, 4c; 18 October 1826, 3c; 25 September 1825, 4e.
9. Est. 1804 by the book trade; see Aspinall, *Politics* 217, 227&n.
10. Carlton dates and identifies 7 items, all signed 'Z', in 'John Dickens;' a further 5 articles concerning the St Patrick's Marine Insurance Company, 3 anonymous and two signed 'Z' also appeared, as follows: 'Z,' 'Irish Joint Stock Companies,' 8 Sept 1826, 3a; [anon.,] 'St Patrick's Insurance Company,' 15 September 1826, 3c; [anon.,] 'Marine Insurance Companies,' 7 Oct 1826, 4a; [anon.] (dated 'Dublin, October 20'), 'St Patrick's Assurance Company,' 23 Oct 1826, 3d; 'Z,' 'St Patrick's Assurance Company,' 24 Oct 1826, 4c.
11. Hall 1.111, Kitton, *Pen and Pencil* 2.132 (To George Lear).
12. Kent seems mistaken to assert that 'the elder Dickens never was a parliamentary reporter at all. He knew absolutely nothing of shorthand' (362).
13. 'Gurney, Thomas (1705–1770),' *DNB*.
14. 'To the Author,' 10, 11 (14th ed., 1817).
15. Chap. 38; my italics.
16. Gurney, xv, xix, 'His Majesty's First Speech to both Houses of Parliament' 9.
17. *The Times*, 4 March 1820, 2d; see Langton 40; Carlton, 'John Dickens' 5.
18. Trevelyan 192, 191.
19. See Carlton, 'Two Tennysons' 173–7 for details of Tennyson's later employment of CD, via Barrow, to help organise election polling in Lambeth (Dec 1832).
20. Collier, Part 2 12.
21. Marcus discusses the models in Brake et al., eds, *Investigating*.
22. *MP* 1832 1. iii; Aspinall, 'Reporting' 227–32; Robson 1–6.
23. Robson 10–14, Kent 366.
24. Crowe 35.
25. See G. D. Squibb's detailed history, *Doctors' Commons* (Oxford, Clarendon Press, 1977).
26. *D*1 89; *PP* chaps 10, 55; *MHC* 'The Clock,' chap. 4.
27. *DC* chap. 33; *P*4 245; *P*1 423.
28. No. 15 Buckingham Street, the Adelphi, near the Strand, which CD shared with James E. Roney, a lawyer and reporter; see Carlton, 'A Companion' 8.
29. Carlton, *Shorthand* 47–48.
30. Langton 100–1; Elwin 1.249–50; Lyndhurst was three times Lord Chancellor; CD is most likely to have reported his speeches during the first of these terms (1827–30).
31. Guildhall Library, London, MS 20778.
32. *D*1 91–92; see Carlton, *Shorthand Writer* 61–6 for a point-for-point comparison.
33. *D*1 196; the trial of Bishop, Williams and May for the murder of Carlo Ferrari, 'the Italian boy,' took place on 2 December 1831; the proceedings were recorded in shorthand and published; Dickens illustrator F. W. Pailthorpe stated to Dexter that the report was by CD, 'and that he had this information from an authoritative source;' MS note to Dex 306 (1), f. 1.
34. Grant, *Newspaper* 1.296–7.
35. Grant, *Random* 2.
36. For CD's satirical account of the bureaucratic stupidities which led to the fire, see *Speeches* 205 (the new House of Commons was not completed until 1852, nor the works overall until 1860).
37. Kent 363; *Life* I.iv (CD's own phrase).
38. Elwin 1.249; see also Bevis, 'Temporizing' 179; *P*6 68; *P*5 127.

39. Note-taking story told first in McCarthy 1.176 but repeated in various later versions explored by Carlton, 'O'Connell'; CD's comment on the variations in the speech, repr. in Fields (Mrs) 177; but see *P4* 194 for a negative opinion.
40. *P4* 605&n (August 1846).
41. See Fields (Mrs) 174–6; also chap. 9 below.
42. *Life* I.iv; *P8* 131; Speeches 347.
43. Shelton Mackenzie, *Life* 46; Grant, *Newspaper Press* 1: 296.
44. *P1*, 10 &n., 33 &n.; see Carlton, 'An Echo' &c.
45. The Bishop of St Asaph, one of various authorities cited by Barrow (see Preface, *MP* 1833.1, iv & 1064); in evidence to the Select Committee on Parliamentary Reporting, Gladstone asserted that Barrow's *MP* 'is the primary record' of its day 'and not Hansard's Debates, because of the great fullness which Barrow aimed at and obtained' ('Report from the Select Committee' &c., 28 June 1878, *Parliamentary Papers*, 1878, XVII).
46. E.g. T. C. Hansard's claim that *MP* 'had its origin in a greedy but miscalculating desire for commercial profit' (*Hansard* XXV [1834] iii); for the trend, see Robson 13–14; Knight Hunt 280–83; Silvester xxii.
47. Carlton, 'Literary Mentor' 59.
48. Harle 51b, Graham Mott 37.
49. Shelton Mackenzie 47, [Taverner] 26.
50. Kent 362–3; Harle 51b; Grant, *Metropolis* 2.108.
51. *Life* I.iv; 'magnificent mansion' is no irony: Grant recalls that the *True Sun's* offices 'were fitted up in a style of splendour which little accorded with the ultra Democratic principles which the paper advocated' (*Newspaper* 2.341).
52. *P1* 6&fn. [date uncertain].
53. Trevelyan, 237–39; Cannon 204–63.
54. Grant, *Newspaper* 2.341.
55. CD did not meet Blanchard formally until late summer 1838; see *P1* 291, 300n., Vivian 328–30, Slater, *Jerrold* 102.
56. On 14 April 1832, 20 of the paper's 24 columns were devoted to the debates; the *Sheffield Iris* noted that a full report of a Lords debate which finished at 7 p.m. had reached Sheffield (160 miles) 'in the incredibly short space of about twelve hours' (*True Sun*, 18 April 1832, 2c).
57. 22 June 1832, 3e (extracts from stanzas 2 & 3 of 4).
58. 12–3.
59. See Carlton, 'Blacking Warehouse' for a detailed account of the rivalry during the 1820s between Robert Warren's Blacking business and his brother Jonathan's (for which CD worked).
60. *Life* I.ii; *OCS* chap. 28.
61. 'Jessie, The Flower O'Dumblane' by Robert Tannahill (1774–1810), the Weaver Poet of Paisley; first published in the *Scots Magazine* (March 1808); for the lyrics (on which 'The Turtle Dove' is clearly modelled), see Item 75 in Tannahill's *Poems and Songs*.
62. *True Sun*, 13 March 1832, 1a (verses 2 & 5 omitted). The other nine advertisements are as follows: 'The Wager,' 19 March, 1a; 'Warren's Address to his Northern Friends/Air, "Scots Wha hae," ' 26 March 1b; 'Juvenile Discernment,' 2 April 1b; 'The Cat and the Boot,' 10 April, 1a; 'Corunna,' 16 April, 1a; 'The Farmer's Yard Dog,' 23 April, 1a; 'Ballad. Air – "Cottage in the Wood," ' 30 April 1a; 'The Persian's Mistake,' 7 May, 1b; ' "Soft Fell the Dew." A Parody,' 14 May, 1b. The series is repeated, not in identical order, from 21 May, until well after CD is thought to have left the paper.

63. See Slater, *Women* 49–55; Haywood passim.
64. 'Peter Pindar' [John Wolcot, 1738–1819] published, amongst much comic and satirical anti-establishment verse, the critical *Lyric Odes to the Royal Academicians* (1782–5) which CD imitates; CD owned his *Poetical Works* in an ed. of 1788–9 (*S*).
65. Partington 200 et seq.
66. *Bell's Life in London*, 27 September 1835, repr. *D*1 70–5; see also *PP* 10 (July 1836) in which Sam Weller is introduced, preparing Jingle's boots 'with a polish which would have struck envy to the soul of the amiable Mr. Warren (for they used Day & Martin at the White Hart).'
67. O'Connell, *Correspondence* 1.375; Grant records that O'Connell donated £1000 towards the *True Sun*'s costs (*Newspaper Press* 2.342).
68. *Thunderer in the Making* 496–7.
69. Fox's leaders (c. 1835–37) 'raised the circulation ... to fifteen thousand copies' (Fox, *DNB*).
70. *P*1 30 &n.; the recess of 1831 lasted 222 days, and averaged 144 days a year in the 1830s.
71. Circulation c. 600, price 2/6; CD recalled his delight at seeing the story published in the Preface to Cheap Edition of *PP* (September 1847).

Chapter 2

1. *To* Mrs Winter, 10 Feb 1855, *P*7 534; Slater, *Dickens and Women* 49 et seq.
2. See Asquith.
3. Webb 95–96.
4. Collier 2.12, 15.
5. Kent 367; for a biography of Parkes, the father of Bessie R. Parkes, see Buckley.
6. Unpublished letter of 6 June 1834; extract from Sotheby's *Catalogue*, 17 December 1981, lot 208.
7. *P*1 196.
8. *P*4 77.
9. Kitton, *Pen and Pencil* 1.133–5.
10. Slater, ed., *D*2 xii.
11. Carlton, 'Dramatic Critic' passim; *P*1 61–75 &nn.
12. Compare the account of CD's emerging 'voice' in Hayter 18a.
13. Pope-Hennessy 39.
14. See headnote to *D*2 Item 2.
15. *D*2 4.
16. Ackroyd 159.
17. Kent 371.
18. Revised text repr. in *D*1 138–41.
19. 'Street Sketches. – No. V. "Brokers" and Marine Store Shops,' 15 December 1834, 6b.
20. See the indispensable Butt & Tillotson 35–61; ditto Schlicke's 'Revisions' passim; Schlicke's forthcoming Clarendon ed. of *SB*, collating the newspaper texts with later eds, will be a landmark in its publishing history.
21. Black published translations of literary and scientific works by Schlegel, Humboldt, Buch, Berzelius and Bohte; his friendship with James Mill is detailed in Mill, chap. 4; Austin (1793–1867) was J. S. Mill's 'Liebes Mutterlein,' and a close friend until his marriage to Harriet Taylor (Hayek 89).
22. See Fonblanque, *England* 3.125 for the motive.

23. See Andrews 2.77–79 for the role of *The Times*, Brock 315–9 for the significance of the Tamworth manifesto.
24. Carlton, 'Story' 69; *D2* 11, 13.
25. The *Times'* secession described by Rintoul, *Spectator*, 3 January 1835; Black's response in *DNB*; see Buckley 124–5 for increased circulation of *MC* throughout reading of the Municipal Corporations Bill in Autumn 1835.
26. J. S. Mill, 12 December 1864 (Elliot 14–5); CD spoke affectionately of 'never-forgotten compliments by the late Mr Black, coming in the broadest of Scotch from the broadest of hearts' (*Speeches* 347) and 'Dear old Black! My first hearty out-and-out appreciator' (*Life* I.iv).
27. *Speeches* 347.
28. CD's health was much undermined by the stresses of political reporting; letters from this period shows him prone to colds, exhaustion, and the torturing 'spasm in my side' he had complained of since childhood; see *P1* 65, 69, 71, 86, 119, 140.
29. Fields (Mrs James) 174.
30. See *D2* Items 3, 6, 7 & 8; *EC*, ed. George Hogarth, CD's future father-in-law, a lawyer and respected music critic; see *P1* 54–55 &nn. for CD's 'claim to *some* additional remuneration … beyond my ordinary salary as a reporter' for a series of articles for the paper.
31. See Maxwell, 'Two *Chronicles*,' &c. 27–8.
32. *Life* I.iv.
33. *MC*, 2 May 1835, 3a.
34. Slater, ed., *D2* xii.
35. *P1* 59 &n.
36. *MC*, 2 May 1835, 3a.
37. Silvester xxii; CD's 'Parliamentary Sketch' (see next) and Grant's *Random Recollections* were both published in 1836.
38. *EC*, 7 Mar 1835 & 11 April 1835, later combined & revised as 'A Parliamentary Sketch' for *SB* (2nd Series, 1836); see *D1* 151–61.
39. See Bevis, 'Temporizing' 175–6 et seq. for a finely developed argument concerning CD's parliamentary satire.
40. *EC*, 28 February–20 August 1835; repr. *MC*, 20 April–26 December 1835.
41. Buckley, 'The Municipal Reform Act' 116–33.
42. *Parliamentary Accounts and Papers*, XXXI (1833), 319. Cited in Buckley 117.
43. *EC*, 14 July 1835; rev. ed. repr. *D1* 20–6.
44. See *D2* 26; *P1* 701.
45. *P1* 106.
46. *D2* 28 (CD was told that he need not 'remain here for the Declaration of the Poll on Monday;' *P1* 109); 'Northamptonshire Election … The Declaration,' *MC*, 21 December 1835, 3f.
47. Aspinall, *Politics* 239–41; Andrews, 2.90–95; Fox Bourne 8.
48. *P1* 220. Buckley details Parkes's frustration with Black (a 'dolt') 143–6, but the anon. *Tait's* article of 1834 compares Black to Socrates and Parkes to a self-seeking 'babbler;' Andrews concludes more neutrally that it was hard for any editor, so long as *MC* remained the semi-official organ of a Whig party in disarray, to offer sound policy (94–95).
49. [Rintoul, R. S], *The Spectator*, London, 3 January 1835.
50. *P1* 122–3 &n.
51. Taverner 37.
52. Strictly, the second part of the tale, N.S. 18 (August 1834) 177–92.

53. See cancelled intro. to 'Scotland-Yard' (*MC*, 4 October 1836) repr. De Vries 169; 'The First of May' passim (*D1* 168–75); or revised ending of 'The Last Cab Driver, and the First Omnibus Cad' (*D1* 150).

54. *P2* 275 &n.

55. CD was on the staff of *MP* during June–August 1834 when the new Poor Law bill was being debated; House's view that CD knew little of Bentham's theories (38) is persuasively countered by Murphy chap. 1 passim, Schlicke ('Bumble' 152), and Stokes's marathon footnote (724–5n.).

56. See Pope 49–60 passim.

57. CD's reporting duties on 18 May cannot be established, but he was in London and 'on call' for *MC*; in *Sunday Under Three Heads*, he describes not only the content but the mood of the Commons debate as a first-hand observer (*D1* 486); opening sentence refers specifically to defeat of the bill 'on the 18th of May in the present year' – hence Edgar Johnson's assertion that the pamphlet was begun shortly after the successful first reading of the Bill on 21 April, and 'was still in press' at the time of its defeat in May, seems unfounded ('Bluenose Legislator' 451, 457, repeated Johnson, *Tragedy* 1.144, 146).

58. *MC*, 19 May, 3c.

59. Repr. Marriott, ed., *Unknown London*, vol. 6.

60. Butt & Tillotson 45–46.

61. Marriott, *Unknown* 6.248; *D1* 491.

62. *D1* 485–92.

63. Beaumont (S. Northumberland; 1792–1848) claimed if the bill got to Committee he'd move an amendment for it to be called 'A Bill for the promotion of cant and humbug' (*MP* [1833] 2.1094).

64. *D1* 477.

65. CD sent a copy to Macrone on 30 June (*P1* 154); excerpts from notices in *The Weekly Despatch*, 3 July; *The Brighton Guardian*, 6 July; and *The Bath Herald*, 9 July 1836; all cited in D[exter] 272–74.

66. *P1* 127.

67. As Patten 64 notes 'Dickens was addicted at this time to legal-sounding double phrases,' but the phrase accurately describes the narrative gambit adopted in *PP* and various of his *Miscellany* contributions, viz. that the written words are edited by 'Boz' from another's writings – the kind of work CD was to undertake in adapting T. E. Wilks's MS of the *Memoirs of Joseph Grimaldi* in 1837.

68. Emphasized in Pope 50; Ackroyd 114, 136–38.

Chapter 3

1. Bevis, 'Temporizing' 181–3.

2. *MC* 23 June 1836, 2–5 (26½ cols); as with 'Bardell against Pickwick,' the report presents a progression of reporting styles, interchanging descriptive, verbatim, and synoptic representation of the proceedings.

3. Critics cited in Bevis 'Temporizing' 181n.; Gash 147–52.

4. From the cancelled conclusion to what became 'Our Parish. Chapter I' ('Sketches of London, No. 4. The Parish' &c., *EC* 28 February 1835).

5. 14: 242 (Pickwick's Whiggery is traceable through the parallels between his 'Corresponding Society' and Brougham's chairmanship of the 'Society for the Diffusion of Useful Knowledge'; see Patten, 'Portraits'); *P1* 161.

6. Chesterton, 'The Pickwick Papers,' *Last* chap. 4; Bevis, 'Temporizing' passim.

7. To be given priority over any 'other literary production;' *P*1 649.
8. *P*1 149 &n.
9. *D*1 xix; *P*1 197, 190.
10. E.g. [James Fitzjames Stephen], 'Mr Dickens as a Politician' *Saturday Review*, 3 January 1857.
11. *Hansard*, 2nd series, vol. 21, 1643–70, cited in Paul Johnson 989.
12. See Hemstedt, 'Inventing.'
13. *Wellesley* 3.5; Harvey 15.
14. *P*1 682.
15. *BM* 1 (January 1837) iv.
16. ibid. 2, 6.
17. No. 480, January 7 1837, 4c.
18. *Wellesley* 3.7.
19. MS British Museum Dex. 306 (2); of the 'Gazette's 8 pages, pp. 1–4 consist of text by CD; see *Dickensian* 26 (1930) 54–56.
20. 'The Pantomime of Life' repr. *D*1 504.
21. Ibid. 505–6.
22. *BM* 1 (January 1837) 49–63.
23. Bowen 89.
24. *BM* 1 (January 1837) 63.
25. *BM* I.105, 115; *P*1 227.
26. At the instigation of proprietor John Walter, *The Times* became one of the Act's 'most formidable and consistent critics;' Rose 79 &f.
27. Barham, *Life and Letters*, 2 vols (1870), 2.24; *P*1 231; Tillotson, intro. to *OT*, footnotes the comment in *MC*, 27 September 1837, that 'Boz has produced so strong an impression ... that in Chelsea ... people have gone about lecturing for the purpose of counteracting the effect of his writings' (xvi); press support for the measure was stronger in the manufacturing North; see Read, *Press and People* 145.
28. Ackroyd 218; Paroissien 5; Patten, 'Serial Author' 141.
29. *P*1 308.
30. *BM* 2 (November 1837) 437–8; see Tillotson ed., *OT* 105–6 &n.
31. Hook's editorial in *John Bull* for 7 September 1835 did not mince its words: 'Amongst the extensive humbugs which so eminently distinguish this very extraordinarily enlightened age, none, perhaps, is more glaring than the meeting of what is called the British Association for the Advancement of Science' (284b et seq.).
32. See Chaudhry for examples: 'the object of Dickens's satire is not just pseudo-science, but social science' of Benthamite inspiration (105).
33. *P*1 339.
34. From the 2nd of 2 letters drafted by Barham to Bentley, as go-between during transfer of the editorship to Ainsworth (*P*1 502n.).
35. *BM* 5 (March 1839) 219; repr. *D*1 552.
36. *1830s* 113, 112.
37. *P*1 207.
38. Patten 77; a fair circulation compared to established rivals such as *Fraser's* which had given its own as 8700 after a year (3 [March 1831] 260), or *Blackwood's* 8000 (Altick 392–3).
39. Chittick, *1830s* 113.
40. *D*1 554; 'Bentley is the real editor. The veto rests entirely with him. I am more restricted than Dickens,' quoted in *Wellesley* 3.11 &n.
41. *BM* 5 (March 1839) 219; repr. *D*1 554.

42. See Chittick, 'Miscellany' 158.
43. Variously, Andrews, 'Introducing;' Chittick, 'Miscellany,' and Mundhenk.
44. *P1* 563–5.
45. *Life* II.vi; *P2* 469; see Patten 106–09 for discussion.
46. *P2* 46, 70 &n; according to Waugh the fall in sales from No. 1 to 2 was 'alarming,' and from 2 to 3 'disastrous' (48); Patten suggests a slower decline from c. 70 000 weekly to c. 50 000 between April and May, and to c. 30 000 by August; even this was unprecedented for a weekly literary magazine.
47. Bowen 143–151.
48. Andrews, 'Introducing' 71; Stewart 45.
49. *P1* 189; Mundhenk 647; Andrews 74; Mudford xx; Bowen 149.
50. 3 February 1839; see *D2* 39–40.
51. *MHC* No. 4, 25 April 1840; later incorporated as *OCS*, chap. 1.
52. Forerunners include Steele's 'Bickerstaffe,' Johnson's 'Idler,' De Quincey's 'Opium-Eater,' Lamb's 'Elia,' Irving's 'Geoffrey Crayon;' followers most notably Poe's 'Man of the Crowd' (December 1840) but also the lawyer Utterson in Stevenson's *Jekyll and Hide* (1886).
53. 6 February 1841, 134–36ff.
54. Compare ll. 203–6 of Wordsworth's Ode 'There was a time' (1807) or the passage in *Confessions of An English Opium-Eater* (1822) where, speaking of his young female companion, a prostitute, De Quincey writes 'But the truth is, that at no time of my life have I been a person to hold myself polluted by the touch or approach of any creature that wore a human shape .... (ed. Hayter, 49–50).
55. Lytton led the way with *Asmodeus at Large* (1833); in the 1840s, CD refers to Asmodeus in *OCS* 33, *AN* 6, *MC* 15 and *DS* 47, and had recently acquired a copy of *Le Diable Boiteux*, ed. Jules Janin (Paris, 1840; *S*); on the trope, see Arac 17–23, 111–13 and Hollington, *Grotesque* 155–56, 167–8.
56. See *UT* essays 'City of London Churches' and 'City of the Absent' (*D4*), and 'All Night on the Monument,' a paper CD commissioned from Hollingshead (*HW* 17 [30 January 1858] 145–58).

Chapter 4

1. Cited *P3* 289n.
2. 23 June 1840, repr. *P2*, 86–9 &nn.
3. *P2* 90–1 &nn.; CD presents himself as a 'plain' and 'practical' (i.e. manly) man; decision to adopt the pseudonym probably from 'a wish to keep Easthope in the dark – this being his first contribution to the paper since his haughty withdrawal from it in 1836' (86n.).
4. See *P2* 301; Gash describes the Reading electorate as 'deeply divided,' eventually returning the 2 Conservative candidates with a majority of 335 votes amongst an electorate of 1945 voters (294–9).
5. *P2* 354n.
6. *P3* 481.
7. 517c; title followed by the suggested tune, 'A Cobbler there was' – in fact a popular 18th-century song text, sung to the tune of 'Derry Down,' an undated English melody included in Chappell's *Popular Music Of The Olden Time* (1855); see *DS* 2.
8. For Victoria's antipathy to Peel ('such a cold, odd man') see Benson & Esher 1.158–9.

9. John Frost, Zephaniah Williams, and William Jones, Chartist leaders sentenced to death (commuted to transportation) in 1840 after the 4 Nov. 1839 rising in Newport, Monmouthshire.

10. Arthur Thistlewood (1770–1820), Cato Street conspirator executed for plot against Castlereagh and other Tory ministers; Edward M. Despard (1751–1803), Irish conspirator drawn, hung and beheaded for plot against George III.

11. *BR* chap. 52; 14 August 1841.

12. *Salopian Journal*, 7 July 1841, cited *P2* 367n.

13. *P2* 379.

14. *MC*, 25 July 1842, repr. in *P2* 278–85, but clearly an article not private correspondence.

15. *MC*, 20 October 1842, repr. *D2* 44–51.

16. Angus B. Reach cited in Knight Hunt, who himself claims 'that the speakers owe a great debt of gratitude to those who place their speeches before the public,' and cites various further examples (280–3).

17. *D2* Item 18.

18. *P3* 462.

19. *P4* 66; 68–9.

20. *D2* Item 20.

21. The passage inspired Hood to start work on a sequel to 'The Bridge of Sighs,' fragments of which were found among his papers (Jerrold, Walter 373, 379–80).

22. *Life* IV.iii; Greville records the 'great rage' of the official Whigs on the *Chronicle's* gradual desertion after 1839 (*Memoirs*, Part 2, 1.179).

23. *P3* 459, 461.

24. *P2* 358 (?mid-August 1841); *P4* 66 ([7March 1844]).

25. 'In reply to a question from the Bench, the Solicitor for the Bank observed, that this kind of notes circulated most extensively, in those parts of the world where they were stolen or forged. – *Old Bailey Report*' (*Life* III.viii).

26. Captains Frederick Marryat, Basil Hall and Thomas Hamilton; Andrew Bell and Frances Trollope had all published critical accounts of America from a Tory perspective in the 1830s; Fielding, 'Notes' 536.

27. *United States Magazine and Democratic Review* (April 1842) cited in Slater, *America* 8–9; *P3* 43.

28. Adopted in Parker; Welsh, *Copyright*; Meckier, *Innocent*.

29. McCarthy, 'Claiming' 2–4.

30. Stone, 'American;' Stevens; but see final paras. of CD's 'An American Panorama' (*Examiner*, 16 December 1848, repr. *D2* 136–7) where frontier life is defined as comprising 'different states of society, yet in transition' contrasted to the *un*moving, if not actually retrograde, English panorama.

31. See Whitley & Goldman, eds; Edgecombe; Stevens.

32. *P3* 76–7.

33. *P3* 90.

34. *P2* 368: in defence of his friend, Dr John Elliotson, controversial pioneer of mesmerism, CD writes: '... when I think that every dirty speck upon the fair face of God's creation, who writes in a filthy, bawdy newspaper – every rotten-hearted pander who has been ... rolled in the kennel, yet struts it in the Editorial We once a week – ... every live emetic in that nauseous drug shop, the Press – can have his fling at such men and call them knaves ..., I grow so vicious that with bearing hard upon my pen I break the nib....'

35. On return to London, CD composed a Circular describing the effects of his campaign, and entreating British authors not to send early proofs of their work

to any but 'respectable' US publishing houses; this was published in *MC*, the *Examiner*, the *Athenaeum*, the *New Monthly* et al. and found widespread British support (*P3* 256–9).

36. See also Patten, *Publishers* 147–48.
37. Sharpe 12–24.
38. *AN* 90; CD considers the methodology in *P2* 402.
39. The long chapter on Boston details visits to the Perkins Institution and Massachusetts Asylum for the Blind, the State Hospital for the Insane, the House of Industry (for providing indoor relief to paupers), the Boylston School for neglected and indigent boys, and to 'close the catalogue,' the House of Correction for the State.
40. Carlson *pace* the arguments of John Hollowell in *Fact and Fiction* (U North Carolina Press, 1977) and John Hellmann in *Fables of Fact* (U of Illinois Press, 1981).
41. See McCarthy, 'Claiming' 1.
42. Ard; CD's letter to Chapman of 15 October 1842 broods over difficulties of address (*P3* 345).
43. McCarthy, 'Claiming' 9; CD's comment 'A Fly-Leaf in a Life' (1869, *D4* 388).
44. Slater, *America* 32–3; Miller, 'Sources' 476.

Chapter 5

1. *P3* 587.
2. Evening paper recently ed. (1837–39) by Laman Blanchard, it had run the gamut of political allegiance from Jacobinism (its founding brief was to popularise the 'Ideas of 1789') to Toryism to respectable Whiggery; Aspinall, *Politics* 101–2, 241–2; Koss, 44–46.
3. *P3* 262.
4. *P3* 266.
5. *P4* 121.
6. *P4* 327–9.
7. *Life* V.i.
8. *Life* V.i: 'it does not fall within my plan to describe more than the issue' i.e. CD's resignation.
9. Markham 164–5.
10. *P4* 411.
11. Garnett 279.
12. Double that of any other London editor apart from Delane of the *Times* (Grant, *Newspaper* II.84) – but CD had been paid 25% more as editor of the *Clock*.
13. Thomas Britton (b. 1828?), formerly office boy, later editor of the *Daily News*; autograph letter of 1912, cited in *The Charles Dickens Archive*, Sotheby's Sale Catalogue, 15 July 1999, 200#.
14. *P4*, 346–7; see also Knight Hunt, 194.
15. *P4* 461; cited first in *Life* I.iv but clearly relating to this period (late 1845).
16. McCarthy & Robinson 12.
17. Thomas Britton, in McCarthy and Robinson 7.
18. *P4* 411: CD's detailed queries to Beard about 'those small correspondents at Madras, Ceylon, and Aden' and their parcelling and addressing procedures (*P4* 415, 446 &n.).
19. W. H. Russell, in Atkins 58; his brother Robert left the *Times* for CD's offer of 7 guineas a week; Easthope's *Chronicle* started offering 9, and captured William.

20. *P4* 427.
21. *P4* Appendix B 701–2.
22. Paxton reported them as 'downright mad at the newspaper office they say it is the *best* thought that ever *occurred* not a doubt of success and they are full of preparation' (undated letter, cited in *P4* 435n.).
23. Tillotson, 'New Light' 89–90; the involvement of Sir William Jackson and Sir Joshua Walmsley in the initial backing of the project (Kellett 29, Pope Hennessy 247, Johnson 1.574, N. & J. Mackenzie 177) is unconfirmed.
24. Crowe, *Reminiscences* 69.
25. Forster engaged James Russell Lowell to contribute from America (MS Houghton Library, Harvard; Forster to Lowell, 3 November 1845).
26. *P4* 444, 451.
27. Staff details and data from Knight Hunt (based on *DN* experiences) 196–202 and CD to Lady Blessington, *P4* 475.
28. Barrett-Browning cited in *P4* 438nn, Macready ditto, 412n, 457n; Dilke anecdote in Kellett, 28; the editor was Joachim H. Stoqueler, in 'Mr Charles Dickens and "The Daily News,"' 6 December 1845, 543a, b; Samuel Phillips's savage *Times* review (27 December 1845) repr. Collins, *Critical* 154.
29. Prince Albert, paraphrasing the stated concerns of Peel, Memorandum, 25 December 1846; Benson & Esher 2.66.
30. Discussed in Cook, *Delane* 20–30.
31. Cf. Kellett 28, 'editorial drudgery [Dickens] could not endure. His manager ... was of little use to him ... . One can hardly imagine Mr Micawber in a newspaper office,' or W. H. Russell: 'if his father was not really a Micawber, he was at all events destitute of the energy and experience of Delane, senior' (W. F. A. Delane was appointed financial manager of *The Times* in c. 1832, a much more responsible position than the post held by John Dickens): Atkins 58.
32. Thomas Latimer, *Western Times*, 31 January 1846, cited in *P4* 480n.
33. August 1855, 211.
34. To Lord Robertson, 17 Jan 1846; *P4* 474.
35. 'Foreign Letters. No. I,' *Daily News*, Monday 19 January 1846 [in fact printed 17 January], 7d; 'Nancy' clearly printed in error for Mamie; series title later changed to 'Travelling Letters.'
36. Markham 173.
37. Barrett-Browning in *P4* 478n.; of 3 pages of advertisements, 1 was devoted to railways.
38. 4a.
39. Fox complains particularly of omissions in the report of a soirée to honour the Radical MP Thomas Duncombe (Garnett, 281).
40. Repr. *P4* 477.
41. Gratton 102 cited in *P4* 480n.
42. *Diaries* 2.320, cited in *P4* 484n.
43. British Museum Add. MS 40, 583, f. 139.
44. *DN* 5f; *P4* 479.
45. Fielding, 'Danson' 156.
46. Garnett, 283; full text of letter given in *P12* Addenda 600 &nn.; Danson's dismissive leader appeared on 9 February, 4a, b.
47. Thus, in an otherwise invaluable article, David Roberts oversimplifies the paper's position in contending that 'for Dickens' *Daily News*, Peel was the villain' (53).
48. See *DN*, 31 January, 4b, c; CD's decreasing commitment to the 'Ten Hour' movement, 1838–46, charted in Brantlinger, *Spirit* 86–90; Roberts's claim that

such opposition in 'a newspaper edited by a novelist who is the embodiment of humanitarianism' is '[s]urprising! Indeed astonishing!' seems wide of the mark, though the ensuing explanation of CD's limited Benthamism is helpful (54–60).

49. Forster to Macready recorded in *Diaries*, 2.321–2 (the latter also doubted Forster's ability as CD's successor); Garnett 282–83.
50. Atkins 58.
51. CD's aim for the *Daily News* to 'shine' in its coverage of Indian affairs was reasonably well fulfilled; see the 'Extraordinary Express' from Marseilles, carrying news of the Battle of Moodkee in the Anglo-Sikh war (23 February, 5–6).
52. *P1* 59n, *P4* 485; Tillotson, 'New Light' 90.
53. Patten 171n. & *P4* 514n, 538n disagree over payments, but together suggest a continuing financial interest until late spring.
54. *P4* 498.
55. Scott, *Journal* 3 April 1829, 2.262.
56. *P4* 648–9; Forster resigned on 22 October, on learning that C. W. Dilke, as business manager, intended simultaneously to raise the price and cut back on foreign news coverage.
57. 24 Jan 1846, 5f (stanza 1 of 5).
58. Wright 178; *P4* 497.
59. 14 February 1846, 5a (stanza 4 of 5).
60. Gatrell cites CD's writings on scaffold crowds frequently and disapprovingly, stressing his 'scape-goating' tendencies, but sources all quotations from Collins's selective discussion, without apparent awareness of their original dates or contexts (59–60 et seq.).
61. *P4* 405, 432.
62. 3 only of the letters repr. in *MP* and *CP*; Paroissien reprints all 5 in *Selected Letters*; all page refs are from this edition.
63. Hazlitt's 'Capital Punishments,' *Edinburgh Review*, July 1821; cited in Paulin 41–2.
64. Paroissien, ed. 245.
65. See *P5* 644–45, 651–54 for CD's 2 letters to the *Times* supporting private executions; Collins, *Crime* chap. 10, interprets 4 of the 5 letters in this way, but his thesis can perhaps now be seen as historically contingent on the intellectual atmosphere of the early 1960s: a liberal phase rather than a resting point. See also CD's 'Occasional Register' (chap. 8 below).
66. For detailed analysis of the article, see Drew, 'Voyages' Part I.
67. Pope 152–64 gives the best account of the movement's history and connection with CD; *First Annual Report of the Ragged School Union* (1845) 19.
68. [Carpenter] 4.
69. *MP* 20.
70. Massingham 42–43; McCarthy & Robinson xvii.
71. Ormond notes that the 'joke is particularly aimed at the work of G. P. R. James' (*PFI*, J. M. Dent, 1997, p. 466) but compare the opening sentence of Scott's *Antiquary* (1816).
72. 21 January, 6e.
73. 24 January, 4c, d.
74. E.g. Mahoney's report on 26 February on the corrupt system of appointing cardinals and approving canonizations of candidates mainly from within the papal states themselves (5e, f).
75. E.g. description of High Mass in the Duchy of Modena (Letter VIII, *DN*, 11 March 1846, 5; *PFI* 354); or, the description of crossing into 'the Papal territory' (*PFI* 359).

76. See headnote to 'The Italian Prisoner,' Article 20 in *D4* (190–9).
77. See Flint, intro. xxiv–xxviii, on the political subtext, Schad *passim* on the subversive encoding of churches, in *PFI*.
78. 26 February, 5a.
79. In the much admired 'Plymley Letters' published in the *Edinburgh Review* Smith allows himself the liberty of laughing at the 'theological errors' of Roman Catholics, but shows determination that such 'nonsense' ought not to prejudice their civil rights; for his influence on CD, see chap. 9.
80. *DN* 26 February, 4f; 2 March, 5b.
81. McCarthy & Robinson 18; others credited to CD's editorship were the establishment of 'a news-gathering alliance with the *Morning Herald*, which was among the first of its kind in the history of the newspaper' (Grubb, 'Resignation' 37) and 'the newspaper supplement devoted to a special subject. This excellent feature was first inaugurated by the *Daily News* in its seventh number, which gave four extra pages, entitled "Some Account of the Corn Laws and their Operation" ' (Symon 189).
82. E.g. 'A Pictorial Rhapsody' (1846) repr. in Hollington, *Critical* 1.306–7.
83. See Davies, *Textual* 64–74; Ormond, 'Dickens and Painting' 131–5.
84. 11 March 1846 6a; *PFI* 353.
85. The traveller's need for 'novelty' in many passages leads him to eschew the role of Baedeker tourist, and adopt that of 'anti-tourist' – in John Urry's definition, 'a "romantic" form of tourist gaze, in which the emphasis is upon solitude, privacy, and a personal, semi-spiritual relationship with the object of the gaze' (43); in his description of the tour party led by 'one Mr Davis' in Rome, moreover, CD also perfectly illustrates James Buzard's additional insight that 'anti-tourists ... *required* the crowd they scorned and shunned,' since 'there is a dialectical relationship between the elaboration of "crowd" ... and the anti-tourist's privileging of "solitude," which is less a valuing of private experience than it is a rhetorical act of role-distancing in need of its audience' (153).
86. *PFI* 301; *P4* xiv, 571.
87. *P4* 660.

Chapter 6

1. CD's semi-reliable recollection as the 'Uncommercial Traveller' (*D4* 140); Solly 162; for Forster's conduct of the *Examiner* see Davies's invaluable *Literary Life*, chap. 13.
2. Duffy 83; Davies 225.
3. Adelman 2–5; circulation increasing to 4900 in 1855 before declining in the 1860s (figs in Davies 225, Ellegard 22, Fox Bourne 2.249); Solly 154.
4. Solly 247–248.
5. *P1* 408 &n.
6. 'The Queen's Coronation,' 1 July 1838, 402c, 403a.
7. 'Prison and Convict Discipline' (10 Mar 1849, 146b–147a), 'Rush's Conviction' (7 April 1849, 210a–c), 'Capital Punishment' (5 May 1849, 273c–274a) and 'False Reliance' (2 June 1849, 338ab).
8. Collins, *Crime* 217.
9. Paroissien, ed., *Letters* 213.
10. *D2* 94–95.

11. *D2* 97.
12. Fielding & Brice, 'Exclusion of Evidence' 40.
13. Historian J. Saville (*1848: The British State and the Chartist Movement*) cited in *D2* 138.
14. 'Judicial Special Pleading,' *D2* 142.
15. Repr. *D2* 154–55; *MP* 146–51 reprints 'The Tooting Farm' and 'The Verdict for Drouet;' Brice & Fielding reprint 'A Recorder's Charge' in 'Tooting Disaster.'
16. *MP* 148.
17. Massie 2c; Mortimer 61b; ibid. 61a; Massie 2a.
18. CD's joint authorship of 'Drainage and Health of the Metropolis' (*Examiner*, 14 July 1849), 'The Sewer's Commission' (*Examiner*, 4 August 1849) discussed in Fielding & Brice, 'Graveyard;' CD's circular 'Appeal to the English People on Behalf of the Italian Refugees' (*Examiner*, 8 September 1849 & other papers) discussed in Caponi-Doherty.
19. See Waters for a stimulating survey of how the 'trade' in death formed part of *HW*'s wider analysis of the emerging 'commodity culture.'
20. *D2* 100.
21. House 139–45; discussed in Drew, 'Voyages,' 84–6.
22. *A Description of the Chinese Junk 'Keying'* (London, 1848). British Library J. F. Dexter Collection, MS Dex 306 (22). CD derives many details from this, paraphrases it three times and quotes directly once; where he suggests however that the 30 Chinese crew of the vessel would have sunk it *en route*, were it not for 'the skill and coolness of a dozen English sailors' (*D2* 100), the brochure clearly states that the former were 'as good sailors on board their ships, as ours are on board our own' (6).
23. Davies 219, 224; similar prejudices aired in 'The Great Exhibition and the Little One,' CD & Horne, *HW* III.361–3, repr. *Stone* 1.319–29.
24. See *D1* 527 and *D3*, 182.
25. Ikime 7, Fage 127.
26. *D2* 124–5.
27. Virtually overlooked in David (xiii, 61), but considered in Brantlinger, *Darkness* 178ff.; CD invokes the words/spirit of 'Rule Britannia!' often in his journalism, always negatively, as representative of the worst kind of national jingoism (see *D2*, 294, 309, 331; *D3*, 217, 291; *D4*, 50, 76, 250).
28. *HW* VII.337–9, repr. *D3* 141–8.
29. See *AN* 144–45, 243–4.
30. E. M. Forster, 1924, chap. 4.
31. *Life* VI.iii.
32. Lettis 118; *D2*, 102–7.
33. 30 Dec. 1848; *D2* 144, 145–7.
34. *Examiner*, 4 March 1848, 147; *Life* IX.viii, para. 2 (both cited in Davies 216).
35. Variously *D2* 161–9.
36. Brice & Fielding, 'Demoralisation' 4.
37. *D2* 89.
38. CD discusses the secret with W. H. Wills (Chambers's brother-in-law), 21 October 1866 (*P11* 258); review repr. in *D2* 129–34; conclusion advanced by Fielding & Lai, 'Poetry' and defended in their letter to the *Dickensian* editor; the implications of CD's review searchingly discussed in Fielding, 'Science?'
39. *D2* 359.
40. Brice & Fielding, 'Demoralisation' 1; 'Graveyard' 120.
41. Fox notes Forster's difficulty in writing daily leaders (Garnett, 283).

Chapter 7

1. *Daniel Deronda* (1876), Bk II, chap. xi (Eliot writes of 'human beings' not periodicals).
2. Lohrli, 3–50, *Stone* 1.3–68, Drew's entries on *'Household Words,' 'All the Year Round,'* 'Wills, William Henry/Dickens as Editor' in Schlicke, ed., *Oxford Reader's Companion.*
3. Ackroyd 592.
4. *P4* 660, 639; *Life* V.vii.
5. *P5* 582–3; CD refers to *Chambers's Edinburgh Journal* (see below).
6. *P5* 622.
7. Jaffe considers the problem in a purely secular light, and finds The Shadow 'a figure of contradictions' (15–16).
8. See, for example, wording of the last sentence of the first volume ed. of *GE*, in which the positive prospect of Pip's remaining with Estella until death is rendered as 'the shadow of no parting from her.'
9. *P5* 622–23; *Life* VI.iv.
10. *P5* 621.
11. For a facsimile, *see Stone*, 1.18, plate 5.
12. *P6* 22; 31 January 1850.
13. The Offices described in Fitzgerald, *Memories* 125; see also inventory in 'In Chancery – cause of Bradbury & Evans vs. Dickens and Another,' in J. F. Dexter's edition of *Life*, British Library, Dex. 316.
14. Sutherland *Victorian Novelists &c.* 170; contrast Collins's analysis in 'The Significance' &c., 56–57.
15. Lists of titles given in Forster's *Life* VI.iv, *MDGH* 214; *Spectator*, ed. Bond, 1.21 (5 March 1711).
16. As Poovey states of the debates in the mid-1850s over the Matrimonial Causes Bill (52).
17. 13 April 1850.
18. A facsimile of an early bank note, accompanying W. H. Wills's 'Review of a Popular Publication. In the Searching Style,' *HW* I.430.
19. *To* Wills *P6* 35; *P4* 110; Al-Ani 7–12 for an overview of the contents of *Chambers's.*
20. Lehmann xi, xiv; Wills received 'the handsome remuneration of £10 a week' for his articles in 1849.
21. Sutherland, *Companion* 113.
22. Est. 2 Jan 1847; cost $1\frac{1}{2}$d.; others included *Eliza Cook's Journal* (est. 5 May 1849, cost $1\frac{1}{2}$d.), *The Family Herald* (est. 13 May 1843, cost 1d.), *The People's Journal* (est. 3 Jan. 1846; cost $1\frac{1}{2}$d.) and *The Penny Magazine* (est. 1832).
23. For a survey of so-called 'Rebel Journalism,' see Kellett, 64–66 and James, *Fiction* 32–50; titles included *Cleave's Penny Gazette of Variety and Amusement* (from 1837), *Lloyd's Illustrated London Newspaper* (from 1842), *The London Journal* ed. GWM Reynolds (from 1845), *Reynolds's Miscellany* (from 1846), and *Reynolds's Weekly Newspaper* (from 1850).
24. Report, 1849, question 1310, cited in Kellett 66; Newspaper Stamp Committee, *British Parliamentary Papers* 17 (1851), 478–79.
25. *HW* I.1; *D2* 178.
26. Fitzgerald, *Memories* 135 and Wills (Collins, 'Letter Book' 25) put the opening number at 100 000; the most detailed attempt to calculate circulation is Buckler ('Success' 198–99 &nn.); Patten 242n. dismisses his contention that

HW sold '950 000 copies weekly' as 'way out,' not realizing this figure is Buckler's estimate of total copies sold over a half year, giving a weekly circulation of a more realistic 36 540 (six months to 30 September 1858). These figures can be refined (following Buckler's method) by including the accounts until 31 March 1859 (Patten, Appendix D, 464), and give an average weekly sale of 37 975 copies (high of 40 075 for the 6 months to 31 March 1853; low, 35 575 for the 6 months to 31 March 1854).

27. *P6*, 83; Patten 464, 243; *HN* April 1851; riposte in *Reynolds's Newspaper*, 8 June 1851, discussed in Peyrouton, 'Chartists,' 78–88 & 152–161.
28. Briefly discussed in Maxwell, 'Mysteries' 202–3.
29. Admirably discussed in Schlicke, *Popular* 190–225.
30. *HW* I.1; *D2* 177–8.
31. *Edmund Yates&c.*, 146; *Athenaeum*, 22 April 1854, cited in Lohrli 22 &n.; *P6* 64.
32. Lohrli 22&nn., *P6* 64&nn.
33. *P7* Addenda 904; Solly 149, 244, chap. 13 passim, 150–51.
34. Cf. references in *OMF* IV.6 and 'The Uncommercial Traveller' paper for 12 September 1863, repr. *D4* 304.
35. *HW* VI.193–97 (13 November 1852), repr. *Stone* 2.443–54.
36. Pascoe xvi.
37. 12 November 1859.
38. Review of *ATYR* I, 5 Nov 1859, 708c–709a; possibly by Morley himself (Solly 248).
39. Gaskell, *Letters* 538; *Memoirs* 2.156.
40. See Clark, chap. 4 '*Household Words* as organ of Reform,' 207f. & passim.
41. *Speeches* 201 (27 June 1855), *P7* 19; the sequence comprises 3 *Arabian Nights* parodies ('The Thousand and One Humbugs' I–III), 'The Toady Tree,' 'Cheap Patriotism,' and 'Our Commission' (21 April–11 August 1855).
42. 'The Metropolitan Protectives' *HW* III.97; 'A Detective Police Party (I)' praised and excerpted in the lofty *Quarterly Review* for June 1856 (XCIX.176–80); 'On Duty With Inspector Field' excerpted in *Ragged School Union Magazine* for September 1851 (II.200–305).
43. *P6* 64; *P7* 439 &n.; W. H. Russell's accounts of the Battles of Alma (20 September) and Balaklava (25 October); Sala's article was held over from the 28 October issue of *HW*, and CD's essay on Boulogne, repr. *D3* 229–41, appeared on 4 November, the day before the Battle of Inkerman.
44. Hollingshead 96; Sala, *Things* 1.80–3; Barrett-Browning cited in *P6* 451n.
45. Straus 117, 122; the original idea was Sala's; he was paid a total of £303 for 250 cols leaving c. £175 for 24 weeks' expenses, assuming the standard *HW* rate of payment; his later complaint that CD failed to pay travel expenses was unfounded (Sala, *Life* 1.375; Lohrli, 158–64,]; *P8* 93).
46. Solly 199; *HW* VII. 145–9 (16 April 1853) repr. *Stone* 2.467–75.
47. In the early years of *HW*, Wills (who, before 1855, received no additional payment for his own writing in the journal) needed to make up for any missing material once the £16 had been spent on contributions for a given issue; see Lehmann 34–36, *P6* 149.
48. Gaskell, *Letters* 113; Sala, *Life* 1.313–4; Solly 241.
49. Crowe 71; see Spencer passim for a sympathetic profile; also Collins, 'Wills' Plans.'
50. Martineau, *Autobiography* 2.420, Lohrli 462.
51. *P6* 69, *P9* 415.
52. *P6* 130 &n.; Lehmann 30–2 for Wills's defence.
53. *P6* 522; Lehmann 74–5.

54. *HW* X. 169–70; *D3* 225–9.
55. CD's 'Office Day' initially instituted on Wednesday (Lehmann 74), changing to Thursdays in 1854 (Al-Ani 133), to Wednesdays by May 1861 (*P9* 415), and back to Thursdays again from May 1868 to May 1870 (*P12* 107, 540).
56. *P8* 98, 99–100.
57. To Wills, *P7* 46–7; CD and Wills both revised Morley's draft, published as 'In and Out of Jail' (*HW* VII.241–5, 14 May 1853), repr. *Stone* 2.477–88.
58. Lai 45. I am indebted to this article for its rigorous interrogation of the extent of CD's editorial control.
59. *P7* 125, 432; *P6* 231.
60. Since the 1940s, a matter of heated critical debate too complex to be summarized here (see, as a sample relating only to *HT*, Smith's selection from post-1948 criticism [331–7], or Engel and Coles for theses built on differing views on whether there is any 'essential difference' between CD's political positions as a novelist and journalist).
61. See Lohrli 5–23 for a generally negative impression of the *HW* brand.
62. See Sanders, Preface ix–xv, for a valuable overview; *Spectator*, 7 July 1832, 632; [CD] *Sketches of Young Gentlemen* repr. in Chesterton ed., *SB* 466.
63. Fielding & Smith 418, 415.
64. *Autobiography* 2.383–5&f; *P7* 438.
65. All by Morley, looked over by CD: 'Fencing with Humanity' (*HW* XI.241–4) 'Death's Cyphering Book' (ibid. 337–41) 'Deadly Shafts' (494–5) 'More Grist to the Mill' (605–6).
66. Martineau, *Factory* 46, 35.
67. *HW* XIII.13–9 (19 January 1856), repr. *Stone* 2.550–62; *P8* 9&n.
68. *ATYR* (26 December 1863) X.419; note followed last instalment of Charles Reade's *Very Hard Cash*; hence Lai's conclusion that we 'have to make a discriminating reading of each article in the light of its author and its context if we are to deduce Dickens's opinions on the topics' in his journals (50).
69. By no means biases which set *HW* apart from the rest of the Liberal press; Jerrold & Thackeray in *Punch*, and Delane's *Times* were likewise strongly against the restoration of the Catholic hierarchy in October 1850; both publications satirized the nascent women's movement, represented by the 1851 Bloomer campaign.
70. *P4*, 611.
71. See the ferocious 'Crisis in the Affairs of John Bull' (*HW* 23 November 1850; repr. *D2* 297–305); the peroration of 'A Sleep to Startle Us' (*HW* 13 March 1852; repr. *D3* 57); CD returns to the theme in 'The Last Words of the Old Year,' *HW* lead for 4 January 1851 (*D2* 310, 315).
72. *Autobiography* 2.420, 422; 'The Yellow Mask,' *HW* XI.217f. (7, 14, 21, 28 July 1855) repr. in *After Dark* (1856); 'A Ghost Story,' *HW* XI.170 (24 March 1855) repr. in *Nothing New*; 'Child's History' &c., Chapter XXX England under Mary,' *HW* 9 April 1853, 'Chapter XLIV England under James the Second,' *HW* 26 November 1853.
73. Mark O'Shaughnessy, cited in *P6* 845n.; anon. review of *LD*, *The Leader*, 27 June 1857, 616–7; for succinct discussion of CD's brand of Christianity, see Slater, *Intelligent*, chap. 6 passim.
74. *Autobiography*, 2.419.
75. 'Chapter XXII England under Henry the Sixth,' *HW* V.613, 11 September 1852.
76. See Welsh, *City* 180–95 for CD's concept of woman as 'Angel of Death.'

77. For CD's support of the latter, see J. C. Parkinson's 'Slaves of the Ring' (*AYR* XX.85–8, 4 July 1868) and CD to Parkinson, *P*12 127–8.

78. VIII.121–3; *HT* chap. x and Eliza Lynn's 'One of Our Legal Fictions,' telling Norton's tale, both ran in *HW* 29 April 1854 (IX.237–42, 257–60); Wills's 'A Legal Fiction' followed another aspect of her case (XI.598–9, 21 July 1855); see Humphreys, 'Marriage' 180–1 &nn. for relations between the parliamentary and *HW* debate.

79. CD's longest leader in *HW* sternly profiles the work of Urania Cottage, the 'Home for Homeless Women' which he had established with Miss Coutts (*HW* VII.169–75 repr. *D*3 127–41); in both *DC* (through the stories of Martha Endell and Em'ly) and *HW*, CD himself emphasizes reclamation through emigration, rather than the harsher fate of redemption through apotheosis (Mrs Gaskell's 'solution' in 'Lizzie Leigh'); see Nead 139 à propos.

80. Commenced/published by R. Dodsley from 1758 & ed. by Edmund Burke until 1790; different versions contd. until 1954; CD owned a set complete to 1860 (S; *P*5 169 &n.) and used it regularly (see *P*2 228, *P*6 799&n., *P*11 287 & 386&nn. and *OMF* Bk 3, chap. 5).

81. 'The Forge' was a rejected title for *HW*, and one CD and Collins toyed with for its successor: 'The Forge …/"We beat out our ideas on this"/ ONCE A-WEEK' (*P*9 16&n.); note also the wording of CD's offer to stand in for Collins during his illness: 'I am … ready … to strike in and hammer the hot iron out' (*P*10 142).

82. The *Narrative* 'was allotted to Forster, and he furnished a substantial portion' (Fitzgerald, *Memories* 124); Morley affirmed that 'Forster does its leading article' (Solly 200).

83. Lohrli 275.

84. Solly 200, Lehmann 165.

85. CD corresponds with Miss Coutts about his disposition of coverage in both publications, *P*6 804–5; his article for *HW* was called 'Trading in Death,' and while toasting Wellington's 'glorious memory' it condemned the revival of costly State Funerals as 'a pernicious instance and encouragement of the demoralizing practice of trading in Death' (VI.241–5; repr. *D*3, 95–105); see Waters.

86. The most famous *Narrative* 'original' is of Jo (*Bleak House* No. 6 [June 1852] onwards), 'discovered' when House (32–3) reprinted the testimony of George Ruby from the January 1850 *Narrative*; Collins, 'Significance' 64.

87. As early as Feb 1854 he had notified the other partners of his 'inability henceforth to contribute literary articles to *Household Words*' (Lehmann 196, citing unsigned Agreement from Wills's papers).

88. *P*7 205, *P*8 Appendix B 730.

89. 'Our Almanac,' *HW* XII.385, 24 November 1855.

90. *P*7 754; *Stone* 2.538–9 prints a facsimile of the wrapper and of pp. 16–17, for August 1856.

91. The rate seems to have been £100 per bi-annual volume; see *P*6 505n., 519; Lohrli 48.

92. Patten, 197n.

93. Grubb, PhD. 287–8, provides the basis for the following corrected but still incomplete breakdown: *Angell et al.*, Vol. I. No. 1 – VI No. 133; *McElrath*, VI Nos. 134–5; *McElrath & Lord*, VI 136 – VII No. ??; *McElrath & Barker*, VII No. ?? – X No. ?234; *J.A. Dix*, X No. ?235 – XI No. ?279; *Dix & Edwards*, XII No. ?280 – XV No. ?370; *Miller & Co.*, XV Nos 371–374; *Miller & Curtis*, XV No. 375 – ??;

John Jansen, unspecified; *Jansen & Co.*, unspecified; *Frederic A. Brady*, XVIII No. ?? – XIX No. 479 (final issue).

94. Barker's extraordinary letter to CD given in full in Buckler, '*HW* in America' 161–3; Orvis to B&E (7 July 1854) cited in Buckler 164; ibid. 160.
95. *P9* 645, Lehmann 164–6 (To CD, 11 June 1855).
96. *P6* 518; 31 January.
97. *P7* 245, *P9* 494; Slater, *Women* 135–62.
98. *P8* 488.
99. In 'The Murdered Person' (*HW* XIV.289, 11 October 1856), CD turned from consideration of the victims of violent crime to the 'victims' of bad marriages: 'The Law of Divorce is in such condition that from the tie of marriage there is no escape to be had' &c. (*D3* 400).
100. See Tomalin 96–115 and Slater, *Women* 202–217 for analyses.
101. See Stone, *Night Side* 292–98; also coded references to 'my little reason' in CD's 'Please to Leave your Umbrella' (*HW* XVII.457–9, 1 May 1858; *D3* 483–8).
102. Fitzgerald, *Memories* 138–9.
103. See Slater, *D3* xv, Patten 263; Fielding suggests however, that although the announcement 'generally had a good effect at the time,' CD 'has often been blamed subsequently ... because the results have been confused with those of the "Violated Letter," published by the *New York Tribune*' ('Bradbury' 74).
104. Straus 134: 'Many newspapers, including the *Daily Telegraph*, printed the statement without comment; a few, the *Liverpool Mercury* in their van, printed it with a more or less stinging commentary.'
105. 'Mr Charles Dickens and his Late Publishers,' inserted in No. 20 of *The Virginians* (June 1859), repr. *P9* Appendix C 565; *P8* 608 &n.
106. Extract from *HW* 'Articles of Agreement,' Sotheby's Sale Catalogue, *The Charles Dickens Archive* (15 July 1999), Lot 169# i; a shorthand report of the Chancery Judgment gives CD's statement that over 500 000 copies were in the process of distribution (Fielding, 'Bradbury' 81); legal opinion from Chancery barrister Arthur Hobhouse, signed & dated 17 December 1858 (ibid. Lot 170# ii); the 'light' of CD's name &c., from Wills's report to CD of the outcome of the hearing, repr. *P9*, Appendix B 564.
107. Gross sales of £2326 5s. 4 d. for the last 8 issues of *HW* (nos 472–79), suggest a weekly circulation of 34 894 even as *ATYR* was being launched (cash account described in *The Charles Dickens Archive*, Sotheby's sale catalogue, 15 July 1999, Lot 169 ii).
108. Patten 269, Sotheby's Catalogue &c. Lot 170# vii, CD's own account of the auction in *P9* 65.
109. Slater, intro. to *D3*, xvii.

Chapter 8

1. *P11* 292.
2. Spencer, 149–50.
3. To James T. Fields, *P12* 18.
4. See Bevis, 'Public' 333, 344 & passim.
5. Aside from *AYR*, 114 'periodicals undertakings were started in London alone' in 1859; Graham 301.
6. *AYR* II.95; see Graves 174 & passim.
7. See Patten, 'Dickens Disappears;' Drew, 'Dickens Reappears.'

8. See *P9* 11n., summarising evidence from Wright, Slater, Tomalin and CD's account book with Coutts bank; Ellen Ternan's last professional stage appearance was on 10 August 1859.

9. US ed. of *AYR*, IV.336 (12 Jan 1861).

10. Terry 67; she calls the publication 'Household Words,' but the dates clearly signal that *AYR* is meant.

11. Subscription of Arthur Hobhouse to engrossed draft 'Articles of Agreement' for *AYR* dated 29 June 1859, quoted in Sotheby's Sale Catalogue, *Charles Dickens Archive* (15 July 1999), Lot 172# iii; see *P9* 84 n. 2 for CD's MS redraft of Article 6.

12. *P9* 98, *P12* Addenda 690, *P9* 252 & 84.

13. *Life* VIII.v; *P9* 16&nn.

14. See *P9* 86–7, 90, 303, 309; see also Fitzgerald's after-comments in *Memories* 200–1.

15. See Elwell for a broad survey of the journal's changing fortunes 1859–80.

16. Knight contributed to vol. I on 23 July & 10 September 1859; Martineau and Hughes's involvement cited *P9* 87n.; Meredith's hostility and Linton's quandary recounted in Lohrli 364, 344; Wills to Patterson, in the *AYR* Letter Book, and cited in Collins's 'Letter Book' 26; Tennyson's pay in Patten 270 and Ricks 1106; George Simpson to Joseph Langford, 16 November 1859, cited in *P9* 161n.

17. Carrow, 'An Informal Call' &c.; CD himself described the Office as 'simply hideous' (18 March 1864) but appears to have ordered linoleum floorcoverings and 'Persian and Turkey' carpets 'for the wear and tear of our 2 rooms' (4 May), see *P10* 373, 390.

18. Details from *AYR* Letter Book, cited in *P9*, 50n.; Fitzgerald, *Memories* 225; *Recreations* 51.

19. *AYR* Letter Book, cited in Oppenlander 49, and Collins, 'Letter Book' 26.

20. Attribution to CD of 'The Blacksmith' (*Life* VIII.vi) is erroneous; 'Our Eye-Witness' items all by CD's son-in-law, Charles Allston Collins, and almost certainly looked over by CD in detail (see *Examiner*, 3 November 1860, for a very favourable review of the volume collection).

21. 'Five New Points of Criminal Law,' *AYR* I.517 (repr. *D4* 12–14); 'Very Common Law,' *AYR* II.253, 301, 522, 554, III.54, 180, 303.

22. 'Occasional Register,' *AYR* I.10–11 (30 April 1859); identified in Kitton, *Minor* 142, together with paragraphs 4, 6 and 10 of the first 'Register' and paragraphs 2, 5, 7, 8 and 12 of the second (I.35–6, 7 May 1859); *P9* 49n. seems unaware of Kitton's identification.

23. Wills to CD, a.m. Thurs 28 April 1859 (as with *HW*, copies of *AYR* were dated Saturday – in this case, 30 April – but went on sale the previous Wednesday), *AYR* Letter book, cited in Collins, 'Letter Book' 25; see also Patten 271.

24. The Volunteer Movement, formed on the plan of 1792, had been revived across the Metropolitan and southern counties in 1859, mobilising 120 000 troops to resist French invasion.

25. Hughes & Lund, 61; my brief discussion here of *TTC* as a serial responds to their valuable analysis in chap. 3.

26. *Liverpool Daily News* reprinted chaps 1–2 of *TTC* on 28 April (the day after the 1st no. of *AYR* had gone on sale in London); *Lloyd's Weekly London Newspaper* repr. the whole of chap. 3 on 1 May 1859 (Hughes & Lund 296 n. 20).

27. Law 184.

28. 12 Nov 1859, p. 458; cited in Hughes & Lund, 65.

29. *AYR* II.49 (*TTC*, Bk 3 chap. 13); for 'A Flight' see *HW* III.529–33 repr. *D3* 62–35, comparing in particular 529–30, or the narrator's fantasy that he becomes a prisoner of state, escaping with a comrade (532–3).

30. *AYR* II.93.
31. Lever's casual approach to the task was partly to blame; perhaps also CD's haste to welcome 'to my open arms' an author whom he knew was considering a similar contract from Bradbury & Evans to write a novel for *Once a Week* (see exchange cited in P9, 190–1&n.)
32. *P12* 443.
33. *P9* 343; Sutherland, *Victorian Novelists*, 170.
34. See Wynne 87–91, and Meckier's chapter on *GE* in *Hidden Rivalries*.
35. Buckler, 'Dickens the Paymaster' makes the case for CD's relative rigidity, in reply to Grubb's somewhat hagiographic 'Editorial Policies' &c.; Grubb's riposte, 'Dickens the Paymaster Once More' points to examples of CD's liberality not so much in payscales but in advances to contributors and readiness to respond to individual circumstances; Hollingshead, *My Lifetime* 1.116.
36. Edwards 78, 75, 97.
37. Collins, 'The Significance' &c., 61; Sutherland, *Victorian* &c. 186.
38. Technically, only a contracted 'privilege,' since rights could not be legally enforced in the absence of an international copyright agreement.
39. Agreement signed, 17 March 1859; terms summarised in Patten 275; T. C Evans so described to Forster, *P9* 36 &n.
40. Wills contracted the Liverpool firm of John H. Green & Sons to receive, insure, pay duty on & forward the 48 lb. package of plates by the Saturday steamer for New York, beginning 16 April (2 weeks before the publication of *AYR* No. 1); see letters of 7, 10 & 12 April 1859 in *AYR* Letter Book (Oppenlander, 51&n.).
41. 19 May 1859; Collins, 'Letter Book' 25.
42. Grubb, 'Charles Dickens' &c., 327; *AYR* American ed., 21 May 1859, I.96.
43. Serialised 7 May – 3 December, Agreement signed by *Harper's* London agent, Sampson Low, on 7 April 1859; see Wills to Sampson Low, and Wills to Evans, 15 April 1859, *AYR* Letter Book, cited in P9 98n.
44. Wills to Evans, 13 August 1859, *AYR* Letter book, cited in P9 36n.
45. Grubb PhD. 328 gives the US price; Wills to Sampson Low, 25 November 1859, *AYR* Letter Book (Oppenlander 52).
46. Grubb, PhD. 328; *AYR* American ed., IV.144 (it is not in fact clear whether Emerson & Co. remained the authorized publisher much after May 1861, as Grubb concludes in 'American Edition' 304); To Sampson Low (Harper Bros London agent), 29 January 1863, *AYR* Letter Book (Oppenlander 53); CD to Wills, *P10* 202.
47. US 'rights' for publication of the Christmas Numbers of *AYR* were separately negotiated; Ticknor and Fields printed *Mugby Junction* in *Every Saturday* (December 1866) 'from the advance sheets' of *AYR* (P11 265n.).
48. *P10* 184, 346; *P11* 133, Edgar Johnson 1061, Patten 301, *Life* VIII.v; *P9* 168.
49. Previous articles in the campaign had been 'The Spirit Business' (*HW* 7 May 1853), 'A Haunted House' (*HW* 23 July 1853), 'Well-Authenticated Rappings' (*HW* 20 February 1858); after further provocation from Howitt, CD returned to the attack with 'Rather a Strong Dose' (*AYR* 21 March 1863); To Alfred Dickens, *P9* 149; Howitt objected to 3 papers called 'A Physician's Ghosts' (*AYR* August 6, 13 and 27), see *P9* 116 &n.; 'The Haunted House,' *AYR Extra Christmas Number* 48.
50. *History of the Supernatural* (1863) 2.413 cited in *P9* 181&n.; Peyrouton, 'Rapping' passim; Thomas, Deborah 75–80.
51. See Ostry 65–70; she singles out particularly the author (C. A. Collins, CD's son-in-law) of the 'Small-Beer Chronicles' (*AYR* 30 August 1862–14 Feb 1863) as a writer who 'curtails utopian notions of scientific progress' and 'asserts the power of the spiritual' in *AYR*'s pages.

52. *AYR Extra Christmas Number* 1859, 30–31; the autobiographical matrix of clusters of images in *UT* and *GE* has been noted: see Foll, 'Sketch Book' and *D*4 Items 12, 15, 16, 17 and 33.

53. Collins, 'Letter Book' 25; over a 14-volume sample, *AYR* features 94 articles on international affairs, *HW* 52 (Al-Ani, Appendix G); an exception is the series of 6 articles on American life and scenery appearing in *AYR* IV Nos. 90–96 (12 January – 16 February 1861), during the serial run of *GE*.

54. *AYR* II.321 (28 Jan 1860); repr. *D*4, 28.

55. Litvack's pioneering survey documents 'a significant volume of articles on Irish subjects' in *AYR* 'encompassing folklore, history, transport, tourism, medical practices, penology, policing and politics,' esp. the politics of the Fenian movement, to which 10 articles were devoted, 1865–7; see also *P*11 474, *P*11 Appendix C 537.

56. 'Uncommercial Traveller' 13 October 1860; *Memories* 227, see also *D*4, 190–1.

57. 'Roman Sheep-Shearing,' *AYR* III.429; CD to Trollope re 'The Sack of Perugia' (*AYR* I.421); even in the modified account, the Pope and the Papal troops 'are totally blackened' *P*9 117–8 &n.; see also *D*4, intro. xiii.

58. *P*11, 237; Thornbury's 53 'Old Stories Re-told' ran in *AYR* from 20 October 1866 to 18 July 1868; they were succeeded by 31 topographical sketches through England, 'As the Crow Flies.'

59. E.g. 'Our Eye-Witness at Woolwich,' 'Ships and Crews,' 'Portsmouth,' 'On Board the Training Ship' (all in *AYR* I, the last 3 by James Hannay); 'Royal Naval Volunteers' and 'Cherbourg' I–III (all in *AYR* II, the last 3 by Hannay).

60. E.g. 17 articles by M. L. Meason on stock market abuses (*AYR* Vols XI–XIV); 5 articles by John Hollingshead on bank and trading frauds (*AYR* Vols I–II); Dvorak shows the freedom allowed to different contributors in their analysis of the ambivalent interaction between commercial matters and public/private morality, but stresses that the extensive coverage raised the debate to one of central significance in *AYR*'s representation of the contemporary scene.

61. Examples are 'Species' *AYR* III.174–8; 'Natural Selection' *AYR* III.293–9 (long and intelligent review of *Origin of Species*); 'Transmutation of Species' *AYR* IV.519–21 (overview of development of evolutionary theories); see also 'England, Long, Long Ago' *AYR* II.562–6; 'Deluges' *AYR* III.40–7, and Wynne 84–7 for analysis.

62. Fitzgerald, *Memories* 196, Hollingshead, 'Fifty Years;' Fitzgerald, ibid., 216; *Examiner*, 5 Nov 1859, 708c–9a.

63. 'A Letter from the Editor to a Friend and Contributor,' repr. in *Letters*, 4.165–6.

64. Thackeray's quarrel with Yates became the pretext for a cold war between the two older men, still waging during the launch of the *Cornhill*; see Edwards 59–66 for a lucid summary.

65. See Harden chap. 7 for full discussion of the 'Roundabout Papers.'

66. To Collins, *P*9 (7 January 1860); *D*4 xv, 26–7.

67. See Drew, 'Nineteenth-Century' 51–7, *Speeches* 290–3 & 172.

68. See Drew, 'Voyages' 76–96, Drew, PhD. chap. 1 passim, Smith, Grahame 80–5.

69. For CD's views on 'progress' see Slater, *Intelligent* chap. 4, and ibid., 'How Many Nurses' for reasons not to read *UT* 'as though it contained chunks of straight autobiography' (253).

70. *AYR* III.278, repr. *D*4 148 in 'Dullborough Town.'

71. See *D*4 Items 15, 10, 12, 28, 29; compare Harden 197 on Thackeray's 'De Juventute.'

72. Hemstedt, 'Later Journalism' 39&f.

73. Cf. 'the dark side of Dickens's later work is ... here ... almost unrelieved' (Fielding, *Critical*, 207); *UT*'s 'almost overwhelmingly morbid gloom ...

surprising preoccupation ... with death' (Schwarzbach 178f.); 'chronicles of sometimes desolate and unhappy wandering, filled with nostalgia, solitude, weariness and melancholia' (Ackroyd 872–3).

74. For the 3 'Mr Booley' papers, see *D3* Item 43 201–12, and *MP* 216–222.
75. For examination of the evidence, see Headnote to *D4*, Item 11, 96–7; a fairly clear example of such fabrication is CD's 'Down with the Tide' (*HW* VI.481–5; repr. *D3* 113f.), a 'report' of a night journey with the Thames River Police that was collated from interviews with various officials invited to the *HW* Office; on the sub-genre, see Adams.
76. *P11* 483, 522; *P12* 108, 130; Fitzgerald, *Memoirs* 2.218; Solly 251.
77. *AYR* XX (28 Nov 1868), *AYR* XX.337 (19 September 1868); CD worried that the larger font 'crowded out' material in his attempts to draw up a standard 24-page number plan for *AYR* N. S. No. 1, eventually adopting Wills's compromise suggestion of running two type sizes in the same issue; the new, larger size became consistent throughout from N. S. III (*P12* 224–5 &n.).
78. 'Dickens's Ammanuensis,' *Tit-Bits*, 2 September 1882, cited in Kitton, *Dickensiana* 482–4.
79. Details of 5 MSs given in *D4* 344, 365, 379–80, 387 & 392.
80. Chesterton, ed., *UT* ix, ibid., *Criticisms* xx; on the 'profoundly unsatisfactory ... want of cohesion' in the Christmas Numbers, and CD's weariness of having his 'own writing swamped' see *P12* 159, 161–2 & 212.
81. Fitzgerald, *Memories* 241; CD had supplied half of the 47900 words of *No Thoroughfare*.
82. *P12* 192, 378.
83. For the subsequent history and modest success of *AYR* (which continued, under CD Jnr's editorship, until 1895) see *D4*, xix–xx and Fitzgerald, *Memories* 244–7.
84. The formal Articles signed 2 May; these and the Will published in *P12* Appendices J and K.

Chapter 9

1. I broadly follow Leech & Short's 'multilevel' approach to questions of style in this chapter ('Style and Choice' 14–38).
2. See, respectively, Beaumont, Wimsatt, Paulin and Nattrass.
3. This applies to articles as well as monographs; of 24 reviewed, only Quirk dealt in any detail with the language of CD's non-fictional prose.
4. 91–3.
5. 74–5.
6. A point underlined by *Stone* 1.64–6 and in 'Interior Monologue.'
7. 5, 7.
8. Cited in Mathew 35.
9. *Charles Dickens* 36–7.
10. 'Our Honorable Friend' *D3* 69, 72; *Times* 31 July 1851, cited in *D3* ibid.
11. *Morning Chronicle*, 17 January 1835 4d, e *King John* V.vii;
12. 24, 17–18.
13. 'On Gusto' first published in the *Examiner* (May 1816), repr. in *Round Table* (1817); CD owned a copy (1841; *S*).
14. *NN* chap. 16 (August 1838); Magnet notes that Gregsbury's speech is a burlesque of a passage from Part 1 of Burke's *Reflections* ('The Situation of France'), in which Burke is praising French prosperity, not English; *Social Order*, 8.

15. See Brent, 'Theory of Reading?'
16. *P*1–12 offer hundreds of examples; to choose at random – see *P*6 220 *To Moncreiff.*
17. Sucksmith 26–7; book acquired by CD prior to May 1844 (*P*4 Appendix C 719).
18. Studies by Stone (PhD.), T. W. Hill, and Collins ('Dickens's Reading') are outdated, given new evidence from *P*1–12 which has exploded Forster's claim that 'there was never much notice of his reading in his letters' (*Life* VI.iii); research is often based around *S*, but Stone rightly guesses that '40% or more of Dickens's library books ... were not listed' in *S*, so what we know of CD's reading 'is always a minimum' (vii).
19. I document elsewhere the various references to these writers (Swift excepted) made by CD, and assess their influence; Drew PhD. 27–30, 34–9.
20. *Speeches* 312; *P*7 592 &n.
21. *P*7 Addenda 789 &n., Drew, PhD. 63–7; *Speeches* 11–12, Drew, PhD. 49–50.
22. See Drew PhD. 39–43; CD quotes Bacon's *Essays* (which he owned in 3 eds) in *BR* 37, *DS* 5 & 17, *P*3 266 and shows detailed knowledge of his work and career in *P*9 209–10.
23. *In and Out* 154.
24. See Oddie; Carlyle's influence on CD's 'Uncommercial Traveller' papers considered in detail in Foll, PhD.
25. *P*7 367.
26. Smith was, of all the men 'whom I never heard of but never saw' the one CD had 'the greatest curiosity to see and the greatest interest to know' (April 1839, *P*1 546); after his death, he became 'the wisest and wittiest of friends I have lost.' (September 1869, *Speeches* 405); see Drew PhD. 45–48.
27. See Nattrass; Cobbett, *Selections* (the edition CD owned) 6.335; Hazlitt, *Table Talk* 57, in vol. 7 of *Complete Works* (CD owned the 2 vol. edition of 1845–6; *S*).
28. Paulin 239, 43, 297.
29. See Cook, 'Hazlitt, Speech and Writing' and Bevis, 'Temporizing' 176 for useful considerations of these in context of a developing media culture.
30. *Speeches* 75, 89; Paulin 79–80; *HW* 30 Oct 1852 (*D*3 88–95), *AYR* 21 July 1860 (*D*4 148–57).
31. Essays from the *Plain Speaker* cited in Paulin 274; CD may recall 'sounding' in its less usual, secondary meaning of 'having full, rich, or imposing sound' (*OED*) from its frequent use in Hazlitt's *Table Talk*, cf. 'On Going a Journey,' 'On Familiar Style' (used twice), and 'On Effeminacy of Character.'
32. For what the Pilgrim editors rightly call 'a remarkable and complex play on words' in CD's note to Forster about his *Examiner* sketch of the Coronation, see *P*1 408 &n.; Burke 110–111; the fate of 'Boz's hypothesis about door knockers in 'Our Next Door Neighbour' indicates CD's ironic stance: 'Our theory trembled beneath the shock' (*EC*, 18 March 1836; *D*1 41–7).
33. For Poole's influence on CD see Tillotson, 'John Poole' and De Vries 170–7; Grillo chap. 4 considers the influence of Egan, Poole, Leigh Hunt and Thomas Hood.
34. Marriott xv.
35. Ibid. xxiii.
36. Butor 2, 5; Andrews, *Grown-up* 44; see Mowitt on the social function of the familiar essay, Drew 'Voyages Extraordinaires,' for development of points summarised in this section.
37. *D*4 382, 116.
38. Hollington, 'Flâneur' 78.

39. *D*4 Items 37, 8, 14, 16 variously.
40. *HW* 1.410; *D*2 269.
41. Miller, 'Fiction' 92.
42. See Schwarzbach, '"Terra"' passim.
43. 'Threatening Letter' &c., *D*2 69; *P*6 & 7 passim.
44. *AYR* NS I.300–3 (27 Feb 1869); *D*4 381–2 'On an Amateur Bent.'
45. *AYR* NS I.61; *D*4 354.
46. *D*4 355.
47. *D*4 362–3.
48. See Holquist 174 for 'the central Bahktinian question' this raises.
49. *AYR* IX.444–9; *D*4 254–5, 259–60.
50. See *D*2 284f., 290f., *D*3 304f.
51. Solly 151; 'Letter from a Highly Respectable Old Lady,' *HW* I.186–7; 'The Good Side of Combination' *HW* III.56–60; Solly 196.
52. *HW* VIII.553–9; *D*3 200.
53. Cited in Butterworth 133.
54. *D*3 207.
55. Reported in Maurice 111.
56. *Speeches* 379, 383; Hudson 2.663–4; for a profile of Curtis see Frank Mott 2.483–4.
57. Sutherland, writing of *AYR*, in *Victorian Novelists* 172, 186.
58. *P*9 395.
59. For a comprehensive analysis of the gendering of women readers of magazines, see Flint, *Woman* 137–83.
60. Anon. review of Wills's *Old Leaves. Gathered from Household Words*, 21 January 1860, 37ab.
61. See *Stone* 2.627–40 for CD's revisions to a sketch of Murray's.
62. See Wiener, 'How New was the New Journalism?' in *Millions* 53, 59, 62–5; ibid., 'Edmund Yates: the Gossip as Editor' in *Innovators* 271; Edwards 1–3, 136, 195; also Fox Bourne's seminal 'Class and Clique Journalism' (vol. 1 chap. 23).
63. See John Morley and Hughes for analyses.
64. *P*9 423; see Frank Mott 2.25–26 for American practice (by 1860, most magazines were either printing authors' names or including them in their annual index).
65. See Law, Table 1.1 (10).
66. As Sala recorded, CD was 'a Liberal of the Liberals' yet 'expressed but very half-hearted approval of the agitation for the abolition of paper duty;' *Life* 1.399.
67. *P*6 32; see his conclusion to a joint article with Mark Lemon 'A Paper Mill' *HW* I.529–31 (31 August 1850) repr. *Stone* 1.137–42; complaint of the Window Tax in 'Red Tape' *HW* II.481–4 (15 February 1851) repr. *MP* 295–302.
68. CD reported in the *Times*, 21 January 1851.
69. *To* Macready, *P*6 586.
70. The Lords' rejection of Gladstone's Paper Duties Repeal Bill in October 1860 was unprecedented; the crisis and stratagem for the subsequent passing of the measure in 24 & 25 Vict. C. 20, is explained in May II.108–112 & n.13.
71. *AYR* V.437 (3 August 1861).
72. CD Jnr. was one of three Directors of the Postford Paper-Making Co., subscribing £500 of its £3000 capital; the firm failed in 1868 (*P*9 508n., *P*12 138ff).
73. *P*6 586.
74. *P*6 36.
75. *HW* I.238–40.

76. Fitzgerald, *Memories* 125.
77. 16 & 17 Vict. C. 63 'An Act to Repeal Certain Stamp Duties' 4 August 1853; Fox Bourne 214, 218, 217; *P6* 423n., A. Andrews, 323–4; T. Milner-Gibson MP, CD's friend, used the *Narrative*'s case in debate on 22 April 1852 (Hansard 3rd Ser. CXX cols. 983f.); see also Wilson's excellent account of the transactions of the Select Committee, 57–74; C.D. Collet, author of *History Of The Taxes On Knowledge: Their Origin And Repeal* (1899).
78. *P6* 586.
79. Curran & Seaton 9, 22, 24, 15.
80. Wiener, 'How new' 50, 56–8; the coinage from Ralph Blumenfeld's *The Press in My Time* (1932) 208.
81. Curran & Seaton 41.
82. Although a welcome corrective to the misleading idealism and subterfuges of free-market historians ancient and modern, Curran's 'Press History' seems unduly hard on the character of the stamped press of the mid-Victorian period, which (to this reader) still seems – even as it mutates – to fulfil the Habermassian criteria for healthy participation in a democratic public sphere.

Chapter 10

1. Mostly male: only 9 of the 69 reviewers whose sex was inferrable, were female.
2. Hensher 41.
3. 'Parson threatens crowd with pistol' [review of D2], *TLS*, 17 January 1997, 18bc.
4. Gardiner 230–231; the para. owes much to this fine essay.
5. See in 'A Fly-Leaf in a Life,' *AYR* NS I (5 June 2869) repr. *D4* 386–391.
6. Hayter 18d.
7. Sutherland, 'the Blair facts' &c.
8. Jessel, 'Dickens' day job.'
9. Foot 27b; the 3 Tory Cabinet ministers named in Lord Justice Scott's report into the 'Matrix-Churchill' arms-to-Iraq scandal as having signed Public Interest Immunity Certificates which prevented the use of documents by the defence in the trial of 3 UK businessmen.
10. col. b; articles of 27 April and 18 May 1850 respectively, repr. *D2* 212–34; Mortimer invokes the thesis of Edmund Wilson's groundbreaking 1941 essay 'Dickens and the Two Scrooges' (repr. Hollington, *Critical Assessments* 1.756–808).
11. 'A Tale of two authors' 31cd–32a.
12. Nayder 365–6.
13. 'His life and hard times' 2c.
14. Nye 18c.

Bibliography

This bibliography is limited, for economy, to works mentioned or cited in the text. MS materials and their locations are given in full in the Endnotes. The place of publication, unless otherwise stated, is London.

Dickens's Works (with their acronyms as used in Endnotes)

References in the text and notes to Dickens's journalism are cited by page number to one of the editions listed below, or to volume and page of their original periodical publication (see 'Periodicals and Newspapers' below). References to his novels and other works are cited by book and chapter, or the number and date of the monthly/weekly part. The sheer variety of available editions makes citing specific page numbers of little value; where these have been given, readers are referred in the Endnotes to an edition specified under its editor's name in the main listing of secondary sources.

AN	*American Notes*
BH	*Bleak House*
BR	*Barnaby Rudge*
CP	*Collected Papers.* Ed. A. Waugh, et al. 2 vols. 'The Nonesuch Dickens.' Nonesuch Press, 1937.
D1–4	*Dent Uniform Edition of Dickens' Journalism.* Ed. Michael Slater (Vols. 1–3), Michael Slater and John Drew (Vol. 4). 4 vols. J. M. Dent, 1994–2000.
DC	*David Copperfield*
DS	*Dombey and Son*
GE	*Great Expectations*
HT	*Hard Times*
LD	*Little Dorrit*
MC	*Martin Chuzzlewit*
MHC	*Master Humphrey's Clock*
MP	*Miscellaneous Papers.* Ed. B. W. Matz. Vols 35, 36 of 'The Gadshill Edition.' Chapman & Hall, 1908.
NN	*Nicholas Nickleby*
OCS	*The Old Curiosity Shop*
OMF	*Our Mutual Friend*
OT	*Oliver Twist*
PP	*The Pickwick Papers*
SB	*Sketches by Boz*
Stone	*Charles Dickens' Uncollected Writings from Household Words, 1850–59.* Ed. Harry Stone. 2 vols. Bloomington & Indiana University Press, 1968.
TTC	*A Tale of Two Cities*
UT	*The Uncommercial Traveller*

Dickens's Life, Letters, and Library (with their abbreviations as used in Endnotes)

References to Forster's *Life* are given in the Endnotes using the book and chapter numbers adopted from 1876 onwards.

Life   *The Life of Charles Dickens*. By John Forster. [3 vols. 1872–74] Ed. J. W. T. Ley. Cecil Palmer, 1928.

MDGH   *The Letters of Charles Dickens, 1833–1870*. Ed. Mary Dickens and Georgina Hogarth. 2 vols. Chapman & Hall, 1882.

P1–12   *The Letters of Charles Dickens*. 'The Pilgrim Edition.' General Eds Madeline House, Graham Storey & Kathleen Tillotson. 12 vols. Oxford: Clarendon Press, 1965–2002.

S   *Reprints of the Catalogue of the Libraries of Charles Dickens and W. M. Thackeray &c*. Piccadilly Fountain Press, 1935.

Speeches   *The Speeches of Charles Dickens*. Ed. K. J. Fielding. [1960] Harvester, 1988.

Periodicals and Newspapers (with their acronyms as used in Endnotes and Index)

All the Year Round, 1859–70 (*AYR*)
Bell's Life in London, 1835
Bentley's Miscellany, 1837–39 (*BM*)
British Press, 1825–26
Carlton Chronicle and National Conservative Journal, 1836
Chambers's Edinburgh Journal, 1850–51
Cornhill Magazine, 1860
Daily News, 1846 (*DN*)
English Gentleman, 1845
Evening Chronicle, 1835 (*EC*)
Examiner, 1838–49, 1859–60 (*Ex*)
Household Words, 1850–59 (*HW*)
Household Words Almanac, 1856–7
Household Narrative of Current Events, 1850–55 (*HN*)
Leader, 1850
Mirror of Parliament, 1828–34 (*MP*)
Morning Chronicle, 1834–7 (*MC*)
Once A Week, 1859
True Sun, 1832–33
The Wellesley Index to Victorian Periodicals, 1824–1900. Ed. Walter E. Houghton. 5 vols. Routledge, 1966–89 (*Wellesley*)

Theses

Al-Ani, Tariq. 'Charles Dickens's Weekly Periodicals: Their Establishment, Conduct, and Development.' Unpublished MA thesis, University of Leicester, 1971.

Asquith, Ivon. 'James Perry and the *Morning Chronicle*, 1790–1821.' Unpublished PhD. thesis, University of London, 1973.

Clark, Harold Frank. 'Dickensian Journalism, A Study of *Household Words*.' Unpublished PhD. thesis, University of Columbia, 1967.

Drew, John M. L. 'Charles Dickens' "Uncommercial Traveller" Papers (1860–69): Roots, Interpretation and Context.' Unpublished PhD. thesis, University of London, 1994.

Foll, Scott [Leroy]. 'Dickens and the "Uncommercial Traveller." ' Unpublished PhD. thesis, Florida State University, 1982.

Freedman, Nadezhda. 'Essays by Boz: The Eighteenth-Century Periodical Essay and Dickens's Sketches by Boz.' Unpublished PhD. thesis, University of Columbia, 1977 DAI 38: 277A.

Grubb, Gerald G. 'Charles Dickens: Journalist.' Unpublished PhD. thesis, University of North Carolina, 1940.

Leavis, F. R. 'The Relationship of Journalism to Literature.' Unpublished DPhil. thesis, Cambridge University, 1924.

Mott, Graham. ' "I Wallow in Words": Dickens, Journalism and Public Affairs, 1831–38.' Unpublished PhD. thesis, University of Leicester, 1984.

Rathburn, Robert Charles. 'Charles Dickens' Periodical Essays and their Relationships to the Novels.' Unpublished PhD. thesis, University of Minnesota, 1957.

Stone, Harry. 'Dickens's Reading.' Unpublished PhD. thesis, University of California, 1955.

Articles, Books and Pamphlets

Adams, Percy. *Travelers and Travel Liars, 1660–1800.* Berkeley LA: University of California Press, 1962.

Adelman, Paul. *Victorian Radicalism … 1830–1914.* Longman, 1994.

Andrews, Alexander. *The History of British Journalism.* 2 vols. [1858]. Richard Bentley, 1859.

Andrews, Malcolm. 'Introducing Master Humphrey.' *Dickensian* 67 (1971) 70–86.

——. *Dickens and the Grown-up Child.* Macmillan, 1994.

Anon. 'Private History of the London Newspaper Press.' *Tait's Edinburgh Magazine* Supplementary Number for 1834 [?Jan. 1835] 788–92.

——. *The Thunderer in the Making 1785–1841: The History of The Times.* Vol. 1. Office of *The Times,* 1935.

Arac, Jonathan. *Commissioned Spirits.* New Brunswick, NJ: Rutgers University Press, 1979.

Ard, Patricia M. 'Charles Dickens' Stormy Crossing: The Rhetorical Voyage from Letters to *American Notes.' Nineteenth-Century Prose* 23 (1996) 34–42.

Aspinall, Arthur. *Politics and the Press, 1780–1850.* [1949] Brighton: Harvester Press, 1973.

——. 'The Reporting and Publishing of the House of Commons' Debates, 1771–1834' in *Essays Presented to Sir Lewis Namier,* ed. R. Pares and A. J. P. Taylor. [1956] Freeport, NY: Books for Libraries Press, 1971. 227–57.

——. 'The Social Status of Journalists at the Beginning of the Nineteenth Century.' *Review of English Studies* 21 (1945) 216–32.

Atkins, J. B. *Life of Sir William Howard Russell.* Vol. 1 (of 2). John Murray, 1911.

Bann, Stephen. 'Visuality Codes the Text: Charles Dickens's *Pictures from Italy*' in *Writing and Victorianism,* ed. J. B. Bullen. London and New York: Longman, 1997. 202–18.

Beaumont, Charles Allen. *Swift's Classical Rhetoric.* Athens: University of Georgia Press, 1961.

Benson, Arthur C. and Viscount Esher. *Letters of Queen Victoria, A Selection from Her Majesty's Correspondence, 1837–61.* John Murray, 1908.

Bevis, Matthew. 'Temporizing Dickens.' *Review of English Studies*, NS 52 (2001) 171–191.

——. 'Dickens in Public.' *Essays in Criticism* 51 (2001) 330–51.

Bourdieu, Pierre. *On Television and Journalism*. Trans. Priscilla Ferguson. London, Pluto 1998.

Bourne, Henry R Fox. *English Newspapers*. 2 vols. Chatto & Windus, 1887.

Bowen, John. *Other Dickens*. Oxford: Oxford University Press, 2000.

Brake, Laurel et al., eds. *Investigating Victorian Journalism*. Macmillan, 1990.

——, et al., eds. *Nineteenth-Century Media and the Construction of Identities*. Basingstoke: Palgrave, 2000.

Brantlinger, Patrick. *The Spirit of Reform. British Literature and Politics, 1832–67*. Cambridge, MA: Harvard University Press, 1977.

——. *Rule of Darkness: British Literature and Imperialism, 1830–1914*. Ithaca: Cornell University Press, 1988.

Brent, Doug. 'Why Does Rhetoric Need a Theory of Reading?' *Proceedings of the Canadian Society for the History of Rhetoric* 3 (1991) 81–91.

Brice, Alec W. '"A Truly British Judge." Another Article by Dickens.' *Dickensian* 66 (1970) 30–35.

——. 'A New Article by Dickens: "Demoralisation and Total Abstinence."' *Dickens Studies Annual* 9 (1981) 1–19.

——. and K. J. Fielding. 'Charles Dickens and the Tooting Disaster.' *Victorian Studies* 12 (1968) 227–44.

——. and K. J. Fielding. 'Ignorance and its Victims: Another New Article by Dickens.' *Dickensian* 63 (1967) 143–47.

Brock, M. *The Great Reform Act*. Hutchinson, 1973.

Buckler, William E. 'Dickens's success with *Household Words*.' *Dickensian* 46 (1950) 197–203.

——. '*Household Words* in America.' *Papers of the Bibliographical Society of America* 45 (1951) 160–6.

——. 'Dickens the Paymaster.' *PMLA* 66 (1951) 1177–80.

——. '*Once A Week* under Samuel Lucas, 1859–65.' *PMLA* 67 (1952) 924–41.

Buckley, Jessie K. *Joseph Parkes of Birmingham*. Methuen & Co., 1926.

Burke, Kenneth. *Philosophy of Literary Form*. New York: Vintage Books, 1957.

Butor, Michel. 'Le Voyage et l'écriture' [1972] repr. as 'Travel and Writing' Trans. J. Powers & K. Lister. *Mosaic* 8 (1974) 1–16.

Butt, John & Kathleen Tillotson. *Dickens at Work*. [1957] Methuen, 1968.

Butterworth, R. D. 'Dickens the Journalist: The Preston Strike and "On Strike."' *Dickensian* 89 (1993) 129–38.

Buzard, James. *The Beaten Track: European Tourism, Literature, and the Ways to Culture*. Oxford: Oxford University Press, 1993.

Campbell, Kate, ed. *Journalism, Literature and Modernity*. Edinburgh: Edinburgh University Press, 2000.

Cannon, John. *Parliamentary Reform 1640–1832*. Aldershot: Gregg Revivals, 1994.

Caponi-Doherty, Gabriella. 'Charles Dickens and the Italian Risorgimento.' *Dickens Quarterly* 13 (1996) 151–63.

Carey, John. 'A tale of two authors' [Review of *D4*]. *Sunday Times*, 31 December 2000, Books 31–32.

——. 'His life and hard times' [Review of *D2*]. *Sunday Times*, 8 December 1996, Books 1–2.

Carlson, Laurie. 'Categorizing *American Notes*: Dickens as New Journalist.' *Nineteenth-Century Prose* 23 (1996) 25–33.

Carlton, W. J. '"Boz" and the Beards.' *Dickensian* 58 (1962) 9–21.

——. 'Dickens's Literary Mentor.' *Dickens Studies* 1 (1965) 54–64.

——. 'A Companion of the Copperfield Days.' *Dickensian* 50 (1954) 7–16.

——. 'An Echo of the Copperfield Days.' *Dickensian* 45 (1949) 149–52.

——. 'Charles Dickens, Dramatic Critic.' *Dickensian* 56 (1960) 11–15.

——. *Charles Dickens, Shorthand Writer. The 'Prentice Days of a Master Craftsman.* Cecil Palmer [1926].

——. 'Dickens and O'Connell.' *Notes and Queries* 188 (April 1945) 147.

——. 'Dickens and the Two Tennysons.' *Dickensian* 47 (1951) 173–7.

——. 'Dickens reports O'Connell: a legend examined.' *Dickensian* 65 (1969) 95–9.

——. 'In the Blacking Warehouse.' *Dickensian* 60 (1964) 11–16.

——. 'John Dickens, Journalist.' *Dickensian* 53 (1957) 5–11.

——. 'Portraits in "A Parliamentary Sketch." ' *Dickensian* 50 (1954) 100–9.

——. 'The Story Without a Beginning.' *Dickensian* 47 (1951) 67–70.

[Carpenter, Mary]. *Ragged Schools: Their Principles and Modes of Operation.* Partridge & Oakey, 1850.

Carrow, G. D. 'Informal Call on Charles Dickens by a Philadelphia Clergyman.' *Dickensian* 63 (1967) 112–9.

Chaudhry, G. A. 'The Mudfog Papers.' *Dickensian* 70 (1974) 104–112.

Chesterton, G. K. *Criticisms & Appreciations of the Works of Charles Dickens.* J. M. Dent, 1911.

——. *Charles Dickens.* Methuen, 1906.

——. *Charles Dickens, the Last of the Great Men.* [1st ed., *Charles Dickens: A Critical Study*, 1906] New York: Press of the Readers Club, 1942.

——, ed. *Sketches by Boz [&c.].* J. M. Dent, 1907.

——, ed. *The Uncommercial Traveller.* J. M. Dent, 1911.

Chittick, Kathryn. 'The Idea of a Miscellany: *Master Humphrey's Clock.' Dickensian* 78 (1982) 156–64.

——. 'Dickens and Parliamentary Reporting in the 1830s.' *Victorian Periodicals Review* 21 (1988) 151–60.

——. *Dickens and the 1830s.* Cambridge: Cambridge University Press, 1990.

Cobbett, William, *Selections from Cobbett's Political Works.* 6 vols. ed. J. M. & J. P. Cobbett. Ann Cobbett, 1835.

Coles, Nicholas. 'The Politics of *Hard Times*: Dickens the Novelist versus Dickens the Reformer.' *Dickens Studies Annual* 15 (1986) 145–79.

Collier, John Payne. *An Old Man's Diary, Forty Years Ago; for the Last Six Months of 1833.* Vol. 2 of 4. Thomas Richards, 1872.

Collins, Philip. *Dickens and Crime.* Macmillan, 1962.

——. *Dickens and Education.* Macmillan, 1965.

——. 'Dickens and the Ragged Schools.' *Dickensian* 55 (1959) 94–109.

——. 'Dickens on Ghosts: An Uncollected Article.' *Dickensian* 59 (1963) 5–14.

——. 'Dickens's Reading.' *Dickensian* 60 (1964) 136–51.

——. 'The *All The Year Round* Letter Book.' *Victorian Periodicals Newsletter* 10 (1970) 23–9.

——. 'The Significance of Dickens's Periodicals.' *Review of English Literature* 2 (1961) 55–64.

——. 'W. H. Wills' Plans for *Household Words.' Victorian Periodicals Newsletter* 8 (1970) 33–46.

Cook, Jon. 'Hazlitt, Speech and Writing.' in Kate Campbell, ed.

Cook, Sir Edward. *Delane of The Times.* Constable & Co., 1915.

Crowe, Sir Joseph Archer. *Reminiscences of Thirty-five Years of My Life.* John Murray, 1895.

Curran, James and Jean Seaton. *Power without Responsibility; the Press and Broadcasting in Britain*. [1981] 5th ed. London and New York: Routledge: 2000.

D[exter] W[alter]. 'Early Propaganda.' *Dickensian* 32 (1936) 272–74.

Daunt, William J. O'Neill. *Personal Recollections of the Late Daniel O'Connell*. 2 vols. (Chapman & Hall, 1848) 1.14–15.

David, Deirdre. *Rule Britannia. Women, Empire and Victorian Writing*. Ithaca, NY: Cornell University Press, 1995.

Davies, James A. *John Forster: A Literary Life*. Leicester: Leicester University Press, 1983.

——. *The Textual Life of Dickens's Characters*. Macmillan, 1989.

De Quincey, Thomas. *Confessions of An English Opium-Eater* (1822). Harmondsworth: Penguin Classics, 1971.

De Vries, Duane. *Dickens's Apprentice Years: The Making of a Novelist*. New York: Harvester Press, 1976.

Drew, John M. L. 'Dickens Reappears' [P11 review essay]. *Dickens Quarterly* 18 (2001) 139–47.

——. 'The Nineteenth-Century Commercial Traveler and Dickens's "Uncommercial" Philosophy.' *Dickens Quarterly* 15 (1998) 50–61, 83–110.

——. 'Voyages Extraordinaires: Dickens's "Traveling Essays" and *The Uncommercial Traveller*.' *Dickens Quarterly* 13 (1996) 76–96, 127–50.

Duffy, Sir Charles Gavan. *Conversations with Carlyle*. Sampson, Low, Marston & Co., 1892.

Dvorak, Wilfred P. 'Dickens' Ambivalence as a Social Critic in the 1860s: Attitudes to Money in *All the Year Round* and *The Uncommercial Traveller*.' *Dickensian* 80 (1984) 89–104.

Edgecombe, Rodney S. 'Topgraphic Disaffection in Dickens's *American Notes* and *Martin Chuzzlewit*.' *Journal of English and Germanic Philology* 93 (1994) 35–53.

Edwards, P. D. *Dickens's 'Young Men': George Augustus Sala, Edmund Yates and the World of Victorian Journalism*. Aldershot: Ashgate Publishing, 1997.

Ellegard, Alvar. *Readership of the Periodical Press in Mid-Victorian Britain*. Göteborgs Universitets Arsskrift LIII, 1957.

Elliot, Hugh S. R., ed. & intro. *The Letters of John Stuart Mill*. 2 vols. Longmans, Green & Co., 1910.

Elwell, Stephen. 'Editors and Social Change: A Case Study of *Once a Week* (1859–80),' in Wiener, *Innovators*.

Elwin, Whitwell. *Some XVIII Century Men of Letters: Biographical Essays*. 2 vols. Murray, 1902.

Engel, Monroe. 'The Politics of Dickens's Novels.' *PMLA* 71 (1956) 945–74.

Fage, J. D. *A History of West Africa*. Cambridge: CUP, 1969.

Fielding, K. J. '*American Notes* and some English Reviewers.' *MLR* 59 (1964) 536.

——. 'Bradbury v. Dickens.' *Dickensian* 50 (1954) 73–82.

——. *Charles Dickens: A Critical Introduction*. 2nd ed. Longmans, 1965.

——. 'Dickens and Science?' *Dickens Quarterly* 13.4 (December 1996) 200–216.

——. 'Dickens as J. T. Danson Knew Him.' *Dickensian* 68 (1972) 151–61.

—— and Alec W. Brice. '*Bleak House* and the Graveyard' in *Dickens the Craftsman*, ed. Robert J. Partlow, Jr. Carbondale: Southern Illinois University Press, 1970. 115–39.

—— and Alec W. Brice. 'Charles Dickens on "The Exclusion of Evidence",' *Dickensian* 64 (1968) 131–40 & 65 (1969) 35–41.

——and Anne Smith. '*Hard Times* and the Factory Controversy: Dickens vs. Harriet Martineau.' *Nineteeth-Century Fiction* 24 (1970) 404–27.

—— and Shu-Fang Lai. 'Dickens, Science, and *The Poetry of Science*.' *Dickensian* 93.1 (1997) 5–10.

—— and Shu-Fang Lai. Letter to the Editor. *Dickensian* 93 (1997) 205.

Fields, James T. *In and Out of Doors with Charles Dickens*. Boston: J. R. Osgood, 1876.
Fields, Mrs James T. *Memories of a Hostess &c.* Ed. M.A. DeWolfe Howe. T. Fisher Unwin, 1923.
Fitzgerald, Percy. *Memoirs of an Author.* 2 vols. Bentley, 1894.
——. *Memories of Charles Dickens &c.* Bristol: J. W. Arrowsmith, 1913.
——. *Recreations of a Literary Man.* Chatto & Windus, 1883.
Flint, Kate. *The Woman Reader 1837–1914.* Oxford: Clarendon Press, 1993.
Flint, Kate, ed. & intro. *Pictures from Italy* by Charles Dickens. Harmondsworth: Penguin, 1998.
Foll, Scott Leroy. *Great Expectations* and the "Uncommercial" Sketch Book.' *Dickensian* 81 (1985) 109–16.
Fonblanque, Albany. *England Under Seven Administrations.* 3 vols. Richard Bentley, 1837.
Foot, Paul. [review of *D1*]. *Spectator*, 14/21 December 1994, 26–7.
Ford, P. and G. *A Guide to Parliamentary Papers.* Shannon, Ireland: Irish University Press, 1972.
Forster, E. M. *Passage to India.* [1924]. Penguin Books, 1989.
Gardiner, John. 'The Dickensian and Us.' *History Workshop Journal*. No. 51 (2001) 227–37.
Garis, Robert. *The Dickens Theatre.* Oxford: Clarendon Press, 1965.
Garnett, R. *Life of W. J. Fox … 1784–1864.* John Lane, 1910.
Gash, Norman. *Politics in the Age of Peel … 1830–1850.* [1959] London and Harlow: Longmans Green and Co., 1969.
Gaskell, Elizabeth. *The Letters of Mrs Gaskell.* Ed. J.A.V. Chapple and A. Pollard. Cambridge: Harvard University Press, 1967.
Gatrell, V. A. C. *The Hanging Tree: Execution and the English People, 1770–1868.* Oxford: Oxford University Press, 1994.
Gettmann, Royal A. *A Victorian Publisher: A Study of the Bentley Papers.* Cambridge: Cambridge University Press, 1960.
Golding, Robert, *Idiolects in Dickens.* Basingstoke: Macmillan, 1985.
Graham, Walter, *English Literary Periodicals.* [1930] New York: Octagon Books, 1980.
Grant, James. *Random Recollections of the House of Commons [1830–35].* Smith, Elder & Co., 1836.
——. *The Great Metropolis.* 2 vols. Saunders & Otley, 1837.
——. *The Newspaper Press.* 3 vols. Tinsley, 1871.
Gratton, C. J. *The Gallery, a Sketch of the History of Parliamentary Reporting and Reporters.* London, Bath, 1860.
Graves, C. L. '*Punch* in the 1860s' in *The Eighteen Sixties*, ed. John Drinkwater. Cambridge: CUP, 1932.
Greville, Charles C. F. *The Greville Memoirs: A Journal of the Reigns of King George IV, King William IV, and Queen Victoria.* 8 vols. 3 parts. Longmans, Green & Co., 1888.
Grillo, Virgil. *Charles Dickens's Sketches by Boz: End in the Beginning.* Boulder, Colorado: Colorado University Press, 1974.
Grubb, Gerald G. 'Charles Dickens's First Experience as a Parliamentary Reporter.' *Dickensian* 36 (1940) 211–18.
——. 'Dickens and the *Daily News*: the Origin of the Idea' in *Booker Memorial Studies: Eight Essays on Victorian Literature in Memory of John Manning Booker*, ed. Hill Shine, 60–77. Chapel Hill: University of North Carolina Press, 1950.
——. 'Dickens and the "Daily News": Preliminaries to Publication.' *Nineteenth-Century Fiction* 6(1951–52) 174–94.

———. 'Dickens and the "Daily News:" Resignation.' *Nineteenth-Century Fiction* 7 (1952–53) 19–38.

———. 'Dickens and the "Daily News:" The Early Issues.' *Nineteenth-Century Fiction* 6 (1951–52) 234–46.

———. 'Dickens the Paymaster Once More.' *Dickensian* 51 (55) 72–8.

———. 'Personal and Business Relations of Charles Dickens and Thomas Coke Evans.' *Dickensian* 48 (1952), 106–13, 168–73.

———. 'The American Edition of "All the Year Round".' *Papers of the Bibliographical Society of America* 47 (1953) 301–4.

———. 'The Editorial Policies of Charles Dickens.' *PMLA* 58 (1943) 1110–24.

Gurney, Joseph. *Brachygraphy: or an Easy and Compendious System of Short-hand &c.* 14th ed. [1750] W. B. Gurney, 1817.

Habermas, Jürgen. *The Structural Transformation of the Public Sphere.* [1962] Trans. Thomas Burger & Frederick Lawrence. Cambridge: Polity, 1989.

Hall, Samuel Carter. *Retrospect of a Long Life, from 1815 to 1883.* 2 vols. Bentley, 1883.

Harden, Edgar F. *Thackeray the Writer.* Basingstoke: Macmillan, 2000.

Harle, W. Lockey. 'John Forster: a Sketch.' *Monthly Chronicle of North-Country Lore and Legend*, 2 (1888) 49–54.

Hartley, John. *Popular Reality: Journalism, Modernity, Popular Culture.* Arnold, 1996.

Harvey, J. R. *Victorian Novelists and their Illustrators.* Sidgewick and Jackson, 1970.

Hayek, F. A. *John Stuart Mill and Harriet Taylor: their Correspondence and Subsequent Marriage.* Routledge and Kegan Paul, 1951.

Hayter, Alethea. 'Parson threatens crowd with pistol' [Review of *D2*]. *TLS*, 17 January 1997, 18.

Haywood, Charles. 'Charles Dickens and Shakespeare; or, The Irish Moor of Venice, *O'Thello*, with Music.' *Dickensian* 73 (1977) 67–88.

Hazlitt, William. *Complete Works.* Ed. P. P. Howe. 21 vols. J. M. Dent, 1930.

Hemstedt, Geoffrey. 'Dickens's Later Journalism.' in Kate Campbell, ed.

———. 'Inventing Social Identity: *Sketches by Boz*.' in Robbins and Wolfreys, eds.

Hensher, Philip. 'A genius at this best and worst' [Review of *D4*]. *Spectator*, 9 December 2000, 40–41.

Hill, T. W. 'Books that Dickens Read.' *Dickensian* 45 (1949) 81–90, 201–7.

Hollingshead, John. 'Fifty Years of *Household Words*.' *Household Words* 'Jubilee Number' No. 26 (May 1900).

———. *My Lifetime.* 2 vols. Sampson, Low, Marston, 1895.

Hollington, Michael. *Dickens and the Grotesque.* London, Sidney: Croom Helm, 1984.

———. Dickens the Flâneur.' *Dickensian* 77 (1981) 71–87.

———, ed. *Charles Dickens: Critical Assessments.* 4 vols. East Sussex: Helm Information, 1995.

Holquist, Michael. *Dialogism. Bahktin and his World.* Routledge, 1990.

Hudson, Frederic. *Journalism in the United States, from 1690 to 1872.* [1873] 2 vols. Routledge, 2000.

Hughes, Linda K. & Michael Lund. *The Victorian Serial.* Charlottesville & University Press of Virginia, 1991.

Hughes, Thomas. 'Anonymous Journalism.' *Macmillan's Magazine.* (5 December 1861) 157–68.

Humpherys, Anne. 'Louisa Gradgrind's Secret: Marriage and Divorce in *Hard Times*.' *Dickens Studies Annual* 25 (1996) 177–95.

Hunt, Frederick Knight. *The Fourth Estate.* [1850] Routledge/Thoemmes, 1998.

Ikime, Obaro. *The Fall of Nigeria; the British Conquest.* London, Ibadan: Heinemann, 1977.

Jaffe, Audrey. *Vanishing Points: Dickens, Narrative and The Subject of Omniscience.* Berkeley LA, Oxford: University of California Press, 1991.

James, Louis. *Fiction for the Working Man 1830–1850.* Oxford: Oxford University Press, 1963.

Jerdan, William. *Autobiography.* 4 vols. Arthur Hall, Virtue & Co.

Jerrold, Walter. *Thomas Hood: His Life and Times.* Alston Rivers, 1907.

Jessel, David. 'Dickens' day job.' *Scotland on Sunday,* 10 January 1999.

Johnson, Edgar. 'Dickens and the Bluenose Legislator.' *American Scholar* 17 (1948).

Johnson, Edgar. *Charles Dickens, His Tragedy and Triumph.* 2 vols. Hamish Hamilton/Boston: Little, Brown, 1952.

Johnson, Paul. *The Birth of the Modern ... 1815–1830.* Weidenfeld & Nicolson, 1991.

Kellett, E. E., 'The Press' in *Early Victorian England, 1830–65.* Ed. G. M. Young. 2 vols. Oxford University Press, 1934.

Kent, Charles. 'Charles Dickens as a Journalist.' *Time* (July 1881) 361–74.

Kitton, Frederic G. *Charles Dickens: By Pen and Pencil.* 3 vols. Frank T. Sabin & John F. Dexter, 1890–92.

——. *Dickensiana.* George Redway, 1886.

——. *The Minor Writings of Charles Dickens.* Eliott Stock, 1900.

Koss, Stephen. *The Rise and Fall of the Political Press in Britain.* Vol. 1 (of 2). Hamilton, 1981.

Lai, Shu-Fang. 'Fact or Fancy: What Can We Learn about Dickens from His Periodicals *Household Words* and *All the Year Round?*' *Victorian Periodicals Review* 34 (2001) 41–53.

Langton, Robert. *The Childhood and Youth of Charles Dickens.* Hutchinson, 1912.

Law, Graham. *Serializing Fiction in the Victorian Press.* Basingstoke: Palgrave, 2000.

Leech, Geoffrey N. and Michael H. Short. *Style in Fiction. A Linguistic Introduction.* Longman, 1981.

Lehmann, R. C. *Charles Dickens as Editor.* Smith, Elder & Co., 1912.

Lettis, Richard. 'Dickens and Art.' *Dickens Studies Newsletter* 14 (1985) 93–146.

Litvack, Leon. 'Dickens, Ireland and the Irish.' Forthcoming in *Dickensian* 99 (2003).

Lohrli, Anne, comp. *Household Words, ... Table of Contents, List of Contributors and Their Contributions &c.* Toronto: University of Toronto Press, 1973.

Mackenzie, Norman and Jeanne. *Dickens, A Life.* Oxford: Oxford University Press, 1979.

Mackenzie, Robert Shelton. *Life of Charles Dickens.* Philadelphia: T. B. Peterson [1870].

[Maginn, William]. Review, Grantley Berkeley's *Berkeley Castle. Fraser's Magazine* 14 (August 1836) 242.

Magnet, Myron. *Dickens and the Social Order.* University of Pennsylvania Press, 1985.

Markham, Violet R. *Paxton and the Bachelor Duke.* Hodder & Stoughton, 1935.

Marriott, John, ed. & intro. *Unknown Early Modernist Visions of the Metropolis, 1815–1845.* 6 vols. Pickering & Chatto 2000.

Martineau, Harriet. *Autobiography.* 3 Vols. Smith, Elder & Co., 1877.

Martineau, Harriet. *The Factory Controversy; a Warning against Meddling Legislation.* Manchester: National Association of Factory Occupiers, 1855.

Massie, Alan. 'Sometimes he agreed with Scrooge' [review of *D2*]. *Daily Telegraph,* Arts & Books, 28 December 1996, 2.

Massingham, Henry William. *The London Daily Press.* [London:] Religious Tract Society, 1892.

Mathew, H. C. G. 'Rhetoric and Politics in Britain 1860–1950' in *Politics and Social Change in Modern Britain: Essays Presented to A. F. Thompson*, ed. P. J. Waller. Brighton: Harvester, 1987, 34–58.

Matz, B. W. 'Dickens as a Journalist.' *Fortnightly Review* NS No. 498 (1 May 1908) 817–32.

Maurice, Arthur Bartlett. 'Dickens as an Editor.' *Bookman* 30 (1909) 111–14.

Maxwell, Richard C. 'Dickens, the Two *Chronicles*, and the Publication of *Sketches by Boz*.' *Dickens Studies Annual* 9 (1981) 21–32.

——. 'G. M. Reynolds, Dickens, and the Mysteries of London.' *Nineteenth Century Fiction* 32 (1977) 188–213.

May, Thomas Erskine. *Constitutional History of England since the Accession of George the Third*. [1860] 3 vols. 7th ed. Longmans, Green & Co, 1882.

McCarthy, Justin. *History of Our Own Times*. 2 vols. [1880] New York: A. L. Burt, n. d.

—— and John R. Robinson. *'The Daily News' Jubilee, A Political and Social Retrospect of Fifty Years of the Queen's Reign*. Sampson, Low & Marston, 1896.

McCarthy, Patrick. 'Claiming Truth: Dickens and *American Notes*.' *Nineteenth-Century Prose* 23 (1996) 1–11.

Meckier, Jerome. *Hidden Rivalries in Victorian Fiction: Dickens, Realism, and Revaluation*. Lexington, KY: University of Kentucky Press, 1987.

——. *Innocent Abroad: Charles Dickens's American Engagements*. Lexington, KY: University of Kentucky Press, 1990.

Mill, John Stuart. *Autobiography*. Columbia University Press, 1948.

Miller, J. Hillis. 'The Fiction of Realism: *Sketches by Boz*, *Oliver Twist*, and Cruikshank's Illustrations.' in *Dickens' Centennial Essays*, ed. Ada Nisbet and Blake Nevius. Berkeley LA & University of California Press, 1971. 85–153.

——. 'The Genres of A Christmas Carol.' *Dickensian* 89 (1993) 193–206.

——. 'The Sources of Dickens's Comic Art: From *American Notes* to *Martin Chuzzlewit*.' *Nineteenth Century Fiction* 24 (1970) 467–76.

[Morley, John]. 'Anonymous Journalism.' *Fortnightly Review* 2.9 (1 September 1867) 287–92.

Mortimer, John. 'Losing patience with the poor' [review of D2]. *The Spectator* 14/21 December 1996, 61.

Mott, Frank Luther. *A History of American Magazines* 1850–65. Cambridge MA: Belknap Press, 1957.

Mowitt, John. 'The Essay as Instance of the Social Function of Private Experience.' *Prose Studies* 12 (1989) 274–84.

Mudford, Peter, ed. & intro. *Master Humphrey's Clock and other Stories*. J. M. Dent, 1997.

Mundhenk, Rosemary. 'Creative Ambivalence in Dickens's *Master Humphrey's Clock*.' *Studies in English Literature* 32 (1992) 645–61.

Nattrass, Leonora. *William Cobbett: The Politics of Style*. Cambridge: Cambridge University Press, 1995.

Nayder, Lillian. [review of D3]. *Victorian Periodicals Review* 32 (1999) 364–6.

Nead, Lynda. *Myths of Sexuality: Representations of Women in Victorian Britain*. Oxford: Basil Blackwell, 1988.

Nye, Robert. 'Breaking the news of Dickens' break up.' [review of D3] *Scotsman*, 9 January 1999, Books 18.

O'Connell, Daniel. *Correspondence*. Ed. W. J. Fitzpatrick. 2 vols. Murray, 1888.

Oddie, William. *Dickens and Carlyle*. Centenary Press, 1972.

Oppenlander, Ella Ann. *Dickens' All the Year Round: Descriptive Index and Contributor List*. Troy, NY: Whiston Publishing, 1984.

Ormond, Leonée. 'Dickens and Painting: the Old Masters.' *Dickensian* 79 (1983) 131–51. *See also under* Schwarzbach

Orwell, George. 'Charles Dickens' in *Inside the Whale*. Gollancz, 1940.

Ostry, Elaine. ' "Social Wonders:" Fancy, Science and Technology in Dickens's Periodicals'. *Victorian Periodicals Review* 34 (2001) 54–78.

Parker, David. 'Dickens and America: the Unflattering Glass.' *Dickens Studies Annual* 15 (1986) 55–63.

Paroissien, David. *Companion to Oliver Twist*. Edinburgh: Edinburgh University Press, 1992.

——, ed. *Selected Letters of Charles Dickens*. Basingstoke: Macmillan, 1985.

Partington, Wilfred. 'The Blacking Laureate. The Identity of Mr Slum, a Pioneer in Publicity.' *Dickensian* 34 (1938) 199–202.

Pascoe, David, ed. & intro. *Charles Dickens, Selected Journalism* 1850–1870. Penguin Books, 1997.

Patten, Robert L. *Charles Dickens and his Publishers*. Oxford: Clarendon Press, 1978.

——. 'Dickens as Serial Author: A Case of Multiple Identities' in Brake, Laurel, et al., *Nineteenth-Century Media*. 137–53.

——. 'Dickens Disappears' [*P* 10 review essay]. *Dickens Quarterly* 17 (2000) 45–51.

——. 'Portraits of Pott: Lord Broughan and *The Pickwick Papers*.' *Dickensian* 66 (1970) 205–24.

Paulin, Tom. *The Day-Star of Liberty: William Hazlitt's Radical Style*. Faber & Faber, 1998.

Peyrouton, Noel. 'Charles Dickens and the Chartists.' *Dickensian* 60 (1964), 78–88, 152–61.

——. 'Rapping the Rappers: More Grist for the Biographers' Mill.' *Dickensian* 55 (1959) 19–33, 75–89.

Poovey, Mary. *Uneven Developments: The Ideological Work of Gender in Mid-Victorian England*. Chicago: University of Chicago Press, 1988.

Pope-Hennessy, Una. *Charles Dickens*. [1945] Reprint Society, 1947.

Quirk, Randolph. *Charles Dickens and Appropriate Language* [inaugural lecture]. [Durham:] University of Durham, 1959.

——. 'Some Observations on the Language of Dickens.' *Review of English Literature* 2 (1961) 19–28.

Read, Donald. *Press and People, 1790–1850*. [1961] Aldershot: Gregg Revivals, 1993.

Ricks, Christopher, ed. *The Poems of Tennyson*. London & Harlow: Longmans, 1969.

Robbins, Ruth, and Julian Wolfreys, eds. *Victorian Identities*. Basingstoke: Macmillan, 1996.

Roberts, Adam. 'Dickens as Journalist.' *Dutch Dickensian* 12 (1990) 34–44.

Roberts, David. 'Charles Dickens and the *Daily News*: Editorials and Editorial Writers.' *Victorian Periodicals Review* 22 (1989) 51–63.

Robson, J. M. *What Did He Say? Editing Nineteenth-Century Speeches from Hansard and the Newspapers*. Lethbridge, Alberta: University of Lethbridge Press, 1988.

Rose, M. E. 'The Anti-Poor Law agitation.' in Ward, J. T.

Sala, George Augustus. *Charles Dickens*. Routledge, 1870.

Sala, G[eorge] A[ugustus]. *Life and Adventures of George Augustus Sala*. 2 vols. Cassell, 1895.

Sala, George Augustus. *Things I Have Seen and People I have Known*. 2 vols. Cassell, 1895.

Sanders, Valerie. *Reason over Passion: Harriet Martineau and the Victorian Novel*. Harvester, 1986.

Schad, John. 'Dickens's Cryptic Church: Drawing on *Pictures from Italy*' in *Dickens Refigured: Bodies, Desires and Other Histories*. Ed. John Schad. Manchester: Manchester University Press, 1996. 5–21.

Schlicke, Paul. 'Bumble and the Poor Law Satire of *Oliver Twist*.' *Dickensian* 71 (1975) 149–56.

——. *Dickens and Popular Amusements*. [1985] Unwin Hyman, 1988.

——. 'Revisions to *Sketches by Boz*.' Forthcoming in *Dickensian*.

——, ed. *The Oxford Reader's Companion to Dickens*. Oxford: Oxford University Press, 1999.

Schwarzbach, F. S. ' "Terra Incognita" – An Image of the City in English Literature, 1820–1855.' *Prose Studies* 5 (1982) 61–84.

—— & Ormond, Leonée, eds. *American Notes* and *Pictures from Italy* by Charles Dickens. J. M. Dent, 1997.

Scott, Walter. *The Journal of Sir Walter Scott, 1825–32*. 2 vols. Edinburgh, 1891.

Sharpe, William. 'A Pig upon the Town: Charles Dickens in New York.' *Nineteenth-Century Prose* 23 (1996) 12–24.

Silvester, Christopher, ed. & intro. *The Pimlico Companion to Parliament*. Random House, 1997.

Slater, Michael. *An Intelligent Person's Guide to Dickens*. Duckworth, 1999.

——. *Dickens and Women*. J. M. Dent, 1983.

——. *Douglas Jerrold 1803–1857*. Duckworth, 2002.

——. 'How Many Nurses had Charles Dickens? *The Uncommercial Traveller* and Dickensian Biography.' *Prose Studies* 10 (1987) 250–8.

——, ed. & intro. *Dickens on America and the Americans*. New York: Harvester Press, 1979.

Smith, Grahame. *Charles Dickens: A Literary Life*. Basingstoke: Macmillan, 1996.

——, ed. *Hard Times*, by Charles Dickens. J. M. Dent, 1996.

Solly, H. S. *Life of Henry Morley*. Arnold, 1898.

Sotheby & Co. *Catalogue of Valuable Letters, Literary Manuscripts &c.*, 17 December 1981.

Sotheby & Co. *The Charles Dickens Archive*, Sale Catalogue, 15 July 1999.

Spencer, Sandra. 'The Indispensable Mr Wills.' *Victorian Periodicals Review* 21 (1988) 145–51.

[Stephen, James Fitzjames]. 'Mr Dickens as a Politician.' *Saturday Review* 3 (3 Jan 1857) 8–9, repr. Hollington 1.162–6.

Stevens, David. 'Dickens in Eden: The Framing of America in *American Notes*.' *Nineteenth-Century Prose* 23 (1996) 43–52.

Stewart, Garrett. *Dickens and the Trials of Imagination*. Cambridge MA: Harvard University Press, 1974.

Stokes, Peter M. 'Bentham, Dickens, and the Uses of the Workhouse.' *Studies in English Literature* 41 (2001) 711–27.

Stone, Harry. 'Dickens and the Idea of a Periodical'. *Western Humanities Review* 21 (1967).

——. 'Dickens and the Interior Monologue.' *Philological Quarterly* 38 (1959) 61–66.

——. 'Dickens' Use of his American Experiences in *Martin Chuzzlewit*.' *PMLA* 72 (1957) 464–78.

Straus, Ralph. *Sala, The Portrait of An Eminent Victorian*. Constable, 1942.

Sucksmith, Harvey Peter. *The Narrative Art of Charles Dickens*. Oxford: Clarendon Press, 1970.

Sutherland, John. 'The Blair facts about Dickens and Politics.' *Independent*, 9 November 1996, 6.

——. *The Stanford Companion to Victorian Fiction*. Stanford, CA: Stanford University Press, 1989.

——. *Victorian Novelists and Publishers*. Athlone Press, 1976.

Symon, J. D. *The Press and its Story*. Seeley, Service, 1914.

Tannahill, Robert. *Poems and Songs*. Paisley: A. Gardner, 1875.

[Taverner, H. T. & J. C. Hotten]. *Charles Dickens. The Story of his Life*. John Camden Hotten, [1870].

Terry, Ellen. *The Story of My Life*. Hutchinson, 1908.

Thackeray, W. M. *Letters and Private Papers of William Makepiece Thackeray*. Ed. Gordon N. Ray. Vol. 4. Oxford University Press, 1945.

Thomas, Deborah A. *Dickens and the Short Story*. Philadelphia: Philadelphia University Press, 1982.

Tillotson, Kathleen. 'Dickens and a Story by John Poole.' *Dickensian* 52 (1956) 79–80.

——. 'March 1846, "at Sixes and sevens": a new letter.' *Dickensian* 82 (1986) 98–99.

——. 'New Light on Dickens and the *Daily News*.' *Dickensian* 78 (1982) 89–92.

——, ed. *Oliver Twist*. By Charles Dickens. Oxford: Clarendon Press, 1966.

Tomalin, Claire. *The Invisible Woman*. Viking, 1990.

Trevelyan, G. M. *British History in the Nineteenth Century, 1782–1901*. Longmans, 1931.

Urry, John. *The Tourist Gaze: Leisure and Travel in Contemporary Societies*. Sage, 1990.

Vivian, Charles H. 'Dickens, the "True Sun", and Samuel Laman Blanchard.' *Nineteenth-Century Fiction* 4 (1949–50) 328–30.

Ward, J. T., ed. *Popular Movements, c. 1830–1850*. Macmillan, 1970.

Waters, Catherine. "Trading in Death": Contested Commodities in *Household Words*.' Forthcoming in *Victorian Periodicals Review*.

Waugh, Arthur, *A Hundred Years of Publishing*. Chapman & Hall, 1930.

Webb, Beatrice and Sidney. *English Local Government*. [1929] Vol. 9 *English Poor Law History, Part II*. Cass, 1963.

Welsh, Alexander. *From Copyright to Copperfield; the Identity of Dickens*. Cambridge, MA: Harvard University Press, 1987.

——. *The City of Dickens*. Cambridge, MA: Harvard University Press, 1986.

Whitley, John S. and Arnold Goldman, eds. & intro. *American Notes*. By Charles Dickens. Harmondsworth: Penguin, 1972.

Wiener, Joel H., ed. *Descriptive Finding List of Unstamped British Periodicals, 1830–1836*. Bibliographical Society, 1970.

——, ed. *Innovators and Preachers. The Role of the Editor in Victorian England*. London, Westport CT: Greenwood Press, 1985.

——, ed. *Papers for the Millions; The New Journalism in Britain, 1850s to 1914*. New York, Westport CT & Greenwood Press, 1988.

Williams, Raymond. *The Long Revolution*. Harmondsworth: Penguin, 1965.

Wilson, Charles. *First with the News: the History of W. H. Smith, 1792–1972*. Jonathan Cape, 1985.

Wimsatt, W. K. *The Prose Style of Samuel Johnson*. New Haven: Yale University Press, 1963.

Wright, Thomas. *The Life of Charles Dickens*. Herbert Jenkins, 1935.

Wynne, Deborah. *The Sensation Novel and the Victorian Family Magazine*. Basingstoke: Palgrave, 2001.

[Wynter, Andrew]. 'The Police and the Thieves.' *Quarterly Review* 99 (June 1856) 176–80.

Yates, Edmund. *Edmund Yates: His Recollections and Experiences*. 4th ed. Bentley, 1885.

Index

This index aims to cover all people, places, periodical publications, and works of non-fiction and fiction handled in the text and endnotes, and to cover a selection of key topics/themes. Unless otherwise stated, all articles, reports, etc. are by (or attributed to) Dickens. Page references in bold type indicate a direct citation or quotation from a given text or author, and/or some substantive discussion of a given topic/theme.